Skate the Thief

For Brittany,
who never gave up on the magic.

Thinklings Books
1400 Lloyd Rd. #279
Wickliffe, OH 44092
thinklingsbooks.com

The Rag and Bone Chronicles, Book 1

SKATE THE THIEF

by

Jeff Ayers

Thinklings

Thinklings Books, LLC
Wickliffe, OH

CHAPTER 1

IN WHICH A QUESTION IS ASKED, A BLANKET
IS ACCEPTABLY CLEANED, AND A DEAL IS
STRUCK.

Skate peered into the shadowy room through the window. She sniffed and brushed a snowflake off the end of her nose, careful not to shift too much of her weight around. Twitch grunted anyway, muttering under his breath. She ignored him. His job was to hold her up, and there was no avoiding some movement, especially in this cold.

Some people liked the snow. *Those people are stupid.*

"Well?" Twitch asked, his small voice straining to both be heard clearly and stay quiet. He managed to do neither, so Skate shushed at her feet while she dug her heel into his shoulder.

She turned her attention back to the dark room. A glow from a light upstairs helped her see shelves upon shelves of books lining the walls, with unidentifiable shapes resting with them. That junk could be valuable, maybe enough for the pair of them to meet their quota for the week, even the month. The books were treasures, but the Boss didn't like trying to find buyers for stuff like that.

"I'll go in and grab what I can."

Twitch nodded his blond head impatiently. Skate pulled a wire from the waist of her shabby pants. She slipped the thin piece of metal through the hairbreadth crack in the window. There were not many windows that this sort of simple device would work on in the area, but this building was old and showing its wear; the stones and large windows showed it to be older than anything around it.

The pair had observed the house for a week and determined that

1

the tenant was a shut-in, an old man who spent all of his time in his upstairs rooms. He only came downstairs to get a new book off one of his shelves. Though elderly, he seemed spry, carrying heavy-looking volumes up and down the open stone stairs set in the wall with ease. His upstairs light stayed lit all night. Twitch had guessed that the old man liked to have it on in case he woke and needed to use the chamber pot. Skate had agreed and pointed out that the white color of the light probably meant it was magical. Magic in the house meant money. It was a good mark, and Boss Marshall would be pleased with whatever they could grab. They just had to get Skate in first.

"I'll leave the window open and toss down what I can. Once I've grabbed my fill, you'll need to help me out—"

"I *know*," Twitch hissed, his voice strained with effort. "J-just hurry up!" He was starting to shake, and it wasn't only from the cold; his muscles were clearly tiring.

"Oh, fine, you big baby," Skate said, and the soft click of the latch disengaging shot through the alley. The window swung outward, and she caught it to keep it from slamming against the outer wall. "Lift up," she said, pulling herself over the threshold and rolling silently into the shadowy den.

As she scanned the room, Skate heard a noise from upstairs: the crinkle of paper. The old man was still awake, and apparently reading. The room was as icy cold as it had been outside, and her breath formed puffs of cloud. There was a fireplace here, with a full rack of firewood beside it, but the hearth was empty, neglected, and forgotten for some time—covered in a thick layer of dust and choked with cobwebs.

Even though the Boss didn't want books, Skate was drawn to them. She ran a finger along the spine of the nearest tome, then shook her head. The trinkets were the better target; besides, she couldn't read any of the stories.

A statuette above the fireplace caught her eye. It was roughly the length of her forearm, and depicted a woman dancing—or maybe swimming; it was difficult to make out clearly from her vantage point in the dark. *Leave it,* she told herself; *get smaller stuff first.*

Three objects were among the books on the nearest shelf: a silver locket, a sheathed dagger, and a delicate-looking sculpture of metal. Skate pocketed the locket in the fold of the thin rags she was wearing, and examined the dagger. It came free of its jeweled leather sheath with silent ease. It was sharp, suffering no signs of wear or neglect. There were markings etched along the flat of the blade.

Skate nodded and put it back into its protective leather. *It should be worth a few scepts, at least,* she thought, smiling at the prospect of handing Boss Marshall more than a month's worth of payments for one night's work. She stuffed the blade into her belt and moved on to the third treasure. The golden thing was a complicated moving sculpture studded with diamonds. The shape warped slightly when she picked it up, but quickly returned to its original circle shape.

The thing was heavy in her hands; the gold was not merely plating. She had never held something so obviously valuable, whatever it was.

Another page turned upstairs.

Skate kept the golden object in her hands as she looked around for more. There was a desk at the far end of the room, on which a small ornate box sat slightly ajar. She was careful that none of her pilfered treasures made any noise as she walked toward her mark. Had the floors of this place been made of wood, they would undoubtedly have creaked. The cold stone, however, made no noise under her practiced feet.

Skate gingerly opened the box the rest of the way and suppressed a gasp of giddiness at its contents: ten polished red stones on black velvet cloth. *A jewelry box.* In the shadowy cold, the gems almost glowed.

Closer examination revealed flaws in the interiors of each, but her disappointment with the faulty goods was short-lived. The stones held images, not flaws. Her nose an inch from an orb, she saw a pair of open hands within, reaching toward some small person.

"Please don't touch those."

Skate dropped the golden thing and squawked at the clatter it made. She locked eyes with the source of the voice.

The old man stood in the middle of the long room. He was wearing a rich dark green robe trimmed in bands of gold and black and matching slippers on his feet. His eyes were heavy with suspicion, and he was holding a heavy tome under his arm. A glint of red flashed in his eyes as he stared her down.

Skate closed the jewelry box and put it back on the desk.

"Come here."

She did not move except to shudder at the cold.

The old man was unbothered. "What do you think you're doing?"

Skate placed a hand on the large chair next to her and glared up at him defiantly. "These are yours?"

The old man ignored her mockery and set the book on the desk. He gestured in Skate's direction, and the golden thing floated off the ground back to its place on the shelf.

She gaped only for a moment. "You're a wizard!" Wizards were not common, even in a city as cosmopolitan as Caribol; producing dangerous wonders was a skill that took years of training and education, and payment for apprenticeships was expensive. Only fools and the mad would try to steal from such a person.

"Did you take a locket? I'll have that back, too." He held out a hand, and the locket was tugged from her pocket. It landed in his hand, and he stuffed it into a pocket of his own. The old man scanned the room and nodded, apparently satisfied. "Right. Now, why were you trying to steal from me, young lady?"

Skate bristled, despite the dangerous situation. *"Young lady"? Make fun of me, will you?* A quieter, darker voice whispered in her head, *He forgot the dagger.* "I was going to sell some stuff in order to pay for a room for the night, maybe a meal."

It was a lie, but not too far from the truth. His face became less severe. "You have nowhere to stay?"

"No. Me and my friend," she said as she nodded toward the open window, "we got nowhere."

The wizard turned to walk toward the window, and Skate took her chance. She charged forward and almost dropped the knife from her belt. She snatched it up and, at the same time, pushed the old man out of her way. The old man grunted as she ran past him through the open window and took a flying leap, hoping to land against the other wall, then blunt the rest of the fall into the snow.

Three feet outside the window, Skate slowed, then stopped. She spun slowly in midair, suspended by nothing. Twitch was where she'd left him and was staring up at her, mouth agape.

"Run!" she said, before flying back through the window. The midnight alley disappeared in a blur, and the window clicked shut behind her as she, for the third time that night, passed through it. Dizzy from the sudden shifts in direction, Skate skidded to a stop near the middle of the room, a few feet from the fireplace with the small statue. She scrambled to her feet and found herself staring into the face of the old man.

She didn't have the dagger anymore; the sheath was lying on the floor a few feet from her. The old man was glaring at her. He impatiently gestured again, this time toward the rack of firewood, and three logs slammed into the hearth. With another flash of his hands and some words that Skate couldn't make out, the old man stretched a palm out. A thick blast of fire flew from his crooked fingers into the fireplace with such force that the logs almost came tumbling out to land on her. They didn't, and the room now glowed orange and red from a crackling fire.

"What were you thinking?" the wizard said, gesturing toward the window. "That is at least eight feet off of street level. You could have broken a bone!" He walked over to the window and looked down below. "Surely, you didn't think the snow would help—"

There was a metallic click against stone, and he stopped talking. He looked down at his side, and in the shadowy illumination, Skate could not see what he was looking at. Then he took three unsteady steps closer, and she gasped. It was the blade, buried right up to the hilt into his side. In her mad dash out the window, it had flown out of its sheath and stuck him.

No blood stained the robe yet. The old man was staring at the knife in disbelief.

A wave of nausea washed over Skate. *Don't think about it. He'll fall, and I'll run. I'll yell for help on the way, and maybe the healers at the church can help him.*

The wizard placed a hand on the hilt and stuck his chin out pugnaciously. "You stabbed me." He stomped right over to her. "You *stabbed* me! What is wrong with you? This could have hurt me!" He pulled the jeweled blade out. It was clean. With another wordless gesture from him, the discarded sheath clattered off the floor and floated over. He put the knife back in its holder and then placed it on the shelf. "Explain yourself!"

"I—I—what do you mean, 'explain myself'?" Already confused,

Skate found a scolding too much to handle. "You're a wizard, and obviously a hard one," she said, waving a hand at the fireplace, "and you'd just caught me trying to nick your stuff. I had to get out, didn't I? I just tried to knock you down, not cut you. And how aren't you hurt?" She pointed an accusatory finger toward the apparently harmless wound in his side. "Is it a fake dagger or magic or what?"

"Don't go trying to change the subject, young lady," the wizard said. Skate felt the flush of heat as her cheeks turned red in embarrassed anger. "You can't just go around stabbing people you're afraid of."

"Who else are you supposed to stab?" Skate asked, throwing her hands up. That she had not actually meant to stab anyone had temporarily slipped her mind.

"Well, if you're going to insist on stabbing other people, then you can cross my name off your 'stab if you feel like it' list, because I won't have any more of it, and it won't do you any good anyway. What's your name?"

"What?"

"Your name." His tone was less offended now, and back to being merely haughty. He ran his hand across the fabric of his robe, and as he did so, the jagged cut disappeared. "You've got one, haven't you?"

"Skate," she huffed, crossing her arms in front of her chest.

"That's not a name."

"Is so. It's the only one I got." *The only one I got now.*

The old man rolled his eyes. "Fine, 'Skate.' Were you lying about a friend outside? I didn't see anybody."

"Yes." Twitch needed to stay away from this man. He hadn't hurt her yet, but no wizard was ever truly safe to be around. Her eyes reflexively darted to the fireplace. "There's no one."

"Why?"

"To get you to go look so I could escape."

"So you could escape by stabbing me."

"I'm *sorry*," she said, and now it was her turn to roll her eyes. "I'm so sorry for stabbing you, mister, okay? Even though it was an accident, even though it didn't hurt you at all, even though it didn't even scratch your clothes for very long, I'm *sorry* for using your own knife—that I stole," she added, seeing him about to interrupt and correctly guessing what that interruption was going to be. "That I stole from you. I am very, truly sorry that I accidentally stabbed you to try to get away from your home. Okay?"

A long time passed in silence. "Okay." The wizard went over to the front door and put his hand on the handle, but checked his movement. He turned toward her, the hint of a red glare still in his eyes. "Do you really not have anywhere to go?"

"No." She could return to one of the Ink's hideouts around the city, but showing up empty-handed after a job was frowned upon amongst the thieves, thugs, and murderers who made up the rank and file of the group. Boss Marshall wouldn't be happy, certainly, especially after she and Twitch had promised a sizable score. The half-truth seemed a safe bet. "I don't. I really was stealing in order to survive." This last part, she took some small pride in, was absolutely true. *Easy to lie with some truth mixed in.*

There was more silence. The old man's hand stayed unmoving on the latch. Skate had the sense that he wasn't really looking at her, but had simply fixed his eyes on her while thinking. His neatly trimmed white moustache twitched. When he spoke, his thin beard bobbed up and down. "Rattle! Blanket!" he shouted at the stairs. Refocusing on Skate, he asked, "Would you like to stay here, then? At least until morning?" His hand dropped to his side. "I find that I can't turn you out into the cold."

Skate opened her mouth, then closed it again. As far as she could tell, he *could* turn her out into the cold and would have every right to do so—or burn her to a crisp, or turn her over to the Guard. She'd been caught red-handed stealing his stuff. *You also stabbed the old man; don't forget that.* "I wouldn't mind, I guess," she said, not wanting to offend him.

"Good. I can't offer much in the way of comfort. Rattle is bringing the only blanket I have down. Here he is now." The blanket came first, but Rattle took all of her attention. For a moment, Skate wished she still had the blade. A yelp escaped her.

Rattle was a swollen bat. That was the only thing her mind could categorize it as. In truth, the leathery wings were where the similarity ended. The wings joined at the top of a lidless eyeball the size of an adult's fist. It looked wet. Beneath the eye were six spindly legs, jittering spider's legs; each one was at least two feet long. The pupil of the eye darted around at random while Rattle descended. It brought the blanket to the old man, who took it with some measure of disgust. The blanket was filthy and full of holes.

Without anything to hold, the spindly legs clicked together as the eye bobbed to and fro in the creature's stationary flight. "Thank you, Rattle. Go back to reading."

The spider-bat turned around and, after sparing a glance at Skate, floated up the stairs.

"That was Rattle," the wizard added unnecessarily as he began to fix the holes in the blanket with passes of his hand.

"What is it?"

"He's a—hmm. I never gave him a name beyond 'Rattle.' I made him. He's a construct, a guardian. Mostly, he just likes to read. He's a lot like me, that way." The dirt and holes faded with each pass of the hand until it resembled something she might have stolen from a vendor in the market. "Here." He held out the blanket for her to take, though she was too far away.

Skate didn't move. "Why didn't you already have the fire going?" Much had been strange since the old man had come down, but this bothered her the most. That fireplace had not been used in a good long while, and warmth was absolutely necessary this time of year. "Magic? I mean, if you've got magic to keep warm, why have a fireplace with wood ready?"

The corners of the wizard's mouth twitched up into a small smile before he said, "You ask many questions for an uninvited guest." He dropped the blanket and turned toward the stairs. "Stay here for the night. Sleep by the fire. I want to talk to you before you go in the morning." As his feet disappeared from view, the jewelry box lifted itself off the table and floated gently up after him.

Skate turned toward the fire. She was warm. The blanket was comfortable enough, and there was a rug. She meant to go to the door, but found herself first sitting, then reclining in front of the crackling flames. Despite her confusion and unanswered questions, she soon drifted off to sleep.

#☿♄☌

Skate shot straight up. There was clicking. The horror that was Rattle was floating by.

Skate rubbed the sleep out of her eyes while Rattle moved through a door in the back of the room, carrying something. The fire still burned, and a few more logs had been added to increase the flame. She noticed with passing interest that there were no fewer logs in the holder.

Dawn was breaking through the windows. Skate's stomach growled as she sat there smacking her mouth to try to get the stench of sleep out. It had been many hours since she'd eaten.

The door to the next room was ajar, and it sounded like the bat thing was hammering metal on metal in an attempt to rouse her from rest. "I'm up!" she shouted toward the open door. Rattle glanced at her as it passed as if to confirm her claim. It then continued on its way, doing whatever noisy task it had started.

Skate was about to yell again when she heard footsteps. The old man had made no noise last night coming down; he should have. He was old. She was good at hearing. Had he cast a spell of some sort—a muffling or silencing enchantment—before coming down the previous night? "I'm gonna go," she said, disentangling herself from the blanket.

"You don't want breakfast?" the old man asked.

Rattle suddenly ceased its clamor and came out of the kitchen, a pot of water dangling at the end of three legs and an empty pan in two others. It looked slowly back and forth between her and the old wizard.

"No, I don't," Skate said.

With a final loud clang, Rattle dropped both the water pot and the pan. Some of the water splashed out onto the stone floor. By the time the pan had settled, Rattle was almost out of view up the stairs, its legs twitching as the bat wings flapped harder than before.

"He likes to cook," the old man said reproachfully. "Even if you're not hungry, you could have let him do the cooking." The old man had not changed his clothes since the previous night; living alone must have left him unconcerned with the normal social niceties of the wealthy.

"Definitely not. I don't know where those legs have been. Besides, it can still cook for you."

"He doesn't cook for me." The old man grimaced, struggling with something.

Gas, she thought, and stifled a laugh. He opened his mouth several times as if to speak, but instead closed it each time. *He looks like a fish out of water.* She failed to stifle the laughter this time.

"Listen," he said at last, ignoring her snorts, "I have an idea. You've got no home, right?"

"Right, thanks so much for the reminder."

"But you're pretty good at...finding things."

She smiled. "Yes, I'm very good at *finding* things." She leaned into the euphemism, trying to make the old man uncomfortable. It didn't work.

"Well, then, here's a business proposition: If you can find me a new book a week, I'll let you stay here. I've got a room upstairs that Rattle could clear out, one that has a vent connected to this room, so the warmth gets in there. Meals, too—and I promise, despite your pro-testations: Rattle's clean enough for you." His face had become impas-sive, a mask.

Skate thought for a moment. She didn't particularly want to live with this strange man, but having an in here could make for a fantastic haul when she decided to cut and run. She guessed Boss Marshall would be happy to hear that, despite her having nothing to show for the previous night. "I 'find' you a book and get to stay out of the cold for a week?"

He nodded. "But it'll need to be one that I don't have. Finding a book I already own is useless to me. And of course, if you get caught, I'll deny everything."

Skate pretended to mull the offer over but had already made her choice; she'd have to be an idiot to refuse the mark's offer to come and go as she pleased. After much feigned deliberation, she spat into her hand and stuck it out. "Deal."

The old man did not spit in his own hand, but he took hers with-out hesitation. "Wonderful! And welcome, officially, to the residence of Barrison Belamy, Skate. Let me show you to your room."

CHAPTER 2

IN WHICH A REUNION OCCURS, A THREAT IS
MADE, AND A GAME OF DARTS IS
INTERRUPTED.

The heavy wooden door of Belamy's house shut behind her. Skate stood in the midday sun amidst piles of snow. The familiar figure of Twitch down the road caught her eye. The shock of wiry blond hair poking out of his wrappings and rags gave him away despite his best attempts at skulking and spying on the house. At the sight of her, he tilted his head two times to the right. By the third jerk, it was clear that this was not one of his accustomed spasms, but a signal.

The mounds of snow made the streets more crowded than usual as Skate navigated through a narrow alley to the next main road. A rat scurried into a discarded basket as she passed. She and Twitch were familiar with most of the main avenues of Caribol, and they had many established meeting places around the bustling city. The one that Twitch had indicated was a walled-off alcove behind a latrine, so the rat's nest was not going to be the most unpleasant thing she would be near today.

Skate squeezed her nose as she approached, one of her rags serving as a makeshift mask and filter.

"W-what happened?" Twitch asked, powering through another involuntary jerk. He had covered his own face. "I thought you was killed."

Not caring for the concerned tone, Skate said, "I handled it. Let's find a beggar; I need to get to the Boss." She turned away from the stink and smiled behind her rag at Twitch's smack of indignation as he

11

hurried to catch up.

"Okay, but where's the haul?" he asked, looking her over for signs of pocketed wealth.

"No haul."

"Boss won't l-like that," he groaned, scratching at the back of his head to defer more spasms. "I thought you s-said you handled it!" he added, lowering his voice as he scanned the streets for a beggar.

"There's no haul *yet.* But I got an in, Twitchy. I got me a home for a while, too—after I steal a book, anyway." Skate explained the deal she had made with the wizard.

"Not a bad j-job, I guess," Twitch said when she had finished, "but you can't go taking deals like that without the Boss's permission. He don't like it w-when we start working for people without Ink approval. F-found one." He pointed ahead to a grungy old beggar on the ground shaking a tin cup.

The gray man was rending the air with ragged calls. "Alms! Money for the hungry! Alms!"

Skate broke away from her companion and leaned against the wall a few feet away. Twitch slid down next to the beggar and slipped six copper coins bearing the image of Old King Rajian into the cup in a particular order: two, then three, then one. "Well-a-day, g-granddad."

"Well-a-day to yeh," the crusty beggar responded in hushed tones. "What'll I do with your gift?"

"Spend it how you w-want, 'cause I know you'll n-never drink." Things changed week to week in the Ink, but this coded conversation stayed the same.

"What do you snots need to know, then?" the panhandler asked. He kept his deep-set eyes scanning the streets for any who might take pity on a broken old drifter.

"Where's the Marshall c-crew meeting this week?" Twitch pretended to be very interested in something under one of his stubby toe-nails, which were sticking out of his rotten shoes.

"The dock house. Be there for the next two weeks at least."

"That's all, then. Th-thank you, uncle."

"Here, boy. You dropped these," the beggar replied, holding out five copper coins.

"You're kind."

"See that you're kinder."

The official business completed, the beggar returned to his shouting. Cries of "Alms! Money for the hungry!" followed the pair of children as they turned the next corner.

"I *know* he don't like it, Twitch," Skate said, once they were out of earshot, "but he'll know it was worth it after I talk to him. You can't believe the stuff the old guy has just lying around. That dagger alone woulda fetched a fistful of scepts, don't you doubt it." Skate was referring to the hexagonal golden coins of the kingdom, each sporting an image of King Rajian's fabled scepter. "And I got a feeling that might've been the *least* valuable thing I got my hands on before he caught me."

Twitch still looked uneasy as they sidled by a wide wagon that had been left in front of a pub. The pub owner was bickering with the wagon owner. "I don't like that he d-didn't go down when you knifed him—and I'm k-kinda surprised you did that at all," he said, cutting his eyes her way. "I didn't think you'd be willing to do that sort of s-stuff to escape. That's more B-Boss Shade's crew, or Kite." The first name was spoken with hushed fear, but he almost spat the latter.

Skate screwed her face up in matching disgust. "I weren't sure myself until the time came, to be honest," she said, looking at the ground. *Let him think it was on purpose. That'll get me a reputation as someone not to be messed with, anyway.*

"Never mind th-that, though," Twitch said, excitement replacing his concern. "How did the old guy not go down? You sure you really stabbed him?"

Skate rolled her eyes and adopted a high-pitched, simpering voice. "Oh my *goodness*, I don't know, I'm just a wittle girl who doesn't know how knives work! Of course I'm sure," she finished, dropping back into her normal tone of voice and glaring at him. She shoved him in the arm, and he pushed back. There was a crowd in front of them with someone talking on a stage. "And I don't know. Magic, I guess. He knows it. Maybe it was some sort of knife that doesn't really stab when you use it."

Twitch shook his head. "What'd be the point of—"

"I don't know; wizards are crazy. Why do they do anything?"

It was an auction of some sort. The hawker was peddling furniture and dishes on the street in front of an ill-kept old wooden two-story house.

"Someone must've died. Hey, look, there's Delly," Skate said, knocking Twitch on the shoulder and gesturing toward a girl in similar rags to their own, moving through the crowd, darting fast hands into pockets and purses whose strings were suddenly too loose. Skate laughed, and they pushed on.

Delly wasn't in the same crew as Twitch and Skate. She worked for Boss Kernisk, who ran pickpocketing and street-begging. There was a lot of overlap between Marshall's crew and Kernisk's; burglars who needed to let the heat fall off of them would move into petty theft to lie low while still contributing, and whenever the cutpurses got more ambitious, they joined up with the house thieves. It was a good system, just like everything the Ink was involved in: no waste, good use of people, profits always up.

The sudden fishy, salty smell of the sea made Skate wrinkle her nose, but Twitch didn't seem to care. He was chattering in halted tones about wizards, but Skate was only half-listening. Cart-pushers started appearing in the foot traffic, peddling cockles and clams and shrimp and crab and mussels and sea bass and mackerel and squid and tuna and eels and every other bounty of the sea, singing their rhymes and jingles. There were sailors about, leathery men and women with powerful arms and stout legs, already carousing and scuffling. Somewhere, a musician was playing a familiar tune, but Skate could not remember the words. The reedy tune fused with the raucous scene, making it all seem somehow connected instead of the mindless, chaotic scramble it was.

The pair stopped behind a redstone building. It was some gambling den or other, but the cellar was why they were here. Skate opened the heavy wooden door to the cellar and hopped down. Twitch followed and let the door slam shut behind them.

The resulting darkness was absolute. They both stayed quiet, since walking blind required concentration.

Twitch arrived first. There was the click of a latch and a low grinding noise as stone rubbed against stone. A crack of light appeared in the stone and became wider as the boy pushed the wall back, revealing a lit passage leading down and left. The door closed behind them.

Skate began talking now that they could see again. "You honestly wouldn't believe the number of books, Twitch. He's got at least double what we cased downstairs. And he keeps lots of shiny, expensive things all over the place. I dunno what they are, but they'd sell."

"Hope the B-Boss is as excited as you are about the whole idea. You know how he is about b-business. He l-likes sure things."

The passage took an abrupt turn into a shut iron door. Skate knocked out the right rhythm. The eyehole slid open, a pair of eyes examined them briefly, and then the eyehole slid shut. With a heavy *thunk*, the door slowly groaned open. Only two or three handspans wide to begin with, the opening began to slowly swing shut as the pair passed through.

"Morning, Bart," Twitch said to the doorman, who grunted and nodded vaguely. He reeked of alcohol, as usual. The Boss let Bleary-Eyes Bart get away with his habits, because the doorman could remember and recognize the people even when apparently blackout drunk.

The tables and stools of the underground common room were scattered around. Various other burglars milled about them, drinking, conversing, throwing dice, or playing cards to pass the time. Two dozen or so of these sneaks filled the room, and the chatter and laughter were only occasionally broken up by a cough or the intermittent thuds of darts landing on the board at one end of the room. Someone else was thumping his table regularly, the thud running through the floor and giving the room the feeling of a cadence underneath the general relaxation.

Pipe smoke hung in the room like a sour fog, trapped and heavy. Skate found the smell a little nauseating, but Twitch took a deep breath through his nose and sighed. He loved the stuff but only rarely had a chance to indulge. He claimed that it helped with his tics, but Skate knew it only made them worse when he was done smoking. "Let's go see the Boss," she said, nudging Twitch and pointing toward the Boss's private area, an office and bedroom separated from this main area by a sturdy wooden door.

"He ain't in," a reedy, nasal voice said, a little more loudly than necessary. Twitch and Skate were passing the thumper's table, and she fought to keep her face blank despite her revulsion. Kite was a tall and thin young man of about sixteen. He was holding a knife, which he had been throwing into the table in front of him, over and over again, leaving groove marks in its surface. He threw it again while he was watching them, and it sank about an inch into the wood. "He's at the monthly."

Skate cursed; the Bosses of the Ink were required to meet with the Big Boss once a month to give a report of dealings, income, losses, recruits, imprisonments, and any other notable developments within their respective crews and disciplines. Boss Marshall wouldn't likely be returning today.

"'Course, if you'd been here, you'd know that. Wasn't you lot s'posed to be robbing a place somewhere in the Old Town?"

Several people nearby had stopped their activities and were watching the conversation. The room at large was uninterested. When neither Skate nor Twitch answered, Kite's deep brown eyes focused on Twitch. "So where's your haul?"

Twitch jerked his head to the side, grimaced, and responded, "We'll t-tell the Boss a-all about it, Kite."

"I bet," he said, taking the knife out of the table and smiling without a trace of humor. "And I bet there won't be no lies in it, neither. Am I right about that?" He put one of his grimy fingernails on the blunted side of the knife and flicked some gunk away. He continued doing the same to his other fingers.

"We don't lie to the B-Boss, Kite."

"Oh, I know *you* don't, kid," he said, jabbing the knife in Twitch's direction, "but your friend there has trouble telling the truth, don't she?" He still wore his snake's smile. He turned his gaze toward Skate, and she did not blink. "She lied to him before, remember? Got her in some *hot* water, if I remember right. And I do. I always do." He wiped his blade on his trousers. "Whatcha say, girlie? Gonna tell the truth, or what?"

Skate felt the heat rising from her neck to the top of her head. She could ignore jabs about getting in trouble, but the intentional reference to "hot" had started her off. She heard roaring flames in her ears, and whenever she blinked, she saw fire. It was the fire that had changed her life, the fire that had put her here in the first place. She heard her voice begin talking, not even sure what she was saying. "I'll tell you something you can do with that—"

"Skate, don't. H-he's a waste."

"A waste, huh?" Kite still smiled, but it was a strained thing now. His voice became thinner. "I could show you lot what a waste looks like." The nasal voice was low and threatening. He held the knife delicately between his two index fingers, looking at the blond boy over the top of it. "I've left people as one of those before, ain't I?"

Thieves who went with Kite on jobs had a nasty habit of sustaining injuries during burglaries, and Boss Marshall wasn't happy with that, but Kite was mostly unconcerned about Boss Marshall's displeasure. He had made it no secret that he planned to join Boss Shade's crew, the crew that handled all the Ink's wet work: assassinations and petty contract killings. It was known, even among the rank and file, that Boss Shade hadn't ruled out the possibility of Kite's defection.

"Enough," a voice called out from the Boss's rooms. The sound carried across the room, because Kite's threats had caught several tables' attention; even the game of darts had ceased.

Kite's smile vanished. "Sure, Haman," he said, dropping the knife into the table once more, "sure. We was just joking around. No harm done, yeah?"

"See that it stays that way. Spilled ink flows both ways."

That was one of the axioms of the gang, warning that blood spilled against a member of the gang would be paid back. The Bosses didn't condone infighting.

Kite dropped his gaze to the knife in the table. Haman turned his attention to the children. "You two. Come see me. Now." He left the door open as he returned to the office. There were a few seconds of silence, and then some chuckles as the room resumed its clinking and thudding and chattering. Kite's eyes followed Skate and Twitch as they moved. The resumed thumping of the knife in the table remained audible until Skate pulled the Boss's door shut.

Haman Vaerion was sitting in Boss Marshall's chair behind Boss Marshall's desk. The lieutenant had put on his spectacles and was examining several pages while taking notes in a book of his own. In the Boss's absence, he alone was responsible for keeping track of everyone's hauls and making sure the Ink got its full share. Recordkeeping was an indispensable part of running any complex enterprise, Boss Marshall was fond of saying, and Haman was skilled at finding "errors" that the various thieves under him "missed." Boss Marshall regularly delegated this activity to his lieutenant even when he was present to run things, simply because the younger man had a better head for numbers. If Haman minded this extra unpaid responsibility, he never let on.

"Take a seat, and I'll begin working on your reports in a moment," Haman said without looking up, waving toward two empty stools across from him. He made a few marks on the page and, apparently satisfied with the end result, nodded and removed his glasses. Skate could not help but feel a twinge of jealousy as he worked. *Reading and writing is power,* she thought while he took a delicate-looking cloth from the breast pocket of his smooth gray-and-red vest and wiped the ink from his fingers, though there was little; the man was very careful with his work.

No one had ever told Skate about the semi-mystical status of being able to understand the written word; no one had ever sat her down and pointed out that it was something the powerful and the wise could do, and that it helped them to stay powerful and wise. It was an obvious fact to anyone who bothered to look at the world. The children of the Ink were all aware of literacy's elevating force; those who could read were above, while everyone else was below.

Once he had cleaned his hands to his satisfaction, Haman placed the papers into a tray on the far end of the desk. "Now, then. You were working on the old man in Old Town, yes?" Not waiting for a response, he pulled a blank sheet of parchment paper toward him. "Let's begin, then," he said, dipping his quill into the inkwell.

"Haman, wait," Skate said, not wanting him to get too far before knowing what had happened.

He raised his head slightly. The angle made his forehead look enormous. "Yes?"

"We didn't st-steal anything," Twitch explained. His voice squeaked a bit at the end; whether this was from nerves or part of the change that boys went through with age, Skate didn't know. Maybe it was both.

"I see." Haman replaced the quill in its holder after tapping the excess ink back into the well. The paper had only a few indecipherable marks at the top. "Why is that?"

Skate tried to read his hawk-like face; he was more curious than angry. Haman had always been a thoughtful man, not prone to outbursts or rash actions. It must have had something to do with the magic he had studied, she decided. Haman was a noteworthy wizard whose skills made him indispensable to Boss Marshall. Word was that he was not only a passable lock-picker in the traditional sense, but that he also had magic to unlock doors, chests, and windows without even touching them. It was his magic and dutiful attention to detail that had made him Boss Marshall's number two, and he had managed to hold that position despite numerous thieves vying for it.

"We were p-planning to—"

"I'm aware of the plan; the Boss's notes were, as always, quite clear. The question at hand is why you *didn't* steal anything."

"Right," Skate jumped in, seeing Twitch jerk in his seat as he valiantly tried to respond. "That's me, Haman. I got in and had a few things gathered, but the owner walked in on me." She relayed the rest of the story, embellishing only the accident of his wounds; she wanted to seem dangerous, so in her retelling she made it deliberate. She also omitted the bargain she'd made for housing.

Haman seemed interested that the old man had a command of magic, and he became even more so when Skate explained that he had not fallen into a heap upon being stabbed. When she finished the story, Haman rubbed his temples.

"Why did you not leave during the night?" he asked.

"He didn't want me to. He would have prevented it."

"Hmm. And what occurred when you did finally stir from sleep?"

"I..." She paused and looked to Twitch, but Twitch was transparently trying to avoid eye contact. She plowed ahead anyway. "I agreed to steal books for him in exchange for room and board."

The proclamation sat heavily in the room. For what felt like minutes, no one said a word. Twitch coughed. Haman leaned forward, looking even more like some sleek and dangerous bird of prey in a nest of paperwork. He pierced Skate with his gaze and asked, "You took a bargain for stealing without checking with either your Boss or his lieutenant?" When she nodded, he settled back into his seat, leaned on the arm of the chair, and rested his palm on the side of his face. "Why?" he asked, in a tone that suggested she had taken leave of her senses. "You could be blacklisted for this, or killed outright. It is bad enough to show back up empty-handed, but that's just a mistake—jobs go bad sometimes, of course, but—"

"Haman, I ain't gonna steal any books for him. It's a con, a way for me to get inside and keep track of all of his stuff so I can pick the best before leaving."

Haman's eyes narrowed, and he pursed his lips slightly. "Did he see your mark?"

"No," she said instantly, though she couldn't be sure; she had flailed about enough that the old man could have seen the gang's tattoo between her shoulder blades. Apparently, her answer had been too quick. Under the wizard's gaze, she backtracked. "I don't think so."

"If he did, then he may now be under the impression that he has hired the Ink for an official, contracted job. If he didn't, then he's not to know whom you're associated with. It's quite possible the man doesn't even know of the existence of our organization. Probable, even." Haman was drumming on the other arm of his chair with his fingers. "This might end up working. If he doesn't know who you are, then he's still a target instead of a client. We need clarification on this before we decide what to do with you—with *both* of you," he added with a glance at Twitch, "regarding your decision to hire out without the Boss's approval.

"The Boss will have to make that call when he gets back, but I have to tell you: he doesn't like it when you house-runners take up clients for yourselves without getting his approval first. You can see why," he said, nodding to the wall behind the kids. The familiar map was there, to the right of the door. It was the entire city, with each district clearly defined and labeled. Different color pins were tacked in at different points: green pins for safe houses, yellow pins for guard towers, and red pins for protected clients. "Don't write where you eat" was another of the Ink's mottos. It was forbidden to steal from someone who either had an open contract with the Ink or was paying monthly dues to the organization for protection. There were many red pins in the map, particularly in the docks district where they were now hiding.

"You steal from the wrong person," Haman went on, "and the Ink's broken a contract. Clients with broken contracts don't like to come to us for business and might get the idea that they can go ahead and rat us out to the Guard. Unhappy clients are bad news. Disorder is bad news."

Haman stood up and replaced his spectacles on his nose, running a hand through his straight black hair and sighing. "You've got to figure out what the man knows, Skate. Twitch, you're on thin ice for failing to get anything out of this last mark. I need ten helms by the end of the week," he said, referring to the square silver coins that bore the image of Old King Rajian's war helmet, "or we'll have to have a very unpleasant conversation about your continued employment and safety. Well, either *we* will, or you and the Boss will. Understood?" At Twitch's emphatic nodding, Haman dismissed the boy with, "Better get to work then. Not you," he added, putting a hand out to stop Skate from leaving. "Close the door on your way out, Twitch."

The boy looked with discomfort at Skate but did as he was told. When the door clicked shut, Haman leaned forward across the desk. "You need to be careful. Those of us who practice the art of magic are not known to be particularly easy to trick or steal from. I'm not even sure what kind of magic he could have employed to prevent the blade you used from hurting him. Did his skin look strange?"

Skate shook her head. "No different than anyone else's. Wrinkly, I guess, and he had some spots on him, but all old people get those things."

Haman looked even more intrigued than before. "I'd be very interested…" he muttered to himself, apparently lost in thought. "Never mind," he said, turning to the bookshelf beside him. He considered the collection for a moment before pulling a medium-sized tome from the shelf and handing it to her. "There. Your first stolen book for the old man." He took another off and set it on his desk.

"How do you know if this is one he doesn't already have? He told me he didn't want copies of things he already has."

"I don't. But you don't either. It's a stalling tactic," Haman explained, taking his seat again, "so you can find out what he knows. If he knows you're Ink, then get back here immediately or try to skip town and disappear forever, because that means you've messed up. If he doesn't, then you can worry about stealing what he wants to give you time to size the place up properly."

Haman noticed that she winced when he mentioned failure.

"Skate, listen to me," he said, pulling his paperwork and the other book back toward him. "This could be a big break for you if you haven't screwed everything up already. And for whatever it's worth, I really hope you haven't. I think you're going to do well here, but we have rules. Order. Without rules, there's no organization. No organization, no business. Do what you need to survive, but stay in the box. Got it?"

Skate stood and nodded. "I don't think he knows." She risked a glance at the cover of the tome. It told her nothing.

"I hope you're right. We'll be in the Old Town next, if you don't get back here before the move. Close the door on your way out."

She did so. While she was leaving, she might have seen a rather satisfied smile play across his lips as he opened his book.

CHAPTER 3

IN WHICH A BOOK IS DELIVERED, A SECRET
IS REVEALED, AND A BACKPACK IS BROUGHT
DOWNSTAIRS.

Skate climbed up into the glare of cold sunlight. Book in hand, she turned down the street toward Belamy's house and crinkled her nose at the fresh stench of the streets.

The walk felt longer on her own; Twitch was out getting Haman's money. The rhythmic thumping of Kite's knife had also been absent when she'd left, and that worried Skate more than a little. He wasn't stupid enough to spill another Ink member's blood, but he could hurt Twitch in other ways. She had told herself that it was a coincidence and hurried out of the room.

None of the eyes of the other thieves had followed her passing. Bart had only given her a cursory glance as he'd brought his bottle to his lips.

Skate wound her way through familiar back alleys, taking pains to avoid the few Guard patrols. She'd had run-ins with them before, especially during her pick-pocketing days a few years earlier, but she had never been caught—not yet. She was out of the docks when a familiar voice called out to her.

"Skate!"

She turned to look and smiled. It was Delly.

Skate waited for the younger girl to reach her. "Hey!" she said, wrapping her arms around her. "How's pickings?"

"Bad," Delly said, rolling her eyes. "None of these rubes keep anything worth having on them. All the rich ones are in the other districts, where the Guards are always walking around. I managed a few blades, though." She reached into her pocket to reveal a handful of brown coins emblazoned with a pair of crossed swords. "So at least I'm not going back empty."

"I had to," Skate replied. She told the other girl the story as they walked. They passed an apple cart, and Delly nicked a couple of sour green ones.

"Y'know," Delly said around a mouthful of half-chewed fruit after Skate had told the whole story, "that's not a bad job, getting a roof and food for stealing a book. Who'd you take that from?" she asked, pointing to the tome in Skate's hands.

"Haman gave it to me to get me started with Belamy."

Delly perked up at the mention of the Ink wizard. "You talked with Haman?"

Skate smiled; Delly had long been enamored of Boss Marshall's second-in-command.

"How is he? Did he mention transferring me?"

"No, you didn't come up, and I didn't wanna swerve the conversation your way, since I was trying to stay out of trouble and all. Did you really want your name brought up while we were talking about 'dire consequences' and 'questions about future employment'?"

Delly looked disappointed. "No, I guess not." They had reached the house. Delly looked it over. "Kinda old, huh?"

"Yeah. Listen, you better scram."

"Yeah, okay. Good luck, Skate." With that, Delly was off to find another crowd or a sleepy-looking mark with a coin purse hanging too loosely.

Skate took a deep breath and moved toward the door. *Remember: He's a wizard. He's dangerous. He's not easy to trick.* She reminded herself of these truths over and over as she approached the door, putting her mind in the right place to deal with Barrison Belamy. She lifted the large brass ring on the door and knocked twice.

The door swung wide, and there stood Belamy, alert and robed. "What is it?" he said harshly. When he looked down and saw Skate carrying her prize, his eyes widened. "Already? Good, good, come in." The room was as warm as it had been this morning; a couple of logs were still smoldering. Everything looked the same as before, with a few key differences. The blanket was gone, as was the small statue above the fireplace. There was also something on each of the three large windows around the long room: little brown boxes that twisted in place occasionally.

Belamy saw her stare and brightened up considerably, his face splitting into a wide grin. "Curious?" She nodded, and he approached the nearest one, beckoning her closer. "They're locks. After your...intrusion, I determined it a good idea to keep these windows from opening to any old fool with a lockpick handy. They move, see?" He pointed at the twitching metallic brown lock. "The innards, the mechanisms—they move around, so that even if someone does manage to bring the right set of tools, they'll have a devil of a time getting the window to unlock. They're magic of course; just made them this morning. Pretty clever, eh?"

Skate thought they were impressive, so she nodded. She did see a glaring flaw in his plan, but was loath to point it out.

"Ah," he said, apparently sensing her skepticism, "I know what you're thinking: someone could just break the glass. Not likely. Here!" he said, taking a glass globe from a perch on the nearest bookshelf and putting it in her grasp. "Chuck that as hard as you can at the window. Don't hold back; give it all you've got!"

The globe sat like a stone in her palm. It could easily break the window, she knew, but Belamy's encouraging smile made her shrug and try it anyway. She threw it with more than enough force to shatter the pane, and braced for the crash of broken glass. She heard instead only a thump, and then Belamy extended his hand and prevented the ball from hitting the floor with his magic. He gently floated it toward its place on the shelf. "No one is breaking in that way again; that glass is hard as stone now. So is this ball, for that matter. But never mind all that," he said, turning to face the girl with a hand outstretched, palm open. "You have something for me?"

"Yeah," Skate said, handing the book over, "but I don't know if it's one you already got." Her mind raced: If he was protecting against thieves, then he didn't know about the Ink's rules about stealing from clients; and if he didn't know about the Ink's rules, then he didn't know about the Ink at all.

Belamy glanced at the cover, and his face fell slightly. "I'm afraid it is," he said, flipping through the pages, confirming its contents. "You'll have to return this to wherever you found it; it's of no use to me." He passed it back without further ado.

Skate accepted it, doing her best to look crestfallen. "I guess I'll just sell it for a room tonight, then," she said gloomily.

"You'll do no such thing," he said, looking stern and animated once more. "That is someone else's property, and you'll return it as soon as possible."

Judging by his face and tone, Skate surmised that he was being entirely serious. "You're the one that asked me to get it for you!" she pointed out. "You knew it was someone else's, and you were more than happy to keep it before you found out you already had one." The wizard's hypocrisy made her abandon caution.

"Calm yourself. I was never going to keep anything you brought me. I want to read and return them, that's all."

Skate shook her head in disbelief. "You're having me st—*find* these things just so you can give 'em back later?"

"Well, yes. I'm no thief."

"No, you're treating other people's libraries like they're your own."

Belamy smiled and nodded. "That's right, and I treat my own library as equally open to anyone who asks. A book belongs to everybody in the end, doesn't it? The stories, the lessons, the discoveries—they belong to everyone, when it's all said and done. Think about it," he said, drawing passionate intensity out of her skeptical expression. "When I read a story, I keep it with me, in here." He pointed to his temple. "It's always there, always at my disposal. Stories and histories are as real in memories as they are on the page. What need do I have to hold the book in hand—or even worse, stored on a shelf—if I keep its secrets with me wherever I go? What right do I have to pretend that I own what's among the pages, just because I lay claim to the pages themselves?"

Skate put her hands up in grudging acceptance. "Fine, I'll put it back where I found it." She crossed her arms over her chest. "Should I keep 'finding' books until I get one you don't have?"

"That seems horribly inefficient. Let me give you a list of books, so you can—"

"I can't remember a whole list of books."

Belamy was nonplussed. "Well, you can bring the list with you, of course; that's no issue."

"I can't read."

Uncomfortable silence greeted this proclamation.

"Oh. Yes." Belamy seemed lost in thought. "Oh," he said, his eyes flashing wide and a smile cracking his lined face. "Oh! I have an idea! Wait here." With that, he bounded up the stairs.

Skate, now alone, moved toward one of the new locks. She brought a hand near it and, after working up her courage, pressed a finger on the textured back of it. She could feel movement within. When it gave one of its periodic jerks, she pulled her hand away but continued watching it, wondering how she could possibly beat it. Hearing Belamy coming back down, she backed away from the strange device.

He appeared at the foot of the stairs, carrying a backpack in his hands, and offered it to Skate with a grin.

She eyed it dubiously. "How is a backpack supposed to help me find books? Is it magic or something?"

"The backpack? No, it's just rough cloth and metal clasps. However," he said, unlatching the clasp that was keeping it shut, "what's inside will help you tremendously." When he opened the pack all the way, a familiar pair of bat wings popped up and began flapping lightly.

Rattle poked its eyeball body out, leaving the spindly legs within the bag. It hovered in place for a few moments, looked about the room, then slowly descended back into the bag. Its eye appeared and disappeared at small holes in the sides of the bag.

Belamy clasped the bag shut. "Rattle will be joining you to help point out books that aren't in our collection. He knows all of mine, so I trust him not to make any mistakes."

Skate took the backpack. It was surprisingly light, given its strange cargo, but she hesitated over putting it on. "This is a bad idea."

"What? Why?"

"'Finding' things takes quiet and quickness. Rattle is not quiet." As if to accentuate her point, Rattle clicked its legs together within the bag. "See? What if it does that while we're finding a book for you, and the people living there come to see what the noise was?"

Belamy waved a hand in front of his nose as if swatting an irritating insect. "He'll be fine, and so will you. And if someone does discover you while you're finding me a book, you just run. Don't try to hurt anybody to get away."

Skate didn't bother reminding him that she had not tried to hurt him when the knife plunged into his side; he would not hear her. "I still want to know why you didn't get hurt."

"Magic."

She pursed her lips and frowned, holding the backpack out as if to return it.

Getting the point, the old wizard made the swatting motion again. "Fine, fine. A better, more accurate detailed answer. The blade cannot harm me, nor will any others unless wielded by an extremely powerful arm or else enchanted heavily—and in the latter case, it would still take a reasonably strong arm to cause a blade to hurt. This is because of certain modifications I have made to my body, preventing harm from certain sources. These changes were made using powerful magic. If I got any more specific than that, then nothing I would start to say would make any sense, as the magic involved is very complex and dangerous besides. Does this answer satisfy you?"

Skate sized the old man up. In addition to being good at lying, she was also quite skilled in determining when others were trading in falsehoods; this was a necessary skill when living among ruffians. Belamy had not seemed to be lying, except when he'd claimed he was not being clearer for technical reasons. There was a subtle shift at that point, a lifting of his voice that told her he had begun warping the truth. He was holding something back, and he wanted the conversation dropped.

The only sounds in the room were the clicking of Rattle's legs from within the bag and the crackling of the fire. Finally, Skate spoke. "Sure. Magic. I can deal with that. And I won't hurt anyone. If I get caught, I'll throw Rattle at them and run away. It'd probably scare anybody worse than a crummy knife would."

At the mention of its name, Rattle pushed its body out of the top of the bag and looked at her. When it heard the last few words, it clicked its legs together rhythmically and bobbed its body up and down. Skate thought this must have been its version of laughing, since Belamy looked at it and smiled.

"Yes, I suppose he probably would." The smile left the wizard's face. "Though he must not be seen. If you are caught while finding and Rattle is seen, any witness would tie him right back to me. Not many know of Rattle's existence, but some do. It would be putting me at risk. You can't do that."

Skate soured at that even as she realized it made sense. How many people, wizards included, had a pet or partner that was an eyeball with bat wings and spider legs? Belamy himself claimed not to know what to properly call Rattle; it was probably utterly unique. Its presence would be a lightning rod for trouble if it were seen.

This complication only made Skate more uncomfortable with Rattle's proposed presence as she worked—in addition to her unspoken but no less pressing major concern: with Rattle around, she was unlikely to be able to continue communicating with the Ink. However, she also didn't know of another way to distinguish which books the old man had and which ones he didn't.

"I'll have to make sure I'm not seen, then, and keep Rattle hidden," she said. The old man appeared satisfied with the answer. "Where should I start looking for these books? Anyone you know who definitely has books you don't have?"

"Oh yes. Oh yes!" Belamy said, brightening as if struck with a sudden idea. "There are several people who have let slip to me that they have rare tomes I haven't been able to find yet. Laribel Ossertine, nearby in the Old Town, is one. Bakurin Gemhide is another. He lives near the docks, though I'm not as confident in him as I am with her. He may have been lying to make himself seem more impressive than he really is; I know he does that from time to time. I've seen Laribel's collection, though, and she isn't lying. Another of interest would be Jack Gherun, who lives near the Baron's Palace."

Skate ran these options through her internal filter, catching the relevant information. Jack Gherun, whoever he was, would be a poor choice, given his living situation near the seat of official governance of the city. Guards would be everywhere.

Then there was Gemhide, who both wasn't a sure thing and lived near the docks. The Boss's map had a lot of red pins around there. Could she be sure that Gemhide's house was not on the list of "protected" properties? The last thing she needed was to have to navigate with Haman the delicacies of a possible breach of the Ink against their own contract with a client, especially with a bizarre creature stuck behind her back hearing every word. The Old Town mark was probably safest.

"I'll try Laribel. She's closest, right?"

"That's right. Rattle can guide you there from within the backpack. And be sure she doesn't know I'm connected to this—that she doesn't even spot you. As my nearest acquaintance, she may have seen you sneak around the neighborhood. Whatever the situation, she is not to be harmed, and you are not to be seen. Understood?"

"Yeah, yeah," Skate said, hoisting the backpack on her shoulders. "I'm gonna go case the place. I've got a few hours until night, and I want to know what I'll be getting into before I do the job."

"Oh, why wait? I have it on very good authority that Laribel will be away from her home, where she lives alone, well into the evening. You should make your way there as quickly as possible. Besides, you don't want to be caught out in the cold tonight, do you?" He had taken on a cheerful disposition, one with a forced nonchalance that was not endearing at all; he came across as more worried than gregarious.

"What authority?" Skate asked, as she heard Rattle do its rhythmic clicking and felt its bouncing in the backpack.

Before Belamy could answer, there was a heavy knock at the door. He looked from the door back to her. All pretension of good humor had vanished. He looked positively stricken.

"Hide! In the kitchen!" he hissed, waving her away. "When I get everybody upstairs, slip out the front. Remember: you must not be seen!"

Confused, Skate hid, sliding into the kitchen and leaving the door cracked, both to hear what was going on and to avoid making extra noise by opening the door when she left. She couldn't see far into the main room, but she could hear Belamy make his way to the door. She heard the heavy door swing open on its hinges, and Belamy broke out in a hearty laugh. "Come in, friends, come in!"

These unknown guests shuffled in from the cold and knocked the snow and ice from their shoes in the entryway. Skate looked down at her own ratty footwear; she had not done the same. A bolt of panic shot through her. Clods of snow and ice almost certainly served as tracks on her way into the kitchen. These guests might get curious if they noticed the incriminating puddles.

"Afternoon, Barrison. Glad you've got a fire going, for once," a gruff male voice said. Judging from where she heard the voice coming from, the man speaking had moved closer to the fire. She heard him clap and rub his hands together.

As he warmed himself, a second voice, this one obviously feminine, added, "Yes, it's much better in here than the last time I paid you a visit." From the sound of it, she was still near the door. "Your downstairs looks like it's actually been lived in, rather than covered up in sheets and dust by servants while the master's away." She had a condescending lilt to her words, and Skate could hear the sneer in them.

"Laribel and Bakurin, you've always been such great wits," Belamy said with much more ease than he had managed before, sounding genuinely sardonic rather than slightly manic. Skate's mouth dropped open at the names. It seemed that the old man's "good authority" had been very trustworthy after all! The list he had given her had not been randomly chosen; they were to be his guests for the evening.

A third voice, this one male, soft, and thin, said something that sent another shock of panic coursing through her: "What are those puddles, Barrison?" Gherun (she assumed) sounded closer than Ossertine had; he must have moved to the fire with Gemhide.

"Oh, I went out earlier. I must have forgotten to clean up on my way to the kitchen." Belamy laughed, then muttered words. Skate could hear him getting closer with each bout of repeated muttering.

"What was this new discovery you wanted to show us?" Ossertine asked, coming from the general direction of the fireplace; all three were apparently warming themselves now. Skate let go of a breath that she had been holding since Gherun had noticed the puddles. They seemed to have accepted Belamy's explanation.

"Oh, it's quite interesting, I think you'll agree," Belamy said. He sounded like he was just on the other side of the door now. "Did you all bring the copies of the book?" After getting three general affirmations, he went on, "Excellent! I believe I've found an odd variation in my copy, and I wanted to compare notes. If Kewpier was as clever as I believe she was, this is no calligrapher's error, but an indication that there is particular attention to be paid to the text. It may even be some sort of clue toward some code she wove into the account, only to be deciphered once enough copies had been found. In fact..."

His voice had been moving away and becoming more indistinct as he talked. Skate heard footsteps on stone and knew that he had successfully moved the party upstairs to ponder his esoteric discovery. She risked a peek into the main room and found it empty.

Before she stepped back out, Skate quietly knocked the remaining slush on her feet onto the kitchen floor. She slipped through the door and saw that her floor puddles from before were gone; Belamy must have been "cleaning up after himself" with all that muttering.

Conscious of Rattle's muted and bizarre laughter in the backpack, Skate crept noiselessly across the room, out through the barely open front door, and into the cold afternoon light.

CHAPTER 4

IN WHICH A DESTINATION IS REACHED, A
TRAP IS BYPASSED, AND A MAN IS KICKED IN
THE GROIN.

Skate hurried away from Belamy's door and across the street, trying her best to stay out of sight of any interested parties. Her breath formed temporary clouds in front of her eyes as she jogged, and the ground was intermittently patched with piles of snow that had not yet melted or been shoveled away. The residual warmth of the old man's house was keeping some of the chill away, but she could feel it dissipating as she darted around pedestrians to cross the busy road.

When she was safely out of sight of the general population, Skate began to slap her hands together and breathe into them. "Where do I go, eyeball?" she said, knowing Rattle could hear her. She felt a light tap on the right side of her back. "Does that mean I need to go right?"

In response, Rattle clicked and tapped twice more, a little harder, on the right side of her back.

"Okay, then, right it is."

Rattle clicked again but did no more tapping, so Skate set off in the direction the odd thing had indicated.

In this way, she was able to find Laribel Ossertine's home easily. Rattle tapped and jabbed to move her left, right, or straight, sometimes forcing Skate to hiss *"Too hard!"* over her shoulder, earning confused looks from passersby. Caribolians, though, were used to a certain level of eccentricity in people walking their streets, and no one paid her any mind beyond initial irritation or confusion. Skate, in return, ignored their stares and went on her way, secretly guided by the strangest thing she'd ever met.

After several more avenues and alleyways, Skate stood across the street from a row of tall and narrow homes. The one directly in front of her was the one Rattle was prodding her toward. "You sure that's it?" she muttered into the alleyway behind her, not caring if anyone else saw her talking to no one.

Rattle clicked once and nudged her forward in the center of her back.

"All right, hold on," Skate said, taking stock of what was ahead of her.

Ossertine's home was part of a set of houses connected to one another. *They look like books on a shelf,* she thought; the thin faces of the homes jutted out like a row of book spines. Most of the street block was effectively one wide, squat structure divided up into smaller living spaces. There was some variation—one house might have an awning while the next did not, and some of the houses rose to a third or even a fourth landing—but these minor instances of individualization did little to set any particular house apart from another. The overall effect was rather the opposite: the small fluctuations in cosmetic choice served to highlight their similarities.

Skate sighed at Ossertine's place. Although there were no lights on within it, nothing else she saw of the house made her think the job of breaking in without attracting attention would be an easy one.

There was, as far as she could tell, one door to the place. There was only one window at the ground floor, and it was blocked by a large piece of furniture on the inside. She would have to go in through the front door, or else climb up to the roof and try to break in through the second-story window. The first option was terrible, since there were people milling around, one of whom was bound to spot her and give a description to the Guard. But clambering into a second-story window was just as likely to attract unwanted attention.

Skate knew the area somewhat, and she thought that there were more houses behind this row, facing the other direction—which meant there would be no back door.

She had never been atop the buildings. There *could* be some sort of roof access. She muttered over her shoulder, "I'm going to try to get to the roof to see if there's a way in."

"Bully for you," a soft, reedy voice responded. She whipped around to see Kite standing there, using his knife to clean his fingernails. He was not looking at her as he worked. He leaned against the alleyway wall with contemptuous ease. "Why you trying to get in, love?"

She tried to stay calm, but her nervousness projected as petulance. "None of your business, Kite."

"The Ink's business is my business. Is this Ink's business?" His voice was disinterested, and he still wasn't looking at her, but she could sense an icy chill in his words. Violence danced just underneath the surface with Kite, always.

Skate grimaced at him. "Yeah, Kite, but you're not a Boss or a lieutenant. I don't have to tell you anything." She turned away from him and moved toward one of the houses that had a ladder up against it.

Kite was a nuisance. He probably thought Skate was on the trail of a big score and was attempting to horn in on the haul. She wasn't going to let him get to her, though. Her mother had taught her that bullies feed off the misery of others, so she'd starve him.

To Skate's annoyance, when she looked back, she saw him occupying the space she had vacated, watching her. *He fancies himself a detective*, she thought, sticking her tongue out at him and beginning to climb up the ladder.

The flat roofs that greeted her were not particularly promising—nothing but straw thatching. She moved over to Ossertine's roof and was pleasantly surprised. There was a wooden trapdoor under some loose straw. It was latched but unlocked. She pulled at it, and the creak was painfully loud. She tried and failed to keep the door from crashing as it opened. It was heavier than she'd expected.

Skate swore as the rumble from the door rolled under her feet. She almost bounded through the hole in the roof due to sheer nerves, but she paused when she saw something dangerous on the lip of the frame.

It was small, and by design very easy to miss: a glyph painted onto the lip. Twitch had taught her to look for such things when entering unfamiliar nice houses, and her wariness had saved her. If she had crossed the boundary made by the trapdoor's frame without first speaking the proper password, the symbol would have released whatever murderous energy it contained. Some such runes would trigger if even seen, though this one wasn't blasting her with any arcane energies. It was probably activated by passing through without a password.

Skate wondered whether Ossertine was capable of making such a trap herself, or if she had hired someone to create the magical deterrent.

Regardless, Twitch had taught Skate how to disarm it. She pulled a metal wire from her clothes. There were two points that she had to touch with perfect accuracy and at precisely the same time. Success would mean the magic within would fizzle out, and she would be able to pass without harm. Failure would trigger it.

Wire in hand, Skate stood up and began to jog in place. Neighbors might hear her, but that bang from the door had dispensed with that concern.

Rattle clicked indignantly in the backpack.

"Shush," she said between heavy breaths. "I need...to get...warmer." Rattle clicked twice within, and then fell to silence, apparently ready to wait and be jostled by her aerobics.

When she felt confident in the warmth she had started to radiate, Skate lay near the wooden frame of the door and bent the wire into position. She took a deep breath, and let it out. She took another, and let it out too. She took several more, steadying her nerves for the task at hand. She took a final deep breath, and she released it. When her lungs were empty, she double-checked the positioning of her hands and pushed both forward to their respective targets. When she felt the wire make contact, she closed her eyes.

Feeling that she was still alive and unhurt, Skate opened them again. She saw only the ward placed on the wood, her bent wire making contact exactly where it should. As she watched, a trickle of energy trailed across the surface of the defeated trap and dissolved into nothing. With a satisfied grin, she dropped down into the house.

Skate landed wrong and had to tumble into a roll to avoid hurting herself or Rattle. She struggled to her feet, the backpack adding difficulty to the process.

Rattle clicked again. Skate ignored it and took stock of her surroundings. She had landed in a bedroom. The late afternoon sun cast a slightly orange glow on everything, making it look warm and sleepy. There were dressers and end tables, and a privacy screen in the corner. The bed was feminine in its decoration, but not distractingly so. Everything in the room had an air that suggested it was relatively new and well-kept. It was very unlike Belamy's home that way; everything in his home had carried a trail of dust from months of neglect—the location of everything unchanging and unmoving, inviolate even as it was forgotten. The only things in his house that did not bear that sense of abandonment were the books. They alone saw care and use, and they enjoyed a hallowed status.

It did not appear that Ossertine held her own books in quite such high regard, because Skate saw no sign of any books in the room, which seemed to occupy most of the second floor.

"Do you know where her books are?" she asked her back in hushed tones; a rooftop thump might have perked up ears, but a strange voice afterward would raise true suspicion, and that was attention she could ill afford.

Rattle avoided clicking but shifted around in the pack and pushed downward with just enough force that her head and shoulders jerked backward a bit. "Okay, I got it," she said, taking the bent staircase down to the ground floor.

This room looked much more promising—like Belamy's study, though smaller. While the upper floor was entirely directed toward accommodating a comfortable bedroom, the ground floor divided its space into two sections. One, which Skate saw through an open door, was an unstaffed kitchen. The study she was in functioned as a den or living room. Rows upon rows of books covered the room's walls, the line of spines broken only twice: once where a comfortable sofa and table with a shaded lamp were positioned, behind which was a small square landscape painting, and again across from it where there hung a huge painting of an unfamiliar figure engaged in battle.

"Okay, eyeball," Skate said over her shoulder, "pick one." She unslung the bag and held it in front of her, afraid that mishandling it might get her stabbed or clawed. She could feel Rattle positioning itself inside the bag, and the heavy cloth of the bag shifted as the bat-winged eyeball spider peeked out to begin its survey.

Its eye roved hungrily over the titles, and if a book lacked one,

Rattle stuck a trio of spindly legs out to open it. If it looked familiar (as the first several did), the book would be replaced on the shelf.

Skate walked with Rattle across the shelves that lined almost every inch of wall in the room, eventually standing on tiptoe to let it read the highest shelf, then bending at the waist to let it read the bottom. The sun moved further down while they scanned every book in the room. As they neared the last of the library, Rattle clicked its legs in irritation, and Skate couldn't help but let out a heavy sigh. Belamy had said that there were books here he didn't have. Where were they?

Her arms were getting tired. After Rattle had pulled and replaced the last of the books and devolved into a clicking frenzy, Skate set the bag down. The sought-after books were not here.

For the first time, Skate let her mind wander from the job. Not having anything else to do while Rattle stewed in its irritation, she found the only thing in the room worth looking at other than the books. The small square painting—the one that she could take out of the room if she wanted to—was dark and foreboding, though not masterfully done. The amateurish brushstrokes created a somewhat blurred image of a small island in a lake, all ground areas lush with various flora. It was evening in the painting, just as it was quickly becoming outside. The island in the middle had the only building in the whole picture: a thin tower with a single light peeking through a window in the top floor. Habit made Skate begin to examine the frame to see if it might be valuable.

Her initial appraisal was not promising. It looked like gold, but a gentle touch revealed wood under paint rather than precious metal. It did reveal something much more interesting, though: the painting would shift very easily from its place, despite its size and weight. She pushed it to the right and caught a glimpse of bare wood behind the frame. Curious, Skate tried to remove the entire painting and found that it dislodged easily. It was also heavy, and she struggled to set the thing down gently. When she had placed it safely on the floor, she saw with surprise that there was a small door the size of a window suspended in the wall. She pulled the heavy iron ring that served as the handle.

It was only as the door began to swing open that Skate thought of how foolish an act that had been; if this oddly placed door opened into the neighboring house's wall, as it must do, she risked being spotted for a thief. Before she could admonish herself for her curiosity, she took in the sight in front of her:

This was not the neighbor's house but a spacious room lined floor to ceiling with books, just like the room she was standing in—except the ceiling was higher, and the room considerably larger. A pair of comfortable-looking chairs and a fireplace interrupted the flow of the books across the room. Skate briefly thought about how dangerous it was to have a fireplace around this many books as she climbed through the door.

An ear-splitting screech rent the air. Panicked, Skate looked at the doorframe and spotted the culprit: another rune, this one designed to alarm rather than hurt. Presumably, Ossertine had not wanted to risk damaging her prized collection, but the noise was sure to attract a huge amount of unwanted attention. "Rattle!" Skate shouted, trying to be heard over the din. "Get out here and find a book! Quick!"

Before she had finished the command, Rattle had darted past her, flapping its dark wings happily as it roved the titles. The thing took less than ten seconds to pick one and clicked happily as it bobbed haphazardly toward the backpack with its prize in tow.

The screeching continued as Skate bolted out of the strange room. She slammed the hidden door shut, hoping that it would smother the noise, but to no avail. She pulled the neck of her ragged tunic over her nose to hide her face, and tied a rag from a pocket across her brow. Then she picked up the backpack, heavier with both the book and Rattle within, and bolted out the door.

Ten feet out the door, she heard a voice cry out for her to stop. She fought the urge to look for the source, since it would be no one she wanted to talk to: the best-case scenario was that it was a neighbor or other witness, and turning would only give them a description.

Skate darted down an alleyway, and heavy footfalls in the snow behind her told her she was being followed. She knew how to lose a tail, and set to work on randomizing her path; if she had a destination in mind, she would make for it eventually, even if she were not consciously trying to. She knew to avoid the house of Barrison Belamy, and so pushed it out of her mind. She took note of which way she turned and varied it at each opportunity: left, left, straight, right, straight again.

As she ran, Skate found a building with outdoor stairs leading to the roof. She bounded up them, still not looking back to see who was chasing her.

While taking the steps three at a time, Skate caught a glimpse of the blue-trimmed tabards of the Guard blowing past and below her. In the fading light, they managed not to see her ascent.

Skate crested the landing and found herself facing a family sitting under an awning. The father of the group shouted "Hey!" and Skate knew she couldn't stay still. She leapt to a neighbor's roof, and then the next neighbor's roof as well.

Skate was on the roof of a fourth house when she heard a Guardsman call out for her to stop again. She spared a glance backward, which proved a mistake: she missed her footing on the slanted roof and went tumbling. As she neared the ground, Skate tried to roll with the fall, but couldn't manage it. She landed wrong on her hand and cried out in pain.

Rattle clicked behind her. It did not sound like its laughter, but she was engrossed in the pain and could not register what Rattle was trying to tell her.

Skate found herself standing somehow, leaning against the building from which she had fallen. Her wrist was either sprained or broken, neither of which was good news. Taking a deep breath, she took off into the night.

#-ᛞ-ᛉ-ᚢ

Twitch had been the one to teach her how to throw off a pursuer. "You're going to end up r-running in a straight line unless you try not to, you know?" he had said, explaining the purpose of the constant changing, "Nothing's easier to catch than somebody r-running straight ahead."

As she was taught, so did she put into practice. It took but a few minutes after hurting her arm to throw the Guards completely off.

Skate was not completely sure where she ended up. She was not near the docks, since the smell of fish was very distant—only detectable whenever the wind blew north. It was possible she was still in the Old Town, but she had no idea where in that district she might be. If she could get to a roof, she would be able to find landmarks among the sleepy old buildings. However, the prospect of getting that high with one arm led Skate to decide that was not going to happen. She was not sure she could even climb one-handed, much less from street level to the top of a building. Her only hope was to walk the streets at dusk and try to determine where her soon-to-be-satisfied patron's house was.

Skate's arm shook with barely contained torment at each step. She focused on the street and its occupants to take her mind off of the incredible discomfort. She saw no vagrants or Guards. That told her she was neither in the slums nor in the Baron's district. Certain areas tended to attract certain occupants, and the absence of these two groups was enough to tell her that she was likely still in the Old Town.

The Old Town had one major avenue, and it was the only part of this section of the city that was consistently visible throughout the night. The lampposts had been lit well before the onset of the evening, the lampmen wanting to be done with their work before the cold became unbearable. It was approaching that point now for Skate as she made her way toward the orange lamps; her skin felt like it was on fire every time a piece of threadbare clothing moved across it, and her feet were numb. "Rattle," Skate whispered behind her, "do you know where we are?"

Before she reached the street, Skate grunted as she was yanked into a crevice between two buildings. The space could not rightly be called an alley; a person may have been able to comfortably walk between the sturdy wooden walls if he were not terribly large, but that was all the space available.

Skate was currently pinned against one of these walls, her feet suspended about two feet from the ground, her dropped bag on the ground. She stared into the cruel lean face of one of the last people she had wanted to see again that day: Kite, who held her against the rough wood with one of his forearms across her chest. His other arm was bent as his hand rested jauntily on his hip. His blades were out of sight. "Evening, girlie," he said with a sneer.

When Skate didn't respond, he contorted his sharp face into a mockery of pain and continued, "Aw, now don't be that way. I's just trying to help, kenit? You was doing pretty good running from the Guards, but that fall looked pretty nasty." He pointed his free hand toward the dropped bag.

He knows the tricks, Skate realized. *He was able to follow me.*

"Wassin there?"

Skate gave him no answer but a forward-jutting jaw and a look that she hoped could curdle milk.

Kite smiled his vicious smile. "I toldja not to be that way once already, didn't I? Come on, girlie, and tell me wassin the bag. If it's Ink business, I got a right to know."

"Not a lieutenant," she muttered, finding it harder to breathe as he increased the pressure on her. "Don't gotta tell you nothing."

Kite still smiled. "I'll make ya tell me, you little *snot,*" he said as he leaned into her. She gasped and coughed; he had brought his free hand straight into her stomach, and hard. Between the pain in her arm and not being able to breathe, she was worried she might lose consciousness. *Stay awake. Stay awake.* She repeated that to herself as her swimming vision came to rest on the singularly unpleasant image of Kite sneering at her.

His face no longer smiled; it was twisted in hate. "What's in the bag, girlie?" His voice was low and dangerous, and she knew he'd continue to hurt her—but never actually draw any blood from her or kill her; even Kite was not that stupid—until she let him in on what she was doing. He had done it to Twitch before, and she knew he had done it to everyone he had ever worked around who was smaller and weaker than he was.

Then Skate saw something over his shoulder that gave her a great idea.

"If you're not going to spill ink, lemme go," she said, pretending to plead. She let her voice turn into a whimper. "Please, Kite, come on." When she saw the familiar look in his eye (the one like a snake about to strike a cornered mouse), and he was about to speak, she kicked her foot straight forward as hard as she could and connected lower than his stomach—which was exactly what she meant to do. Kite's arm loosened. "Now!" Skate said and dropped down to the ground, crying out as the movement hurt her arm.

A whirl of black lines and flapping wings filled her vision. Rattle's white "body" bobbed in the air as it brought its legs to bear, slapping and stabbing the young man, who could not understand what he was seeing, much less fend it off.

"Get off!" Kite yelped several times, his voice slightly higher than normal. Rattle slapped him across the face, drawing a thin red line and sending him twisting against the wall. The thin legs poked through Kite's clothes, pinning him up against the wall. It had a leg pulled back to strike at his throat when Skate yelled, "No!"

Rattle paused, and twisted slightly toward her, its eye shifting to the right and left in a quizzical gesture. "Don't kill him," she said, grabbing the backpack off the ground. "No killing," she added emphatically as it turned its attention back to Kite.

"What…" he muttered, his arms dangling uselessly off to his sides as he tried to make sense of what he was seeing. "Wassis?"

"Get outta here, Kite; I dunno if it'll kill you or not if you don't."

Rattle pulled its legs out of the wall behind Kite and let him settle back on his feet. Skate saw with relief that the blow to the face hadn't actually drawn blood, though it had broken the skin.

Kite stood stunned for a second before his feet began to take him down the narrow space between buildings. He did not look back.

"Thanks," Skate said to Rattle. In response, it bent one of its legs and patted her twice on the head. It then flapped over to the bag and crawled back in. "You could probably fly the rest of the way, now," she said. Rattle just clicked again and brought a leg out to tap on the straps. Skate sighed and scooped the pack up as she stepped into the only well-lit avenue of Old Town.

CHAPTER 5

IN WHICH A PARCEL IS DELIVERED, A ROOM
IS EXPLORED, AND A PANCAKE IS DROPPED
ON THE FLOOR.

Once Skate found her bearings on the main road through the Old Town, reaching Belamy's house was simple. Her arm still hurt, but her breathing had returned to normal since Kite's assault. By the time she found Belamy's stone-block home, she was bitterly cold. The fire burned low downstairs, but she could not tell if any of Belamy's guests were still there. The white light was on upstairs, but that told her nothing on its own.

"Rattle, do Barrison's friends know about you?" She felt a poke at her back, which she took to mean "yes." She tapped the bag and said, "Good. Go inside and tell me if the coast is clear to come in." She heard the flap open and the flutter of Rattle's wings as it extricated itself from the bag. It puttered over her shoulder, letting its slender legs clack playfully as it went to the house's front door. It hooked two of its legs around the handle and flapped its wings fitfully to get it open. Once the door was cracked enough for it to get through, the thing slipped in, leaving Skate utterly isolated in the cold. With nothing but the pain in her arm for company and nothing to do but wait, she thought over the confrontation with Kite.

He had seen Rattle and would not likely forget what the thing looked like. With some snooping, he would be able to determine its origin and owner. He would know the next time they met whom she was working for, and he was smart enough to puzzle out that Belamy was either hiring her out as a member of the Ink, or that he was soon to be a mark for thievery. If he decided it was probably the former, she would be fine; Kite did not care much for rules, but he knew better than to interfere with a contract. If he correctly guessed the latter, he would almost certainly decide to steal from him first, ruining her plan and landing her in hot water with the Boss. Any mark that wasn't part of a contract was fair game for whomever got the goods first.

Skate took a deep breath and let it out as a sigh. The next time they met would be unpleasant; Kite was not the type of person to let personal injury or insult go unanswered, and his answers to such things were usually escalations. She had once seen a new Ink member (she'd never learned his name) muscle past him in a hall in one of the safe houses. When Kite and this neophyte had later gone on a job together with a team, the job had gotten done, but the hall ruffian had been the only one caught by the Guard. He'd never left their custody, and was found dead in his cell two days later. The magistrate's official decree on the matter was "mysterious circumstances," and no more investigation occurred into the death of the lowly thief. It was whispered that Kite had had something to do with it, but there was no proof, or even a hint of it, so the Boss let him be. She did not like to think about what he would want to do to her for her well-placed kick.

As Skate was ruminating on these dark considerations, Belamy's front door creaked a bit wider open. A thin black leg poked out and bent upward three times. Skate took that as a sign that it was safe to enter, and crossed the street. The cold was quite painful now, in the dark, and even a low-burning fire would be of immeasurable comfort.

The fire crackled intermittently, casting a low reddish glow around the room. There were no lanterns lit downstairs anymore. Belamy sat behind the desk at the far end of the room with a book open. He was tracing a line across the page with his thin finger, reading in the shadows. As she watched, he traced the same line several times. She guessed he must have been memorizing the text. Not wanting to interrupt, she moved toward the fire without a word and began to warm herself in its glow. She lifted a log from the rack and dumped it into the embers. The thud as it hit jolted Belamy out of his trance. He looked up and smiled.

"Welcome back to the conquering heroes!" He laughed as he stood up and walked around to the other side of his desk. "Rattle has filled me in on your progress, of course," he said as he rubbed his hands together. His eyes were fixed on the bag. Skate handed the backpack to the old man and sat back down in front of the fireplace, enjoying the increased warmth as the new log caught. "Oh, yes, wonderful! *Bereziah's Chronicles!* Good find, Rattle. And good work, Skate. I'm going to get started on this right away. Rattle, take that." He pointed to the open book on his desk, and Rattle clicked its legs together and obeyed, flapping over to retrieve the text. The flying eyeball made its way upstairs, leaving Skate and Belamy together in the now much brighter room. Skate leaned forward, letting the warmth from the fireplace roll over her as she gingerly explored the damage to her arm. She could move it, but it hurt. Hopefully that was something that would disappear in time.

"You don't have to stay in here, you know," Belamy said without raising his eyes from the pages in front of him on his desk. Skate turned her head to look at him but did not answer. In the yellow-orange light from the fire, he looked very old indeed. His nose was large, his cheeks were sunken in and shriveled, and a liver spot marked his forehead. His hands were equally wrinkled, his fingers appearing to be little more than bones with skin covering them. She thought of the last time she had stayed too long in water, and how it had caused deep and winding waves on the skin of her fingers; his whole body looked that way to her, of what she could see.

"How old are you?" The question came without her bidding, and she blinked several times after she asked it, not even sure if she had spoken the words aloud. Belamy took his eyes from the page with a quizzical look.

"How old are *you?*" he responded pointedly.

"Nine years," she said, "and it'll be ten on New Year's Day."

"You were born on New Year's Day?"

"Dunno when I was born, do I? So I just call it New Year's Day and be done with it."

Belamy seemed to consider the answer, then nodded in acceptance. "A reasonable way to handle it, I suppose."

"So how about you?"

"Oh, I wasn't born on New Year's Day."

"But how old are you?" she said, rolling her eyes.

"What's wrong with your arm?" he said, moving out from behind his desk, a look of concern on his features.

"Don't change the subject." Skate held her arm in her other hand and shifted it away from him, as if she meant to play a game of keep-away. She didn't believe his concern was genuine, but merely a way to avoid telling her something personal.

"I'm not changing the subject, I just—"

"Get away!" she said, more loudly than she meant to, scrambling to her feet and cradling the wounded arm in her good hand.

"Will you stop? You could hurt—"

"How old are you?"

"I'm a hundred and seven!" he shouted back at her, his eyes wide with concern. "I'm a hundred and seven years old. Now stop jumping around. Is your arm hurt? What did you do?"

Skate smiled through the wince as she dropped her hand to her side. "I think I landed on it wrong," she said, mimicking a trip to get her point across. "You don't look a hundred and seven."

"Clean living," he said offhandedly as he moved to one of the bookshelves. He pulled one of the decanters being used to help the books stay upright off the shelf, and the end book fell over. He paid it no mind as he uncorked the delicate-looking glass. It held a dark blue liquid. "Hold out your arm."

"Why?" Skate said, reflexively bringing the injured arm up to be held by the other arm, wincing again as another wave of pain shot through her.

"I want to help."

She eyed him suspiciously. "How do I know it won't hurt me?" she asked, shooting a swift glance at the bottle. "How do I know it's not a trick?"

Belamy's lined face fell slack for a moment; his expression might have been one of surprise. Then he restored himself to a look of irritation. "Young lady," he began, using that term that Skate was sure was being meant to belittle and mock her, "if I wanted to hurt you, I would be using a far less expensive method to do it. I don't invite people into my home only to injure them for a lark."

"You invite them over to steal from them."

"Borrow!" he insisted, "to *borrow* from them. And I invited them over weeks ago, before I'd ever met you. It was just a happy coincidence that they were—never mind!" he said, shaking his head. "It doesn't matter. It's not going to hurt you. I promise."

He held the dark blue liquid out, offering its contents again. Gingerly, she put her arm forward, careful to hold it limp to avoid more pain. Belamy tipped the decanter, being very careful to control the amount that left the bottle. As the dark blue stuff poured out, Skate had time to notice that it flowed much like water before a trickle landed on her sprained wrist. She yelped as it landed, feeling more pain. She cut the yelp short, though, because she realized she was only feeling the coldness of the liquid rather than the burning she had first thought. The dark blue disappeared into her skin as soon as it landed. Belamy lifted the decorative glass bottle back up after the brief contact the liquid made with her skin. He had been careful not to spill a drop on the floor or himself. "Better?"

Skate looked at her arm. It didn't feel any different, but she had been holding it in that position on purpose. She risked a contraction of the muscle and brought her hand up a fraction of an inch. It responded without sending any warnings to her. She clenched her hand into a fist. No pain there, either. "Wow!" she said, forgetting her mistrust of the old man. "It's perfect." She bent her arm and threw it in a wide circle with abandon. "It's like I never hurt it at all!" She had never encountered such an immediate relief from pain before. "What's in that stuff?" she asked, casting an eye on the bottle.

"Magic," Belamy responded with a satisfied smile as he replaced the bottle on the shelf. "A gift from a priest, a healer, years ago. For minor injuries—cuts, bruises, sprains, that sort of thing—it does the trick. As long as I don't use it all at one go, it always refills itself. It's been enormously useful over the years, though recently—well, I'm glad it helped."

"Is that how you got to be a hundred and seven? Using that stuff?"

Belamy locked his expression into that satisfied smile. "No. The potion does nothing to help fight aging. Clean living," he repeated with a wave of his hand, dismissing further inquiries into his longevity. He walked back to his desk. "Now, if you're ready, you know where your room is. I had Rattle clean it when you left this morning, so it should be ready for you. There may be some dust that evaded cleaning, but it will certainly be better than sleeping on the street." He returned his attention back to his book and said no more to her.

Knowing a dismissal when she heard one, she turned toward the stairs, then stopped. "And Rattle really cooks?"

"Rattle really cooks."

Skate tried to gauge the old man's reaction to her question. As far as she could tell, there was none. He was utterly engrossed in his reading. She felt a question forming in her mind, and she was divided about it. As she looked at the book and saw the joy and concentration on the old man's face, the question glowed hotter in the back of her brain. She pushed it down, away, where it would not come out into the world unbidden:

How do I read?

Skate turned away and made her way upstairs, leaving behind the old man brooding over his new book. The air got noticeably colder as she ascended, but not nearly to the point of freezing that it was outside.

The stairs led directly into an upstairs hallway with three doors. The one on the left went to Belamy's room, and the first on the right led to the other study. She could hear the soft flapping and clicking of Rattle moving about the latter, presumably either replacing books on the shelf or else taking one down for itself. The remaining room was to be her own.

When she'd been here that morning, Belamy had opened a creaky door into a room that looked untouched for decades. Everything in the room had been caked in a considerable layer of dust. There were some unidentifiable pieces of furniture that had long ago either been broken into kindling or else rotted away into useless debris. The room had been suffused with a smell like moldy clothing, and Skate had been glad that there had not been warmth to make the odor overwhelming. "Don't worry," Belamy had said, "Rattle will clean this up before you get back. I'll have him take care of it immediately, in fact." He had closed the door on a room that Skate did not look forward to inhabiting.

The room as she now saw it was unrecognizable. The floors had been swept, and nothing was broken. The room held an empty desk with a chair, a bed with an end table with a white-lit lantern on it, and a dresser. It was this last piece of furniture that she gravitated toward first. She had never stayed in a room that held such a thing. She had nothing to place inside it, but thinking of the tall, heavy wooden set of drawers as being in some way her own felt exhilarating. *It's not mine,* she reminded herself, *not really.* But it was hers to use while she stayed here.

It did not look particularly old. She opened the empty drawers, relishing the feel of the grating wood as she slid them open and shut with successive light bangs.

Skate moved to the bed next. It was set on sturdy legs, the mattress soft but having some resistance to it. Further investigation revealed a wicker latticework to support the soft pallet on top. The bed was not fabulously decorated, nor particularly expensive-looking—if she had been burgling and came upon a room with this type of bed, she'd likely move on to bigger and better marks—but getting to sleep in such a bed was an enormous extravagance. In the safe houses, she slept on mats on the floor or in dingy hammocks strung up between beams. She had only slept on a proper mattress before the fire of her earliest years.

Skate pushed away the unexpected and painful memories, and went to examine the desk. It was a simple affair, with a drawer in the front and nothing on its surface. She knew immediately that it was a thing of age, unlike the other two pieces of furniture in the room. The top was mostly smooth, with a few small pits scarring it where an over-zealous writer had pressed through the page with their quill—or else someone had used it as a convenient surface to cut something. Skate could feel each divot as she ran her hand across the top, each scar like a message from the past. *There are memories here; there is* history *here.*

She opened the desk drawer. Inside was a black slate, somewhat worn around the edges. She had seen these before, but they had always been accompanied by a stick of chalk. She could find nothing of the sort within the drawer. She did notice more marks in the drawer, though. These were not sporadic as the marks on the top had been; they were deliberately carved in the lower right-hand corner. She brought the lantern closer, its magically created light illuminating the drawer completely. She recognized the carved things as letters, though she had no idea what their significance was.

Skate replaced the slate in the drawer and closed it. She noticed a small washtub, bucket, drying cloth, and privacy shade in the corner. The tub was near a vent in the wall; she felt hot air blowing through, just as Belamy had said it would. The water in the bucket wasn't hot, but it wasn't cold either; the hot air had kept it from turning to ice.

Skate hadn't bathed in weeks. She decided to change that, leaving her filthy clothes on the floor.

The water was cold, so her bath was quick. She dried off with the cloth, then bent over the tub and dipped her filthy rags into the water. When she had swished them around to her satisfaction, she laid them out flat in front of the vent. By morning, they would be dry, and hopefully not frozen.

Skate put the cloth down too and quickly got into the bed; the room had felt fairly warm before the bath, but felt significantly less so now. Snuggling in, she fully shuttered the lantern, extinguishing all light in the room.

Under the warm blankets in the pitch darkness, it did not take her long to fall asleep.

#⌂☼⅄◌

The next morning, Skate saw that her tub and bucket had been taken away. The fact that she had not awoken during what she assumed must have been Rattle's visit impressed her. She had been trained through several years of company exclusively among thieves to wake at the lightest sound. Whatever Rattle was, it could be very quiet when it needed to be.

Skate's clothes were folded neatly on the foot of the bed. Her washing had done little to improve the state of them; they had gone from a dark brown grunge to a dark gray splotch. But they didn't smell as bad as they had before, so she felt fine as she put them back on. She jumped as a voice growled from the vent at the floor. She couldn't make out what was being said, so she moved closer.

"Hello?" Skate asked, peering into the dark. She could feel more warmth emanating from within but saw nothing but darkness.

"Skate," the voice said, and she could recognize Belamy's voice as it bounced through the metal tube to her room.

"Yeah?"

"Are you awake?"

"Are you making a joke?"

She thought she could hear the smile in his voice when he said, "It was an attempt, yes. Rattle is ready to make breakfast. Do you like pancakes?"

"I don't know."

She heard Belamy talking, but could make nothing out until his voice became clear again with, "...before. Skate, you'll love them. Come down whenever you're ready."

No more metal-warped words came toward her, so Skate got off the floor and walked down the stairs. Pots and pans were banging around behind the kitchen door. Belamy himself was seated at his desk, apparently entirely stationary through the night. The book in front of him was more than one-third read, and he didn't show any signs of pausing as Skate made her way toward the fire, which was crackling merrily. The supply of firewood looked as full as ever, though the fire was crackling hotter than it had when she had retired.

"Did you sleep at all last night?" she asked, warming the backs of her legs near the fire.

"I don't sleep during the night," he replied without taking his eyes off the page. "Did you enjoy your rest?"

"Yeah, thanks," she said, turning back toward the flame and warming her hands. "It made me glad I made the deal."

"Happy to hear it," he muttered, tapping his finger lightly on a word on the page. "I don't know who this is."

"What do you mean?"

"I don't know who this person is. She just appears in the story without any explanation. She's not in the story before this point, and I don't recognize her from other histories on the topic. I don't know who she is," Belamy repeated, pulling a smaller open book toward him. He dipped his quill into the inkwell and made some marks in the smaller book before tapping excess ink back into the well and laying down the quill to dry. "Very strange."

Skate wanted to ask more questions but was interrupted by the kitchen door banging open as Rattle announced breakfast with a clatter of clicks. It brought Skate a plate with flat brown things on top. "Pancakes?" she asked, picking one up before the piece she was holding tore off, dropping the rest of it on the floor. Rattle clicked in irritation at the wasted food and moved to retrieve it. "Sorry," she muttered after it as it disappeared back into the kitchen.

"Pancakes," Belamy confirmed, "and they're very soft, as you can see. If you like them, Rattle will make as many as you please."

Skate gingerly picked another up, making sure to hold it flat in her hand. As soon as her tongue touched the sweet bread-like food, her eyes went wide. She *did* like pancakes. She reflected that she was glad to get a nicer place to stay as she took another fluffy bite.

CHAPTER 6

At the conclusion of breakfast, Rattle flapped in and took Skate's plate away. She heard it bang into the other dishes as the door shut behind the flying eyeball. Belamy had no plate to take.

"Did you already eat?"

He gave a noncommittal grunt as he continued reading and taking notes. Because he clearly wanted the matter dropped, she persisted.

"If you don't sleep at night, when do you sleep?"

He gave no answer but continued reading silently. Skate thought she saw a hint of irritation on his wrinkly face despite his best efforts to remain impassive. Rattle began to live even more up to its name as it moved the pans and plates around in a cleaning frenzy behind the shut door.

"You don't really eat at all, do you?"

"No."

The frank admission threw her off, but only for a moment. "Same for sleep, right?"

"Right."

"How? Magic again?"

"The same as before," he said as he looked up and made a gesture toward where he had been wounded the night before last. "The magic I've done keeps me from needing things like sleep or food or even breath."

Why? she thought but did not ask. Belamy spoke as if she had asked the question aloud anyway.

"Time," he said, taking a thin wooden slat and placing it between the page of the book. "I did it for the sake of time. Think of how much of it you have to waste each day worrying about food and drink and sleep and exhaustion and soreness. Think of how vulnerable you are right now to a thousand thousand random occurrences." He waved his hand as he began to list examples: "The air could be sucked out of the room—or it could be flooded—or filled with deadly gas, filling your lungs. The fire might go out and not be able to be lit again. You will get hungry again, and tired and sick. You might get a cough; you might get cold; you might get uncomfortable and need to move around. You could get something in your eye or have to scratch an itch. Think of how much these things must occupy your time and attention. And it only grows worse with age: the body aches, the eyes become cloudy, the hearing fades, and the simplest of tasks become challenges to complete. I could not afford these distractions, so I did away with them."

"You did this so you could read more?" Skate asked in disbelief. *"That's* why you magicked away hunger and sleep and all that?"

Belamy's expression shifted from thoughtful to amused. "No, that's not why. I needed full use of my time, and then when my task was done, I needed to fill my time. The books became a useful occupation. Now they are how I pass my time, with Rattle and any other guests." As if on cue, Rattle banged another pot, and a splash could be heard through the door.

"What did you need all that time for? What was so important?"

Belamy grew stony-faced; though he kept his smile, it hardened somewhat. "I had my reasons. There's no need to say more than that."

Skate shifted weight back and forth on her feet. She could feel the discomfort settling in the room like a wet blanket in the summer heat, stifling and smothering. More to change the subject than out of curiosity, she asked, "What's that about?"

Belamy saw that she was pointing to the open book on his desk. "Ah. It's a history generally known as *Bereziah's Chronicles,* from the first line of the text: 'Here follow the chronicles of Bereziah, servant and protector of King Mehu of Agonia.' That's a translation, of course; the Agonianites didn't speak or write in our language."

"Those are funny names," Skate said, looking at the text. It looped and swirled, like it was all written without taking the quill from the surface of the page.

"I'm sure they'd have something to say about 'Skate' and 'Barrison' in return," Belamy said with a chuckle. "But yes, the names seem strange to us. Much of what the elves left for us to ponder seems strange."

"Elves?" Skate repeated, her voice and face revealing her disbelief. "There's no such thing as elves; they're just stories made up to scare kids and stuff."

"No, not at all! They're very real. Or they *were* real, rather. They left ruins behind, and books," Belamy said, tapping the page in front of him, "and tools, too. Yes, they did really walk among us at some point in the distant past. It is believed that everything we know of magic either came from the elves or was developed from what they left us. Their records are real, and that means they must have been real, too."

"Did you ever see one?" Skate asked. She wasn't fully convinced, but the mention of the elves sparked wonder, and she was curious despite her misgivings.

"Oh, no," he said, chuckling, "no, I never have seen one; nor has anyone in living memory. Even when I was a boy, a century ago, they were the stuff of ancient legend. Scholars like me are divided on just how long ago they were around; it could be as recently as the past five hundred years, but I'm of the opinion that they disappeared well over a thousand years ago. Most mentions of them after that point smack of invention rather than recollection, details added to stories to make them more interesting."

"What happened to them? Where'd they go?"

"We don't know. It's one of the great mysteries of those who study elven histories. No contemporary records exist explaining where the elves might have gone, and there are no writings that warn of some dire impending doom that only made the elves disappear. King Mehu," he said, motioning to the book in front of him, "was not the last of the Agonianite line, since this account lists several offspring and potential heirs to the throne. But this is the last known record of that kingdom's goings-on. I haven't read to the end, but I know there won't be a direct explanation for any forthcoming 'end of the elves'; I've talked to other scholars who have read it, and they've told me as much."

"So...they just disappeared?"

"They did. We don't know if they all packed up and traveled or were destroyed or something else entirely. We've never seen *any* of their physical remains, which deepens the mystery further, since we've had access for centuries to burial sites they built to stand the test of time. The structures themselves are relatively intact and resistant to the forces of nature and ravages of the centuries, and many treasures have been found within, but no bodies. This, despite the placement of receptacles for corpses being present. The old bodies are just gone. As I said, it's one of the great mysteries to those who study history."

"You said they invented magic?"

"Yes! Well, I'd say they discovered it more than invented it, but it comes out to the same thing." Belamy gestured toward one of his shelves, causing a book to float his way. "This," he said, spinning the green book slowly in the air, as if it were suspended on an invisible string, "is one of the most basic texts aspiring wizards are almost universally required to read as part of their education. It details what magic is and how to capture it for useful purposes, and it even lists specific spells for beginning wizards to learn. It's a translation from Elvish. The anonymous author of the book is largely responsible for magic as we know it for at least the past thousand years."

Skate gingerly took the book from the air. There were letters on the front of the book and on the side. "Just reading this can teach someone magic?"

"If the reader grasps what she's reading, yes, she will gain enough knowledge to enter into a larger world of energies and forces most people only whisper about." Belamy looked at Skate with a knowing smile.

Skate put the book down on the desk a little harder than she meant to in her rush to separate herself from what suddenly felt very dangerous. "What's happening in that story?" she asked, feeling herself blush as she rapidly changed the subject back to the other book.

Belamy's smile widened somewhat. "The company of Bereziah is on a quest to stop a war with a rival elven nation. Bereziah seems to believe that this other nation, the Kemelite nation, has misunderstood some action of King Mehu and is preparing for war because of it.

They're currently crossing a mountain range and have lost some of their number. The author is taking note of available food stocks, and is expressing concerns about their ability to cross the mountains."

Skate thought for a moment about the events described. "Sounds kinda boring."

Belamy chuckled. "I suppose it probably would be for someone with no interest in the topic. But do you know what I've found?" He leaned forward conspiratorially. "If you attempt to become interested in things, they become more interesting. And," he added, pointing an accusatory finger Skate's way, his face suddenly stern, "people who have interests in things are themselves more interesting. Have you ever met someone who thinks everything is *dull?* They're miserable to be around!" He threw his hands up in exasperation. "Don't let your hesitancy or disinterest linger, young lady. People who do that become unbearable and find no joy in anything." He settled into a more relaxed position again. "I've known people like this, Skate. I'd hate to see you get that way. It would be an absolute waste of your potential."

Skate found herself frowning. She didn't like being scolded. "It sounds like you just don't like your dumb book being made fun of." Before Belamy could respond, she turned and bolted out the door. It slammed shut behind her as she stepped into the cold winter street.

Skate was fuming. "Tell *me* what to do," she muttered, kicking a lingering snowdrift to splatter onto the street. She began stomping away in no particular direction. Rattle's food was in her belly, so she wasn't hungry. She didn't feel much of anything except anger, and the chill of the out-of-doors.

After a few minutes, her anger had cooled. She didn't know whether it was simply that time had passed, that she was beginning to feel guilty about her outburst, or that the cold kept her from staying angry, but she began to think about what to do next instead.

"Young lady…" she mocked, turning toward the docks.

#⚡︎⚡︎⚡︎◈

Skate entered the main room of the docks hideout. Boss Marshall was sure to be in this time, and she wanted to make a report about what she'd learned about Belamy and what he might have in his home. Haman was in the nearly deserted common area. Bleary-Eyes Bart was off duty, and so had given himself completely to the bottle; he was passed out on a table in the corner. A pair of burglars Skate knew by sight but not name were chatting over a large piece of parchment. Skate saw that it was a map of a building, and guessed that they were planning a heist. No one else was in the main room.

She approached Haman's table, where he had several stacks of papers around him like a half-built wall. He was busy writing on a scroll, his dexterous hand scraping across its width as he left trails of looping marks in its wake. His handwriting was thin; he wrote so much on each line that by the time he started back at the beginning, the ink of the previous line had dried. His hands were almost entirely clear of black smudges.

Haman finished his current page and glanced up over the top of the glasses resting at the end of his thin nose as he waited for the final line to dry. "Good morning, Skate," he said, pulling a blank page from one of his stacks. He settled it in front of him, next to the finished page. "Trouble with your mark?"

"Nothing I can't handle." She hoped she sounded more confident than she felt; she was not sure Belamy would even let her back in the house after her outburst. "I wanted to fill the Boss in on stuff I've learned about the old man."

"Great, I'll go in with you," Haman said, taking the finished page off the table. "I'm interested in this wizard of yours, Skate. I have…well, let's say I have some suspicions about who he really is."

Haman moved to the Boss's door and gave the particular series of knocks worked out by lieutenants and Bosses each week. Skate heard the Boss say something, and Haman opened the door. He waved her in first.

The room looked just as it had the day before, with the exception of who was sitting behind the fine desk. Boss Marshall filled out the chair much more than Haman had; his sides brushed against the arms as he leaned backward languorously, bringing a pudgy hand to the side of his bearded face. He looked suspiciously at Skate, but his countenance softened when he saw Haman closing the door behind her and taking a seat in front of the desk.

Boss Marshall's eyes narrowed until they disappeared as he smiled a trusting grin Haman's way. When he spoke, it was soft, deep, and strained, like heavy stones pushed slowly across metal.

"To what do I owe the pleasure, Skate?" he asked, turning his grin from his lieutenant to his underling. His grin shrank to a more manageable size, though he was obviously still in good spirits. "I'm told you've got a big job set up, huh?"

"Yeah, Boss. He's got loads of stuff, and he's letting me stay in his place. I guess he trusts me," Skate concluded with a shrug.

The Boss's smile widened again. "His mistake, eh?" He laughed a hearty laugh that quickly became a hacking cough. His belly and arms shook from the effort. After two or three bouts, he gathered control of himself again, and his quaking ceased. "Well, what're you here for? Shouldn't you be scoping the place out?"

"I wanted to tell you some stuff I've found out. Don't worry," she added quickly, seeing concern creep into the Boss's face; "he don't know I'm here, or that I'm in the Ink."

"Good, good," Boss Marshall said, his pudgy face relaxing considerably. "It wouldn't do for him to learn of that, would it? Well then." He leaned back into the chair, resting his face in his open palm. "Report away."

"He keeps a lot of his stuff out in the open, and it looks like most of it would fetch a nice price with our fences. He's gone and put weird locks on all the windows, but that won't matter to me none, seeing as how he's letting me in the front door. He's got books for days, and it's all he cares about, I think," she said, feeling the note of bitterness in her voice and immediately quashing it. She smiled to hide it and went on. "I know those are worth a lot, but they're heavy. I could maybe make it out with two or three of them when I do decide to cut and run; more if I get guys on the street. I've been thinking, I could toss books out the window upstairs if there's someone below to catch them. We'd get a better haul of them that way."

Boss Marshall looked at the ceiling as he considered Skate's plan. "Yes, I'd guess so. My concern, though, is time. It doesn't matter how many clods you got on the street ready to carry a haul away if you can't get them out of the building fast enough, does it? Your man don't leave the house much, does he?" he asked, directing the question to her while cutting a knowing glance to Haman.

Skate shook her head. "He didn't when we were watching his

house to start out with, and he ain't gone out once since I've been around him, either."

Boss Marshall was nodding sagely by the time Skate finished speaking. "So the amount of time you'd have to get the books out would be low. Too low to make it worth much of an effort. What else?"

Skate agreed, and remembered that Belamy claimed to need neither food nor rest, which would also complicate the theft. She decided to hold on to that piece of information for the time being. "Well, he's got magic stuff, too. He's got lanterns that never go out, a bottle full of some stuff that heals you, a stack of firewood that never runs out. I'm sure there's loads of magic kit that we could make a clean getaway with if we tried. 'Course, if I'm gonna be working on my own, I'll need to figure out what's worth what and take the best thing he's got. I'm pretty sure there's loads of stuff I haven't even seen yet, so it'll take some time to narrow it down."

The Boss was smiling congenially at her. "You're a fine thief, Skate. I've known it since you first joined us. Your smarts and instincts are top-notch. You probably won't get a chance to clean house, so you're absolutely right: find the best thing he's got and then get him for all he's worth by taking it away. Don't take too long, though; every second you spend in the home is a chance that you're discovered, and it will all have been wasted. It sounds like you may be able to take care of your dues for the next many weeks if this works out for you." He smiled again, his eyes disappearing behind his puffy cheeks.

Skate smiled herself, glad of the Boss's praise. "Yeah. It won't be easy, though. The guy doesn't sleep."

"Sure he does, girl; everyone sleeps. You just gotta find out when."

"Nah, Boss. He really doesn't sleep, ever. He says he don't have to. Says the same thing about eating." As she explained her earlier conversation with Belamy, the Boss's face became more and more confused, and he looked to Haman more and more. In turn, Haman's narrow features became more and more strained and pale. Skate began to feel uncomfortable, understanding that these two were silently coming to a conclusion to which she had no access. She pressed on and finished explaining what the old man had told her.

Boss Marshall's face was drained of color, save for two bright pink patches on his round cheeks. He wasn't looking at Skate anymore, but only at his lieutenant. "Haman."

"Yes, Boss?"

"Do you know of any magic that can do what she's describing?"

"Yes and no, Boss." When Boss didn't say anything else, Haman took that as a cue to expound. "Well, you see, I know of spells that can stave off hunger, and I've read of trinkets that can feed your body without your ever having to actually eat anything, but I don't know of any magic that can eradicate the need to eat entirely. Similarly, I know of spells to help one stay awake, but extended use of such magic leaves one feeling drained and could eventually kill the recipient if used too much." Haman licked his dry lips and removed his glasses, taking a soft cloth out of his breast pocket and rubbing the lenses. There was a tremor in his hand as he worried at the glass. "Skate," he said without looking up from his polishing work, "you've never seen him sleep or eat?"

She shook her head. "No. Pretty sure he stayed in one spot for an entire night." The memory of seeing him in exactly the same spot that he had been the previous night flashed through her mind, with a third of a huge book apparently read in one sitting. "I'm sure he didn't sleep," she said, with renewed confidence.

Haman's polishing continued with increased jerkiness, but he said nothing.

"Haman?" Boss Marshall prompted.

Haman jumped as if stung, and looked around dazedly. "Yes. Well. As I said, I know of no spells that could make these things true, but there are...ways to get around the common needs in life." He gingerly replaced the glasses on the end of his nose. He took a deep breath, and his composure reasserted itself. "If your mark is not *alive*, he would need none of these things."

Skate shook her head, not understanding. "What do you mean, 'not alive'? I just talked to him this morning, and he talked right back. He moves; he reads; he talks; he can do magic. I don't know a lot, Haman, but I know dead people don't do any of that stuff."

"He didn't say he was dead, Skate." Boss Marshall had not gained his usual color back, but his deep grating voice was calmer, at least. "He said 'not alive.' There's that in the world what's neither living nor dead and never was, like stones and water. But there's else that's been one and not passed into the other. Eh, Haman?"

"Just so, Boss." Haman placed his paper gingerly on the edge of Boss's desk, and Skate could see that sweat had bled onto the page where he'd been holding it. "And based on what we've seen and heard, I think our Mr. Belamy may be one of these. There are huge varieties of these half-dead, and some need to eat still, though many don't. They don't sleep; they don't breathe. They don't pass on from old age."

This last characteristic echoed in Skate's ears. *I'm a hundred and seven,* he'd said, though he was able to do much more than a man so old could be expected to do.

"Could they survive a knife to the ribs?" she asked, already guessing the answer.

"Yes," Haman said, gingerly pushing his glasses further up his thin nose, "I imagine most of them could."

The three of them sat in silence. Haman held his chin in one of his hands, deep in thought. Boss Marshall drummed his fingers nervously on his desk. Skate sat looking at the floor. *Maybe they're wrong,* she thought. *Maybe he's not a half-dead. Maybe he's just healthy for his age and uses his magic to get past things he finds inconvenient.* It was certainly possible; Haman said he knew of no such magic, but Haman didn't know everything. He could be wrong. And Boss Marshall relied on Haman for all of his information about magic. *Maybe they're wrong.*

Staring at her feet, Skate felt in her heart that they were not wrong. Barrison Belamy was a man who had died but was not dead. The kind old man who liked to spend his days reading was some sort of monster who would not die. He was an unnatural thing. It was the only explanation that made sense of his idiosyncrasies—oddities that not even magic explained properly.

"He doesn't act like a monster," was all she finally said, looking at her feet.

"The undying are many and varied," Haman intoned, settling into a pedantic affectation that helped his composure. "Depending on what he is, he may be able to control his nature for short or even extended periods of time. A vampire—"

"Vampire?!" Skate exclaimed, jerking upright, her fingers gripping the hard seat of her chair. Twitch had told her stories of such monsters, and Skate had consoled herself by deciding they were just stories, imaginary things made up to scare children like her. Haman's mention of them with regard to Belamy shattered that feeble comfort. "You think he's a vampire?"

"He may be. Or a haunt. Or a ghost or a lich or a revenant or a ghoul or any of a dozen other horrors sent by the demons to torment the living. My best bet right now would be a vampire or ghost, since he never seems to leave his home. He may be a particularly reclusive and inactive lich, I suppose. It's all conjecture until you learn more."

"I gotta go back?" Skate imagined trying to sleep in the bed given to her by her host, imagined sharp fangs glistening in moonlight, Belamy's face feral and long as his mouth opened entirely too wide. She shuddered.

"Oh yes, Skate," Boss Marshall said, leaning forward and dropping into a comforting tone, "you must. You owe the Ink, remember? You were supposed to rob that place days ago to meet your quota for the week. That debt is deferred only so long as it takes you to successfully steal something of great value from the fellow. You'll be out if you fail to pay, and you know what that means—to say nothing of what will happen should you outright refuse." His rough voice was little more than a growl, his wobbly smile nowhere to be found. "I've protected you, Skate. You know that. I've made sure you were always among the best among us. But that protection only works if I'm still in charge. I've GOT to make money. The Big Boss, he...well, he's got reasons to be upset with me right now, Skate. If I start reporting a dip in income— which is exactly what I'll have while you're not bringing anything in— I'm gonna have to explain that to him."

The Boss leaned back, his wide eyes moist with tears. "I'm sorry, but you have to." His soft smile did not reach his eyes this time. "I hope you don't fail. I don't want you hurt. But the Ink needs its funds, and anyone not doing their part gets blotted out. We'd take away the mark on you, and you'd be on your own in this city. You'll go back to the old man. You have to." He wiped his eyes. "No matter what."

Skate looked to Haman and saw no support there. His narrow eyes showed perhaps sadness, but no help. No willingness to intervene.

She was trapped.

Skate felt herself starting to cry. She blinked hard and swallowed.

It was her father's voice she heard in her head, a voice she had not heard in years. *Be strong*, it said. *Cry later, away from these men. Be strong.* It helped her. It surprised her, too. She took strength from the memory.

After a steadying breath, Skate said, "All right. I'll pay what I owe. I'll do it, monster or no monster."

The Boss grinned his toothy grin, and Haman nodded. "I knew you would, girl," said the Boss. "I knew you'd do what's smart. You're a survivor, aren't you? That's what I've said about you since I met you. Ain't that so, Haman?"

"Just so, Boss."

"Sure, 'Skate's smart and a survivor'; that's what I say. Well, you better get back to work," Boss Marshall said, motioning toward the door, "while I take care of more business with Haman. And, Skate," he added as she put her hand on the handle, "don't give it away. It'd be bad enough for a wizard to find out who you work for, but I don't want to deal with something that fought death itself and won. Be smart, like I know you are."

Skate took the final words as the dismissal they were and stepped back out of the room. She closed the door behind her and saw a familiar shock of blond hair headed her way through the shadows.

Twitch was alone and seemingly in good spirits; he had a bounce in his step even though he seemed lost in thought. Skate whistled at him, and he perked up at the sight of her. He smiled and changed course from the Boss's door to her.

"Boss is meeting with Haman," she said, taking a seat at one of the tables, "so you gotta wait."

"No—no problem," he said, sitting near her in another chair, "I can wait. I made a great haul." He patted a bag at his hip. "Nicked some silver off a vendor, then got some spices out of a warehouse. Already took 'em to Rog," he explained, naming one of the Ink's approved fences, "and I got more than enough to cover my quota this week. Even after the—the Ink gets their cut of the leftovers, I'll have a nice bit of silver to hold on to."

"Nice one," Skate said, holding her hand out to examine the bag. Twitch handed it over, and she felt its weight. "Yeah, you'll be fine." She smiled and gave it back.

"Yeah. So how'd it go with your guy? Did you find something worth stealing from him yet?"

"Nah, not yet, but I found out some stuff." Skate explained what she'd learned and what Haman and the Boss thought it meant. Twitch looked horrified.

"They can't make you go back if he's some sort of monster! Well, I-I guess they can, but they shouldn't!" His good mood was gone, replaced by anger and indignation. "It's dangerous. Way t-too dangerous."

"Everything we do is dangerous," Skate reminded him. His discomfort bolstered her somehow. "It'll be fine. If he wanted to hurt me, he could have done it last night. Although..." She trailed off, thinking of the less-than-friendly conversation they had had before she left. "It'll be fine," she repeated, deciding she'd cross that bridge when she came to it.

"If you say so," Twitch said, looking into his bag and counting the coins. "You can han-handle yourself."

"No doubt about it." Skate smiled at her friend, who was engaged in counting his money. She knew he was genuinely worried about her, and she also knew he genuinely had confidence in her ability to stay alive and take what she could. His apparent lack of concern was a show of his belief in her. The blind trust puffed her spirits up; Belamy did not seem so dangerous anymore. "Thanks."

"For what?"

Before she could answer, the Boss's door opened, and Haman walked out. He saw Twitch and Skate and cut his eyes toward the door to signal that the young boy could go in. Twitch scooped up his bag to deliver his payment firsthand, leaving Skate alone. She decided to make her way back to Belamy's house. Before leaving, though, she needed some more information. She walked over to Haman's table, where he had again taken his seat behind the great wall of paperwork.

"Skate," he said without looking up as she approached, his eyes shifting between whatever he had brought in to the Boss and the blank page in front of him, "is there something I can do for you?"

"Yeah, Haman. How can I tell if he's a vampire?"

"Garlic," he said, putting the finished page on the table next to the blank one. "Vampires don't like garlic or sunlight. There would also be a coffin somewhere nearby that he'd spend time in. He'd need to...eat, as well, so you should be able to find some evidence of that."

"Okay." Skate felt confidence rising in her like steel, an unbending bar of willpower to face whatever she needed to face, including asking this next question: "Have you seen Kite?"

Haman blinked and shook his head. Skate saw a flash of dislike in that action that was quickly replaced by Haman's calm, neutral expression of polite disinterest. "No, not since he paid his dues two days ago. Why? I never got the sense that you wanted to work with Kite or even liked the fellow." After he spoke, he drew one flat palm across the blank page in front of him while the other hand pointed at the words on the marked page. As his palm moved down, the exact same marks appeared on the blank page as on the marked one. He flipped both pages over and began the process anew.

Skate smiled. "Just wondering." That meant he hadn't told Haman or the Boss about their little meeting. *He's probably too embarrassed,* she thought. How could he tell anyone without revealing that he had failed to bully a nine-year-old girl? He would sound like a lunatic if he mentioned Rattle to anyone who had not seen it, so he had not told anyone. "Thanks, Haman." She stood and turned back toward the exit. "Tell Twitch I'll see him around, and not to spend all his money on tobacco."

"I'm not your messenger, Skate," Haman said in a bored voice as he lifted the newly written page, examining it for copy errors.

Skate smiled again and began to walk down the hall.

"Skate." Haman's voice echoed down the hall as she prepared to turn the corner. He had set both pages down and was looking at her. He took his lenses off and held them in his hand as he leaned forward, his head framed by the documentation surrounding him. "Stay safe. The Boss doesn't want you to fail, and neither do I."

Skate nodded and left the hideout. There was something in Haman's voice that bothered her. It was only after she had stepped back into the open air behind the tavern that she was able to determine what it was: sympathy.

She rolled her eyes and made her way back to Belamy's old stone house in the Old Town, reminding herself to make a quick stop by a spice vendor on her way.

CHAPTER 7

IN WHICH A THEORY IS TESTED, A SECRET
ROOM IS EXPLORED, AND SOME SOUP IS SET
ON THE FLOOR TO COOL.

Skate stood once more at the door of Barrison Belamy's home as the afternoon sun disappeared behind a few blanket-like clouds. She wondered briefly how best to enter, and decided a knock at the door would be most appropriate, given that she was not sure she was still welcome as a guest. She banged her fist on the heavy wooden portal, listening carefully for approaching footsteps or a call to enter. She heard the familiar sound of Rattle's legs clicking together, and moved her head away from the door. The latch clicked, and the door slowly swung open, though not all the way. Rattle moved away from the door, so she went in.

Belamy's bottom floor was much as she had left it that morning, though the scant light streaming in had shifted as the day had passed. A purplish light was bouncing off the walls into the room. No orange glow escaped the fireplace, which sat cold and untended. Skate saw the ends of Rattle's legs as it floated back upstairs, perhaps to read or perhaps to clean. She also saw her host in his usual spot behind his desk at the end of the room, his book open and his head bent over it.

The room had chilled to the outdoor temperature, and Skate's breath puffed into clouds when she spoke. "Evening, Mr. Belamy," she said, making a concentrated effort to keep her voice steady and calm.

"Good evening, Skate." He did not take his eyes from the page in front of him. His voice was cold and cordial, uninviting and lacking any of his usual warmth. As the silent seconds ticked by, Skate's sense of discomfort grew. Whether he was a monster or not, the awkward cloud hanging in the air was unbearable, and she was ready to get back on speaking terms with the person in front of her.

"Sorry I called your book stupid." The apology was feeble and a little silly sounding, and she knew it, but she didn't know a better way to phrase it. "It's not stupid. I just don't understand any of it."

Skate thought she saw the corner of his mouth twitch a fraction of a hair upward. Belamy raised his head so that it was no longer hovering over the pages. The cold edge was gone from his voice when he spoke. "That's all right, Skate. Forget about it. I understand that this sort of information is not interesting to everybody. The fault was mine for trying to lecture you when you are my guest, and a welcome one. Would you like a fire going?"

Soon, the room shimmered with orange-red flames as the fire-place crackled and popped with Belamy's endless supply of wood in the hearth. The old man had called Rattle down to cook dinner, and the flying thing was now happily banging away in the kitchen, preparing whatever it liked for Skate to consume.

"How's the reading going?" Skate asked, having to raise her voice to be heard over the cacophony.

"Quite well!" Belamy said, rising from the desk and gesturing at the open book. He appeared to be halfway through the text, a wooden bookmark resting on his current page. "The account is very thorough; Bereziah seems to have been quite a stickler for specifics and details. A catalog of rations, injuries, deaths, and so on for pages and pages. Very interesting—to some people," he added with a smile.

Skate smiled back, and it took several seconds before she remembered she was almost certainly smiling at a monster, a creature from a children's tale come to unlife. It reminded her of her plan, and she felt around in her pocket until she found something round and ridged. She closed her fist around it.

"Hey, Mr. Belamy, catch!" she said, tossing the object at the old man, easily enough that he could catch or escape it. He chose the former, shooting a sleeved arm out to catch the item in mid-descent. He brought it close to his face and sniffed.

"Garlic?" he asked, curiously turning it over in his hands. "Why did you give me this?"

"For Rattle to cook with," Skate said immediately. It was the lie she had concocted on the way over, and she was pretty proud of it. If he had been a vampire, he would have been exposed and she could have run away. If not, she could just claim she'd gotten it to eat. "I figured that since you don't eat much, you must need stuff like that from time to time while I live here."

The old man laughed—a throaty, windy sound. "Oh, we'll do all right, don't you worry. Come on, I'll show you." He walked into the kitchen, still chuckling and causing the noise of Rattle's preparations to get louder for a moment until the door swung shut again behind him. Skate followed him in and felt heat before taking in the scene.

She had only seen the kitchen once before, and it had been dark. At the time, she had also been focused on Belamy's guests, and hadn't had attention to spare.

The room was narrow, with a countertop and a wood-burning stove. Rattle sprawled in front of this latter fixture, all legs fully extended and doing the different tasks required to prepare the meal. With one leg, it stirred a pot, while two more rolled out dough behind it on the counter. The three remaining arms were busy cutting up a series of vegetables and dumping them into the boiling pot. Skate stood agape, struggling to follow each of the different activities. She shook her head and turned her attention to Belamy, who was reaching toward a pair of cabinets.

The wizard swung the doors open to reveal a jumbled assortment of spices and seasonings; small green, yellow, orange, brown, white, and red jars; bottles; canisters; cups; and bowls from top to bottom—all drunkenly leaning on one another, some sideways or upside down. Skate could see small labels with writing on each container. The effect of the contrasting colors and general disarray was overwhelming to both the eyes and any sense of order. Belamy chuckled as he put the bulb into the cabinet and shut it. "Thank you, Skate; it looks like we were running low after all."

Skate stood, temporarily stunned. That amount of spice would cost a small fortune; spice merchants were among the wealthiest of that class in all of Caribol, and that was in large part because their wares were sold at a dear cost. "How... *why* do you have all of that?"

She pointed an accusatory finger at the old man. "You said you don't eat! And the eyeball there doesn't even have a mouth!" She poked a thumb at the bat-winged chef-thing. "Why did you spend the chestful of scepts it must have cost to buy all that stuff if you don't even eat?"

Belamy nodded. "I don't get much use of them now, it's true. I did, however, get quite a number of delicious meals out of my stock before I did my magic. I used to *love* food, you see," he said, patting his belly, "though you might not guess it by looking at me. Not as a glutton enjoys it, though; I didn't gorge myself, and I didn't spend all of my wealth on it. But I loved *good* food, and so I made sure I'd never be too far from it." He looked wistfully at Rattle as it worked. "I never learned to cook myself, but Rattle has the touch and the practice to compete with the finest chefs in the land."

"How long ago did you make yourself not need to eat?" Skate asked nervously, hoping the distance between now and then was not terribly long.

"About twenty years or so. Why?"

Skate stuck out her tongue in a look of disgust. "You mean it's been cooking with stuff that's more than twenty years old?" She gagged and spluttered at the thought. "I ate some of that!"

"Yes, and it was delicious, wasn't it? Here," Belamy said, reaching into the cabinet and pulling out a bottle containing fresh-looking, sharp-ridged green leaves. "Smell. Go on, take a deep breath."

Skate skeptically looked between the bottle and the old man before gingerly sniffing the contents. The smell was inviting. She sucked in deeper, and her nostrils felt pleasantly chilly. "Okay, what is that?"

"Mint leaves," Belamy said with a satisfied smirk as he recapped the bottle and placed it in a random place in the shelf. "Mint leaves bought fresh and bottled two decades ago."

Skate looked at the cabinet. "Magic?" she asked as much as stated.

"Of course!" the old man said with a laugh. "Anything placed in these cabinets will last indefinitely, refreshed as the day it was put in with each new rise of the sun. I'm glad these flavors will be enjoyed by someone instead of sitting here trapped in an endless cycle getting a day stale and reverting again. Had I thought more about it at the time I was preparing to go through my experiment, I might not have bothered with the preservative spells for food, but..." He waved the thought away and pointed to Rattle. "I know Rattle's glad to have some more cooking to do. The pots had been unused for years."

Rattle fluttered its bat wings to show approval before turning its attention back to the tasks at hand. Most of its legs were now being used to steady the heavy pot as it continued stirring. The smell coming from within was delicious; Skate thought she detected the aroma of meat, either beef or pork. "It is good at it," she said, more to herself than to her host. "I had a question," she added as she moved to the kitchen door, the heat from the stove becoming too much to bear. "You've got a lot of money, right?"

Belamy looked taken aback by her forwardness. He stuttered a few times, and finally managed to say, "Well, I, ah, don't know about 'a lot,' but I have enough to live quite comfortably." He looked around the room as he spoke, a shine coming to his watery eyes as he looked on his books, his fine desk, and his comfortable chair. "Yes, quite comfortably. Why?" He arched a feathery white eyebrow as he tried to size up his guest.

"I was just wondering where you got it from," she answered easily, another lie prepared well before she'd broached the subject. "Did you inherit it or win it or work for it or what?" The thin draft poking through a closed window gave her some relief from the boiling cauldron that was Rattle's kitchen.

"A combination of working and winning, I should say," the old man said, clasping his hands behind his back. "In my younger days, I was something of a treasure hunter. As I grew older, I had acquired enough wealth from those travels to 'retire' from such a life and begin selling my services as sage and wizard to the local population. Of course, only the nobles of the city and the wealthy merchants who had begun to rise in stature could afford the cost of magic, so these were my clientele. They could afford much, so that's what I charged them. I still do occasional alchemy work or spellcasting, but more as favors to old friends and clients than any real need for the work or the money."

Alchemy? Skate thought but did not ask; instead, she said, "Old friends? You can't have too many friends as old as you. No offense."

"None taken." He smiled as if to reassure her. "You're right, of course. The friends of my youth are long gone, though I have made many enduring connections in my older years with those of the younger generations. Some of them pay visits every so often; the trio you evaded two days ago are among them. Wise and capable, and magic users in their own right, they have much to offer even a well-read old coot like me." He smiled contentedly, a vision of pride and gratefulness. "I've known them for years," he added, moving back toward his customary seat at his desk.

"What's alchemy? Is it magic, too?" This was what she was more interested in, since she had no idea what the practice would even look like. Magic she understood at a rudimentary level: wiggle your hands and say some words, and stuff happens. This new thing was unknown in even that limited sort of way.

"Not exactly, no." Belamy seemed to consider something, and then rose again from his seat. "Here, follow me again." He moved toward one of his bookcases along the wall beneath the stairs and pulled a book off the shelf—except that as soon as the book leaned forward from the rest, the bookcase swung forward on unseen hinges.

A bark of surprised laughter escaped Skate's lips. At Belamy's curious expression, she felt the need to explain herself. "It's just...I've never seen a hidden stairway behind a bookcase before. It's clever." Belamy smiled back, satisfied with the explanation, and began his descent into the dark spiral descending stair. Skate felt fine about the lie, because the truth of her mirth would have revealed her association with other thieves, which would needlessly complicate her job.

The real reason she had laughed was because this kind of misdirection was well-known among burglars, and its reputation brought nothing but ridicule. "A good thief," Haman had once told her when the topic had come up in a common area of one of the hideouts, "knows exactly how to find such 'hidden spots.' They're pitifully simple to find; just look for a place where there should be space but isn't." The nearby table that had been discussing the concept laughed uproariously as the mocking conversation continued. Skate had only been paying attention to Haman at the time, and did not notice the rest of their words.

"You probably won't ever see one," Haman had said, resettling his spectacles and reviewing the page in front of him, "since they fell out of style ages ago; people in this city learned fairly quickly what poor protections they were."

Belamy had never gotten the notice, it seemed—unlike in Ossertine's home, where the space had been a product of magic, a passage
that should have led into the neighboring house but had not—this
entrance was entirely mundane.

Another giggle threatened to burst out, but Skate was ready for it
this time and suppressed it.

Belamy brought a magical ball of light out from somewhere down
below and called up to her. She responded and began her descent. The
stair was narrow, and the white light from below cast a grayish hue on
the cut stones of the wall. The ghostly color made Skate pause. The
thought that had been floating in the back of her head surged forward
again. *He's probably a monster. I'm going underground with someone
pretending to be alive.*

She stood on the top step. If the bookcase swung shut, she might
be trapped.

She took a deep breath. *If he wanted to hurt me, he could have
fifty different times.*

Skate knew her reasoning was solid, but her sense of dread grew
as she took the next step. *The Boss wants a big score.* That did little to
ease the deepening pit in her stomach as she placed a steadying hand
on the inner wall of the spiraling stairs, though it shifted the target of
that ill ease toward Boss Marshall.

She came to the end of the steps.

In front of her was Belamy, a ball of light floating over his open
hand. He was fidgeting with a latch on a lantern in one wall. He turned
toward Skate and jerked his head behind him. "Open that one, will
you?"

Skate saw in the other wall a lantern identical to the one Belamy
was trying to open. She moved toward it, keeping a wary eye on the old
man's silhouette as he struggled with the latch. She got to hers and
immediately saw the problem: the metal had started to rust. She took
one of the thin pins from her hair and tried scraping the corroded
metal away. It came off surprisingly easily, and within a minute, she
had flipped the latch open and drawn the metal shade upward.

Skate squinted, eyes watering, as more white light streamed into
the room.

The squeak of metal behind her made the light grow stronger still. She turned around to see Belamy smiling at the lantern he had bested, wiping his hands together to shake the red rust off. It fell in clouds until it dispersed from vision entirely. He shook his light-bearing hand, and the ball of light disappeared; the magical lanterns provided more than enough for comfort's sake.

Skate took in the room, then. The heat from the main room's fireplace had not made it down to this hidden part of the house, and she was not sure it ever would, even if the fire were kept burning for days.

This room was roughly half the size of the room they had entered from, though it looked slightly larger than that for the lack of bookshelves lining every wall. Instead, there were three workbenches with open shelving overhead for each one. Directly in front of each workstation was a metal tube with a single handle that hung down about two feet from the ceiling.

The work surfaces were mostly clear, though each one held a bizarre instrument or two that she did not recognize. Metal canisters, stunted bottles, and other sundry oddities were stacked and lined up in rows along the high shelves. There was a hole in the wall, under which was a sizable basin. A considerable amount of dust covered everything in the room.

"I haven't been down here in years," Belamy remarked in reminiscent tones. He took a deep sniff, seeming to savor the smell. Skate tested the air a bit more gingerly, and wrinkled her face in distaste. The room smelled like something sour, and the peculiar aroma stung her nostrils.

Belamy went to each workstation and pulled its handle. Skate heard a grind of metal within each tube as he did so. "Probably better to open the vents now that we're down here."

Skate looked around at the different tools and containers, some of which were empty, some of which were full. "I don't get it," she said, shrugging.

"Oh, let me give you a demonstration!" Belamy walked to the foot of the slender staircase and shouted, "Rattle! Water in the lab!"

A few moments passed as Belamy took a pair of small bottles from a nearby shelf and poured some of the contents of one onto the surface of a workstation. It looked like salt. Water began to trickle from the hole in the wall into the basin, presumably from upstairs at Rattle's direction.

Belamy then added some of the contents from the second bottle onto the first pile. Skate saw that the second bottle's contents were also granules of whitish stuff, though of a slightly darker hue than the salt stuff. The old man swirled the two together with his finger, then pushed the mess he'd made back into a respectable and thoroughly mixed pile. He took an empty glass from a shelf and dipped it into the small pool forming at the bottom of the basin. "Ready?" he asked, and Skate nodded, not sure what she was looking at.

Belamy poured a small amount of water into the mixed pile. For about two seconds, nothing happened, and then there was a flash of yellow light and a small bang. Skate yelped at the sound. In the enclosed space, she could feel the sound of the small explosion in her chest as the shockwave traveled across the room.

"That's alchemy," Belamy said with a chuckle. There was little left on the workbench after the blast—a black mark and a smattering of granules that got swept by the old man's hand onto the floor. "Mixing reagents together to get a reaction. Most of it can be done without any magic whatsoever. There are several practitioners around town, though they're all under contract with the Baron and the Guard, and they don't offer services to the public except for special exceptions, or ameliorative antidotes and balms. Anything dangerous like this"—he casually gestured at the black mark—"would be out of the question. However," he said with a conspiratorial air as he lowered his voice, "some of the more extravagant merchants of the city have an eye for impressive defensive measures when they travel. I've made stocks for several families across the years, all for a handsome profit."

Skate had sufficiently recovered from her shock to ask, "How does it work?"

"Scholars disagree. There's plenty of speculation among those that study and work with the practice. Some say it's spirits within the ingredients that long for or detest one another, causing the violent or combining reactions we see in the course of the work. Others say it is an act of God, or of gods, who cause the reagents to form something new upon mixing. Still others say that the question is meaningless or totally unanswerable because it's some quality of the reagents themselves; the reaction occurs because that's what the reagents do, just as a stone is solid and water is wet. I'm not sure where I stand on that question." He thoughtfully crossed his arms and looked down.

"So you can do other stuff with it?" Skate asked, seeing that he was lost in thought and unlikely to snap out of it on his own any time soon. "Not just explosions?"

"Oh, yes. Artificial antidotes to poisons, traps, torches that work underwater, powerful acids, lubricants, adhesives—all sorts of useful tools and tricks. One must be very careful, however," he added, his eyes wide with warning, "because any slip-up could be disastrous. Had I grabbed the wrong bottles just now, the room could be filling with deadly fumes or full of burning tar—or any number of other horrible fates. Alchemy is not to be entered into lightly or carelessly. It's much like magic in that regard."

"So this is how you made your money."

"Yes. Well, this and offering my services as a wizard to those able to pay."

"Is there anything behind here, or is it a storage closet?" she asked, moving toward the one door in the room. She tried the handle and found that it would not budge.

"That is the room that I use to dispose of dangerous leftovers from the alchemical processes. Best left locked when I'm not working. Come on, let's get back into fresh air," Belamy said, moving to each metal tube and pulling the handles back to their original positions.

Something about Belamy's demeanor struck Skate as odd. He seemed perfectly at ease as he spoke and moved, but there was an artifice to it, as if he were putting on a very convincing but still unreal show. She had herself done the same thing when she needed to sell a lie; and so long as the person she was trying to deceive was not focusing all of their attention on her at the time, it usually worked great. However, Belamy *was* commanding her whole attention, and not just because he was the only other person in the room; she was watching for signs of one of her greatest fears, after all.

Belamy smiled as he brought another light into being out of nothing, and began walking upstairs.

"Should we shutter the lamps?" Skate asked as she moved behind him, looking back at the locked door. She did not really care about the lamps, but wanted an excuse to look back in the room for a little long-er. Boss Marshall's granite-filled voice echoed in her head. *Find the best thing he's got and then get him for all he's worth by taking it away.* She had a sinking feeling that the locked room might have something like that behind it.

"No, don't bother," he said, moving fluidly up the steps—much more gracefully than a man of a hundred and seven years should be able to, she noted—carrying the ball of white light in his open palm. "They'll just get stuck again. Besides, being down here brought back an itch to work in the lab. I may come back down here later, and I don't want to have to mess with the lights to get started. By the way," he add-ed as he reached the landing back into the main room of the ground floor, "have you thought of where you're going to be getting your next book from? By my count, you've got about six days to work on it."

Skate followed him out of the narrow tunnel of a stairway. "Yeah, a little." The truth was that she hadn't thought much about it, but she now realized she needed to. Her best bets were Belamy's other two friends, Gherun and Gemhide. However, it was unlikely that Belamy had another helpful meeting planned to get either of them out of their homes. She needed to begin scoping one of the places out to try to get a handle on the target's habits, his patterns, his schedule. She had six days, but she needed to use that time to study the next mark instead of sitting around talking with Belamy about magic and alchemy and his-tory and whatever else the old man decided was worth wasting his time on. There was also another pair of questions she wanted to ask him, but she was not sure she would be able to.

"Good! Plenty of time to get it done. I'm not looking for anything specific, so Rattle should be able to find a suitable book with relative ease. Speaking of Rattle," Belamy said, glancing inside the kitchen, "it smells like he's just about got your dinner ready. Will you be taking your dinner by the fire or in your room?"

"The fire, I guess," Skate said, sitting in front of the crackling flames. After being in the stale cold air of the basement laboratory, the warmth was a great comfort. Besides, she wanted to ask one of her questions before she went to bed, and that was not going to happen if she went and barricaded herself in her room.

Belamy nodded and took his seat behind his desk. He pulled his large book closer to him and began reading silently as Rattle floated into the room carrying a bowl of fresh hot soup. It offered the bowl to Skate and bounced happily back into the kitchen. The soup smelled inviting, but it was too hot to eat, so she set it on the floor to cool.

Skate stared into the fire. *Find the best thing he's got and then get him for all he's worth by taking it away.* Yes, she was sure there was something special in that room. She thought of what else might be very valuable, a single object she could take and escape with when the time came.

The statuette that had been above the fireplace when she'd first tried to steal from Belamy had not been put back in its place. Could that have some high value she did not know about? There were also the ten red gemstones Belamy had told her not to touch that first night; she had not seen those again either. Both of these objects—the statuette and the jewelry box, wherever they were—could very well be the type of thing she would need to find and escape with when the time came to cut and run. They were both small and presumably lightweight, so escape would not be a problem; and they seemed to be so valuable that Belamy, who kept very expensive books within easy reach of his guest, deemed it prudent to relocate them to a safer, undisclosed location. *Behind a locked door in a basement behind a trick bookcase, maybe.*

Skate took up her soup, which had cooled some, though she still needed to blow the steam off the top in order to make it safe to eat. When she tilted the bowl upward, the warm brothy water was at just the right temperature; she could taste every bit of it, and the heat was pleasant and soothing to a throat sore from the cold. Rattle really was a good cook.

After a few small gulps, Skate lowered the bowl again, not wanting to make herself sick by eating too much at once. The Ink's food was okay when you could get it while it was warm, and for members in good standing, it was readily available most of the time. When Skate had first joined, she had been ravenous and had gorged herself far too quickly on the meat offered to her. The stomach pain and the hideous expectation of being sick for the next few hours had taught her never to make that mistake again.

Skate wiped her mouth with her perpetually dirty sleeve. She thought the fire was lacking, so she took a sizable log from the ever-full rack of wood and tossed it on top of the other logs. It landed with a heavy *thunk* and sent a few embers spraying out, spiraling like flecks of dust in the wind and landing safely in the old stone fireplace, nowhere near the precious books or the soft rug Skate stood upon.

As she watched the small flames lick the sides of their new meal, her mind drifted to a night that had been in many ways like this one.

#♌♌♌♌

It had been a cold night near the middle of winter, and there had been snow on the ground then, too. It had still been falling from the sky in small packets, flakes swirling and crashing into one another on their way to the welcoming earth below. She remembered falling asleep looking at it through the smudged window of the room that had been her family's home.

They had been in the slums, a part of town even worse than the docks, both then and now. They lived on a plot with ten other families, most of whom had no more than a tent and the ragged clothes on their back to try to make it through the night. Every morning after a night like this, the first children up went peeking into tents to see who had survived and who had not, taking the departed family's best things for themselves before announcing the passing to the group at large. It was a matter of survival; nobody wanted anyone to pass in the night, but if it happened, all the better for your own family.

Her mom and dad had managed to get a rudimentary shack built before winter, complete with that one dirty window. They had even secured a ratty old mattress to serve as a family bed. Her parents had been talking quietly to each other as she drifted off. She could not hear what they were saying and did not care to try. She was warm from the cold under the thick blanket, and they had managed to have a hot meal a few hours earlier.

It was later that the fire came. A couple of men from nearby families tried to start a bonfire in the plot of land, in a suitably open area where the flames should have stayed far clear of the tents and sheds and sleeping bags. They were successful, and the warmth of the red flames was a great comfort for this disaffected and despondent crew. There would not have been any problems had a drunken argument not resulted in someone jostling the fire, sending a stray log rolling to one of the tents.

Skate was asleep for the inciting incident; she pieced together what had happened the day after, when she heard some of her neighbors talking in hushed tones.

"Poor dear," she overheard an old crone whisper to a neighbor, "to lose her parents that way."

Throughout the day, Skate could add a chorus of alternately sympathetic and callous remarks:

"—can't take her in, of course, can barely feed me own, can I?"

"—rescued her but then rushed in to find the mother. No one saw—"

"Anybody call dibs on her parents' stuff yet?"

"It all burned up, stupid."

"—better that she had passed as well than to suffer so..."

Skate heard these things but felt nothing. She had been numb since waking up in the snow, her father telling her to stay there and wait. He had been a rough-looking man, a sailor by trade, though unable to find work for most of the year because of an old injury. In the cold, he could barely walk.

He tried that night to move, hobbling away from her into an inferno. It was then she had noticed that the world was burning. The orange and red flames climbed impossibly high into the night, and she might have even called them pretty in a different situation. However, there and then, they meant death.

She never saw her father again; nor did her mother ever surface from the firestorm.

And so, over the next few days, Skate sat there. She never moved, just stared at the spot her home had been, hearing but not listening to the chatter around her as the world passed by. She believed that last voice, that there was little point in trying to survive now that she was without home or kin. If she had living relatives elsewhere, she knew nothing of them. She was alone, and the world was careless.

Then Haman appeared. He sat next to her without introduction. He was in training, still, as a wizard. He bore the insignia of an apprentice on his breast. He did not say anything for a long while, and Skate did not care, for what use had she for any comfort a stranger might offer?

When he did speak, his voice was somber. Reverent. "There is no loss without mourning, and mourning is no small thing. But your mourning is useless without a life to sustain it." It was then that he turned to her and spoke directly. "Do you wish to go on?" The question had been simple, but it felt like hours before she nodded.

The rest was much a blur. Haman eventually introduced her to Twitch, and they had both been present when she swore to the Bosses to serve with loyalty, on pain of death or exile, and received her tattoo. That had been four years ago.

#ᚢ☩ᛉᚨ

Skate shook the memories away and turned back to her soup. There was plenty of it left, and the temperature was now comfortable. She took several more gulps and looked back into the fireplace. There were marks on the mantle she had not seen before, and closer inspection revealed them to be stylized letters of some kind. "What does this say?" she asked, pointing to the writing.

"It's in the language of the dwarves," Belamy answered without looking up from his reading. He spoke some words that sounded harsh to her ears, with many hard "K" sounds and noises from deep in his throat. He then translated, "'Speak my name, then a color you want.' It rhymes in the Dwarvish."

"What does it mean?"

"It's a set of instructions. That fireplace was made for me by a craftsman of those folk who was skilled in the magic of the dwarves. If you're near the fireplace while a fire is burning, you need to say the Dwarvish word for fire, and then the Dwarvish word for a color of your choosing. If you do it right, the fire will change color."

"Does it work?"

"Of course."

"I want to try it."

"Certainly. What color would you like it to be?"

"Blue."

"Then stand in front of the fireplace and say, *'Gerunk kekonda-hash.'*"

Skate had to twist her mouth around the words to get them out, and she did not feel like she had been able to get them correctly when she heard herself say them. *"Gerenk kekondashash."* Belamy corrected her, and she said, *"Gerunk kekondahash."*

As soon as the last syllable left her mouth, the orangish red flames flashed out for a moment, as if a great wind had blown from behind the fire, and then the room was awash in a bright blue light. The temperature remained unchanged, but the dancing shadows looked darker than they had before, and everything looked colder. It was a pretty shade of blue, though, and Skate was in awe of the result.

"That's amazing!" she said. She caught herself, though, and bottled up her excitement. She decided to try to appear more detached and asked nonchalantly, "So, how do I turn it off?"

"Gerunk haktha."

Skate spoke the words correctly the first time and the flash occurred once more, rebathing the room in the normal glow of orange and red hues. The shadows became less cold-looking as they shimmered in the moving light of the flames, no longer tinged with the cooler shades of blue. Belamy rose out of his seat, his acquired book in hand. "I'll leave you to it, if you'd like to practice the words."

Skate thought to ask him for more colors, realized she had no chance of remembering more than a few, and so let the question dissolve in her mind. It was not the question she had meant to ask anyway, and that question was weighing heavily on her. As Belamy reached the middle of the stairs, she called out. He stopped and turned, his bushy eyebrows raised in polite curiosity and attention.

"I—" She stopped because asking for help was a sign of weakness, and she was planning to steal from this man before long. She did not like asking close friends for any kind of help, much less strange old wizards who were demon-sent unliving monsters. "I want something."

"More food? I'm sure there's plenty left, or I can get Rattle to—"

"No, not food. I..." She swallowed hard. "I want to learn to read."

Belamy's face fell into an expression that revealed nothing. "I have had no students for many years, young lady. Why do you want to learn to read?"

Skate shrugged, not wanting to voice what was in her heart. Reading was her ticket up and a sign that she was not a nobody. "It'd help me find books for you, and I wouldn't have to worry about Rattle anymore."

Belamy smiled. "We can work something out tomorrow. Good night, Skate." He turned back up the stairs, and Skate heard a door close. She turned to the fire and spoke the words. Sitting in the blue light, she knew she should go to bed, and she would, but she wanted to enjoy the flames a while longer.

She stared into the dancing tongues as they consumed the wood, and she smiled.

CHAPTER 8

Skate woke up in the warm bed to see snow falling outside. It was not the small pellets of ice that would sting someone unfortunate enough to be caught in their path; nor was it the furious downpour of blinding white that signified a blizzard. Instead, she saw fat gentle flakes drifting lazily past her window, swirling in various directions as updrafts and downdrafts took their turns at play with the puffy-looking snow. She was glad to be indoors for the moment, though she sighed as she thought of what she needed to do for the day.

Whichever mark she chose (she had all but decided on Gherun over Gemhide because she was not going to risk stealing from someone who might be under the care of the Ink; such a breach of contract would be disastrous), she needed to begin watching today. She only had a five-day window left to work, and she did not want to wait until the last minute.

Skate perked up at the memory of her conversation with Belamy; they would need to discuss her learning to read today. She hopped out of bed, glad once again of the vent in the floor for the heat it funneled in.

Before she dressed, Skate moved to the desk in the room and proudly pulled out the slate. After she set it down on the surface of the desk, she threw on her freshly laundered but irredeemably tattered clothes and bounded down the stairs.

To her surprise, Belamy was not at his desk. There was a plate of fried eggs and a pancake topped with some red fruit sitting in front of the fire, which was burning much as she had left it the night before, blue and crackling happily. Skate called out, first to her host and then to his chef, but heard nothing in response. With a shrug, she sat down and picked up the pancake gingerly, unsure of how warm it was going to be.

As soon as her finger touched the food, Belamy's voice filled the room. She dropped the pancake back onto the plate and jumped to her feet. So deep was her shock that it was several moments before she realized the voice was saying something intelligible.

"—to my supplier to get the necessary tools. I see you've found Rattle's work for the morning; enjoy that. We'll be back soon. Stay out of trouble until then." Belamy's cheerful voice drifted away, and then the room was quiet once more. Skate recognized it as some form of magic message left for her. She took a deep breath to push the startled excitement out of her and returned to her seated position, retrieving the pancake.

Skate enjoyed the warmth of the fire as she ate, moving on to the two eggs when she was done. She ate them the special way Delly had shown her earlier that very year, taking the fried egg between her fingers and placing the entire morsel in her mouth at once. "Thab 'ay you bon't spill aby yolk on yer mug," Delly had said, chewing happily. Skate did the same now, savoring the internal warmth as the yellow of the egg burst out of sight without any mess.

When she had all of her food down, Skate watched the blue flames for a few minutes more before rising and beginning her work for the day. She could hardly believe her luck. Belamy's message indicated that they would be returning soon, so she did not have much time. If she could pull her heist now, she would not have to worry about stealing any more books for Belamy. She would not be able to learn to read either, but that seemed unimportant in the adrenaline of opportunity.

Besides, if she worked hard enough for the Ink, she might one day become one of the lieutenants, who had to learn to read as part of their responsibilities; running an organization like the Ink was a complicated affair, so all the Bosses and their assistants had to be able to read and write to keep the work going smoothly.

Skate moved over to Belamy's desk. There was a drawer attached to the underside, which she tried to open but found locked. She pulled her pin from her hair and began trying to pick the small lock embedded in the desk, then stopped when she remembered the locked door downstairs. She bolted to the bookcase and began pulling books. When she found the right one, the secret passage opened up, and she made her way down.

The lights were on as they had left them, and the smell was as acrid as it had been before. Skate blew out of her nose and moved to the door, kneeling down to try to figure out the lock mechanism. She prodded the frame around the handle and tried the door several times to see if she could pinpoint where the lock was engaged. It seemed to be equally focused all along the side of the door near the handle. She scanned the jamb and noticed small markings all up and down the space where the door rested against the wall.

Skate swore under her breath. She recognized the marks as a magical lock. Twitch knew how to get past these things, but Skate had not figured them out yet. She knew that she needed two small metal bars, but she didn't know what to do with them.

As she was trying to figure out what she was supposed to do, a resounding banging noise echoed down the stone steps. She jerked around and bounded up the steps two at a time, slamming the bookcase back into place behind her. She spun to put the bookcase behind her as she looked at the front door, from where the banging continued to issue throughout the room.

"Barrison!" a feminine voice called, and Skate recognized the voice of Laribel Ossertine. "Barrison, are you all right? Have you fallen down? Barrison!" She was obviously concerned, and Skate was worried that she might break the door down in her zeal to help her friend.

"Mr. Belamy isn't here right now!" Skate called, moving toward the door to make sure she was heard. "He'll be back soon!"

Ossertine was silent for a moment, then responded in more even tones. She sounded dangerous in her sudden serenity. "To whom am I speaking?"

"I'm Skate. Mr. Belamy's letting me stay here."

Another tense pause. "You stay here." Ossertine stated it as somewhere between a declaration and a question. "And you are called Skate." Not fully trusting of these facts, the woman said, "Unlock the door, Skate. I would like to come in."

Skate bit her lip. She did not know if she had Belamy's permission to let someone in, but she knew that Ossertine and Belamy were at least acquaintances. She did not want to be rude, but she did not want to let someone in whom Belamy did not want inside. Especially considering that Belamy had her stolen property upstairs, likely open where he had last left off. "I don't know if I'm supposed to let anyone in," she said finally, deciding rudeness was better than the possibility of her finding out about the theft.

"Skate, listen very carefully." The threat was even clearer in Ossertine's low voice. "I don't know you. I don't know where my friend is. For all I know, you've murdered him and are standing over his cooling body as you speak to me. If you don't let me in, I will come in anyway by breaking down Barrison's very sturdy and expensive door. If he's alive, it will be your responsibility to repay him for any damages that result. Will you let me in, or will I have to come in on my own?"

Skate looked at the door. It was finely made and would be costly to replace, and it *would* be her fault if Ossertine thought she had to break it down to help a hypothetically dying Belamy. "Okay, okay, hold on," she said, disengaging the latch on the door and swinging it open to allow Ossertine free passage in. "There," she said, looking her full in the face and huffing, "I'm telling you, he's gone, but he said he'd be back soon."

Ossertine was standing with arms crossed over her chest. A woman in her late thirties, Skate guessed. Ossertine was thin of face and body, much as Haman was; but where Haman had eyes that could vary in expression from cold and calculating to warm and sympathetic, Skate only saw the former in Ossertine's catlike gaze.

Ossertine was dressed in warm furs, snowflakes getting caught in the delicate animal hairs as she stood on Belamy's old stone stoop. Her auburn hair, obviously quite long, was tied up into a tight bun on top of her head and draped in a light scarf that trailed behind her in the soft wind. She was very pale, but the chill of the air had brought a pink to her cheeks. Skate thought she had a pretty face, though it looked cruel at the moment.

"We shall see whether he's gone or not," Ossertine said, delicately lifting the hem of her furs off her feet as she crossed the threshold into Belamy's home. The haughty timbre that Skate had first heard when she had been hiding in the kitchen was in full force, and Skate had to deliberately push down the anger she felt at the imperious woman.

Ossertine surveyed the room, looking for any sign of foul play. Not finding Belamy's body anywhere in the main room, she focused in on details she could see. Her eyes lingered on the used plate on the floor, on the crackling blue fire, on Skate's dingy clothing. The woman appeared, with much effort, to suppress a sneer as she broke into a venomously polite smile. *"Krykyull dur angatak Morshkinok?"*

Based on her expectant expression, Skate assumed it was something she was supposed to respond to. She had no idea what Ossertine had just said to her, but it sounded like the language that Belamy had called the language of the dwarves. Not knowing what else to do, she said one of the two phrases she had been taught: *"Gerunk haktha."*

When the blue flame flashed away, Ossertine smiled a bit wider, and her face softened. "Very well. You can't speak the language, but you know how to operate the fireplace. I doubt very much that you learned how to do that from anyone other than Barrison, so I believe you. You must be his guest. Fetch me a chair. I wish to warm myself by the fire. And clean your plate; you're a guest in this house, and so must be expected to do your small part to keep it clean." She was no longer looking at Skate but appeared lost in thought while staring into the flames, drawing her furs closer for increased warmth now that she was safely out of the cold.

Skate, frowning, picked up one of Belamy's chairs along the wall and set it down harder than was strictly necessary behind the woman. Carrying the poufy chair had been somewhat awkward for her, and she had taken no care at all when setting it down. She then picked up her plate and walked into the kitchen, where she dumped it into the water that Rattle had left in the basin.

When Skate walked into the main room again, Ossertine had taken her seat, upon which she had draped her fine coat. She was using it as extra cushioning as she enjoyed the heat from the crackling fire. Without looking away, she said, "You did not wash that plate, dear."

Skate did not move, but said, "No."

"Why not?"

"Rattle will do it."

"Rattle is not here." Ossertine's tone had become harsh in addition to haughty. "And it is incredibly rude of you to assign it extra work in its absence. Clean your plate." She had never taken her eyes from the flames as she talked, and now she returned to her silent contemplation.

Skate, for her part, had not moved yet since the woman began talking. Now, however, she deliberately and slowly walked past the sitting woman. She felt the anger burning in her chest, forcing her to refuse the woman's demands for no other reason than because she did not want to do what she was told by someone she knew not at all.

Skate went straight to the stairs, formulating several biting retorts in her head to anything the woman might say to her, but Ossertine was unconcerned with Skate's obstinance, staring into the fire as she had been for the last few minutes. Skate moved up the stairs, satisfied that she had won that confrontation; by not obeying the command, she had proved she was not to be commanded. Years in the Ink had taught her not to instinctively heed commands given by adults, a tendency that had to be trained out of the younger members of the group. After all, a burglar who actually listened to the Guards' shouted demands to halt, stop, and wait was only good as bait to let others escape.

When she got to the top of the stairs, Skate turned toward her door, then paused. There was not much to do in her provided living space except stare at furniture, so she released her hold on the handle and turned instead toward the upstairs library, which she found unlocked, as Belamy had told her it would always be on that first morning here.

Skate closed the door behind her, figuring that Belamy could deal with his new guest when he got back. She had seen the room earlier this morning and several other mornings beside, but had paid little attention to it. Now, though, she canvassed it for anything valuable. Her first scan of her surroundings revealed Belamy had far too many books, and the two objects that Skate thought were likely to be his most valuable possessions were not in here. The fact that the jewelry box and the statuette remained hidden only further convinced her they would probably be the items she needed to look for when she finally made it out of the house for good.

Her targeted goods being absent, Skate continued peering around the room, which was packed floor to ceiling with texts. *Being dead must be an incredibly dull affair*, she thought as she considered the fact that the old man had probably read and reread everything in here at least twice. That explained why he was so desperate for new reading material. Finding something unread must be a rare event indeed for the man.

There were several trinkets on the shelves in this room, as there were in the main room downstairs, and some glass spheres and metal gizmos. Most of them appeared to her as rather dull, however detailed, stone trinkets and paperweights.

Tiny gargoyles and little lions, diminutive dragons and small dogs, beasts of every description stood in silent watch over the books that towered behind them. Skate picked one off the shelf. It was a life-size representation of a toad, squat and grumpy-looking as its blank stone eyes stared off into nothing at either side of its triangular head. She wondered where Belamy had gotten all of these; for the most part, they were of the same make and style, even seeming to be of the same material, despite being images of very different animals. She placed the toad back on the shelf, but almost dropped it when she heard a whisper in her ear.

"Ungor."

Skate spun around in a panic—a panic even more profound than what she'd felt earlier in the basement. She did not know the voice; it was male, but she could not decipher more than that from the very quiet message. She could not find any source for it. "Hello?" she said quietly to the empty room, hoping to draw out the source of the unwelcome intrusion. Nothing greeted her in response.

A few minutes passed in utter silence. *Did I imagine it?* She definitely *thought* she had heard something. However, the continuing silence was doing an excellent job of convincing her otherwise. She waved her hand in the air, guessing that she had felt a breeze under the door and ascribed a word to its whistle. She returned her attention to the little toad and readjusted it, fixing its position, which she had ruined in her worried shock.

"The toad's name is Ungor."

Skate spun around again. She still saw no one, but there was something different about the room. A glass bauble near the single window of the room, which had been clear before, was full of gray smoke. The smoke churned before her eyes, neither excited nor languid.

Skate swallowed hard and took a step toward the bauble. "Are you talking?"

There wasn't an immediate answer, but a few moments later, she heard unmistakably another whisper from the direction of the ball. *"Yes."*

She moved closer and asked, "How?"

Another pause. *"I'm in the glass ball."*

Skate got within inches of the ball and looked into its depths. She saw no one within. Indeed, she saw nothing but the churning gray fog. "I don't see you."

Another pause. *"Pick up the ball."*

Skate thought this an odd request but did as she was asked. As she took hold of the sphere, the fog began to thin ever so slightly. The color within took on a blue tone as something moved closer to the surface. She saw a pair of eyes, wide-set and deep, under a dark brown brow. Nothing else appeared to her, not even the rest of the face.

"That's much better, thank you." The voice was no longer whispering but talking in a calm and friendly tone. The eyes were expressive—or perhaps Skate was simply ascribing that to them, because she had nothing else to work with. "As I was saying, the toad's name is Ungor. If you were curious."

Skate regarded the eyes with suspicion. "How could you tell I was looking at the toad?" she asked, looking back at where she had been standing. "How could you see anything?"

"I can see out of this even when you can't see me," the half-face said, drawing back into the blue-gray fog of the sphere. "You see? I can see that arched eyebrow you're shooting my way, even though you can't see my handsome face."

He moved back into her vision, parting clouds as he came, still revealing only eyes and the bridge of his nose. He looked how some of the burglars dressed when doing a job, though she'd never seen someone dress that way using smoke before. "Anyway, I know it's strange to talk to someone you can't see, so I wanted to make it easier for you."

Judging by the slight lift of the skin under the eyes, the man was smiling as he spoke.

"That's not what's strange about this conversation."

The man laughed. "No! No, I suppose it isn't, is it?" He laughed again, a rather nervous sound, and cast his eyes around the room. "Tell me, are you here because Belamy told you to be in here?"

"No," she said hesitantly, "but he didn't say I couldn't be in here." The eyes in the globe gave an encouraging nod, and she continued, "He has a guest waiting for him downstairs, and I don't like her, so I came up here."

"I see, I see." The eyes bounced again as their strange owner nodded some more through the blue smoke. "So you are also a guest of Barrison Belamy, yes?"

"Yeah; he's letting me stay in the empty bedroom up here."

"I see," the voice repeated, interested and encouraging. "That's wonderful. Do you know why he's doing that? I've never known him to have guests stay more than a few hours at a time."

Skate did not answer immediately. "I guess I'm more...hired than just a guest."

"Oh? Mr. Belamy doesn't have much need for a housecleaner, so I guess you're a gopher?"

"A what?"

"Oh, you know," the eyes said, narrowing and rolling in mock exasperation, "a gopher. An errand girl. He tells you to go for something, and you go get it; that sort of thing."

"Yeah, something like that." Skate did not feel the need to go into detail about the nature of the things she was sent for.

"*That* makes sense. He wouldn't want to be going here and there for what little materials and supplies he needs when he could be reading instead. Though, that does raise the question: If you're his errand girl, where's he gone?" The eyes were quizzical now, one arched high while the other dipped in low toward the unseen nose.

"Gone?"

"You said his guest was waiting for him."

Skate realized she had said exactly that. This person was a good listener, and a quick thinker besides. Such a person was dangerous to someone like her, who was trying to maintain a secret. "He didn't say what he was going for. He just said he was going and would be back soon."

"I see, I see." The man in the glass ball seemed to use the phrase as the verbal equivalent of a nod. "That's not like him, you know. He almost never leaves. He spends almost all of his time reading in here. I've noticed the past few days, though, he hasn't been in this room. Do you have anything to do with that?"

"Some of it, sure." She affected a more relaxed posture, worried that she may have put the man in the glass on his guard by her body language. "He's spent some time showing me around the house and stuff."

"Yes, I saw you when he showed you his wonderful little library," the man said, darting his eyes about the room as he talked.

"What are you?"

"A friend."

"Uh-huh."

"It's true! Or at least, it might be. But listen, since Belamy clearly hasn't directly introduced you to me, it might be better not to mention finding me, hmm? At least until I've had a chance to talk to him?" The man looked rather worried at the prospect that she would not agree, so much so that Skate found herself agreeing before she had time to consider. "Good, good. Now, before you put me down, what were you planning to do when you came in here, anyway?"

"I was looking at...the books."

"You can read?" He looked skeptical at the suggestion.

"No, not yet. But Mr. Belamy has agreed to teach me."

"That's wonderful!" The eyes went wide, and though they were quick to hide it, Skate detected not excitement but genuine shock at the pronouncement. "It's good to know how to read, especially if you're working for such a ravenous reader as Belamy." The man within the glass seemed to consider something, and then spoke again. "Listen, there's something I feel you should know. Barrison Belamy is...well, he's different, er, health-wise."

"I know he's really old," Skate said, though she guessed that this conversation was heading in a darker direction.

"Yes, he is that. But I mean he's—well, I suppose if he hasn't told you, I shouldn't be the one to explain it. No, no, I shouldn't." He suddenly looked worried again. "Forget I said anything, that's a good girl. In fact, go ahead and put me down, nice and gently, back by the window."

Skate walked him over to where she had found him and settled him into his wire frame.

"There we are," he said, his eyes falling backward into the fog. "And remember: let me talk to Belamy about our talk, eh? That's the ticket." His voice fell away as Skate moved her hand away from the glass.

Skate stepped back, wondering who this strange person was and why he was in the glass ball in the old man's library. She felt that he had been about to confirm Haman's and the Boss's suspicions that Belamy was not alive in the technical sense, but had shied away from the revelation out of...fear? It had certainly seemed like he was afraid of the consequences of their conversation. She decided, for now, that it was best to stand by her promise not to reveal the conversation to Belamy when she saw him.

Skate left the library, no book or trinket in hand, glad not to have been caught stealing anything. She had not, after all, known she was being watched when she had entered.

Skate heard the heavy front door open and close, and heard Belamy's surprised exclamation at seeing his friend sitting in front of his cheerily crackling fire. She hid out of sight at the top of the stairs to listen to their conversation, which had only just begun.

Belamy spoke first. "...pleasant surprise!"

"Yes, I thought I'd check up on you with this dismal weather, especially since I know how loath you are to light your hearth, even in the bitter cold. But I see that I needn't have worried."

"Oh, no, I'm fine, just fine. Rattle, go fetch Laribel something warm to drink—tea, yes?"

"Lovely. Thank you, Rattle, dear."

Skate heard the clink of her dish as Rattle carried it into the kitchen, where, presumably, it would shortly have a kettle roaring to make some twenty-year-old tea. There was another scrape as Belamy scooted a chair, probably near where Ossertine was resting. When she spoke, a heavy note of disapproval weighed down her words. "I met your other guest, earlier."

"Oh yes, young Skate."

Ossertine gave a noncommittal grunt. "She's a rude child."

"Well, she's not used to dealing with another's houseguests, I'm sure. Whatever rudeness she showed to you, simply charge it to me; she's my guest and my responsibility. I hope it was nothing that cannot be mended."

"No, on the whole, I suppose it was minor. Think not of it." There was a creak as the kitchen door opened and closed, then opened and closed again. "I take it by her…attire, that this is some urchin you've taken in off the streets?"

"She's without a home, yes."

"Oh, Barrison, you mustn't begin taking in strays. Soon you'll have every manner of hanger-on and beggar at your door, believing they've a right to a warm bed and a hot meal."

"She's not a stray, Laribel. She's working for me. Helping me get things I need around town, that sort of thing. I don't know if you've noticed, but I'm not exactly a young man, ready to go out and take on the world. She's been quite helpful these past few days."

"But you were just out there!" Ossertine protested, and Skate heard the beginnings of a whistling kettle from the kitchen. "You have your new employee made dinner by Rattle while you go out into the snow for writing supplies."

"She worked very hard yesterday," he replied sheepishly, "and she's still very young. She seemed to need her rest."

"And you don't?"

"I'm fine, Laribel."

The resulting silence told Skate that Ossertine was skeptical of that claim but did not wish to press the issue. "I also came to warn you: my home was burgled recently. There's a book thief out and about, and he may try to target you next."

"Yes, I knew there had been break-ins in the area. That's why I began to take precautions."

"Oh, yes, I hope they help."

Skate guessed they must have been discussing Belamy's bizarre locks on his windows.

"Who else has been stolen from?" Ossertine asked.

"Some of the shops around have been dealing with thieves for a while, but it's mostly been out in their streetside goods. The neighbors were not forthcoming about *what* had been stolen, so I decided to take precautions regardless. I'm glad I did, since your thief seemed interested in taking books specifically."

"Book, not books," Ossertine corrected. "The thief took only one of my books. A rare one. They seemed to know where to go in my home, as well. Perhaps having an extra pair of eyes around your home may help you further to avoid such unpleasantness." There was another creak as Rattle opened the kitchen door once more to bring tea to Belamy's guest; Skate only then realized the whistling had stopped. "After all, the burglar only struck after I had left my home."

"I'm confident in my locks," Belamy responded, "and in the fact that I almost never leave my home. I thank you for the warning and the concern, though. Have you warned Jack and Bakurin yet?"

Skate noticed with dread the sound of Rattle moving up the stairs toward her, its wings flapping and its legs clicking lazily together, like thin wooden wind chimes in a breeze. She was hidden only by virtue of the landing of the stairs blocking view of her from the main room and had nowhere to hide from someone actually coming up.

When Rattle popped into view, Skate put a finger to her lips in a pantomime of shushing. Rattle looked right at her and continued on as if it had not seen her. It floated past, into the upstairs library, and shut the door behind it.

Skate released the breath that she had held since she'd heard Rattle's approach. She had missed part of the conversation because of all her fretting over being caught. Belamy was saying something.

"...neighbors or not, they should probably be made aware of the issue. If the thief finds both of our homes too well-protected, they're likely to move on to more easy pickings, wouldn't you say?"

"I suppose you're right. However, I'm not interested in walking all that way in a snowstorm. Getting here to you was inconvenient enough, and we're practically neighbors ourselves. Besides, I'd hardly call the mansion that Jack lives in 'easy pickings.'"

"I guess the weather should give us some pause." There was silence after that for a while. When they did begin speaking again, it was on some esoteric topic in their reading from the previous meeting, and Skate decided she had worn out any particular interest that this conversation might carry. She went to her room, opening and shutting her door with absolute silence—the result of years of practice at hiding her passage through occupied houses.

Skate had not been in her room for more than five minutes before there was a soft knock at the door. She opened it to find Rattle flapping in place, holding a small cloth bag in three of its legs. It tossed the bag to Skate, who almost dropped it in surprise. Then it floated over to Skate's desk. It opened the drawer, pulled out the slate within, and tossed it onto the desk lazily. The slate bounced lightly before coming to rest on the wooden surface. Rattle then floated back out of the room without looking at Skate. It left the door open when it left.

Skate opened the cloth bag to find several small squares of white stone. When she touched one of them, it left a powdery residue on her fingers.

Chalk.

Rattle came back in carrying a small book in its legs. It floated to the desk and scooted the slate to the edge of the desk. It then set the book down gently and opened it up. After flipping a few pages delicately, it stopped on a page with care. It floated across the desk and turned around, putting the desk between Skate and itself, looking at her directly as it fluttered in place. It pointed first to the page, then to Skate, then to the empty black slate near the edge of the desk. It repeated this motion three more times, then pointed to the desk.

Skate smiled. Rattle was clearly communicating to her, and she thought she might understand what it was saying. "You want me to copy the page onto the slate?"

Rattle neither confirmed nor denied her suspicion, but gestured her closer to the desk. More specifically, it seemed to be gesturing her to the open page.

When Skate got to the desk, it gently traced one of its legs down the open page, then did so again, and then a third time. It repeated this process as well.

Skate realized that it was tracing specific symbols on the page; there were three columns of different symbols on the open page, with writing above and beneath this set of symbols. Rattle was not pointing to anything but the columns of symbols. "You want me to copy the symbols here?" she asked, tracing the symbols exactly as Rattle had done with its thin leg.

Rattle bounced a little more energetically in the air, and pointed from the bag in Skate's hand to the empty slate. "And you want me to do it using the chalk in the bag. All right, eyeball, I get it."

Rattle bounced in the air enthusiastically again, and then moved toward the door.

"Wait!" Skate said, putting a hand out to stop it. It obliged and looked back at her curiously. "Why?"

Rattle just looked blankly at her, and she realized that it would be very difficult for the eyeball-spider to answer a question of that type. To her surprise, however, it made a move to answer. It brought a leg to the page, this time tracing the writing above the column of symbols, then pointing to Skate's head. It was a surprisingly gentle motion, and Rattle looked at her after the pantomime to see if she understood.

Skate nodded. This was her first reading lesson.

CHAPTER 9

Skate drew her new clothes more tightly around her as she watched the illuminated windows of Jack Gherun's dining room. Unlike Belamy or Ossertine, he owned only a portion of the building he lived in: a selection of three connected rooms on the top floor of a building with other tenants around and below him. The building, according to passersby she had been able to corner and badger, belonged to Baron Richefort himself, though some seemed to remember rumors that the Baron had sold it to a nephew or cousin at some point to pay for some trinket or other that one of his mistresses desired.

Some people cared a great deal about such rumors; the Ink was particularly interested in direct confirmation of any salacious stories of the rich and powerful, which it could then store up for the day when the organization needed to force compliance or demand other information or just to make some quick money for another project. This sort of thing was boring in the extreme to Skate, of course, and it was all hearsay besides. She never met a single person who could directly corroborate the whispers, so she safely ignored them in order to better focus on the task at hand.

This was her third time analyzing Gherun's patterns this week. The first two had been as uneventful as this innocent clandestine observation, which was the point. She was studying her mark's behaviors, his tendencies, and his schedule, and there should not be anything exciting about that idea. *The thief's work done right goes unnoticed for as long as possible.* The nugget of wisdom from Boss Marshall made her smile.

Also making her smile were her comfortable new clothes. When she had informed Belamy of her need to follow and track her mark for days before trying to gain entry to the home, Belamy had remarked that her clothing would tip off any interested parties to her presence, because the poor were at best barely tolerated there under typical circumstances. Staying in roughly one place while spying on a resident of the neighborhood was not "at best" or "typical circumstances." So, recognizing her need to blend in, Belamy had sent Skate out to pick the best clothes for the job.

Given the neighborhood in which Gherun lived, Skate had decided upon a dress that allowed movement, work, and play, a dress that could be worn with the powerful pride that the rich exuded wherever they went—clothing that both invited questions and at the same time put them off. If anyone asked, she planned to claim to be the daughter of a newly wealthy man trading wares out of the untamed region of Edge, a daughter who was easily entertained and tonight had chosen the large building as the focus of her disingenuous "attentions." Of course, there was no guarantee that such an excuse would keep her out of any direct trouble, but it might cause enough of a distraction that she could give any over-curious Guard the slip, ready to head back to Belamy's house until she was safely forgotten.

The thick coat and new dress were not her only sartorial boons; she was comfortable standing in the snow in new boots, and felt that she could have stayed right where she was for hours without needing to go elsewhere.

Skate had, over the past few days, learned much of Gherun's lifestyle. He lived alone, without so much as a pet or plant to keep him company, and he had no other company call on him in the time that Skate had spent watching and learning.

He was also fastidious in keeping his living space clean; after he took his meals, he immediately placed the dirty dishes into the hallway, which the servants who maintained the entire building quickly took away to the building's lower floors. When he read, which he did at almost exactly the same time every night, he placed a bookmark (he favored thin strips of cloth that hung outside the pages, trailing behind the book whenever he moved it like ribbons did in the rich girls' hair) after about an hour of reading, and replaced the book exactly where he had taken it from to begin with.

Skate noted with annoyance that he always checked to make sure the row of books he'd disturbed was unmoved at the end of his efforts. What annoyed her was not so much that such attention to detail meant she would leave some noticeable evidence of her crime; that would best be avoided, of course, but some amount of detail was bound to slip her mind. No, she'd decided that she simply did not *like* Gherun for his obsession with organization, with order, with minute control of his living space. She couldn't place why she found his fussiness so irritating, but her lack of clarity did nothing to mitigate the effect.

A useful aspect of his disdain for all things disorganized was that he kept a very rigid—and therefore very predictable—daily schedule.

Every aspect of the man's life followed a pattern: for the three days Skate had observed him, she'd noticed nothing different at all about his habits or schedule. He didn't have any visitors (aside from the help staff) during her observations. When she asked Belamy about Gherun, the old man informed her that he was a private man, and a wealthy one. It was why he could afford such luxurious living in an expensive part of the city without having to work to keep it. Belamy said he had inherited his wealth. "He prefers the company of books to that of people," Belamy said, "though he can function quite well in a crowd. Given the option, I think he'd choose a book over conversation nine times out of ten."

As she stood in the snow, her new boots wrapping snugly around her feet, Skate decided her only hope was to break in while the man was asleep and sneak back out before she was noticed. That would have to wait until the next night; she had an idea how to get in, but it would take some planning. She did not have Rattle with her, anyway. It needed to be with her, but she hoped that would not be the case for much longer; her lessons were going well.

As she turned on the spot and began the dark, muffled walk back to Belamy's home, she reflected on her progress. That first lesson had been the simple mockery of letters. When Belamy had finally come up after saying farewell to Ossertine, he had explained that all words were made of these letters, and that beginning to read would require knowing these twenty-six symbols by heart. So her lesson was to practice writing each of these letters and naming them when shown.

Rattle was there to help for most of it, with Belamy monitoring silently from the corner of the room, a book ever open on his crossed legs. After a long while of these exercises (she thought it must have been hours), he rose from his seat and told her she could rest for the day. Rattle had prepared food for her while she'd grilled Belamy about her target.

Skate turned a corner at the sight of a trio of Guards; she was not doing anything wrong by being out this late at night, but a young lady alone on the streets—even a well-dressed one—was sure to cause suspicion, and she would rather avoid any probing questions.

Around the corner, Skate found another almost-deserted street, the plentiful lamps of the castle district casting a happy but subdued light as snow began to lazily fall to the earth in wispy, wind-stirred pellets. There was a pair of finely dressed people on the other side of the street, a man and a woman huddled close together. Instead of being engaged in conversation or whispering loving trifles in each other's ears, though, they were purposefully walking faster than normal and avoiding eye contact with the other person on the block: a poorly dressed girl, who was weaving and bobbing as she walked, apparently in the throes of delirium. Skate noticed the urchin but didn't think anything of it; she was used to seeing kids her age who had spent money on or been given alcohol. Of course, Ink members were not to indulge on the job, and the Bosses usually did not let any kids in their teams drink before they were at least fifteen. Skate had never found anything about alcohol appealing, and had never indulged.

This girl had had a lot of it, by the look of her. As she stumbled closer, Skate could smell the booze; it was as if the other girl had bathed in it rather than drunk it.

When they were about five feet apart, each girl's eyes opened wide in recognition. It was Delly, and judging by her sudden alertness and stillness, she was not actually drunk. She eyed Skate's attire curiously, and motioned toward a small space between nearby buildings.

Skate looked around and saw that the nervous young couple must have beaten their retreat very hastily, as they were nowhere to be found. She followed Delly into the cramped area, no longer worried about her disguise being blown.

"What's with the costume?" Delly said without preamble once they were out of view. "You moving up to a lieutenant already or something?" Alert or not, the girl reeked of alcohol, and the stench was almost overpowering up close.

"Nah, not likely. Haman's doing great, and the Boss don't need any more help. What have you been drinking?"

Delly laughed. "Nothing but the boiled water they give us in the hideout with meals. This is just to throw off the Guards if they catch me and start asking questions about what I'm doing, see?" When Skate shook her head in confusion, Delly rolled her eyes. "I been picking! You know, bumping into people and nicking purses and coins. I'm 'drunk,' though, so they don't think nothing of it except to worry about the poor kid in such a bad situation." She laughed at the pity she had been getting. "Most of 'em don't care, though. Most of 'em just want the stinky little rat out of their way, 'nd I am alls too gladsh to do sho." She began slurring her words and giving a mock salute, falling easily into the cover story. "And if tha Guardsh wanted to shee me, I just tell 'em I'm not sure where my homes is at. No questions, and a swift kick out of the district. They only rough ya up a little when they gotta do that, since most of 'em don't really want to hurt a kid."

Skate nodded, very familiar with the casual cruelty of the Guards, a cruelty born not of any real malice, but of simple day-to-day irritation building up over time and spilling when dealing with the criminal element. "Scum, the lot of them," she said, spitting into the snow. "They don't know what we gotta do to live. They don't gotta starve. They don't die on the streets for not having clothes."

"Speaking of clothes," Delly began, motioning toward Skate's fine raiment, "you didn't answer me. What's with the nice stuff?"

"I'm doing a job," Skate said. She explained her situation, and how Belamy had decided finer clothes might help with her disguise. "You shoulda seen the faces of the tailors when I walked in with a bag of scepts and picked out a coat from the rack." Skate laughed; the shock and obvious discomfort mixed with greed at the sight of the gold coins was a sight Skate would not soon forget.

"Wait, wait, wait," Delly said, waving her hands in front of her, "the guy you're stealing from—"

"*Going* to steal from."

"—going to steal from, whatever. That guy gave you money to go buy clothes so that you could steal books from someone else?"

"Yeah. Nice, huh?"

"Is he an idiot?"

"No." Skate thought after she had answered. "No, I think he's pretty smart. He just...cares about some stuff more than others. Like, things that most people don't care about as much. He's got money, and he can easily get more of it, it looks like. But he really loves books, and he's always after more. So money spent on a thief to get books he doesn't have is a job well done, to him."

"Sounds like an idiot to me."

Skate shrugged, not having anything else to say to discredit the assessment. "If he wants to spend money, that's no problem for me. How's picking going?"

Delly smiled and patted a pocket in her ratty clothes. There was the unmistakable clink of coins beneath. "Oh, I'm doing fine, don't worry. These dummies just walk around with their purses and fine bags out and unprotected. I'll be able to pay up with Boss Kernisk for months at this rate." She leaned back and laughed. "Boss says I got a gift for picking. Says I'll make lieutenant well before I'm twenty. Think of that, Skate! Me, a lieutenant to a Boss. I'd be one of the ones running this city, then, you know? Someone important, someone the local dips would know to respect; someone who could pay her own way; someone who could buy fine clothes all her own." She ran a hand on Skate's shoulder as she spoke. "I'd be able to read, then, Skate. Could read a story, could learn stuff about history, could learn the old stories, new stories, could learn math good. I could write, then, too, and people'd have to read what I wrote. I'd matter, you know?" She wasn't looking at Skate anymore, but up at the dark, starless sky as a few fine pellets of snow made their way between the roofs of the buildings. "But I gotta work to get there. Gotta give the Boss his due. Gotta take from them what's got too much already, right?"

"Right." Skate knew that Delly wasn't just bragging or wishing nonsense. She had seen the younger girl at her work, dipping between rubes who could not notice slender fingers digging into pockets or slipping around belt loops. Delly never failed to make a weekly quota; others in Boss Kernisk's crew had told Skate as much with more than a hint of jealousy in their voices. Delly would be lieutenant well before her twentieth year, Skate decided—at least three or four years before then. She was too good at what she did to be held back for much longer than that. Even though she was young, younger even than Skate, she was one of the most determined people Skate had ever known.

"Speaking of," Skate said, "I need to get back to my mark."

"Oh, yeah? Gonna make your move tonight?"

"Nah, I gotta steal a few more books for him before I get in good enough to find the best thing to steal *from* him."

"I hear you. Well, good luck, madam," Delly said, dipping into a low bow to mock her fancy dress, "and may your feet be ever soft."

Skate returned the ridiculous bow and said, "And your fingers always be swift."

"You know it, dummy." With that, the girl resumed her swaying. "I dunno why anybody drinks this stuff," she muttered before she left the alleyway. "It stinks just wearing it." She teetered into the street and took a moment to "steady" herself against the wall, as if the sudden change of direction had disoriented her, and then hobbled away the direction she had been going before their conversation. Skate waited a few minutes before heading out herself.

The streets remained mostly empty, and the snow increased its tempo. It collected in small piles at the edge of buildings, where street and wood met, making the cities' buildings look like needles pushing through tight-woven white cloth. The snow had begun to sting Skate's nose and ears by the time she reached Belamy's heavy front door. She did not bother knocking before opening it, stepping into the welcoming warmth of the main room. She spoke half of the Dwarvish words she knew, and the room was suddenly awash in blue, rather than natural yellowish-red, light.

The master of the house sat in his customary spot downstairs. *No, not customary*, Skate thought. When she and Twitch had been observing Belamy before their attempted robbery, they'd never seen him sitting downstairs. He had only begun to sit in that desk regularly when Skate had begun to stay here. *Maybe not,* she told herself. *You only watched him for two days. All he does is read, and he may have chosen any number of places in his house to read on a given day.*

Her mind returned to her first night here. There *had* been something at the table that night: those red stones, whatever they were, that Skate had not seen since—stones that she was sure were behind the locked door in the cellar. Belamy was very trusting of his new student, but there were some things he was clearly unwilling to risk losing to a too-curious, already-caught thief. *Still,* she thought, *he is down here almost all the time now.*

Belamy looked up from his reading, smiled by way of greeting, and returned his attention to Ossertine's book. He appeared nearly done with the *Chronicles.*

"How goes the reading?" Skate asked, breathing in the warm air. There was a whiff of Rattle's earlier work in the scent; the creature had made a delicious tomato soup, the twenty-year-old ingredients as fresh as ever. It had helped keep her warm, though the new clothes had helped considerably more.

Skate moved in front of the desk and leaned forward, looking at the words on the page. She was seeing them upside down, but it made little difference; the elves, Belamy had informed her, did not write using the same letters as Caribolians. The night their lessons had begun, he had explained the concept of not only letters and words, but the existence of totally separate sets of symbols that other languages used. Caribolians—Skate included—spoke Thervonian, "an old tongue with a long history," as Belamy had described it. He said that the Thervonian language used its own letters, and writers of many other newer languages had found it convenient to copy the same letters for their use, though they often added their own bits and pieces along the way, and changed the pronunciation and usage for their own purposes.

Belamy smiled again and said, "It's going very well indeed. Bereziah and his entourage are returning home, their mission complete and mostly successful. However, several problems still face them: harsh terrain, unfamiliar groups not present at their first passing-by, and general malaise at being gone from home for so long. His use of emotional language here is quite moving, especially since such displays of emotion are comparatively rare in the extant elven literature; they seem to have a cultural taboo against such expression in writing that they breached only at the most poignant moments."

"What, they were never happy or sad?" Such a way of living seemed impossible. "They didn't feel anything?"

"Presumably, they did *experience* emotion. After all, Bereziah felt it appropriate to display emotions in this section," Belamy said, pointing to the large block of text in front of him; to Skate, who was only just now learning the Thervonian alphabet, the elven writing looked like random squiggles on a page. "They just very rarely thought it appropriate to express such feeling in writing. I'm not as sure about what they were like in person. Their skittishness about revealing powerful emotion may have been confined to the written word."

Skate thought of Haman, then, as he went about his work for the Ink: always serious, rarely showing anything on his face other than polite disinterest. "I bet they were like that in person, too," she said.

Belamy smiled indulgently. "Very possibly." He marked his place and stood. "Are you ready for your lessons?"

Skate nodded. This had been the pattern each night: Skate returned after hours and hours of observation of Gherun, and then had her reading and writing lesson with Belamy and Rattle. They had agreed that Belamy's fee for such generous tutelage would be an extra book each week, with the option to defer book delivery up to one week as needed. She planned to take far more from Gherun than she had from Ossertine, which should not be hard. Belamy was not interested in any specific books of Gherun's; just any that he did not already have. Rattle, who had already devoured many times over the whole of Belamy's library, would be able to quickly pick out new books for Belamy's enjoyment.

"I plan on doing the next job tomorrow night."

"Good!" he said, motioning her toward the stairs and gathering his book to follow her up. "And you're sure you'll be able to move around unheard and unseen? Laribel wasn't home when you visited her house, remember," he said for perhaps the fifth time.

"Yes, I'm sure," she responded a fifth time. "I'm actually really good at moving around without getting caught." She began walking up the stairs.

"I caught you."

Skate stopped in her tracks, one hand on the decorative banister as she glared at the old man. "Yeah, I guess you did." The old man's face was impassive, but she thought she saw dancing laughter in the darks of his eyes. "How'd you do that, Mr. Belamy?"

The old man smiled. "I have excellent hearing," he said, gesturing again for her to continue up the stairs. "Excellent hearing perfected with years of practice."

"You 'practiced' hearing better?" She turned and moved up the stairs as she spoke. "Doesn't make any sense," she muttered under her breath.

"Of course it does," Belamy said from the bottom of the stairs.

Skate spun around to face him. With the crackling fire and the sound of her footsteps on the stone, it should have been impossible for the old man to hear her murmur.

Before she could say anything, he pressed on. "The ear can be trained to hear better just as the eyes can be trained to see better, the tongue to speak, the hands to manipulate, and on and on. A musician knows her craft because she has trained her body—and in particular, her ears—to be most in tune with her work." He smiled, arms spread in a welcoming gesture, inviting a discussion on the matter.

"Okay, yeah, you can be trained to *listen* better," Skate said, rolling her eyes, "but I meant just 'hearing.' If something hurts your ears, there's nothing you can do to get your hearing back. There's no exercises you can do, there's no 'training' to get them back where they need to be. Ears are either strong or weak, and that's all there is to it. You just have strong ears."

"Ah, but I'm old. Old people have weak ears, don't they?"

Skate thought about that. He was old, but his hearing was very strong—probably stronger than her own, if this conversation was anything to go by. Skate reminded herself of the most likely true reason for his impressive hearing abilities: something about the transition from life to unlife had made him better at it.

"If they're alive, yeah." She was not sure why she said that out loud; she had not been aware of making the decision to do so.

The old man did not look surprised; instead, his eyes narrowed, and he nodded. "Say more. I'd hear your reasoning, please."

Skate swallowed before speaking. "You move too...neatly for an old man. Too loose. You sit for hours at once without griping about soreness. You don't eat. You don't sleep. You don't breathe. You don't use the latrine. You don't even get tired. You aren't bothered by the cold—at all, even though it's the dead of winter. The only thing you want is books and their stories—things that last forever, or at least last a really long time. I know there's things that move and think and talk even though they're not alive anymore. I think you're one of them." She took a steadying breath. "I think whatever magic you did to yourself killed you, kind of."

The same narrow-eyed expression stayed on Belamy's wrinkled face. He answered, "I can do magic. Isn't that as good an explanation for all of it as anything? Why do you go so quickly to assuming I've somehow cheated death?"

"I don't know," Skate answered half-honestly. She herself knew little, but Boss Marshall and Haman had been fairly convinced. She could not readily cite them as sources, though, given the context of the conversation. "But it would mean magic does way more than I thought it could."

The suspicious expression expanded to a smile. "Yes, that's probably true. Nevertheless, you're right. The reason I don't draw breath, eat, sleep, tire, or shiver is that I'm not alive. I haven't been alive for about two decades now. I'm a lich."

CHAPTER 10

Silence greeted Belamy's confession. Skate knew the word; Haman had mentioned "lich" while listing the different varieties of monsters that the old man might be. Belamy could not know about that, though, so she chose not to react. He had confirmed her suspicions, at least partially; while not a vampire, Barrison Belamy was no longer counted among the living. Looking for something to say, she asked, "What's 'lich' mean?"

Belamy's face neutralized somewhat, changing from the oddly proud and interested expression to that of the practiced lecturer as his voice fell into a more pedantic pattern. "It's the name of a particular group of undead who have willfully chosen to avoid the ravages of the grim reaper by escaping, through the use of magic, into a state of half-death. As such, I am no longer bound to the limitations that most people have to deal with, as you've so thoroughly explained.

"My body will continue to age and will, in fact, begin to decompose much as a dead body does if left unattended until I've been reduced to a moving skeleton. However, I've so far staved off most of the results of such decay with preventative magic, and should be able to continue to do so for the foreseeable future. I stand before you today in as good of shape as I was the day I died—er, stopped living, as it were. Better, actually, since my joints and muscles no longer feel the weight of years." He gave a demonstration of his ease of movement by executing a passable, if not exactly graceful, full squat to the ground, then standing straight up with no sign of pain or discomfort.

"So you're a monster." Skate said the words as her mind raced; Belamy was standing between the door to the street and her. She could not hope to jettison herself out of the downstairs windows with Belamy's locks on the latches, with the magical reinforcements he had placed on them besides, and jumping from the higher floor would be outright suicide. If this revelation was a prelude to an attack, she was not sure she could get away from him. Outwardly, she tried to show nothing but casual indifference, but she knew her body was betraying her; the hair on her arms was standing straight up, the tension in her legs aching, and part of her mind was screaming *Run!* over and over again. Her voice wavered as her throat constricted out of pure terror.

"Some would call me so, yes." Belamy nodded, either not noticing her fear or not caring about it. "But I don't think that's quite fair. I'm not hurting anybody. I didn't have to hurt anybody to get to this point. I wasn't ready to die, and old age wasn't waiting, so I made a change. It's true," he went on, sweeping an arm through the air vaguely, his loose-hanging sleeve billowing softly in the current that it caught as it moved, "that most people who go through this process must lose something of their humanity in doing so. You wouldn't believe some of the horrible things I found in my research leading up to the execution of the deed." He gave what appeared to be a genuinely involuntary shudder. "Anyone who found such paths and followed them would be truly monstrous."

"You did."

"No!" His eyes went wide as he spoke, the passive tone replaced by vehement denial. "I told you, I hurt no one. I did my own research; I found another way. Because of what they had to do in order to reach this state, most of my kind deserve death, *real* death. But I did not do what they have done. *My* way hurt no one. I am not a monster, Skate."

She was standing still. She had begun to actually be calm as he talked, though she was not fully relaxed. Belamy's confession did not seem to be a prelude to an attack, but now that she knew for a fact he was not a living thing, she did not know if she could ever be relaxed around the man again. "So you're not a vampire."

Belamy laughed once, throwing his head back with the effort. "No, of course not. What do you know about vampires?"

"Only what my friends have told me in stories. They drink blood, they're really strong, and they don't like garlic."

"Wait, is that—?" He laughed again. "Is that why you brought me garlic?" He laughed again, a full-throated sound this time. "You've had suspicions for quite a while, haven't you?" He laughed a bit more, then settled down again. "They also can't go into sunlight, cross running water outside of their coffins, or be close to silver for extended periods. So, no, I promise you I am not a vampire. However, that raises a question: you brought me that garlic almost a week ago. If you've been worried that I was some sort of monster waiting to kill you, why have you been staying here the whole time?"

Skate considered a moment before giving her answer. She needed to disguise at least part of the truth—*I'm trying to find something really good to steal*—so she decided to cover up that deception with a truth. "I really want to learn to read. And also not be out on the streets in the cold." These things were true, though they would not, by themselves, have been enough to convince her to stay with a monster. "That, and the fact that you've had plenty of chances to harm me if you wanted to."

"I don't."

"I don't think you do. You don't act like a monster to me, despite whatever you are." It was a bizarre thing to say to someone who'd just confessed to be a thing that was not alive but pretending to be, but she did mean it: Barrison Belamy had shown no interest in hurting others. Whatever else he was, he did not seem to be sadistic. "Why would you tell me any of this?" she asked. "Why not tell me to mind my own business, or just lie?"

He shrugged. "It's bad form for a teacher to lie to his student, or to discourage curiosity for selfish reasons. The most dishonest I've been with you is in how I look." He waved his hands at his body, indicating nothing in particular. "Despite my best efforts to preserve my body, I still find that people immediately recognize something off about me that deeply unsettles them. I've learned to take certain precautions about my appearance, a simple trick of magic to smooth over the parts of me that would keep me entirely incapable of going out in public."

"What do you mean, 'a trick'? What, you can change the way you look?"

"Yes, exactly. Here, I'll show you." He snapped his fingers, and she was no longer looking at an old man. Instead, he appeared to be a young soldier, wearing dark metal armor wrapped at points in leather and no more than seventeen or eighteen years of age. He looked nothing like the man she knew—this image was much rounder and softer than Belamy. He also looked a little taller. "See?"

"Something's weird about you."

"Well, yes, I did just transform right in front of your eyes. I imagine that must seem passing strange."

"No, I mean, I think there's something wrong with your trick." She blinked hard and rubbed her eyes. It was difficult for her to explain. "You look...blurry." That wasn't exactly the issue. In fact, every facet of his new appearance was crystal clear when she looked at him. If she had time enough, she could probably count the hairs on his newly full head. It was only when she wasn't looking at a part of him that she noticed the blurring, or the shaking. When she looked at his face, his arms below the shoulder started to blur at the edge of her vision. The effect was hurting her eyes and giving her a headache.

"Ah, right," he said, snapping again and resuming his more familiar appearance. "Your eyes are detecting the trick because they saw it happen. Your mind knows to look for the difference, to look for what's beneath, despite what your eyes are telling you when you focus with them. The young man disguise doesn't work as well because it's a drastic departure from my true appearance. This one's almost identical to my actual appearance. I've simply modified the small details that, when added together, unnerve anyone looking at me undisguised. Because it's closer to what's real, even though I've told you it's not real, it shouldn't give you any problems."

Skate did not notice the effect anymore after his reversion to normal. "How long did it take you to figure out how to do that?"

"Not long. It's a fairly simple spell. It's also one of the most useful of a wizard's talents, to be able to disguise himself and slip into the crowd when he needs to." Belamy chuckled, clasping his hands behind his back and staring wistfully at nothing in particular. "I remember a wizard I once knew who took to street performances to earn extra money for experimentation, eating, savings, and whatever other odds and ends he might need to spend some coin on. If one of his shows started to go poorly, he'd just bolt into his crowd, change his looks when he was two or three people deep, and blend in with his audience until the crowd began to disperse. He'd leave town shortly thereafter. He told me he sometimes had to heckle himself in order to speed the process along, when a poor crowd would mill around for an hour with no coin forthcoming."

Skate laughed. "I didn't know there were any busking wizards."

"There aren't many. It's considered by most who study the discipline to be a waste of the power and scholarship of magic, to turn what should be esteemed and high-minded pursuits into a crass entertainment stream. It doesn't bother me; after all, a person's got to eat, and it can be hard to get food in your belly with nothing but the knowledge, however vast and impressive, in your head about history, art, literature, religious doctrine, or the like."

It had never occurred to Skate that there could be hungry wizards. People with such skill always found work for those who appreciated their abilities, or so the thinking went. "I don't blame them either."

Belamy nodded. "That's because you've lived it. You've been hungry. Most who study magic never have been. It's not an area that's easy for the unfed to get into. A man like Gherun has never had to deal with want, and his opinions on such matters are far less charitable than yours. He's not a cruel man, but his mercies are limited by his experiences."

Skate thought about that for a few moments. "You told me he inherited most of his money." Belamy nodded. "He's never been hungry." More silence, and a confirming shake. "I don't like him."

"I didn't think you would. But he is a friend, Skate. When you decide to take from him, I expect you to honor your promise not to hurt anyone you borrow from on my account."

Skate rolled her eyes and nodded. "I don't just go off and hurt people I don't like."

Belamy raised an eyebrow. "You stabbed an old man once, as I recall."

"An old man who couldn't even feel what I'd done."

"You didn't know that at the time."

"I didn't do it because I didn't like you! I didn't even know you. I only did that—on accident, mind you—because I was afraid."

"I know." His tone was gentle, but his eyes were iron. "What I'm telling you is, if for any reason you fear similarly around Gherun, I need you to remember that you made a promise."

Skate rolled her eyes again. "Fine, I promise to remember my promise."

Belamy smiled. "That's all I ask. Shall we begin your lesson for the evening?"

"Yeah." She continued up to her room, where Rattle was already floating with a piece of chalk in its claws.

The next half hour passed quickly, with the first part of the time spent on recognition of letters, and the next part spent on practicing writing them. Belamy did little, only occasionally offering bits of advice like "Your first line of that should be longer," or "That takes two strokes, not three." For most of the lesson, he simply listened and read. It was not until Skate's eyes had begun to droop with exhaustion that he closed his book and joined Rattle and Skate at the desk.

"You've done very well, to have learned so much in just a week. It's not often I've had a student with such a willingness to work and ability to learn so quickly."

"How many students have you had?"

"Never mind that," he said as he smiled and tapped her chalk-board. "I had an interesting conversation while you were gone this evening."

"Oh yeah? What about?"

"You."

Sweat immediately broke out along the palms of her hands, which she nervously wiped on the nice new coat she'd taken off and set across her legs. "Yeah? Who you talking to that knows me?"

"I think you only met him once, don't worry. He lives in my library."

"Oh. Yeah." She assumed the man in the ball had taken the oppor-tunity to talk to Belamy; he had seemed very concerned that Belamy should know about the discussion from him. "What'd he say?"

"He mentioned your interest in the books in the room, and the fact that he's the one who instigated the conversation, as well as the effort to withhold information about it from me—"

"Now hold on." Her sweaty palms were now clenched into fists. She wondered why she was so nervous about this, when she knew she had not done anything wrong in the first place by talking to the strange man. "I wasn't withholding anything—"

Belamy patted the air to reassure her. "I know, that's not what I meant. I mean that he asked you not to tell me about it, and you politely obliged."

"Because he was going to do it himself."

"Yes."

"And he did."

"Yes."

Silence stretched out, broken only by Rattle taking the board from Skate and tossing it into the interior of the desk. Its task complete, it left the room with the gentle thud of the shutting door.

"Who is he?"

"A guest."

"In a ball?"

"Yes."

"Why?"

"Because he can't get out. So I give him a place with a view, and Rattle lets him read when he can."

"Does he have a name?"

Belamy nodded. "Petre. Petre Hangman."

"He's a hangman?"

"His father was, and his father before him. He's not sure how far back the family business goes. He never took up the trade."

"How did he end up in the ball?"

"He was imprisoned there by magic." Belamy shook his head. "It is dangerous to cross wizards, Skate, and our friend Petre did so. The ball was the wizard's punishment for his crimes."

Skate was a little taken aback but not too concerned. How many thieves did she know who got caught on the job and done in for their trouble, after all? "I guess he's lucky the wizard didn't kill him."

"I don't think Petre would share your assessment," he said with a half-smile. "Anyway, I brought all of this up to let you know you're free to talk with him whenever you want. Just be careful not to drop him; if his ball breaks, it will be the death of him."

Skate nodded and stood, draping her coat across the back of her chair. Belamy took his book with him out the door.

"Hey!"

The old man stopped and turned to face her.

"What did he steal, anyway? From the wizard."

"Oh, he didn't steal anything. He was put in there for murder." Belamy left then, leaving Skate alone with the information.

More snow was falling outside the window. It would be a foot thick by morning.

CHAPTER 11

IN WHICH A DISGUISE IS EMPLOYED, A PLAN
IS ALTERED, AND SOMETHING EXPLODES.

"You'll need to stay here," Skate explained to Rattle, "and wait for me to open up the window. It'll be that middle one on the very top." It was still snowing, and snow was piled thick all along the road, save for a narrow strip that had been carved out diligently by the servants of the wealthy residents of the neighborhood to allow the passage of small wagons and carriages. In the small alley that the two crouched in across from Gherun's home, it was not so bad; the buildings' overhanging roofs had kept most of the snow out.

Rattle looked in the direction of her pointing finger and clicked once, which Skate took as confirmation of understanding.

"It will take a while; I've gotta double back, then get changed, then get into the room. Will you be okay in the cold?"

Rattle clicked once again. "Okay, then. Find somewhere to hide until you see that window open." With a third click, Rattle fluttered closer to the street and let itself fall heavily into the nearest pile of snow. It burrowed its way deeper into the pile until Skate saw some skittish movement on the other side. A thin leg poked through, pushing some snow out. Rattle had successfully made itself a peephole to wait and watch.

As it put the finishing touches on its snow hole, Skate saw Gherun's light go out in the window above. She knelt down to where Rattle waited. "Remember, come as soon as the window's open." A muffled click let her know that Rattle was as ready as it could ever be.

119

She left it there, hoping to be in position to let it in soon.

Skate went back the way she and the flying eyeball had come, turning down this alley, then the next, throwing any would-be witnesses off of what she was doing skulking through this part of town at this time of night. The Guards were out, though they tended to stay huddled together in their thick cloaks, trying to finish their rounds and get out of the storm. The snow had come down unabated since the previous night and showed no signs of slowing. The Guards probably assumed that any criminals out and about would freeze to death before they had a real chance at hurting anybody or stealing anything.

Gherun's home stood like a monolith four stories high in front of her. He did not own the whole building but owned space within it permanently, according to Belamy. The bottom floor only had a few smaller rooms for residents; most of the ground floor was occupied by a lavishly decorated common room where the Master of the House organized the affairs of the whole building: managing staff, issuing orders for meals, paying and receiving payments. This would be Skate's entrance point. At night, the Master's post was occupied by a stand-in, who was less skilled at the job and seen as mostly ineffectual by the other workers. Eavesdropping through briefly opened windows as workers went about their business throughout the day had told her as much. The scullery maids had very colorful terms to describe the night manager, which was what had planted Skate's current plan into her head.

The snow crunched softly under Skate's week-old boots. The ornate wooden doors stood as silent guards at her approach, carrying the universal message of all such doors: "You are not good enough to enter here; be glad that you have the pleasure of even looking at the exterior to such a place."

Steeling herself with a deep breath, Skate pulled outward on the handles, opening both as wide as she could to make her grand entrance.

The room was empty, save the oft-maligned night manager. This was not unexpected. There were only a few servants active at this time of night to attend to the two dozen or so permanent residents' sporadic needs. Skate had been counting on the manager's solitude to better sell her lie.

He looked up from a stack of papers on the expansive serving counter that doubled as his workspace. A confused expression flashed over his face before he consciously replaced it with dignified attention to the unfamiliar girl now in his foyer. The cause of this transformation seemed to be her clothing; his needling eyes scanned her quickly as she stomped his way.

"Good evening, young miss," he said. His whining voice set Skate's teeth on edge. *No wonder no one likes this guy.* "What can I do for you?"

"You can get me into my room, immediately." She affected the imperious, high-sounding voice she had heard people in the neighborhood use when talking to servants. "My journey has taken hours longer than planned, and I'm very, very tired." She had concocted her story over the past few days; its success depended entirely on the competence—or rather, the lack thereof—of this second-rate manager.

"I'm sorry, your room?"

"Yes, yes, hurry up! Why are we still talking about this?"

"I—I don't—who are you, miss?" He added the last word as an afterthought. He was obviously confused and irritated, which was exactly what Skate needed him to be.

With much rolling of the eyes and scoffing, she said, "My word. Are you the owner of this place?"

"No, miss, but I will be glad to help in any way I can. May I have your name, please?" He was being cordial and calm now, though there was still confusion in his eyes.

"Dodonna Malthessier." The surname was that of one of the more prominent merchant families in the city, one of the cadre of families that acted as bankers and lenders for the elite and powerful. That position gave the family influence and control over most of those who controlled the city; even the Baron himself was rumored to be enmeshed in dealings with the Malthessiers. "My father secured me a room at this location months ago. Are you telling me *you* have lost my reservation?"

"I—"

"Unbelievable! This is your job, isn't it? If you've given away my room to someone else, Father will hear of it, you mark my words. Do you keep no records?"

"Of course, Miss Malthessier, but—"

"What, you keep them in your head? You have it all memorized?"

"Not at all, but—"

"Then check!" She waved her hand vaguely behind the man, where she assumed the older records were kept separate from the stacks of day-to-day paperwork in front of the manager. "And hurry! As I said, I'm quite tired from my journey, and I need a bath and a bed, and it's *late!*"

The flustered man sputtered a bit more before bowing awkwardly and backing into the back room.

As soon as he was out of sight, Skate bolted to the right, where the servants' staircase was; her spying had paid off. She snuck down the steps. The servants' door may have been guarded day and night, but the hallway she found herself in was unlit. When she tried the first door, she found what she was looking for. Inside was the servants' changing room. She left the door open to allow whatever feeble light she could to come in, but she was still essentially groping in the dark until she found her prize.

The laundry basket was stacked with servants' uniforms. It took her several minutes to find one that fit. The owner must have been a very small woman indeed, because it was not nearly as loose as Skate was prepared for it to be, though the unexpected snugness was likely more a product of the blanket she had wrapped around her stomach than any particular daintiness of the uniform owner. She put her nice clothes in one of the bare cubbies. On her way out the door, she grabbed a mop and empty bucket to complete her disguise. She did not expect to pass anyone this late at night between this room and Gherun's suite, but better to be prepared and not need it.

The servants' stairs were an out-of-the way alternative to the central staircase of the building that let off at every floor, allowing the cleaners and couriers to slip in and out of the halls with as little disruption to the tenants and their guests as possible. It was also a very convenient route to go if you were otherwise interested in not being seen, especially late at night when even the servants were not bustling up and down the steps.

The building was asleep around her, all its occupants well tucked in for hours before her arrival; there was no one to mark her passage, and had there been such a person, they would have had no inkling of her existence.

The trip to the fourth floor was without incident. The wooden floorboards of the hallway stayed silent at her passing. There were only two suites on this floor, and one of them was uninhabited; it was that empty set of rooms that had first given Skate the idea of sneaking in and "expecting" a room made up for her.

She stood in front of Gherun's closed door, carefully scanning the frame of the doorway for hidden traps, particularly those of a magical nature. She had not noticed any particular sign given by other servants as they entered the room, or by Gherun upon their entrance, but after the shrieking nightmare of an alarm that had greeted her at Ossertine's home, she did not want to take any chances.

Her search revealed nothing, even as she slowly opened the door and looked for similar signs on the other side. So she slipped in, setting the mop and bucket down silently afterward. The door did not creak at all when she just as deliberately closed it behind her.

The dim light from the hall lamps winked out when the door shut, leaving her in a dark ameliorated only by lamplight reflected off of snow four stories below. *I hope Rattle can see well in the dark.* She stifled a mad urge to laugh when she realized it probably could, since seeing was all a giant eyeball could be expected to do well.

The creeping walk across the central room to the designated window was interminable. The only small consolation was that Gherun slept with his door closed.

Darkness shrouded the room, but with Gherun's finicky refusal to have anything out of order and her own monitoring of the room from various nearby rooftops, her trip across was uneventful, albeit painfully slow.

The window swung open easily and noiselessly, and the ambient light of the room increased ever so slightly as the illumination from the lamps slunk its way in with the cold air.

Skate gazed into the snowy landscape. The slanted rooftops of the city were doing their job of deflecting snow to the ground, though not perfectly. The rooftops were edged in white, and the ground below was covered in the same. The orange lamp lights gave the illusion of warmth to the empty canvas the packed snow was providing. It was pretty. For a moment, Skate could see the appeal that some people found in looking at snow. The consideration lasted as long as it took an errant snowflake to poke her in the eye.

As she rubbed the offended spot, movement caught Skate's good eye. Rattle was flapping its way toward her through the drifting flakes. The occasional breeze sent Rattle moving erratically every few moments, but it seemed comfortable enough despite the cold and difficulty. It was taking care not to let its legs touch one another as it moved. Slipping through the open window proved simple, though its wings were making a dangerous amount of noise in the otherwise dead silence.

Skate motioned for Rattle to land, which it did immediately with an almost imperceptible click. She cut her eyes to Gherun's closed door, ears straining to hear any motion. The only sound that met her was Gherun's soft snoring. She let a breath out that she had not realized she had been holding, then motioned toward the bookcases and slowly crept that way. Rattle followed her, its spidery legs spread out and taut. She had to look away from it; the movement was more than a little unsettling, especially considering Rattle's size. It was like a spider's movement, and the languorous motion of its legs made her feel like it was hunting her, or that she was caught in a web waiting to be devoured. She worked through an involuntary shudder as she reached the first bookcase.

Skate could recognize many of the letters but read none of the words yet. Many of the books were not even in the right script, or else were so stylized that they were indecipherable in the dim light. She needed Rattle.

The eyeball bat reached the bottom of the bookcase and began to move its body slowly across the row of books there. Finding nothing, it raised itself several inches and began the process anew, going the other direction for the next shelf. While it was busy searching, Skate withdrew her blanket from inside the blouse and laid it gently on the floor, making sure to spread it out as much as possible.

A single tap sounded behind her. Rattle had found a suitable book. Skate turned and reached for the indicated tome, careful not to allow for any scraping as it left its position, or any thudding as the other books fell to fill in the gap. It took half a minute to get the heavy book off the low shelf in this manner. Skate did not trust Rattle with this part of the plan; its legs were capable of intricate movements when needed, but practicing in Belamy's library had shown it incapable of moving books quietly. The failure had taken much of the energy out of the bat-winged eyeball. "Don't worry," she had said; "I'll teach you to do it before the next time." The promise had seemed to cheer the eyeball up considerably. At the moment, Rattle was focused on finding the next book while Skate worked.

When the book was free, Skate laid it down softly on the old blanket in complete silence. She turned and waited for Rattle's next choice. She wanted to get at least four books to cover the next two weeks of lodging and lessons. When Rattle tapped another book on the very next shelf up, her hopes grew. If it had been able to find another suitable book that quickly, they might be able to get out with more than planned for. She went through the same process of painstaking pilfering, taking another half-minute to remove the book from its place without a sound, and then placing it on top of the other book, beginning a stack. A third tap, and a third book. They had not even moved on to the next bookshelf yet, and had already found three of the four books they had come for.

It struck Skate as strange that Gherun had not set up any defenses for his precious library, seeing as it was the only thing besides tobacco that he seemed to enjoy. *He must think being high up will keep him safe.* It was true that random break-ins were easier at ground level, but heights did little to discourage targeted jobs like this one. A bit of planning was all it took for someone like Skate to figure out how to get in, take what they wanted, and get out.

She placed the third book in the stack. The weight of more than four might be too much. She tested the three they had already; she could lift them, but it was a more strained effort than she had expected. The books met the floor silently, thanks both to the soft blanket and to Skate's care.

Can we do more than four? Four had been the plan, but Gherun had far more of a variety than they had expected. There would almost certainly not be another chance to take from the rich bachelor; when he woke to find his supposedly safe home short of several books, it was safe to assume he would pour a considerable amount of time, energy, and money into making sure such larceny never happened again. Having only one shot at such a wealth of books made taking more than planned a tempting proposition.

It was a temptation Skate could not resist. After Rattle picked out the fourth and would-be final book, she put it in its place and put a hand out to stop her partner in crime from flying down to the street.

Barely breathing, Skate placed a hand on either side of Rattle's bulbous body and brought it very close. It felt, to her surprise, as if it were made of glass; the wet shine of its body was not on its surface, but underneath. "How many can you carry in your claws?" Even in the absolute silence of the room, the words were all but inaudible.

Rattle spun its eye in her hands to look back at the bookshelf, then met her gaze and brought a leg up to tap on her shoulder. One. Two. A pause, another look back. Three.

The third tap had felt far less firm than the other two. She took that to mean two, maybe three. In that perfectly quiet way, she said, "Get two more."

The eyeball bat looked from her to the stack and then back again several times. She also looked at the haul and realized its concern. *That's an old blanket. It may not be able to hold more than four.* It certainly would not hold six heavy books from here to Belamy's place, but would it hold for the few moments it would take to get the make-shift bag down to the street? *We're gonna find out.* She nodded to Rattle to show she understood, then pointed back to the shelf to indicate she was good with the risk.

When she let it go, Rattle landed softly again, and began its slow creep to the second shelf. Within a few minutes it had made a fifth selection, and while Skate was getting that one off its place, it made the sixth. *Worth the risk,* she decided.

After both books were added to the taller-than-expected stack, Rattle crawled back to the window and perched on the ledge. Skate wrapped the blanket around the stack and tied it, making a passable bag out of the old cloth. There was not nearly as much room as she wanted to grab the bundle by, but that was the trade-off of taking more books.

Seeing the bag made and ready, Rattle jumped into the snowy night air. Besides a brief rush of air as it took off, the creature's exit was as silent as could be hoped for. It would wait for Skate and the bag in the street below. Originally, it had been just going to go with Skate to help as her lookout, but with two more books in tow, it would now be helping to carry the load.

The load in question was considerably heavier than had been accounted for in their planning, which made the next part of the job much more difficult. The books had to be tossed out the window to land safely in the snow. "The snow and the blanket should protect the books well enough," Belamy had said when Skate had explained her plan to him, "and I should be able to fix any damage that might occur anyway." With the extra weight and lack of any meaningful way to get a sufficient grip on the blanket bag, it would end up being less of a throw and more of a shove out of the open window. But as long as the bag stayed tied on the way down, it would be fine.

Skate strained to get the bag up onto the ledge, which groaned under the weight of the books. The noise conjured rustling from Gherun's bedroom. Swearing mentally, Skate gave a great push (or a push as great as her small frame would allow) and sent the tied bag tumbling over the edge. She closed the window with as much care as she could in her haste, and bolted back for the door. Her hand was on the handle when she heard another door open.

"What the devil are you doing?" Gherun's low voice was groggy and angry. She assumed his expression matched how he sounded, but did not stop to check. His door slammed behind her on her way out of his neatly organized home. The scramble down the servants' stairs was both undignified and noisy. There was no time to change into her first set of clothes. *Can't leave 'em, though. Even an idiot would be able to trace those things back to Belamy if they took the time.* Seeing how much money was represented in a place like this, there was little doubt at least one idiot would, in fact, take the time, so the clothes had to leave.

Skate was passing the second-floor landing when she felt steps other than hers in the narrow corridor. She stopped and listened. They were not fast or coming from above. She cut back and turned out on the second floor, throwing her back to the wall to let whomever it was pass. The night manager's unpleasantly whiny voice mumbled past her as he ascended.

She caught only small bits of his irritated muttering: "Bully...entitled...useless..." Gherun must have rung for a servant rather than chase her himself. Judging by his plodding speed, the night manager was unaware of the nature of the call. After he had gone a few steps past the landing, Skate jumped back down the stairs, taking them two or three at once to get to the servants' dressing room.

The servants' floor was as dark as she'd left it, but she knew where her destination was this time. That knowledge, combined with her rejection of stealth in favor of speed, made her trek in and out of the dressing room much faster than her previous visit. She threw the nice coat on and stuffed the boots and dress into the servants' blouse that she was going to end up keeping, apparently. The gloves, she took a few seconds to don in order to gain some protection from the cold. Then it was back up the stairs, though mercifully only one flight. Her clothes were bulging weirdly in her uniform, and every step brought a toe of one of the boots digging into her ribs.

On her way up, she heard a fast rumbling from above. The night manager had apparently been apprised of the situation and was hastily making his way back to the ground floor; whether he meant to chase her down himself or only alert the nearest patrol, Skate neither knew nor cared. She had reached the ground floor ahead of him.

She shot out into the main common room and slammed the stairway door shut behind her. A heavy table sat nearby, which she heaved in front of the closed door. It wouldn't stop anyone from getting through, but might slow them down. She brought her shoulder and arm down to bear the impact of pushing open the heavy front door.

The night outside was cold, snowy, and quiet. Skate knew about where the bag would be, and knew that she had only moments to get to the books before the area was swarming with Guards and servants out to stop her.

She rounded the corner of the impressive building, cringing as the snow filled in the low-resting servants' shoes with each step. In the lamp-lit street, it was not hard to find the blue blanket-bag.

It had not split or spilled on its way down, and Skate would have shouted for joy if she'd had the breath and senselessness to attract attention to herself. Instead, she ran through the snow and, after getting as good a grip as she could, hefted the haul over her shoulder, stomping through the snow toward the alley where a familiar set of thin black spider's legs hung half in shadow and flapping bat's wings caught her ear.

Two feet into the shadows, Skate dropped the blue bag with a heavy thud; more snow caught by overhanging rooftops meant less cushion on the ground below. She quickly untied her makeshift bag and turned to Rattle.

"Get two of them, go as high as you can to stay out of sight, and get yourself back to Belamy. I'll meet you there. Get in through the window to my room. Got it?"

The thing flapped in agitation and pointed a leg at itself and then to Skate.

"I'll be fine. I'm from these streets, remember? I can get there safe enough. Go on!"

Skate hoisted the top two books in her arms for Rattle to gather more easily. This time, it accepted the load without any objection, though the wings began to flap with effort rather than anger or concern. Skate dropped back down and tied up her bag again, giving herself a much easier amount of empty bag to grab hold of. Rattle disappeared with surprising speed into the night sky.

A whiny, irritating male shout broke the silence of the night air: "Guards! Thief! Guards!" The night manager had evidently acquired a bell before getting outside, because a ringing clamor accompanied his panicked call. She heard another voice; the manager had brought out the servants' entrance door guard to aid in his hollering. The shouting and ringing followed Skate while she made her escape, but got quieter and quieter the farther away she ran; the night manager had not given chase.

Exhilaration, giddiness, and fear mixed and shot through her as she snuck around corners and through narrow openings. The thrill of escape was always a heady sauce, and being nearly caught only made the effect better and worse. Being terrified and alert and successful all at once made her legs pump with ease despite the cold, made her hearing sharp despite the blood rushing like a river behind her ears, made a tangled knot in her stomach even as she fought back fits of laughter. The wave of contradictory and intoxicating sensations was familiar, but never had they felt so intense. *Is it because of the mark being so rich, or the worth of the goods, or something else?* she wondered as she backed against a wall, having heard heavy steps moving quickly down the next street.

There was no time to consider it further; the patrol going past failed to notice her crouching form at their backs. It turned the next corner, running to the now very distant sound of ringing in the streets behind and leaving the young thief a clearer path to her destination. She crossed the open street and passed out of the Baron's district, with its plentiful Guards all in a stew in wintery midnight.

The transition into the Old Town was not immediate; many buildings she skittered past were well-built and fairly new, sturdy architecture bought by deep purses with an eye toward beauty as well as functionality. However, such art became less pronounced and more haggard as she progressed, showing more signs of age, neglect, and wear the closer she got to Belamy's home. The Old Town was, after all, old, so the gradual dilapidation was a handy way to determine how far away she was from the more ascendant denizens of the Baron's district.

It was only when the notably old and rundown buildings mixed with the new and rundown buildings that Skate began to get a clearer sense of her exact location in the sprawl of this part of the city. Belamy's home was in such a place, sticking out as a finely made statue might when tossed into a pile of rubbish. She soon found the home, an aged and refined edifice among the new and sloppily thrown-together cabins and shacks.

The front door was unlocked as usual; the warm orange glow of the fireplace was a welcome change from the cold white of outside. She dropped the books and without preamble threw off the useless house shoes she'd taken from whatever unlucky servant happened to be close to her size. The boots that had been jabbing her every step of the way were dug out of her shirt and thrown next to the blanket-bag, which was wet from the melting snow. She handled the dress with more care, refolding it delicately and resting it on her shoulder.

Belamy wasn't downstairs; he must have either been reading upstairs or working in the lab below.

Stretching out in front of the fire brought enormous relief from the lingering bite of the cold. Her tingling toes were giving renewed signs of life, previously muted by exposure to the hoary elements. Eventually, she got comfortable enough that she hooked one leg on the other and lay all the way down on the stone floor, which had been warmed by the crackling flames for hours before she'd gotten here.

Her mind wandered, still fluttering with the exhilaration of the heist well done. *Three weeks of lessons. Three more weeks to find the goods. Three more weeks of warm meals, breakfast, lunch, and dinner.* Rattle should be ready to whip something up soon.

"Rattle!" Skate scrambled to her feet, scooping up her dress as she went, and bolted up the stairs, running as fast as she could into her own room. Sterile white light poured out of Belamy's library, but she didn't pause to greet him or make herself known as she passed; the rest of the load was stuck outside in the snow, and she had to let it in.

Sure enough, silhouetted in the dim light from the street below, Rattle bobbed back and forth in the night air, tapping against Skate's window at regular intervals, bumping the bulk of its body against the glass to be let in. When she opened the window, it flew in calmly, setting the two books on her empty desk. It gave a great shake to remove any clinging snowflakes, then bobbed out of the room with bat wings on still air.

"Rattle."

It turned toward her, single eye fixed squarely on her face.

"A snack?"

It clicked once, and moved off for the staircase.

Steps approached, and soon Barrison Belamy, the lich in disguise, poked his head into the room. "I take it the hunt went well, then?" he asked, nodding at the short stack on the desk.

Skate nodded, and pinched the blouse she was wearing. "You might want to get rid of this, though. If anyone finds the stuff I had to take from that place here, you'd be in trouble."

"We'll burn the clothes in the fire and drop a bag of helms by their door in a week. That should be enough." He waved at the pair of books on Skate's desk, and they floated off after Rattle. "Get changed and bring them down; we'll destroy the evidence tonight. Well done!" He clapped her on the shoulder and left.

Alone again, Skate hustled to get the finer clothes on after throwing the servant's uniform off. She was barefoot but didn't mind; she'd have her feet by the fire again soon enough. She gathered the discarded clothes in a bundle and went to meet the wizard downstairs.

The sound of cupboards opening and closing reached her ears first, followed by the popping fire and the heavy thud of books landing on a desk. Belamy had taken all six books and placed them in one impressive stack on his desk. He was bent over reading the titles, chuckling and smiling as he went. When he noticed Skate, he turned toward her and said, "You were very productive this time! I thought the plan was to only take four."

"I thought of a way to take more. Rattle helped."

"Well and good." He turned his attention back toward the books. "A fine haul indeed. I knew Gherun was holding out on me; every time I've asked for any new books, I've been rebuffed. 'I'm sure your collection is more extensive than mine,' or 'My library's a pale imitation of yours, Barrison,' or a dozen other flattering lies. But I knew!" He laughed and slapped his knees. "I knew it, and I was right. He had more, didn't he?"

"Had more that aren't in your collection, you mean? Yeah, probably. This is just from two of the shelves, and they were the first two we looked at."

"What a cad!" Belamy slapped his knees again. "Selfish, lying cad. Well, the truth will out, won't it? That's the wisdom, anyway." He fell into muttering to himself as he scanned the titles again, as if to commit the names to memory. Rattle brought out a small plate of crisp bread and thin slices of cheese, which Skate took with a nod of thanks.

"I'm sure you're happy, then," Belamy continued. "Not a bad night's work, with three more weeks of home and hearth at your disposal, and lessons alongside to boot."

"Yeah." *Three more weeks to find what you've hidden.* "So what did we get anyway?"

"Four that I'm familiar with, but two I've never even heard of. *An Account of the War of Five Kings*—that one's a history of an ancient war between the elves and the dwarves by a dwarven scribe. There's *The Kiyilid,* an epic poem from the ancient land of Jyone about a king off to war. *Fire: Theory and Practice* is a book on magic theory, specifically how to use fire in creative ways. The fourth is another history, *The Reign of Kas Tomir,* about the life and times of a dwarven king centuries ago." Belamy moved each one into a second stack as he named them. "These next two are unfamiliar. One's Elvish, and I don't recognize the script of the second." He picked the Elvish one up and examined the spine, where text was etched into the hard leather, flowing loops that crisscrossed one another, looking nothing like the twenty-six letters Skate was getting familiar with.

Belamy spoke slowly, translating as he read. *"The Last...Days of the...Burithim*? I don't know what that means, 'Burithim.' It's a plural noun, but that's all I can draw from it. Reading the text will clarify that, I'm sure." He set it on the pile with the rest, and picked up the final, unknown book. Its title was not on the spine but emblazoned on the cover. Unlike the Elvish script, this book's language appeared more jagged, with hooks and sharp curves on almost every character. "How strange. This isn't just stylized Elvish or Dwarvish; it doesn't look like any language I'm familiar with. How intriguing. See?" He held out the book, the front facing Skate directly. "This," he said, pointing to the first character, "could almost be an 'A,' if you squinted at it and used your imagination, but I don't see anything else in the title that could be mistaken for a letter common to men, dwarves, orcs, goblins, or elves. How odd." He moved around behind his desk and put the book down.

Skate, curious to be part of the discovery of what she and Rattle had claimed from Gherun's home, looked at the upside-down tome.

Belamy opened the cover and revealed a page with many similar runes all over the page. "No, wait—"

Belamy's voice was drowned out as a flash of red heat engulfed him. The fire raged outward toward Skate, but she was moving far away, shoved back by an invisible, powerful hand pushed into her chest. She grunted as she landed against the stone wall, and spinning blackness took up her vision. She thought she could hear the sound of wind, and then knew no more.

CHAPTER 12

Hearing came first. Wings were flapping softly nearby. Then came feeling. She was in a bed. The back of her head throbbed. The soft pillow she was lying on helped somewhat, since it felt worse if she tried to move; but the pain was there, dull and constant, even if she relaxed.

Skate opened her eyes, desperate for vision. A white light shone nearby, the same light that she and Twitch had noticed in Belamy's upstairs library. She was seated slightly upright, with an easy view of her surroundings. She tried to sit all the way up and groaned for the effort before flopping back down not on one pillow, but on the several that kept her propped up.

Rattle turned toward her at the sound. It was floating by her bed, a book open on the desk. Seeing her awake, it left the book behind and flapped out of the room. "Hey," she groaned after it, but it didn't stop, and her head ached from the effort, so she stopped calling after the first try.

Alone and unable to move without tremendous effort, Skate became utterly bored within seconds of Rattle's exit. The book was too far away for her to even begin to try to recognize anything within, and so it offered no possibility of alleviation. Not having anything else to do, she looked for a problem to work through, and found one: she didn't know how long she'd been unconscious. Judging from the lack of light outside, it had either been a short amount of time, or else far longer than she would have first guessed. Snow still flew past the window, though it had slowed since her outing.

So, I've either been out for a couple hours, or for a whole day. She ran through a list of clues that would tell her how long she'd been out. *I'm not hungry. I'm only a little thirsty. I don't have to pee.* A few hours only, then.

Her door, which had been left open, creaked and caught her attention. There stood Belamy. He appeared whole and healthy—though the latter part of that was an illusion, anyway—and unburned, despite the conflagration from the strange book. He was stone-faced, his expression frozen into one of grave concern. He said nothing.

Skate spoke, and this time the pain was less pronounced. "Did you fix your clothes with magic again?"

His look softened, and he managed a smile. "No need. Ever since you started using the fireplace, I've been prepared for unexpected fire outbreaks. The flames washed over me and my clothes with what felt like a cool breeze. So, I suppose I *protected* with magic, rather than *repaired.*"

"Lucky you."

He nodded. "A bit of preparation makes the easiest luck, I find."

"The book was trapped?"

"All six of them were." He pointed to the book on the desk. "Unlike Laribel, Jack took the time to have retributive glyphs inscribed on the first page of each book, which were set to explode in the face of anyone who opened them without first speaking the protective word. It was an ingenious trap, really; the flames were designed only to burn the opener of the book and anyone nearby, but not the book itself or any other books that might be around. The flames did singe my desk, but a little work cleared it right up."

"Why do I not feel burned? The fire was coming right at me."

"Well, I managed to, uh, throw you back," he said, scratching the side of his head. "Though in my haste, I may have flung you a mite too hard. Here, lean up."

She did so. The pain was there, but she was prepared for it this time. She winced but managed to stay up. Belamy poked and prodded the pillow behind her, then ran a bony finger on the back of her head. That hurt, but again she only winced.

"Okay, back down. Gently," he added after she flopped backward. "Well, you've got a healthy bump but no blood. You should be fine."

"I thought getting knocked out was bad for you." She knew thieves who liked to brawl in their spare time for extra money, and the most avid pugilists went funny in the head after a few years. Haman said it was because getting knocked in the head too much bloodied the brain.

"It can be. Here," Belamy said, raising a hand with four digits extended, "how many fingers, Skate?"

"Four." She chuckled at the silliness of the question.

"You're probably fine." He smiled at her mirth, and moved to collect the book on her desk.

"I'd like my lesson again tomorrow."

"Of course." He took his lamp out with him, leaving Skate in the wintery dark. She groaned as she rose and put her dress on the back of the chair, then flopped back into bed. The pain was almost entirely gone now. It wasn't long before she drifted away, this time into a natural, restful sleep.

#-�ʊ-ⴋ-◊

Skate woke to the familiar sound of Rattle's cooking bouncing up the heat vent in the floor. As she got dressed, she ran a hand on the back of her head and felt the tender welt there. *Lucky he thought quick.* Burns would have been much more unpleasant than a tiny bump on the head.

Skate moved toward the stairs and froze. Familiar voices reached her ears; Belamy and Gherun were talking. As she had with Ossertine, she snuck to the edge of the stairs and listened.

"...telling you, Barrison, I was targeted! These people went out of their way to steal from me in particular."

"You don't know that, Jack. For all—"

"I don't know it?" Gherun's thin voice was agitated and sounded more like a growl than anything else. "Barrison, I live on the fourth floor of one of the most exclusive buildings in the most well-protected portion of the city. I could name on one hand the number of places it would be more difficult for a random thief to get into in all of Caribol, and two of those belong to the Baron himself. This was not random!" He punctuated the last word by slamming his hand down hard on something, presumably Belamy's desk.

"Okay, Jack, fine. Someone deliberately went to your home in particular and stole some of your books."

"My *rarest* books! They took some of my rarest books, which aren't set apart in any special way from the rest. I'm telling you, I've been marked. This is a message from someone, a message that I'm not safe."

"Come, now, you don't know that for sure. Did they leave you a message of some sort? A note or a messenger?"

Jack groaned. "No, they didn't leave me any kind of message. That's what I'm telling you—this burglary *is* the message. 'Make a deal or lose all your books.' That's why they didn't take more."

"Make a deal? Make a deal with whom?"

There was a pregnant pause, wherein Skate heard only the crackling of the fireplace and Rattle's banging in the kitchen. Jack's voice was quieter when he spoke, but no less emotional. "There are...people I know, Barrison. Rough people, though they can put on a veneer of gentility if they need to." His sneer could be heard with every word. "They approached me last month. We'd met at a party put on at Lady Flandel's to celebrate her birthday, and they seemed like very fine people. I don't know how they know Lady Flandel; they were invited, though. They wouldn't have gotten in without an invitation. They must have her in their clutches already.

"Anyway," he said, and the sound of one of Belamy's chairs scooting on his floor squeaked out, "we got to talking in the parlor, where the gambling tables had been set up. We played several hands of Fleece, then moved on to Tiles. They were wonderful conversation partners, and I thought we'd gotten on fine by the end of the night. I don't know whether I came up on top in our games overall or not, but it didn't matter much. This man and his friends were perfect gentlemen, come win, lose, or draw."

"Who were they?"

"I didn't get a straight answer other than names out of them; the leader of the trio called himself Lord Hajime, and he was my principal partner and opponent as we played. Even when matched with others at the table, he sought me out for conversation—you know, comments and quips about the game, or observations at this lord's shoes or that lady's bodice, the sort of normal fare at such a gathering. The other two

were untitled, though they had rather common names: Marshall and
Haman. The former was a large fellow, and seemed a bit rough in character, though dressed quite well, while the latter chap was too quiet to
get much of a sense of him, though he seemed much more refined than
the other. As I said, Hajime was the leader of the troupe and my main
acquaintance for the evening. I do not know over what province he
kept a lordship or if he was involved in any other distractions than
parties and soirées."

Skate's breath had caught at the mention of the name "Hajime."
That was one of the aliases the Big Boss used in public. Lowlings like
Skate didn't know his real name, but they were familiar with his most
common sobriquets: Hajime, Doughton, Kingfisher, Ouriole. At the
mention of Marshall and Haman, all doubts disappeared: Gherun had
met with the Big Boss, and Skate assumed the Big Boss had used that
meeting to insinuate himself into Gherun's life in order to lean on him.
It was a very common tactic among the thieves of the Ink: introduce
yourself, imply a threat, and suggest a monthly payment for "protection." Haman called such agreements "extortion," but Skate thought
the protection racket was smart. It was free money, and you didn't
have to do anything to get it; just say some stuff and rake in the scepts.
And someone like Gherun would have a lot of scepts to hand over each
month.

"A few months later, they showed up at my home. I was glad to
welcome my new friends, but the conversation took a most unwelcome turn very soon. They began to talk about how vulnerable I was,
how easy it would be for people to come take what wasn't theirs. They
told me—*he* told me—they could prevent that from happening, but I'd
have to pay, since such services 'did not come for free, even for
friends.' Friends, indeed."

Skate smiled. She knew exactly how the Bosses' minds worked,
including, apparently, the Big Boss himself. Gherun must have been a
hefty mark indeed to draw the audience of the BB, and she found that
she took some pride in the fact that she'd managed to successfully steal
from such a bigwig.

"Did you pay them?"

"Of course not! To be set upon by ruffians in disguise in my own
home, only for them to demand money out of me every month? Ridic-

ulous. I told them where they could stuff their offer, that I was not interested, and that I didn't wish to see them anymore."

"Did you inform the Guard?"

Gherun clicked his tongue. "No. After I'd expressed my disinterest, Lord Hajime intimated that I ought to avoid doing that. 'We've ears amongst the law,' he said, 'and we don't like them getting involved in our affairs so unnecessarily.' A common ruffian is all he is!" His voice was suddenly booming and full of hate rather than nervous and agitated. "I doubt he's lord of anything save vice and thievery. He said they'd 'be in touch.' This has been their touch, Barrison; I'm sure of it."

Barrison demurred. "If you say so. What will you do?"

"I'll have to get back in contact, I suppose. Lady Flandel knows him, so she must know how to reach him. That will be the end of it. I may even be able to get my books back."

Skate brought her hands up in silent celebration. This was amazing news; she had managed, on her own, to push a client into the hands of the Ink whom the Big Boss had taken a personal interest in. The Boss would be thrilled, and the King of Thieves in the city of Caribol would know her name and would be glad of her service.

"A small price to pay for my peace of mind."

"Jack, no," Belamy said, his voice sad. "There's no need to fall in league with these people. You'll never be free of them if you agree to their demands. You'll be under their thumb until they say otherwise, which will never happen so long as you pay more money."

"What am I to do, Barrison? They know where I live. They've shown that they can get in and out whenever they please. I'm not safe."

You will be with the Ink, Skate thought. She whispered, "Shut up, shut up, shut up," hoping Belamy would let the matter drop.

"Let me investigate further. Let me be the one to contact Lady Flandel about Hajime and the rest. I don't mind meeting with ruffians; I can handle myself, even in old age."

"Oh, Barrison, no, I can't ask you—it's far too dangerous, and not your problem—out of the question—"

"Jack." Belamy's voice had grown harder. More resolute. "I will be contacting the lady, and I will be investigating this on your behalf. Go home, and keep your door locked. Hire a wizard to ward your place from unwanted intrusions; I know you can afford it."

At the top of the stairs, Skate was pulling her hair in frustration. *"No,"* she hissed to herself, *"take it back, take it back, shut up, shut up."* Belamy was going to ruin everything with his insistence on "borrowing," and now he was trying to keep his friend from falling into the Ink to boot. *"It's his problem, shut up, shut up."*

By the time she had quieted her muttering to the point that she could hear, Jack was already out the door, his voice heavy with emotion. He was thanking Belamy over and over again, promising to stay at home and shield himself better, and so on. "You don't know what a weight this is off of me, Barrison, you really don't," he said with a sniff as Belamy's door opened and let in a blast of cold air.

"I have some idea," Belamy said, gently corralling Gherun out the door and shutting it when he was gone. He walked back to his desk and, after a few minutes, called out for Skate.

She sighed before answering. "What?" she asked, adding *you bloody fool* in her mind after the question.

"Oh," he said, looking at the top of the stairs. He couldn't see her from his position, but her voice must have clued him in that she was very close. "Come on down; your breakfast is almost ready. We need to talk about getting Jack's books back to him."

Skate let her head hit the wall before she stood up and walked down to meet her tutor and benefactor. The smell coming from the kitchen was very inviting; fresh-baked dough wafted through the half-open door, and an unfamiliar sweet smell came with it. Belamy was sitting at his desk, Ossertine's book open in front of him. He had only a few more pages to get to the end of the text.

He looked up at her approach. "How long were you at the top of the stairs?"

"Long enough to hear about thieves and messages and payments," she said, more grumpily than she intended.

"Hmm. And do you know anything about the people he's talking about? I imagine you'd at least have encountered some rogues of their like in your time on the streets."

She chose her words with care. "I'd heard the name 'Hajime.' Your friend is right to call that guy dangerous. Anytime I heard anyone talk about him, they said he was ruthless and smart. He must've went after your friend because he's rich. Hajime's supposed to be in charge of a lot of thieves and tough guys. If he said he wanted Gherun's money, he's gonna want that money still."

"Well, well," Belamy said with a sigh of his own, "but that's a problem of its own. We'll at least able to get his books back to him. After I've had time to read them, of course," he added with a wink. "Speaking of which," he said as he gestured to the open book in front of him, "it's almost time to get this back to Laribel."

"How are you going to do that?"

He looked at her, his face slightly slack, his mouth parted in confusion. "Well—you're going to get it back into her home."

"I am?"

"Of course you are! I can't very well just hand it to her, can I?" His face had gone from an expression of confusion to consternation. "We talked about this already. I told you they'd need to go back to their owners when I was done with them."

"Yeah," Skate said, turning from him to sit in front of the fire, "you did say that, I remember."

"So why are you behaving like you've never heard any of this?"

"I'm just confused; where'd you get the idea that I was supposed to be bringing them back?" She opened and closed her toes in front of the fire. "We never talked about that, I don't think."

"We never—it was implied!"

"Implied?"

"Yes, implied. I meant that you were to take them back."

"But you never said it?"

"No, but—"

"Then how in the world was I supposed to know it?" Her feet were warm enough that she pulled them back and sat cross-legged, watching the wood crackle and burn. "I never agreed to do something like that, and I don't see how it's my responsibility to get them back where you want them. One book, one week of shelter or one week of lessons. That was the deal, right?"

"I—"

"And that's what I've been working under, and how I've paid my way to stay in your home and eat your food."

"But—"

"That was what we agreed on. I never agreed to more, did I?"

Belamy spluttered, caught by the truth of her words. He stopped and closed his eyes. "This is true. I suppose you never did agree to do more. Your part of the bargain is complete, for housing and education, for three weeks." He looked up with a half-smile, sardonic and humbled all at once. "What will it take for you to return these to their owners, then?"

Skate grinned and closed her eyes against the drying effect of the flames. "How about two weeks per book returned?"

Belamy's face registered only a moment of surprise, then fell back into his amused expression. "One week per book returned."

"Deal."

Skate got to her feet as Belamy moved toward her, hand outstretched. She didn't bother spitting in her hand this time. The handshake was brief and firm from both sides.

"You knew what I was going to ask for," she said bluntly as they both let go.

"I had an idea. I did not expect to need to haggle over the issue, but I feel that you got exactly what you wanted anyway."

She shrugged. "Either you'd take the high offer because you were desperate, or you'd haggle over it because you had something we both know I want. No reason not to aim high, right?"

"You thought this through," he said, though there was no malice in the accusation. If anything, he sounded amused and surprised. "This was no spontaneous deal, was it?"

"I've always got to be thinking of ways to stay off the street, Bel— Mr. Belamy. This place is better than any other hole I've had to sleep in, don't you doubt it. I've never had anyone to make me any kinds of meals before, when they come at all. So, yeah, I've been trying to think of how to stay here longer without going back to the streets. You can't begrudge me for thinking about that in the meantime."

"Far from it," he said, the humor gone from his face. His expression was now blank; there was nothing there to read. "I'm impressed with your foresight. Most children your age wouldn't think that far ahead."

"You'd be surprised how many kids there are like me, and how smart they can be. You gotta be smart to survive, Mr. Belamy, make no mistake. Living on the street doesn't give you a choice."

Rattle came into the room carrying a steaming bowl of soup, which it placed on the floor beside Skate. It plopped a spoon into the bowl, and the splash was almost large enough to get on the floor. It floated back into the kitchen to clean up. Skate stirred the soup thoughtlessly for a few moments.

"You may be right," Belamy admitted. "But I also know a quick learner when I see one. Your progress learning your letters is quite impressive; with the three weeks ahead of you, I have no doubt you'll be able to have the basics of reading down. That's uncommon for someone your age. I've taught many people to read over the years, but few have kept your speed and progress. Don't underestimate your own abilities."

"If you say so." She began slurping the warm broth down by the spoonful, her headache getting lesser and lesser with each swallow. *Must be the heat.* "Speaking of reading," she said between slurps, "what are we working on today? More letters?"

"No, I think you've got those. We need to move on to sounds with each letter; I think you're ready for that."

Skate unceremoniously wiped her mouth on the sleeve of her almost new dress. Belamy flinched and muttered some words with a lazy wave of the hand. The food that Skate had left on the inside of the fine sleeve disappeared. "Thanks," she said, heading toward the stairs.

"Take better care of that thing," he called after her. "Are you getting ready for today's lesson?"

"Yeah," she called over her shoulder, "just gimme a minute to get ready."

Skate reached her room and pulled out the board and a piece of chalk. She had written the first three letters of the alphabet in gnarled shapes when a loud thud on the window broke her concentration. There was a splash of white powder stuck to the glass. She opened the window and looked out, only to be smacked in the face with another snowball. It was not tightly packed, so it exploded completely on impact.

Skate spluttered and wiped the snow off her face and hair before glaring down at the alley below. It didn't take long to find Twitch, looking quite sheepish after his well-aimed throw.

"S-sorry!" he shouted, and she shushed him.

In as carrying a whisper as she could manage, she said, "Go away! You'll ruin everything!"

"Gotta t-talk," he said in slightly more subdued tones. "Important stuff."

She groaned in frustration, looking from side to side. "Go wait by where we were searching this place out," she hissed, "and I'll be there quick. Go!" she said, cutting his response off and slamming her window shut. She went back to wiping any remaining snow off of her, crossing the room to leave. She opened the door to find Rattle and Belamy there, the latter holding a small bound leather book she didn't recognize.

"Oh!" he said, surprised that the door opened before he could knock. "Good. Shall we begin?"

"Uh, no, actually," she said, sliding past him toward the stairs, "I kinda feel like going for a walk first."

"A walk? It's freezing outside."

"Yeah, I know, isn't it great?" Skate said, babbling in the hopes that he'd just take her word for everything. "It's always refreshing to be out in the cold, knowing you can come back in, you know? So I'm gonna get some fresh air." She bounced down the steps toward her boots. "After that, we can do the lesson, okay?"

"Yes..." Belamy said, giving a questioning look at Rattle, who lifted two legs out to its sides in a passable facsimile of a shrug. "Why is there snow in your hair?"

"That's what made me want to go out! I opened my window and flakes were falling and I just couldn't stand it," she said as she strained to get the second boot on. "Anyway, it may be a long walk, so I'd just go back to reading, if I were you. Could be out a while, I mean."

"Okay...." He and Rattle had made their way downstairs and were watching her as she swept the heavy coat from the rack. "And everything is all right?"

"Great! Bye," she said as she swung the door shut behind her. She missed another concerned look between Belamy and Rattle and another imitation of a shrug as she began tromping into the cold winter day.

CHAPTER 13

IN WHICH A REPORT IS MADE, A CHANGE OF
PLAN OCCURS, AND A BRAWL BREAKS OUT.

Twitch was right where she'd told him to be, skulking beneath a bowing awning at a diagonal to Belamy's home. The familiar shock of wiry hair poked out of familiar shabby wrappings, and the familiar smile spread wide at her approach.

"How you been?" he said, waving her closer. "I haven't s-seen you in a couple weeks. I was about to get n-nervous." He was looking her over and picking at her dress with his fingers. "L-looks like I didn't need to worry. Where'd you get them clothes, then?"

"The old man paid for them to help with a job."

"Nice. He let you k-keep the clothes?"

"Yeah, sure. What's he gonna do with 'em?"

"I guess." He kicked a nearby snow pile. "So, you're good? No troubles with the old guy?"

"No, he's all right. Looking for the big score, still, but I've bought myself three more weeks to look."

"Th-three weeks?" He ran a hand over his face. "Skate, I think they're expecting s-something this week."

Her mouth fell open—but only briefly. *It's been a week since I've talked to them*, she reminded herself. *It's no wonder they have expectations for a delivery soon.* "Right. I got something to report anyway, so let's get going." He didn't respond beyond looking unsure. "What?" she asked, confused.

"Skate, if you d-don't have anything to give them, it's n-not a good idea to go back."

"I'll tell you what's not a good idea, Twitchy," she said, crossing her arms over her chest and frowning, "and that's staying away from the Boss when I promised money and he ain't seen me in a week. *That* is a bad idea."

He nodded, though not entirely enthusiastically. Brightening slightly, he asked, "Hey, word on the street is someone hit a place by the Baron's. I know a lotta rich guys live over there, and they got books. Wazzat you?"

"Yeah, but don't go spreading that around, you hear? The Guard was buzzing all over looking for me, and I'm sure they'd still love to have a talk if they found out who did it. I'll tell you about it on the way to the hideout."

Their trek through the city streets was a long one, with huge snowdrifts taking minutes to get over or else around on the way. By the time they reached the cellar door, they were both out of breath and red-faced from the exertion of tromping through powder, though Twitch was laughing at Skate's retelling of her exploits.

"So w-what is it, anyway?"

"Rattle? I dunno. It's something the old man 'made,' whatever that means. I'm guessing it's some sort of magic doll or something that he turned into a living thing. Even though it looks like something you'd have nightmares about, it's actually really nice. Good cook, too."

"I cannot believe you got this fool to cook meals for you."

"He doesn't. Rattle does."

They said their hellos to Bart and made their way to the rowdy common area. The snow had driven most of the ruffians indoors to wait for a melt, or for the street to be more cleared by the city. A huge barrel had been set against one wall, and a crowd of men and women shuffled around it, waiting for their turn to pour a drink. A game of darts was on, and someone had brought a guitar. It was playing a merry tune as the thieves and ruffians caroused. The Boss's door was open, and he was sitting behind his desk, laughing and talking to two people seated across from him; it was difficult to tell looking only at their backs, but they didn't look familiar.

She and Twitch made their way toward the Boss's room but stopped short of it to snag seats at a crowded table near the door. The other brigands were paying them no heed, being too busy joking and arguing and gambling.

"Do you h-have any good news, then?"

"Yeah, I think so. I may have got the Ink a new customer, but it'll take some work to get there."

"What? The g-guy you stole from?"

"Yeah, Gherun's the name. He thinks the stealing was a message from the Ink to get on board or get out of town. If I keep that up, it's as good as the real thing, isn't it?"

"I g-guess so."

"It's the same thing," she insisted, irritated at his reluctance, "and the Boss will be glad for the work done. It's just as good as bringing money myself, ain't it? Of course it is," she said, not waiting for a response. "Of course it is." She leaned forward and lowered her voice, though it remained audible over the general din of the room and the more immediate noise of their tablemates. "And this was a big one, Twitch. The Big Boss himself was intent on making it happen."

"How d-do you know that?"

After she explained Gherun's story, he whistled and shook his head. "This is b-big important stuff, Skate. Big and important. S-stay smart when you're talking t-to the Boss. If you bring up the B-Big Boss, it'll get his attention real quick, and p-probably make him nervous." He nodded at the door as the Boss's two guests shuffled out.

Skate was right; she didn't know either of the leather-clad men who emerged.

"G-good luck."

Skate slapped the table lightly and stood up with a grin. "Thanks, Twitch." She knocked on the Boss's open door, and he waved her in, the smile from the last meeting still hanging on his face. *At least I caught him in a good mood.* She slipped in and sat in one of the vacated chairs. "Hey, Boss."

"Hey, yourself, my little spy. How goes the inspection of the old man's home?" The gravelly voice was as congenial as it had been when he'd been speaking to his guests. *He's not too mad, I guess.*

"Good, Boss, good. I'm having trouble finding space to look when he's not around, though; he hardly ever goes anywhere. But I'm pretty sure I've at least found where he keeps the valuable stuff."

"That's good, Skate, very good," he said, stuffing a fat pipe with tobacco leaves extracted from a vest pocket. "I have been hoping for good news on your job for a week, now." He took his lighting stick from the flame of the oil lamp and brought it to the tobacco, puffing gently to coax the flame.

"And I got news to give, Boss, but it might not be...exactly related to my job."

"Oh?" He wasn't looking at her but was focused on getting the tobacco to light. As Skate spoke again, it caught, and he took a deep breath.

"I may be able to get Jack Gherun into business with the Ink."

Boss Marshall spluttered and coughed as his eyes went wide. "You—you what?" he managed to get out between hacking, rumbling coughs. He took a swig from the glass near the edge of his desk, which helped to settle him enough to receive an answer, though his great belly trembled from residual small coughs.

"I stole from him as part of my job, to get more time with Belamy and his goods, you see, and it turns out, he thinks the theft was part of a plot from the Ink to get him on board. He thinks I—we—were trying to send a message with the burglary. If the Ink were to make contact, quickly, I think we'd have him."

Boss took another drink and cleared his voluminous throat. "Skate, how can you know what the likes of Jack Gherun thinks or fears? He's a wealthy, well-respected man. I can hardly believe he would somehow confide in you, the thief of his belongings, all of this information."

She explained the conversation she'd overheard when Gherun came to Belamy's home. "They're friends, you see!"

"Ha!" The Boss had been listening attentively, and the laugh shook his cheeks. "A friend indeed, to send a burglar into his home. Still, if you've heard it from his mouth directly, that's enough for me. The meeting he described did happen, so I'll believe you got it from him." He saw someone behind Skate and waved them in. "Oh, this is great news, Skate. At least, I hope it will be. Well done."

Haman now stood beside her. He gave her a nod of acknowledgement, then handed a stack of papers to the Boss. "Haman," Boss said, "Skate may have inadvertently helped get Jack Gherun into business with us!"

The young mage's eyes widened at the news, and he turned to regard Skate more closely. "That would be a feat, Skate," he said, his tone indicating a desire for clarification. With encouragement from the Boss, she retold the stories of the burglary and of the meeting with Belamy.

"But there's a problem," she said when she got to the end of the latter tale. Their expressions soured a bit at the unwelcome turn, but the Boss motioned for her to continue. "The old man, Belamy, he doesn't want his friend messing around with 'ruffians.' He wants the books returned when he's done with them, no Ink involved. He doesn't know nothing about the Ink, though," she added in response to increasingly disappointed faces. "As far as he knows, it might as well just be you two and the Big Boss. Those are the only names he's got, so my cover's still good."

Neither man's expression improved. Haman spoke first. "Skate, while it's good news that he knows nothing of your connection to our organization, the fact that he has a name and description of us from Gherun is not good news. Not at all."

"What do you mean?"

"Wizards can find people," Boss Marshall said, puffing several times on his pipe and frowning, "wherever they go. Strong ones can, anyway. And information helps them do it. Name, description, piece of clothing, a bit of hair—any and all of that makes such searching easier. If your mark is serious about investigating the Ink, we may be in some trouble."

"It might be wise to take precautions, sir," Haman said, rummaging through his pockets and producing a small badge; a brief glimpse of it before he handed it over to the Boss showed a golden eye, wide and lifelike.

"Big Boss has his own ways around it, but I'll inform him just the same." Boss Marshall placed the badge on his vest and returned to puffing. "You did well to tell us this now, Skate. Hopefully, we've caught it soon enough to avoid prying eyes. If you can convince Gherun that the Ink was, in fact, threatening him with that burglary, you'll have won a great prize, one the Big Boss himself wants. Before making a move on Belamy's goods, you need to make that a priority."

The smoke he blew out smelled dark and somewhat sweet. "That rich idiot's monthly contribution would make a fine credit to your name, girl, a fine credit."

She wanted to ask, *How much of one?* but thought better of it. Instead, she asked, "How do I do that?"

"Why," Haman said, leaning slightly to put a hand on her shoulder, "I'm sure the mastermind behind the heist that spooked him in the first place should have no trouble figuring that out. Right, Boss?"

"Just so, Haman, just so," the Boss said with a chuckle that blew out more of the dark, sweet smoke. "You'll figure it out just fine, girl, don't worry. Smart one like you will do just fine."

Skate accepted the compliment with a sheepish smile and looked down. "I'll do what I can."

"That-a-girl," Boss Marshall said, picking up the packet of papers Haman had brought in and scanning the page with half-interest. "And make sure that old fellow doesn't catch on to whatever you choose to do."

"Oh, that's another thing," she said, snapping her head up. "I found out what he is. You were right—he's a dead thing. He said he was a lich." Boss Marshall's eyes went wide, and he set the papers down. Haman sat back in his chair and took a deep breath, which he blew out in a steadying sigh. "He said it was something wizards turned themselves into to keep from dying."

"That's correct," Haman said, nodding, his expression revealing as little as possible. That was a sure sign he was bothered. "And what a terrible thing to do. I am not familiar with the specifics, but all the literature I've read has emphasized the heinousness involved in enacting such a transformation. Vile magic, vile." He shook his head as he spoke. His façade had fallen, and disgust was plain on his face. "I've done that which I'm not proud of, but if the hints as to what is required of lichdom are a reliable indication, your host is a monster beyond compare."

Skate was silent. *I am no monster, Skate. I found another way.* That had been the claim. She found that she couldn't match the horror on Haman's face with her image of Belamy. Whether it was deception or not, she believed Belamy was more than a monster.

She kept this to herself.

"So what, Haman, he just won't die of old age now?" Boss Marshall continued to puff as he had before, but his wide eyes betrayed a deep fear of the subject. "That's a handy trick, no doubt."

"More than that, I'm afraid. A lich does something quite unnatural with its soul during the process. It sort of...tethers its life force to a physical object outside itself. As long as that object survives, the life cannot truly be destroyed."

"What do you mean?" Belamy had not gone into such detail when discussing the situation with Skate; she was eager to learn whatever he had kept from her.

"So, think of it this way," Haman said, leaning further back into his chair and rubbing his chin in contemplation. "Your soul is tied to your body, as is every other living thing's. When a living thing dies, its soul is wrenched away from its body. That connection between soul and body severs, and that's what we call death. A lich, though, chooses an extra tether, an extra link to its soul. If the body is destroyed, the soul does not fly off to whatever infernal reward such a creature must surely deserve, but instead flies toward this selected object, where it resides over a period of weeks until the lich's body re-forms. Then the original connection is reestablished. This soul container is the lich's greatest treasure and must be protected from all harm, else the undead thing finds itself vulnerable to destruction, just like everything else."

Skate's mind flashed to objects that Belamy had carefully hidden from her, to a locked door in a hidden basement, to red stones and a fine statuette on the fireplace. "I think I might know what Belamy's tether is."

"Oh?" Haman leaned forward. "What's that?"

"One of two things, really," she said. "It's either a little statue that he used to have over his fireplace but took down once I started living with him, or it's a little red gemstone that he keeps locked away."

Haman sat back again, a hand on his face as he considered the possibilities. Boss Marshall popped the pipe out of his mouth and looked at him. "What do you think? Those the types of things a lich might attach his soul to?"

"It can be anything," Haman responded. He was tapping his temple as he spoke. "It's certainly a possibility. You say he keeps these things out of sight?"

"Yeah, but he didn't before I moved in. It's like he doesn't care if I see anything else he owns, but those two things are gone now."

"I think you're probably right, then," Boss Marshall said, taking the pipe back into his mouth and puffing again. "Sounds like he's taken what's most precious to him and hidden it from you. Can't say I blame the fellow; if I had a known thief in my home, I'd want my soul protector thing stored safely out of reach. What say you, Haman?"

The young wizard continued looking pensive. After a moment, he said, "I say that a man who has something treasured is a man who may be controlled."

Boss Marshall did some leaning back of his own. "Go on."

"Think of this, Boss: when we put pressure on people to get them to pay us for protection, we always do so in their homes, or their businesses, do we not? The reason that's so effective is that by making the offer in that place, whatever it may be, the new customer gets a visual, inescapable reminder of what they stand to lose if they refuse."

"Sure," the Boss said, waving his hand impatiently to get him to continue.

"That works because the people treasure things: their homes, their work, their families, and so on. And once these are threatened, they'll do anything to protect them. They effectively put themselves under our control to avoid losing whatever it is they treasure." He stood and placed a hand on Boss Marshall's desk. "What may a man willing to become a monster fear to lose?"

"The thing he wanted to protect more than anything," the Boss answered, picking up the thread of Haman's thinking. "Yeah, Haman, that's good. A man willing to do anything to save his own life would be easy to handle if we held that which contained his own life, yeah? We get the object he's tethered to, we may have ourselves a new special weapon." He turned his attention to Skate. "There's your target, girl. Find out which object he values most—not necessarily the most expensive thing, you understand—and make that your priority."

"You mean to take him prisoner?" The question was genuine, not rhetorical; these men had been all but quaking in their boots a few moments ago at the thought of the terror they assumed Belamy to be, so the jump to trying to force him into service seemed a bit rich. "You think that'll work?"

"I do, Skate, I do." Boss Marshall was now sagely puffing away, his eyes narrowed and his tone that of a lecturer holding forth to an imaginary rapt audience. "This is a man who so feared his fate that he was willing to do whatever it took, however horrifying and wicked, to escape it. If we can threaten such a man with the only thing he fears, is there anything he won't do to save himself? I think not," he concluded with a chiding chuckle. "After all, who among us, at our best, has stared the specter in the face and refused to quail or shudder? That he has been willing to so degrade himself in order to stave off the final waking tells me he'd take to such a threat like vermin to garbage. I'm sure of it."

"Has it changed your mind?" Haman asked. "Does this slight change in your goal in the burglary make you rethink what you need to do?"

"No." She said the word automatically and was surprised to find that she somehow felt dishonest in doing so. Stealing something, even something extremely pricey, from the old man had not bothered her, but the idea of trapping him in servitude put a small knot in her stomach. *It's just a job*, she tried to tell herself, *and he's just a mark. What's it matter?*

It mattered. She didn't have time to explore why right now, but it mattered. "No, it just means I gotta find the things I was looking for anyway."

"Good girl," Boss Marshall said, nodding to her. "Better get after it, hadn't you?" Skate took that as the dismissal it was, and ducked out of the room in a hurry. "Haman, get the door, will you?" The wizard nodded and smiled ever so encouragingly as he closed the door after her.

Twitch was where she'd left him, but he'd stuffed his small pipe with tobacco and was producing a cloud over his head as he played cards with another thief, one many years his senior. He talked without taking the pipe from his lips as he gambled, alternatively laughing, cursing, and trading insults with his opponent.

"You're a fast dog, aren't ya?" the grizzled thief asked through several missing teeth.

"Was a fast one that f-fathered you, sir," Twitch said back, throwing his cards down and pulling the piled copper coins toward him, winning the hand.

"Hark at him! The pup's cut his teeth, make no mistake," the grizzled thief said to another thief sitting nearby. The other thief took a large gulp from his cup, belched, and laughed.

Skate waved the unpleasant cloud away as she took her seat. The tipsy fellow dealt another hand and did his best to reveal nothing about his cards. Being drunk, he found this a more difficult feat than he'd anticipated, and Twitch coughed to cover his smile. There was little wonder that the man thought the boy to be such a master of the game, which relied on bluffing and misdirection, when his own faculties were so impaired.

"How'd it g-go?" Twitch asked, tossing some coins in the pot.

"Not nearly so bad as what you was worried for," Skate answered. "They took my news well and changed my job a bit, but nothing too hard. Hurry up here, so I can tell you about it."

Twitch puffed twice more, then went all in; the drunk took the bait and followed suit. He stared dumbfounded at Twitch's hand as the boy scooped up the coins into a grubby sack. He cursed and muttered as he went away, leaving his companion to his rotten burps, which were endlessly amusing to their supplier.

Skate laughed and shook her head, patting Twitch and pointing to the door. Twitch emptied the ash and straggles of tobacco from his small pipe and pocketed the dirty thing. Once he'd put away his winnings as well, the two made for the tunnel they'd come through.

Only when they were almost out of the smoky, boozy crowd did Skate notice a pair of eyes, eyes that reminded her so much of those of a snake, following their progress. Kite was watching the two of them, and it was anyone's guess as to how long he'd been doing so. He did not avert his gaze at her notice, but continued to watch their movements.

Someone broke the line of sight between the thin young man and Skate, and Kite disappeared.

Skate took Twitch by the arm and hurried him out of the room.

"Ease up, w-will ya?" Twitch had been trying to watch the darts match as they went, and the sudden lurch of her insistence pulled him away.

"Kite," was all she said, and his indignation melted into understanding.

They moved through the dark tunnel quietly, each understanding without communication that they needed to listen for any following steps. They heard nothing but their own breathing, but that was no comfort. Kite was a skilled sneak and could move as silently as the air when he wanted.

Skate picked up her pace as the light from the doorman's lamp peeked around the corner ahead. With a wave and a nod, they were gone, and would surely hear the creak of the door if anyone followed them out.

The midday sun was doing nothing to help the cold of the wintery day. The snow had stopped falling and sunlight came through the breaks in the clouds, but warmth was still hard to come by. Out in the relative safety of the open city, the pair felt the stifling call to silence lift.

"W-what do you think Kite wanted?"

"Nothing good. I think he wants payback for me embarrassing him the other day."

"Embarrassing?"

"He cornered me while I was on a job, and I...got him to leave me alone." Twitch, she decided, didn't need to know about Rattle's attack. "So, he's probably still mad."

Twitch looked over his shoulder to see if they were being followed. "Just s-so you know, Boss is moving hideouts to the s-space in the warehouse." The warehouse hideout was in the Old Town, close to Lady Ossertine's home. Half of the building functioned as an actual warehouse, while the other was set aside for the use of the Ink. It comfortably held the ruffians of a single Boss's crew at a time, and they would be unbothered in the space; the owner of the warehouse had been a thief himself before he'd made the purchase, and was more than happy to give his structure for the use of his fellow thieves. The Ink paid him for his trouble, which meant he offered storage at discounted rates. All things considered, it was a good deal for everyone involved.

"That's where I'll bring the news when I have it, then."

"So what're they getting you to d-do?"

She sighed. "I'm still stealing from the old man, but the target has changed. Instead of looking for the things that'd be worth the most in gold or gems, I'm supposed to find the thing that's most important to him and steal that. They wanna hold it over him to get him on board with the Ink."

"They're trying to ex-extort from a wizard? Are they c-crazy?"

"An undead wizard," she clarified. "He made himself this living corpse so he'd never die for real, but it all depends on a single object. That's what I have to find. That's what's most important to him."

"This s-sounds really dangerous, Skate."

"Yes, it does." The third voice came from their left, from one of a myriad thin alleyways between buildings. Kite stepped into the light, looking as vicious and arrogant as ever. "Too dangerous for the likes of you, brat." He spat into the snow. His arms were crossed over his chest, which put his hands within easy reach of a pair of knives strapped under his arms. These were new.

"What do you want, Kite?"

"Nothin', girl. But what you're jawing about sounds too good to ignore. I got no idea why the Boss thinks this is worth wasting any more time on, but I guess he figures you wouldn't be doing much of anything else useful, huh?" He smirked, then relaxed a little as he leaned back against one of the sturdy buildings he'd been loitering around. "So, you're supposed to be helping the Boss catch some old monster, are ya?"

"None of your business, Kite."

"Listen, spit," he growled, coming off the wall with surprising speed, "anything's my business if I want it to be, got it? So what's he doing with the old man? Why's he want him for the Ink?"

"Why do you care?" Her instinct was to step back from him, but she knew any sign of fear would only encourage him. "What the Boss wants, the Boss wants."

He bent down so that he was just above eye level with her. "Let's just say the Boss ain't the only Boss, is he?"

Skate frowned. "What, you're spying for another Boss now? Is that it?"

Kite straightened and rolled his eyes. "Think of it as 'insuring co-operation across complex organizational structures.' That's how Boss Shade put it." The mention of the cruel Boss in charge of the Ink's wet work put ice in her spine. Kite must have sensed this, because he smiled that predatory, joyless smile and continued. "He's got an inter-est in Boss Marshall's dealings. And he ain't the only one, is he? Some of the other Bosses are concerned about Marshall's state of mind; he's been acting jumpy at meetings and such. Word is the Big Boss ain't happy with him. And ain't no one can have the Big Boss mad at them for long, is it?"

"You s-saying Boss Marshall ain't the Boss for m-much longer?" Twitch had his hands balled into fists, and his chin was pointing out; as idiotic as the proposition was, he looked ready for a fight.

"I'm saying I don't give a rip what Marshall is, because he ain't my problem anymore." The dropping of the title of "Boss" before the man's name upset Skate more than she'd have expected. "Alls I wanna know is: what's he up to? What's he planning?" Kite crossed his arms again, once more putting his knives within easy reach. "My new Boss sure would like to know."

"Your n-new Boss can ask him hisself," Twitch said, spitting on the ground in the same place Kite had earlier. "That's what Bosses do, ain't it? There's s-supposed to be talk, giving h-help where it's needed. That's how the Ink runs."

"Maybe that's how it used to run, but the Bosses—even the Big Boss—might be reaching their limit with Marshall. He's been falling behind on promises, kids; and if the other Bosses can't stand something, it's broken promises. Now, you gonna tell me what I wanna know, or is this gonna get ugly?"

"Can't be any uglier than you." Skate saw Kite for what he was, and so wasn't afraid. She might have been afraid if she'd stopped to think about what his defection might mean, or that insulting a man with weapons while she was unarmed might be a bad idea, but disgust overthrew her good thinking. "You coward."

Kite tensed up, his hands becoming clawlike as he edged them closer to the blades. "What wazzat, spit?" His face hardened into the unmoving mask of indifference he took on before he hurt people. The only indication of his rage was the dancing hate in his eyes. "What did ya say to me?"

"I'll say whatever I want, *coward.*" She moved closer to the dangerous young man, her eyes not dropping or blinking, despite the water she felt in her stomach. "You can't use those nasty knives of yours. We're still in the Ink. Boss Marshall's still a Boss in the Ink. Keep your stupid threats behind your jagged teeth, because they don't mean nothing."

The hate remained behind his eyes, but it settled somewhat and became colder. "Oh, she's smart, isn't she. Clever little spit, dolled up in clothes that ain't hers, telling me what I can and can't do. So, so clever." He uncrossed his arms and cracked his knuckles. "You're right that I can't use weapons in fights with Inkers. Did you forget that I'm two feet taller than you and four stone heavier?" He lunged for her, and several things happened at once.

Skate, who'd been banking on him charging straight at her, charged right back at him. His eyes widened when she dove right under his grasping hands and connected her shoulder with all her might right into his groin. His hands did manage to find her then, but he could only feebly push her away as he bent over in pain.

Meanwhile, Twitch had backed up a few steps. Seeing Kite doubled over, he took a running start and kicked both feet out to the side at Kite's head. The older boy had enough sense to try to bring up a hand to stop Twitch's attack, but it was no use: his feet shot over the weakly raised arm and connected solidly with Kite's mouth and temple at once.

The blow floored him, and Twitch immediately ran over and began kicking Kite wherever he could find an opening in the flailing in the snow. Kite was trying to get up and keep from getting hit at the same time, spewing invectives from a bloodied mouth. "You spits, you worthless spits, you—"

One of Twitch's kicks connected with the head again, and Kite stopped his bellowing. He was thoroughly dazed, and could only mutter and groggily bring his arms in front of his face. Twitch reared back for another kick, but Skate ran up and pushed him back. "Come on, he's done, let's go."

Twitch looked at the other boy, who was half a decade his senior, and shook his head. "What a…" Whether because of his stutter, or just a lack of vocabulary to accurately describe what exactly Kite was, Twitch left the thought unfinished. He jerked, then nodded at Skate, and the pair left the older boy to recover his sense in the snow and debris of the alleyway.

CHAPTER 14

Skate took a seat at the bar of the pub. The sign outside had an image of a snake crawling out of a pile of pillows and barrels, so she guessed the name of the place was "The Sleepy Drunken Serpent," or something like that. It was in the Old Town, several blocks away from Belamy's house; and it was off the main avenues, settled comfortably in the back alleys where one could find a place to eat and sleep without worry of large crowds or patrolling guards.

She ordered some of the soup and coffee, throwing a square silver coin (bearing the familiar image of the helm of the Old King) onto the bar. Twitch had left her about an hour ago, citing a need to find some pickings before the end of the week. "Look out for the s-skinny idiot," he'd said, referring to the battered Kite. She'd assured him she would, and he'd gone off into the city to make his fortune. Skate, for her part, had bumped into a passing courier and relieved him of a loose-hanging purse that ended up containing several copper blades and a few silver coins like the one she'd just made use of. *Next time, he'll keep his purse closer to him.* Somehow, the usual rationalization wasn't making her feel better about the sleight of hand. She never did like pickpocketing; something about having to look at the person she was stealing from always bothered her. That was the main reason she'd taken to burglary instead.

The barman brought her food and dark drink, scooped the helm off the table, and counted out seven copper blades in change. Skate slid all but one toward herself and flicked the other toward the man, who picked it up with a wink. *Be open with your gifts.* That was one of the most important lessons of the ethos of the Ink. Stinginess rarely opened doors, and a budding thief never knew where or when a piece of information might be found—and an easy lie told to the Guards as a distraction might be expected if she only had the foresight to be kind with her coins. One of Boss Marshall's favorite stories to tell was of how, as a young man, he'd ducked into a familiar diner while running from the Guard only for the owner to tell the pursuers "That little thief just ran out the back!" The Guardsmen had run right past the bar that Boss (then, only "thief") Marshall had been hiding behind. The owner had never brought it up again and the Boss frequented his shop to this day, even though it was the owner's son running it now.

Skate slurped the soup off her spoon and winced at the heat. If what Kite had said was true, then Boss Marshall was in trouble. If he was in trouble, then his whole crew was in trouble. Boss Marshall might be relying very heavily on Skate's job to get back into the Big Boss's good graces. Especially now that the job had changed from "steal the most valuable thing Belamy owns so it can be hocked for money" to "steal the object Belamy stores his soul in so we can control him for our own ends."

The soup wasn't bad, once it cooled down. Skate continued slurping, wondering why this new prospect bothered her so much. *Because you're not just stealing anymore*, the voice in her head explained. *If you do the job like the Boss wants, you're selling Belamy into slavery.* The idea put a knot into her stomach that had nothing to do with hunger or the soup. It was a sensation she did not feel often, but she was familiar enough with it to name it: guilt. The idea of selling Belamy into slavery filled her with guilt.

"Stupid," she muttered to herself as she brought the warm, blackish drink to her lips. Why should she feel guilt about it? *If he's stupid enough to let me do the thing, then it falls on him to deal with the results. That's the way it works.*

Running over these truths of the world did not help the unwelcome sensation go away; the knot tightened. "He's a mark," she muttered to herself out loud.

He's your teacher.

She downed the rest of the coffee and stepped out of the Snaky Barrel Pillows or whatever the owner called his place. The cold was bracing, but her coat kept it from being as painful as it would have been in her old rags, and the boots were doing their job as well. *Boots and coat bought by your teacher.* She shook her head and started walking aimlessly through the streets, frowning and fretting.

"He's a monster." The knot loosened not a whit.

He's not. He might have been, but he chose not to be.

She turned a corner as a patrol crossed the intersection ahead of her, and hitched a ride on the back of a passing carriage. She was light enough and skilled enough that her boarding went unnoticed. The rhythmic clopping of the hooves helped as a focusing point to get her thoughts in order.

You don't know he's not a monster. He could be lying. The knot loosened a small bit. She took the train of thought further. *Why's he got a man trapped in a ball? He says the guy committed murder, but how do you know that's true? What if he's got him trapped so he can eat his soul or something?*

The idea that Belamy was lying to her about important matters alleviated almost all of the guilt she'd been experiencing. Almost all. She still found the idea of forced service too gross to accept. The knot wasn't gone completely. *If he's keeping someone trapped against his will, doesn't he deserve it himself?*

Maybe.

Skate left her perch on the back of the carriage and almost fell as she landed on the packed ice of the road. She caught her balance quickly and looked around, trying to find her bearings after paying no attention to where she'd been going. She thought she might still be in the Old Town, but there was nothing immediate or obvious to confirm or deny the idea. She started walking, knowing she would figure it out eventually.

She wasn't in the slums; the buildings were too well-kept for that. The smell of the sea was distant and faint enough that she had to search for it, so she probably wasn't in the docks. That left either the Old Town or the Baron's Quarter. Lack of patrols probably meant the former.

She finally came across a familiar sight: the main avenue near Belamy's house. She kept to the side of the street, barely noticing the passage of horses, buggies, wagons, carriages, and trolleys. Despite the ice, business carried on. Men and women in uniforms of gray and black, members of the City Keepers, had been doing their best to keep the streets clean. She passed one of the Keepers on the way to the old man's house. They moved around the city, almost unseen, taking care of what needed care. Of course, they mostly restricted their activity to the Baron's and the Old Town, working only at the edge of the docks and then through the busiest streets therein. They avoided the slums altogether.

The Keepers had been the current Baron's father's idea; Caribol had begun to grow by leaps and bounds toward the end of his life, and the streets were becoming filthier and filthier with the accumulated waste as thousands turned into tens of thousands in a few short years. So the old Baron had, with the help and blessings of the city's new wealthy elite, devised a system to keep it clean: hire citizens to work directly for the betterment of the city itself. The Keepers had been the city's custodians and functionaries for the last three decades, according to Boss Marshall. If a street was in dire need of cleaning, they did it. They lit the night lanterns, cleaned up spills, helped put out fires, and on and on. The only major duty they didn't seem to have any part in was the policing done by the City Guard.

They had been busy throughout the morning; Belamy's avenue was clear enough that wagons could pass each other with space to spare. Of course, the snow had to go somewhere, and the Keepers had piled it on the edges of the streets where pedestrians usually held sway; Skate had to stomp up and down surprisingly solid hills of the piled-up stuff to get to the front door. When she arrived, she entered without knocking or announcing herself.

Belamy was in his customary seat at his desk at the far end of the room, but he did not have any book open in front of him. Instead, he was alternating between staring into a ball of glass and staring into some spinning yellow thing, both of which were set in the middle of his desk. There did not seem to be anything interesting about the ball of glass, though it was set on a delicately made and ornate wire frame. The yellow device caught light as it seemed to spin in every direction at once, flashing first one way, then another. The old man did not acknowledge her entry, so Skate took a moment to take off her snow-covered coat and boots. With that done, she walked over to where he was seated, stopping on the way to toss another log into the low-burning fire.

The yellow thing continued to spin, and getting closer revealed that it was a golden light flashing every second or so, not just yellow. Recognition hit her suddenly: this was the delicate yellow hoop she'd tried to steal that first night in Belamy's home. How Belamy was getting it to spin at such speed without touching it was a mystery. She assumed the answer was magic.

The old unliving wizard did not look up from whatever he was trying to do, even though there was no way he had not noticed her. Guessing that he did not want to be disturbed, Skate walked upstairs to the library. Rattle was there, flapping over an open book on one of the small tables. It looked at her and clicked once as a greeting, then returned to its perusal of the tome.

"Do you know what he's doing down there?"

Rattle gave the motion that might have been a shrug in response, and did not turn from the book.

"Would he care if I talked to Petre?" she asked, pointing to the cloudy blue ball by the window. When she mentioned his name, she could see the smoke within the glass stir with more energy than before.

Rattle turned this time. It looked first at Skate, then at the blue ball. It shrugged again, but with a stiffness that had not been evident before.

"You're concerned, though, aren't you?"

Rattle waited, then clicked once.

"I'll take responsibility for it. He hasn't told me not to talk to him."

It clicked once again and turned reluctantly to the book. Skate moved over to the window and gently picked up Petre's globe. The blue fog parted almost immediately to reveal the quizzical, nervous eyes.

The eyes of a murderer, she reminded herself.

A murderer who can't hurt you or anyone, she added to her own description.

"Good afternoon, Petre."

"And to you as well, young Skate, the girl who would be a thief."
The appellation carried no accusation, but there was a playful mockery
in his eyes as he spoke. "To what do I owe this wonderful pleasure,
hm?"

"Do you know what Belamy is doing downstairs?"

"I don't know anything other than what's going on in this room.
However, I've spent enough time around the old fellow to tell you what
he's probably up to if you describe what you saw."

She told him about the glass ball and the spinning golden instrument, and he was nodding before she'd finished. "Oh, yes, I know what
that is. He's trying to spy on someone."

"Spy on them? How?"

"Magic, of course. With the glass, he can see anyone he's ever met
or heard of or has a good description of or has any other tenuous connection to. If he's got the amplifier going, he must be having a hard
time of it."

"Oh." Haman had been right to put up his protections, it seemed;
the Boss and his lieutenant were successfully evading the wizard's prying eyes. "Do you know who he's looking for?"

"I'm afraid I haven't the, uh, foggiest idea." Petre offered an apologetic chuckle at the pun, and even sent the smoke in the glass over his
eyes to make sure she didn't miss it.

Skate smiled—it was a little funny—and he looked pleased. "I think
I do," she said. "If I'm right, he's trying to find someone in order to protect his friend."

"Yes, that sounds like him. He's fiercely loyal to people he takes a
shine to. Always has been, as a matter of fact."

"Is he? What I mean is, is he truly loyal to them? On the one hand,
he's got me stealing from his friends. On the other, he's spending his
time trying to track down dangerous people in order to protect those
same friends."

"Oh, I see what you mean." Petre closed his eyes and nodded sagely. "Yes, he's loyal, but he's loyal in his own way. What I mean is, he
sees nothing wrong with taking things from his friends without permission—but only because he fully intends to return them. That is the
nature of your arrangement, is it not?" She nodded. "So, in his mind,
he's not really stealing, and he's not betraying them at all. You see?"

Skate thought about it before answering. Belamy was technically stealing, but he just considered it borrowing. "It's still stealing."

"Oh, yes, definitely."

"And he knows it's stealing."

"On that, he might disagree with you. Though, I do wonder, why does an aspiring young thief such as yourself care? You seem to be very preoccupied with his larcenous ways for someone so willing to do stealing of your own."

She frowned at the image in the ball, but he didn't back down. He looked as he had for most of the conversation: curious and intelligent. "Never mind," was her answer. "You said he's always been like that. How long have you known him?"

"Oh, years and years. Decades, in fact." His eyes dropped a bit. "Decades and decades. Since before the war."

"What war?"

"Oh, it was well before your time. Before your parents' time, too, I'd wager. It was a war between Jero and Filtir to the south. It was over trade disputes or some silly thing like that."

She screwed up her face in confusion. "He fought in a war?"

"Oh yes. King Hilan called for all able-bodied men to be fielded, and that included wizards. Of course, Barrison went willingly; he wanted to protect his home and—and his friends."

She noted the hesitation in that statement, but let it pass by without comment. "I guess wizards would be useful in a war."

"Too true. Dangerous men and women, wizards and witches. Turned to war, their art is terrible to behold. Barrison was skilled enough in tactics and strategy to be given command of his own battalion. I think his military rank was 'lieutenant colonel,' or something like that. With his mind turned to logistics and planning as well as the most destructive uses of his magic, he gained some fame in Jero—and infamy in Filtir—though few learned or bothered to remember his actual name. Instead, he became known in bar tales and hushed whispers by his nickname: Iron Wind."

Skate said nothing. Rattle had been reading, though throughout the conversation, the pages had been turning with a slowing pace. The floating creature seemed to be trying to listen to the conversation without giving itself away. She didn't know how it could follow the train of the discussion, since she was pretty sure it couldn't hear Petre's half.

"Of course, I'm sure it's been years since he's heard that name. I don't think he'd be particularly glad to, either, so don't go calling him that."

"Why not? If I had a name like that, I wouldn't mind it. 'Iron Wind' is a great name."

Petre's expression turned more melancholy and reflective. "His memories of the war are not fond ones. He went to war to protect his country and those he cared about, remember. Over the ensuing months, even though he was nowhere near the head of command of the effort, he came to understand that the crown had not been entirely forthright with the motivations of the conflict. Jero, as it turned out, was the aggressor, marching armies into the border with Filtir as an escalation of force to end the dispute with the neighboring kingdom." Petre shook his head. The motion agitated the fog around his eyes. "I think he told himself that he was doing what was right to keep himself going. He was directly and indirectly responsible for a lot of deaths, you see. It weighed on him. It is not an easy thing to take a life, even less so many. But if he could tell himself it was for a better cause..."

"Stealing without stealing."

"Eh?"

Skate understood how Belamy's mind worked a little better after hearing the story. "He wants to do what needs to be done, but it's bad. So he comes up with a reason for it to not be so bad. Just like with the stealing; he calls it borrowing and plans to return it, so it's not so bad. Stealing without stealing."

The eyes wandered the room, and nodded in consideration, or else acceptance. "Yes, I suppose it's sort of the same thing. Anyway, by the time he had teased out the real nature of the war and the king's orders, the war was already all but won.

"Barrison's battalion was called home, and he was showered with praise and rewards. He was even granted an audience with the king himself. King Hilan praised his skill on the battlefield and ordered a set of tailored robes that bore the royal seal. In a bid to please the king, the Royal Magician offered to enchant the robes with powerful magic when they were done, and the king ordered that done as well.

"The only things Barrison spoke throughout the whole ordeal were a word of greeting upon entering, a word of thanks for the extravagant gift, and a word of parting when his audience ended. He was perfectly polite throughout the entire meeting." Petre's eyes narrowed conspiratorially, as if giving away some great secret. "A typical courtier watching the exchange would have thought Barrison was being properly deferential to his king, but those that knew him understood the truth of it: the wizard held no more love for the king or his politics."

He sighed. "The war changed him. When he returned home, he became more distant from those he knew, though no less kind. In fact, that quality seemed to become more part of his everyday life. He became more willing to offer charity to the needy, and gave whatever any friends asked of him with no questions or expectations. But time spent among his friends became much more sporadic. Eventually, of course, his old friends passed away. He appeared at the funerals but avoided conversation with his fellow mourners.

"His rare conversations were warm, though he bristled at any questions of the war. He refused to discuss that time of his life. His real name did not become latched on to his martial moniker; word of his exploits continued to spread, while almost everyone around him had no idea that the Iron Wind himself was in their midst. I knew, as did his other apprentices, but few else did."

"He had apprentices?"

"Oh, yes," Petre said, nodding again, "for many years before and after the war. He taught five students overall, and I...well, he didn't take any more after me." He suddenly looked embarrassed and cut his eyes toward Rattle, who was still "reading."

Skate looked between the two. "What is this?"

"Hm?"

"You're looking at Rattle. Some things you're not supposed to tell me?"

His eyes darted back and forth between Rattle and her. "Well, you see—what I mean is, he's entitled to his past, isn't he? If he hasn't told you, it's certainly not my place to have that discussion with you. We are both his guests, after all."

Skate narrowed her eyes at the man in the ball. "You're a guest." It wasn't a question, but she did not mean it as an affirmation. Judging by his continued discomfort, he understood that perfectly well.

"That's right."

"Mr. Belamy told me something about you. About how you ended up in the glass ball."

The curious gleam came back to his eye, though it was more suspicious. "And what exactly was that?"

"That you murdered someone."

"Ah. Right." His discomfort became too much for him, and he let his face become obscured by the fog in the glass again. "I think I can talk about that without offending our host." His voice was as close as it had been before, but was much more subdued now that the subject had shifted to him and his own sordid history.

"Is it true?"

"Yes, it's true."

"You killed someone."

"Yes, I did. And I've regretted it ever since."

"Why?" She could not imagine this man, who seemed to be all conversation and friendliness, as a cold-blooded killer.

"Selfishness, Skate. Pure, cowardly selfishness." He did not elaborate, and they sat in silence broken only by the flapping of Rattle's wings and the occasional turn of the pages.

"It was Mr. Belamy who put you in there, wasn't it?"

"It was."

"How long have you been in there?"

He paused before answering. "It will be fifty-three years next week."

The thought of sending Belamy into servitude to another did not seem quite as monstrous as it had before. "Half a century of imprisonment? You don't look anywhere near fifty, much less older than that."

"No, the prison keeps me at the age I was when I was put in. I should be a man well into my seventh decade, or else dead before. The prison gives me youth eternal, though there's nothing I can do with it, of course."

"And how long is he going to keep you there?"

"Pardon?"

"In your prison. How long is Belamy going to keep you trapped in your cage?"

"Belamy doesn't keep me in here, Skate." The eyes came into view again, and he was looking directly into her own. His stare lacked any of the life she was used to seeing from him. He looked like a man defeated and hopeless. "I was not referring to myself as a guest of Barrison's as a euphemism; he's no jailer. I am trapped in here by my own choice, and I will stay here until I have done penance for the terrible thing I did."

"You're here on purpose?"

"Yes, though this was my second choice." He blinked hard a few times before speaking again. "I...asked for something else before this, but Barrison refused."

He wanted to die instead. "Oh." They sat in silence for a few more moments—though it felt like minutes to Skate, who was trying to find something, anything to say. "So you decide when to leave your prison?"

"Yes. I am here as a guest of Barrison. This prison is my own."

"How long will you stay...trapped?"

"By my reckoning, the person I...I killed had as many as seventy years of life left. When I have been here that long, then I will consider ending my punishment. Not before."

"What'll happen to you when you get out?"

"I don't know. I don't give it any thought."

Skate moved back over to the window. "I'm going to go see Mr. Belamy and try to figure out what he's doing. I also need my lesson for the day, so there's that, too." She struggled before asking, "Why didn't he...do what you wanted the first time?"

Rattle inadvertently clicked a few times as it turned toward them. It didn't move other than continuing to flap to stay airborne, but only stared.

"I honestly don't know. He had every right to, but chose this instead." His eyes fell into a sad smile. "He's very odd, you know."

"Yes, I think he is." With nothing else to say, Skate placed him back on his perch near the glass. Fog swirled around him as he turned from her, and soon, nothing was visible within but the gently rolling smoke. Rattle returned to its reading—in earnest this time—as Skate left the room.

She found the lich as she had left him, focused on an empty sphere of glass and the spinning golden contraption. When she approached his desk, he heaved a great sigh and leaned back. The golden thing slowed its spinning.

"Good afternoon, Skate. I'm glad your long walk didn't keep you from us entirely today." The golden hoop continued to slow, and stopped abruptly when Belamy put his hand on it. "I hope your time away did you some good?"

"Yeah, feeling pretty good now, thanks." Her eyes lingered on the golden device. "So, what's this?"

"Oh! Well, you see, a wizard can use certain tools to scry certain— oh, that means—"

"Seeing somebody who's far away, I know." Belamy's surprise was evident, so she quickly explained: "I talked to Petre."

"Ah." His utterance was heavy with curiosity. However, instead of asking questions, he went on. "I'm looking for the people who bothered Jack. Normally, if I've got a name and a description, I can just use the ball"—he gestured to the clear glass orb—"and it works like a charm, so to speak. If I'm having particular difficulty, the enhancer pushes through the rest of the way." This time, he pointed to the spinning golden thing. "You have a good eye for value, by the way; that object is quite expensive. You wouldn't have needed to steal again for months to pay for the finest room in town if you'd have gotten out with it and found a buyer."

"Oh yeah?" She bent down and looked at it. "Maybe I ought to take it now, huh?"

"As if you'd miss out on Rattle's cooking." He leaned forward again. "I don't think either of the tools is broken, so I don't know what the issue is."

"Maybe you're doing it wrong," Skate suggested with a hint of mockery. "You know, maybe you're out of practice."

"I most certainly am not!" The old man seemed to be only playing at being offended, though Skate guessed there was at least a kernel of actual indignity in the proclamation. "Here, take a seat and watch." He pointed to a nearby chair, and Skate moved it to the other side of the desk and sat. Belamy said nothing else, but stared unblinking at the clear glass ball. Nothing happened.

"What's supposed—"

"Shush. Wait."

"But what—"

"Shh."

"What—"

He held up a quieting finger, then placed his hand into a more relaxed position and continued his concentration on the ball. Skate rolled her eyes but said nothing else.

Minutes passed. She was about to interrupt again and ask what exactly she was supposed to be waiting on when the glass ball took on a frosty character, as if invisibly treated before her eyes. The haze receded, and a shape began to take form in the glass. It was Rattle upstairs, and the sounds of its flapping wings and clicking legs were coming not from the staircase but from the glass ball containing its moving image. It was still reading, and even the sound of the turning page came through as clear as if it had been happening on the desk itself. The library itself appeared to be spinning, which made Skate feel slightly nauseous, but she realized that the whole room couldn't be moving while they were under it. *It's more like we're floating in the room and circling around Rattle while it reads.* The adjustment in her understanding of the perspective helped the sick feeling.

"There, you see?" Belamy asked, not breaking eye contact with the glass ball. His voice was measured and less animated than normal; Skate assumed that to be the result of his needing to concentrate. "The tools work perfectly fine, and I'm *not* out of practice." He leaned back, and Rattle's image faded first to the smoky haze, and then to crystal clear nothing once more. "I don't know why it's giving me such trouble trying to find the trio who threatened Jack."

"Well, what would you do if you didn't want to be found this way?"

"There are a number of ways to thwart such unwelcome viewing. There are charms and spells that could be shielding them, if they know someone with the skill to make such things or cast the magic. Either option would be expensive, but if they're a particularly successful set of thieves, it may be within their ability to acquire the tools or hire the spellcasters. There are also those who simply cannot be found with such magic, though that is exceedingly rare. Old King Rajian and his line were said to possess such a power; I'm not sure that's true, since many other royal lines of all stripes make similar claims, but it's certainly possible that it's more than just a legend spread by the royal court to discourage attempts by the curious or the bored. And finally," Belamy said, standing from his chair, "there are those who have been trained to notice and even push away such attempts through the pure exertion of the will. Many wizards go through this training as part of their tutelage, and I have heard tell of monastic and martial orders who exercise the effort for the sake of discipline and security."

"Someone can just fight it off?" Skate asked, looking into the clear ball.

"Yes, but they'd need to know it was there first, and would almost certainly need some practice at it before they could be said to be able to scuttle these magical reconnaissance tactics." Belamy walked to the bookshelf and pulled a small, leather-bound tome off the shelf. "I believe you were ready to move on to phonetics lessons, now that you've mastered your letters."

"Yeah, sure." She was still peering into the clear glass ball. "So which of those is messing you up?"

"I can't say for sure," he said, flipping pages and nodding with a look of satisfaction, "but what I've just described are the only means I know of to beat it. I think the 'natural' option is the least likely. I've never heard of any thieves who go through the strenuous process of learning to feel and defeat scrying, either, but I've never made it a habit to make such rabble conversation partners—no offense," he added, looking up from the page and smirking over his large nose. She made a sarcastic laughing gesture, and he smiled all the wider. "No, my guess is that the first option is most likely: they've hired a wizard to cast spells of deflection or create trinkets to keep me from finding them." He closed his book and tucked it under his arm. "You have your chalk and board upstairs?"

"Yeah, in the desk."

"Good. Let's get to it, then."

Skate followed him up the stairs. "Have you ever done it to me?"

"What?" He stopped and turned. "Scrying? Heavens, no." He turned back around and continued his climb. "It's a horrendous invasion of privacy."

"But you're trying to do it—"

"I have more than enough reason to violate the privacy of someone trying to bully one of my friends for money. They're lucky it's me searching for them, and not the Guards. I just want to talk, not arrest or hang them. They should be so lucky to have it be me who finds them." They turned into Skate's room. "Let's begin."

CHAPTER 15

IN WHICH A NON-WORD IS WRITTEN, A
TITLE IS READ, AND ART IS ADMIRED.

The next four days passed uneventfully. Skate got to eat three hot meals each day and spent her time studying the secrets of how to put the letters of the alphabet together to form new sounds. After the first lesson, she was disappointed that words were not yet the focus of the lessons.

"How am I supposed to be able to read if I don't learn words?"

"Patience," had been the old man's only response. It was frustrating, but she trusted him to know how to teach reading, because he knew how to do it. After the second lesson, her frustration boiled to the surface again, and the wizard pointed out that she could start practicing what they'd already discussed. She stuck some of the letters together on her board at random and sounded them out with laborious effort.

"'Thhhhhaak.' I wrote 'thak.'" She showed him her work, and he nodded with a smile. "That ain't a word, but it's what I wrote. Does that count?"

"Of course. You're practicing what you've learned so far. That's all words are, after all: sounds pressed together that mean something. If you work on the skill of blending the sounds, you're halfway to reading anything you want. In this language, anyway," he clarified.

When she wasn't eating, bathing (a luxury she'd been able to experience only, at most, once a year before now), or studying, she was talking with Petre, trying to tease some more information out of him about

Belamy. Anything the imprisoned man could tell her about the lich might give her a clue as to which item might be the storage box of his soul. However, Petre was very reluctant to speak more about Belamy, always steering the conversation to familiar waters or changing the conversation entirely.

On any subject that wasn't Belamy or himself, Petre was very willing to answer questions and ask them freely, wanting to know about the goings-on around town, about Skate, about Belamy's friends, or about any other topic of any possible amount of interest. His view of the street outside did not give him much in the way of specific details about the world passing by.

"It's slightly maddening at times," he said when learning about rumors of price gouging from some of the merchant families. "I like to know these things from my own efforts, so I sometimes ask Rattle to crack the window so I can hear snippets of conversation, but I can never catch more than half a sentence before the people chatting below have moved on or are else drowned out by a passing carriage or hollering salesman."

"You could ask to be freed and walk down yourself to ask them what they're talking about."

He scoffed. "It's not much of a penance if I end it for every passing fancy, is it?"

Skate was still very curious about the specifics of his crime (Whom had he killed? And why, besides "selfishness," whatever that meant? And why come to Belamy for judgment?), but he had offered no more information, so she had not pried. *Leave the man in a glass ball whatever privacy he still wants,* she'd told herself. *It's not like it matters for your job, anyway.* Even though he was less than forthcoming about the old man and his secrets, he still made a fine conversation partner.

On the fifth morning, as Skate ate her scrambled eggs and a seared slice of a sugary meat (ham, she guessed), Belamy came downstairs carrying a burlap sack wrapped around something heavy-looking and squarish. He plopped the sack down next to her with a thud.

"Wassat?" she managed to get out around the large bite she'd just taken.

"Laribel's book. The *Chronicles.* It was most informative, and a riveting read, but it's time for it to go back to its owner. And of course, you'll get another week of food and lodging, as promised. Or lessons, as you prefer."

Skate swallowed and smacked her lips. "Sounds good, then. When do you want it given back to her?"

"With all speed. Tonight, if you can."

She thought about it. The streets were more slush than snow, now. The sun had been out and shining, bringing with it a warmer wind that helped to dissipate the collected piles of white nuisance.

"Not a problem." She scooped up her empty plate and took it to the kitchen. "How do you want it given back to her?" she said over her shoulder.

"It doesn't matter to me, so long as she gets it undamaged and anonymously." He came to the doorway to speak to her, keeping an eye on Rattle as it floated about doing the work of cleaning up. It deftly snatched Skate's plate from her hands as it passed, causing her to jump a bit and laugh. "I mean it, young lady," Belamy said, mistaking her light mood as unconcern. "She's seen you and knows you've been here with me. The last thing I need is Laribel knowing I borrowed one of her books without permission."

"I get it; it'll be fine." Skate laughed again as Rattle went through a small juggling act with the plates before dropping them in the water in the basin. She slid past Belamy into the main room and sat down by the fire, which she changed to a blue color with the Dwarvish words.

"Good, then. Be sure to do so. And make sure my door is shut when you leave. Rattle will let you in." Belamy moved toward the front door. "Rattle will oversee your lesson for the day, as well. Just practice the sounds you've learned so far. Eventually, it will become a matter of automation for you. But you've got to practice to get there."

"Wait, you're leaving?"

"Yes," he said, stopping with his hand on the handle of the heavy door. "Is there a reason I should not?"

At a bit of a loss, she said, "Well, no, I guess not. It's your house, ain't it? You just never leave, is all."

"True. I rarely have a need. But today, I'm off to meet with people who might help me track down the unpleasant trio bent on extorting money from Jack. I should be back before evening comes, but I can't say for sure."

"Who you gonna talk to for help with that?" It was unlikely he'd have any contacts with the criminal underworld if he didn't know the name "Hajime," but it was possible that he might be able to find something out about the Ink if he looked hard enough.

"Various hedge wizards who may have supplied them with the spells or trinkets. I'm also going to pay Lady Flandel a visit, since she apparently felt comfortable enough inviting them to her soirée. Wish me luck." Without waiting for the wish, he swung out the door and swept into the cool morning. The door shut behind him.

"Good luck!" she called out. "You're gonna need it," she muttered, turning back to the kitchen. "Rattle!"

The eyeball turned toward her at the call, somehow hearing over the din of the dishes it was cleaning in the basin. It didn't stop cleaning as it turned, and the effect was disconcerting. Its legs continued to shift the dishes around and clean them even though it was not focused on the work.

Skate shook her head and forced herself to remember what she'd come in here for. "Did Mr. Belamy tell you what the plan is for the day?"

It extracted two of its legs from the chaos long enough to click them together before shoving them right back into the wash without missing a beat.

"Well, I'm going to be in the library until you're ready, all right?" Another quick shuffle and click. Skate nodded and left it to its work, and she saw the eye swinging back to the washing as the door came shut.

She went up the stairs and found the library as it had always been. Normally, she only came in here to talk to Petre, but this morning she thought to try her hand at a challenge. She scanned the rows of books until she found a spine with a title she could make sense of.

"*Th...e L...a...ast Dra...g...on...*" she sounded out aloud. It was not the entire title, but it was enough to get her to gingerly take the book off the shelf and place it on the nearby empty desk. She opened it up and took in the first page. "*The Last Dragon*," she said again, smiling because she knew she'd gotten it right; at the bottom of the very first page was a detailed illustration of a dragon reared up on its powerful hind legs, breathing fire and snarling. Underneath the words she had read were five more. "...*O...f...th...e L...o...st Br...ink...*'is lands'? What's 'is lands'?" Not having an answer, she read the words over and over again to herself. "The Last Dragon of the Lost Brink Is-lands." Rattle's clicking told her it was coming up the stairs, so she read the words one last time before closing the book gently and putting it back in place on the shelf. She met Rattle in the hallway, and they both went to her room to continue her lessons.

#♅⅞◯

It was early afternoon when Skate needed a break. Her eyes were tired, and the chalk Rattle was using to mark the board was worn down to a near-useless nub. Rattle moved to the kitchen to prepare lunch while Skate rubbed her face in front of the blue flame in the main room. The past few hours had consisted of an interminable series of letters together on the board, with Skate sounding out the noise they made together. After the second hour, she found herself not needing to think about the letters individually anymore; this must have been part of what Belamy had meant when he talked about it being a matter of "automation." By the third hour, she hated everything and wanted to be doing anything else. She thought they must have been in there for at least five hours but wasn't sure.

Rattle brought out a plate of cheese and fruit. She took it and set it down. "Thanks," she said, taking her hands from her face. "That's probably enough for the day, you think?"

It did its imitation of a shrug.

"I think it's enough for me. I'm gonna go lie down after I eat this. You go read or something," she said, taking a bite out of the hunk of cheese.

Rattle clicked once and floated up the stairs. Skate took a few more nibbles of the cheese before moving to the little purple fruits. She didn't get to eat fruit much, and she supposed very few got to eat fruits at all this time of year. Belamy's cabinets were a marvel. "Work of genius," she muttered to herself, savoring the sweet juice in each berry. They complemented the cheese flavor nicely. She set her plate down and realized with some surprise that she was alone. With Belamy out of the house, this might be her best chance to explore that "storage closet" in the basement.

Skate moved to the bookcase and put a hand on the false book that acted as the lever. She pulled the lever and pressed the bookcase with all her weight, keeping it from banging open upon being released. This also had the added benefit of keeping that release mechanism from making any noise. She waited a few seconds, fearing the sound of curious flapping wings, but the quiet sound of Rattle's floating came no nearer, and she heard a page turn. Undiscovered, she made her way down to the cellar, which was still lit up from the last time she'd been down there without permission or anyone else's knowledge.

With practiced silence, she moved to the locked door, ignoring the instruments and bottles stacked along the walls and cabinets. She pulled her wire out and began her work. This, too, was both familiar and quiet, with only an occasional and almost imperceptible click accompanying her efforts. Seconds turned into minutes as she explored the tumblers of the lock that kept the door shut, blindly shifting them where they needed to be by the feeling and sounds of the clicks.

Skate felt the last tumbler fall into place, and the door swung open from the latch in its frame. She caught the door and continued to open it slowly, careful to keep it from squeaking. The light from the lab poured into the unexplored room and cast bizarre-looking shadows on its walls. She stepped in.

Belamy had called this a storage closet, and to his credit, it did appear he had been using it for that exact purpose. Unused cleaning tools were piled in one corner, and a large, scratched chalkboard sat discarded on one wall. There were cracked and burnt alchemical tools on a worn-looking cabinet. *Why not throw those out or fix them?* She didn't have time to consider the question too deeply before her eyes were drawn to the center of the room.

There was a large glass display case that would have dominated the room in better lighting. Within, a mannequin stood on a single metal leg draped in one of the most intricately decorated pieces of clothing she had ever seen. It was a robe, a rich red robe bedecked with blue stones along the hem and cuffs. Red rubies peppered the chest and waist. All around these stones swirled interweaving and precise lines of gold. She tried to follow the path of a single line of the golden thread, but she soon got lost and had to abandon the attempt. In the process, another detail of the fabric caught her eye: the red fabric was also inlaid with swirling patterns of a deeper red color. Staring too hard at the design made her dizzy, so she backed away from it.

At the latch of the collar, which looked unyielding, Skate saw the royal seal on either side of the metal clasp: the scepter, helm, and blades of Old King Rajian. "The war robes," she muttered to herself. She realized she was looking at the extravagant gift from King Hilan to Belamy for his military service. She reached out a hand to rest on the glass. It felt cold.

She frowned, working out what to do with this new information. *Is this the thing he tied his soul to?* If Petre was to be believed, it was certainly valuable enough. Did it matter that much to Belamy, though? He had taken the care to enshrine it here in the room but did not seem interested in watching over it too closely. He was using the room for garbage, after all.

Skate stepped back from the glass. She couldn't know for sure if it was the focus of her search or not, so she couldn't make any decision yet. As she turned back to the open door, a glint caught her eye. She moved in that direction, taking care not to trip on any of the clutter on the ground. The glint was curved, as if shining off of something round and smooth. When she reached it, she recognized it for what it was, and her breath caught in her throat. It was the statuette from the mantle of the fireplace.

She picked it up and held it in her hands. It was weightier than it looked. It was carved out of some dark gray stone and was a figure of a woman in the midst of performing some kind of dance. One of her arms was outstretched toward the ground, holding an intricately carved wand or rod, while the other hand was lifted in a flourish, her flowing dress sweeping around her in a graceful arc. The stone lady's face was pensive, as if in deep concentration on her task. A multifaceted blue gemstone was set in the tip of the wand in her outswept hand. Even though the scant illumination barely managed to reach this corner, the stony figurine managed to catch the light and reflect it beautifully, especially the precisely cut blue stone.

This could work, Skate thought. It looked valuable enough in its own right, and who could say what sentimental value the old man placed on it? *Plus*, she reminded herself, *he took the trouble of taking this out of the room and keeping it away from me.* That may have been enough to convince her that this was what she'd been searching for, except for a nagging voice that brought objections from the back of her mind. *He didn't show you the robes, either. And what about the gemstones in the cushioned case?* It was true that there was more than one item he'd kept hidden from her (one of which he had specifically told her that first night not to touch), and she had no way to tell which was his most cherished possession. She racked her brain, trying to remember anything that Petre had told her that might hint one way or the other. *He didn't care very much about the robes when he received them. He has them deliberately displayed in a place he cares nothing about and hardly visits.* On the other hand, she knew nothing about the statuette, not whom it might be depicting or what attachment Belamy had to it other than wanting it out of sight with a known thief in the house. *And he put the statuette down here, too,* she reminded herself. If he truly didn't care about what went into this room, then neither of these objects was a likely candidate, otherwise valuable or not.

Getting this wrong would be disastrous; two unclear options was not really an option at all, much less three. She could take the robes and the statuette both, but what if neither of these was right? She would have blown her cover, and Belamy would remain out of the reach of the Ink forever. And there were still the red gemstones she was not allowed to touch, and which she had not found. The location of these gemstones was, she decided, worth waiting for.

The only other room that had not been open to her up to this point was Belamy's own bedroom; the door had been, as far as she knew, closed and locked since her first night here.

What need did a lich have of sleep? *He's not alive, so the bedroom is probably storage, too.*

Skate placed the statuette back into its place in the pile of rubbish where Belamy had chosen to store it, making sure that its position was no different than when she'd found it. The blue glint of the woman's wand shone after Skate as she walked, as if winking at her. She caught herself looking back several times on the short trip to the door.

Skate stopped in front of the tall display case and looked over the magnificent red-and-gold robes again. It seemed a shame that this piece of uniquely beautiful clothing was relegated to such ignominy, that it was deliberately on display to no one. It was a piece of art—and powerful and magical besides, according to Petre. "Iron Wind," she muttered, before turning back toward the lab. She watched as the stream of light into the room shrank to a beam that seemed to hesitate as it crossed the robes before it shut out altogether as the door clicked shut. She tried the handle to make sure the lock had reset. Finding the door unyielding once more, she left the "storage closet" behind, and chuckled to herself as she took the short spiral stair up. *I'm probably one of the only living people around who can say they've seen that stuff.*

After she reached the main room and gently closed the bookshelf behind her, she made her way up to the library. She heard the turning of a page as she approached the second floor. Rattle was reading, and had placed Petre near itself. Rattle kept looking between the foggy sphere and the open book. It took Skate a moment to realize that Rattle wasn't the one reading; Petre, having no hands to speak of, needed someone to turn the pages for him. She cleared her throat and got their attention.

"I'm going back to my nap now," she said, feigning a yawn—or trying to, as the attempt turned into a genuine example. "Try not to get too crazy in here, okay?" Rattle looked at the blue sphere and shrugged, then clicked at her to let her know they'd heard her. The flying eyeball bat returned its attention to the open book, and Petre must have done the same, because Rattle very soon turned the page.

CHAPTER 16

IN WHICH GRAFFITI IS DISCUSSED, A TRAP IS
SPRUNG, AND CAKE IS NIBBLED.

Skate awoke several hours later. She had not actually meant to fall
asleep, but only to rest her tired eyes. Her body had betrayed her,
though, and she had slept. She had dreamt, too, and it had been a good
dream: she brought the robes, the statue, and the gemstones to Boss
Marshall, and Twitch was with her. She was laughing; Twitch, the
Boss, Haman, and even Kite were there laughing; and the three things
turned into a pile of gold coins, the scepter of King Rajian stamped on
each one. It was a growing mountain of gold, and Belamy was suddenly
there, seated in the corner reading a book. He lifted his hands and
more gold flowed out, a fountain of coins from each of his loose-
hanging, red-and-gold sleeves. He was wearing the robes somehow,
and he, too, was laughing. He said something, but she couldn't remember it now. The rest of the dream was fading, and the more she tried to
remember of it, the more it dissipated. She shook her head and tried to
forget it. Real life was calling, and she had no time for dreams.

Skate looked out the window to see the sun much closer to the
horizon than its zenith. It had done its work fairly well for the day,
making the snow piles smaller and the puddles of water larger. These
would freeze overnight and melt again tomorrow, unless the warm
breezes stopped, which was bound to happen soon. Winter was less
than half over, and more snow was sure to come to shut everyone in
once more.

Through the door, the ruffling sound of a page turning told her that Rattle and Petre were likely right where she'd left them.

Skate put her bare feet on the floor and walked over to her desk. She pulled out her slate and began mindlessly running through her letters, writing small enough to fit all twenty-six on the smooth black surface. After her third erasure using her discarded old rags, she decided it was time to get Ossertine's book back to her.

Skate put the slate and chalk nub back in the drawer of the desk and stopped. The letters in the back corner of the drawer caught her attention again. This time, she could read them. It was two large letters together. "AB," she muttered, saying the names of the individual letters." *Is "ab" a word?* She thought about it and decided that if it was, it was a stupid one. She'd never heard of any such thing, so she guessed it to be letters carved into the wood as some sort of sign or mark, not a word.

She closed the drawer and went to the library. "What's AB?" she asked, standing right behind Rattle and Petre. The bat thing turned, but Petre's prison remained smoky. She assumed he'd turned toward her, but couldn't be sure; she'd found that he couldn't make himself seen at all until his home was held, and could only make himself heard with great effort if he wasn't in your hand. She walked over to him and picked him up, and his eyes came into view.

"What?" he asked, confusion plain on his face. "They're the first two letters of the alphabet. I thought Barrison said she was an expert with the letters by now." He looked at Rattle for confirmation, but the flapping creature only clicked once and stared at her.

She rolled her eyes. "I know that. I mean, is it a word?"

"Is 'ab' a word?" Petre repeated, his eyes narrowed in concentration. "No, I don't think so. Well, it is in the language of the dwarves. It means 'and.' Have you been trying to read some bizarre translation where they kept the original word in place by spelling it out in a different alphabet?"

"No, nothing like that. There's some letters carved into the drawer of my desk. It just says 'AB.' Capital letters, kinda jagged, up in the corner."

Petre and Rattle shared another look, this one heavy with meaning. Petre retreated into his smoke while Rattle looked back at her.

"I wouldn't worry about that, Skate. Just some graffiti. Surely you've got more important things to worry about, right?"

"Well, yeah, but—"

"Best get to it, then, eh? Deliver your book, and all that?"

"You're acting weird."

"No idea what you mean. Off with you, now."

Skate put him back on his perch. Rattle looked between the pair of them, then slowly turned back to the book. "I'll just ask Mr. Belamy about it when he gets back." She had a finger on the glass, so she'd be able to hear what Petre said.

"You do that," he said, feigning disinterest. She took her hand away and walked down the stairs.

Ossertine's book was right where Skate had left it that morning. Her plan for returning it was straightforward: bang on the door as loudly as she could, drop the book on the stoop, and haul tail to a near-by alley where she could watch and confirm that the haughty woman had found the package. It was a much easier proposition than getting the book out had been.

Skate pulled on her boots and wrapped her fur-lined coat around her to brace against the chill outside; while it wasn't unbearable, there was still a bite to the air when not in direct sun. She put the book and burlap in her pack, then put the pack over her shoulder and went out into the street. Maybe Rattle would have dinner ready by the time she got back.

The streets were busy, but few were stopping to chat or dawdle. Carts and wagons and carriages trundled down the streets, and the pedestrians of Caribol swarmed around one another in tightly gripped cloaks and coats, scarves and hats twitching in the comforting warm breeze that occasionally died out entirely, leaving everyone to attempt to wrap up tighter still. Ossertine lived much closer than the other marks had, so the shivering crowds were not a notable concern. The walk to her home was uneventful, and Skate found it as she'd left it, nestled tight in a row of homes just like it. Some of the stoops had been cleared of snow, while others had kept a slathering of the stuff at their doorstep, their owners too busy or unconcerned to bother pushing it away. Ossertine was among the latter, though a warm bouncing light through the window told Skate the woman was home and had lit her fireplace.

Skate walked to the doorway with a practiced ease, a deliberate way of moving that neither invited suspicion nor tried to deflect it; in a sense, she walked as others did, as if she were doing whatever normal people went about doing—visiting a relative, perhaps, or delivering something to a friend. The window was iced over, since it had not received any appreciable sunlight.

Skate pulled the burlap sack out of her pack and set it down gently. She banged on the door twice as hard as she could, then turned to flee into the shelter of the alley across the narrow cobbled road. An unexpected problem arose, however: upon turning to flee, she found herself unable to take another step. Indeed, she could move not at all. Her arms, still out to her sides, bent slightly with the turn. She could not put them down. She could not speak.

Panic welled up within her and crashed around like a wild animal. Her eyes darted around, searching desperately for an answer or an escape. She saw light, blue and cold at her feet. The sight calmed her, not because it was a welcome development, but because it was an explanation. She'd been trapped by magic, some sort of snare obscured by the unshoveled snow.

This calm was tempered with a new shock of fear as she heard the door open behind her. *I can still hear. I can still see. I can breathe.* These truths were something to hold onto to keep the wild animal calm, and her thoughts somewhere near rational. The familiar and expected voice sounded pleased when it finally spoke. Ossertine sounded as imperious as ever.

"A pleasant afternoon, thief. Won't you join me inside for a cup of cider? Or warm milk, perhaps?"

The world shifted around Skate. She was off the ground and moving backward. Into Ossertine's house. No one had grabbed her, and this, too, was a familiar sensation; it felt exactly as it had the night she'd tried to jump out of Belamy's window and been caught by his magic. Ossertine had magic of her own, it seemed.

The door, her escape, closed in front of her when she landed back on the ground, like a statue picked up and shifted. She maintained her standing position, but she couldn't be sure if that was because of Ossertine's magic or her own stance. She did not see the burlap bag anymore.

"Let's have a look at you, then, shall we?" Ossertine moved in front of Skate, surprise and recognition evident on her face. "Why, you're Belamy's pet urchin, aren't you? I'd never have recognized you without your ratty...clothes. Well, get seated and you can calmly explain why I shouldn't hand you over to the Guard for flogging or whatever it is they do to children who take what's not theirs from their betters."

Before Skate could even begin to try to respond, her view shifted again. The rest of Ossertine's narrow living room opened up in her field of vision. There was a thud as the back of her foot caught the small table in front of the cushioned sofa she was being forced onto, and the pain made her want to cry out, more from surprise than the actual discomfort. All she could manage was a sharp expulsion of breath.

"My apologies. I'm not used to guests that I need to arrange like this." Ossertine walked into view from Skate's left and smirked as she continued past her out of sight once more. Skate could do nothing but stare ahead and wait. She decided to take stock of her surroundings as much as she could, one sense at a time.

She started with the least helpful: taste. There was little to know from it since she had no control over tongue or mouth. All she could taste was salt and dryness; shock and fear had scoured all else away.

Smell was more helpful: other than the dusty odor from the last time she'd been here, she caught a surprisingly comforting aroma. Ossertine was making coffee, and the warm dark flavor of the beans had wafted into the living room. It was accompanied by a sweeter smell she didn't recognize but found no less appetizing.

Feeling, too, gave her something to work through. She was no longer in her awkward standing position, but had been placed like a doll into an unassuming and polite sitting posture. Other than the dull intermittent throbbing of her leg, she was comfortable.

While the smell of coffee and sweetness got stronger, Skate moved on to the big senses: seeing and hearing. Sound was not hampered as her vision was, but there was little to hear. There was the clinking of glasses and the sound of liquid pouring from the kitchen, an occasional pop from the crackling fire, and the rush of blood pounding in her ears.

With her least inhibited tool unable to discern more, she scanned the room. Being prevented from moving her head a hair's breadth in any direction, she nevertheless found plenty to see. The closed door she'd bolted out of over a week ago had not changed, though she supposed Ossertine could have placed some new traps around it. The table in front of her had likewise been here before, a delicately designed thing with thin curving legs and intricate patterns etched along the sides. On it were two oil lamps not yet lit. Most of the light in the room came from the fireplace to her right. Skate could only see the very edge of the hearth, and even that took considerable straining. She assumed the painting she'd had to move was back in place behind her, covering the small passage into Ossertine's hidden library. In front of her were the woman's more common books and a much larger painting.

The thing was massive, taking up all the space between the two rows of bookshelves from floor to ceiling. Skate'd seen it before, of course, but had paid it no mind. She'd been here for books, not art. Now, however, she found herself engrossed in its examination.

Its principal figure was a long-faced man clad in metal armor from head to toe. It was neither chain mail nor the scaled armor meant to mimic the body of fish, but the full plate mail worn only by strong knights on horseback. Such armor was absurdly heavy and cumbersome, which made it ill-suited to someone without a mount, as this fellow seemed to be. Nevertheless, the long-faced man wore it well, unconcerned with the five stone of metal weight. Emblazoned on his chest was a design that she didn't recognize, but she knew the type well enough to pick it out as heraldry. It was a black bird of prey in flight, talons extended and beak gaping downward in a permanent silent shriek. It was set against a blue field which itself was bounded by a gold-and-black border. Full plate armor was expensive, worth hundreds of scepts; an art piece like what the man was wearing would have been worth many thousands.

He bore no shield before him, but carried a blade and polearm. He glared and gestured with his blade off toward the side of the painting. There, a horde of shadows was charging toward him, eyes red and full of hate and teeth long and bared in snarls and bites. Nothing else about the figures was given any definition, with the effect being that of a dark blob of teeth and eyes opposing the armored man. To the right of the painting behind the man stood a high hill, and perched at its top sat a magnificent walled city, shining with white and yellow light—a contrast to the dark forces on the other side of the man. In the middle where he stood, the bright and dark intermingled in the sky as roiling gray clouds.

The hand that did not hold the blade held a spear upright—or rather, downright. He was standing atop something she'd at first mistaken for a nondescript mound of earth, but the spear was imbedded into it and drew red from where it struck. The mound of earth was actually some great slain beast of sinuous scaled body rolled in on itself. Where the man had struck looked like its neck, since its pointed, monstrous head was nearby and still attached.

Skate had no idea what specific event this was referring to, but the meaning of the painting was clear enough to her: the brave warrior in the middle had slain some monster and fought off an army of enemies alone to defend a city.

Art theft, particularly that of paintings, wasn't encouraged by Boss Marshall, so Skate knew little about the value of the thing in front of her. "They're too easy to ruin, and they're a pain to hock," he'd told her once, when she'd first started working for him. "They're too easy to trace, see? If some Lord Tiddlewinks buys some Lady Bumfart's stolen masterpiece, he's gonna want to display it, and word gets around that he had to have gotten it from a thief. And that comes back to us, eventually, doesn't it?" This one looked well done enough to her, but that didn't mean it was worth anything. Why Ossertine had this particular piece of art was anybody's guess, but she was obviously quite proud of the piece, considering how prominently it was displayed in her home.

The smell was stronger. Ossertine came back in from the kitchen and sighed contentedly as she sat down next to Skate. She placed a plate of dark brown cakes onto the table in front of them. The glint of a ring caught Skate's eye, which she took note of without being conscious of the effort; years of thievery had ingrained the behavior into her as a reflex, as automatic as drawing breath. It was of a silvery metal and held a dark green stone set within. *It's not fake,* she thought. *Or if it is, it's a good fake.* Ossertine did not strike her as the type to wear costume jewelry if she had access to the real deal.

"Well, now," the woman said, "this won't do unless you're able to talk. I'm going to set the charm on your body loose. When I do, you're not going to make any attempt to flee or assault me in any way. You'll stay seated, and we're going to talk. Do you understand?" She paused as if waiting for an answer. "Know that I can force you to stay if you try to leave, and I can hurt you if you try to attack me. I hope you'll be smart, though I wouldn't mind trying out some magic I rarely get to use if you're not."

At the last word, Skate felt her body relax as if she had been set on the couch unconscious, her limbs becoming looser and more flexible. Her head even lolled, as she had stopped trying to keep it in position, since there was no need and the effort had become more of a distraction than anything. She put her arms beside her legs to steady herself on the cushioned sofa, and shot a hateful glare at the woman. She made no other movements.

"I see that you are intelligent after all," Ossertine said, smiling and gesturing to the brown cakes. "A sweet treat?"

Skate said nothing, but shook her head. *Like I'd take anything made by you. It's probably poisoned or enchanted.* She didn't know what Ossertine would have to gain by poisoning her, but she took no chances. Ossertine took her silence for the refusal it was, and went on.

"Very well. I've got coffee brewing in the kitchen, so maybe you'd like some of that when it's ready. Or perhaps you'll continue to refuse good things offered to you like a spoiled child. The choice is yours, I suppose. In the meantime, let's get to the heart of the matter. Why did you steal my book?"

Skate looked away. "Dunno what you mean."

"I'm being perfectly clear."

"No. Do you mean, 'Why did I steal from you, instead of someone else,' or 'Why did I take that book in particular,' or 'Why am I stealing books at all'? How am I supposed to know which one of those you meant?"

"Cute." Ossertine took a brown cake from the plate and nibbled at the edge. "All three. Answer all three of those questions." When Skate said nothing, Ossertine swallowed the piece of cake she'd bitten off and said, "If you don't want to talk to me, I can hold you while the Guards come. Maybe you'd rather have the conversation with them. Or," she said, grabbing Skate's face in a clawlike hand and turning her to face her directly, "I'll just draw what I want out of your mind, like pulling thread from a frayed dress."

The woman's face was iron. Her eyes searched Skate for fear and saw a bit that leaked through her façade. She smiled. "It hurts. The mind is not meant to be pulled in such a way, but will yield to the magic just the same. It starts as heat in the back of your head...." When she trailed off, Skate felt the burning, and it did hurt. "It will only get worse as it spreads through the rest of your mind, tearing and pulling—"

"Okay!" Skate shook her head from the woman's hand, and the heat dissipated. "Okay, fine." Ossertine said nothing, but took up her cake and gestured for her to continue. "I stole from you because I figured you'd have books if you were friends with Mr. Belamy. I stole that book because you hid it better, so I figured it was worth more. I'm stealing books to make money. I got a buyer who throws scepts away for those stupid things," she said, waving at the books on the shelf.

"Hmm," Ossertine said, as she brought a thin finger to her thin lips, either to buy herself time to finish chewing, or to consider Skate's reasoning. "I'm not so sure," she said, smacking her lips once after swallowing. "Why would you go looking for my more valuable books at all when I had so many here in plain view?" She walked over and drew one at random from its place on the shelf. "Any of these, even for the stingiest of purchasers, would be worth at least ten scepts on their own. Why would you not grab and go as quickly as possible?"

Skate didn't answer immediately, but looked at the fire. "It's not my first time robbing a place." The woman said nothing, but waved at her to continue. "Books are heavy. At most, I'd have got out with two, maybe three if they were small. I didn't plan to make any repeat visits, so I took my time looking for any sort of hidden cache you had. If you had any rare books, you wouldn't have them out sitting in your living room where any old moron could walk in and take them. So, I looked, and I found it." She took a cake, convinced that it wouldn't hurt her after watching Ossertine enjoy one. "Not my first time robbing a place," she said again around a mouthful. It was shockingly sweet, and she had to force herself not to shove the whole thing down her throat at once.

"You said you knew I was friends with Barrison. How?"

"The night you came over, I was hiding in the kitchen. I heard your conversation, so I knew you'd be out of the house."

Ossertine took another cake off the tray. "About that: how'd you know where my house was?"

"I've seen you before," Skate invented wildly, desperate to avoid mentioning Rattle. "I've been doing my work for a couple years in this neighborhood, so I've got a pretty good bead on who lives where."

Ossertine chewed and considered. "You've known where I lived for years, but you only now decided to steal my very valuable books?"

"How was I supposed to know you had any? Like I said, only reason I went after your stuff was because I knew you knew Mr. Belamy. Plus, my buyer's new."

"If you're after books, why didn't you just steal from Barrison?"

"There's a saying a friend of mine likes: 'Don't burn where you read.' Mr. Belamy gives me shelter and food. He's not likely to let me stay around if I'm stealing from him, is he? And with that flying bat thing always hanging around, there's no chance of me taking anything without getting caught anyway."

"And how do you think he'll react to your theft of my personal belongings?"

Skate said nothing, but looked at the burlap bag.

"For that matter, why did you—oh..." Ossertine trailed off and brought a thin palm to her forehead. "That's why you're here, isn't it? He's made you bring it back before you could sell it." Skate did nothing to correct that misconception, as it was exactly the connection she'd wanted the woman to make. "So he knows he's housing a thief, and he's making you come back and say you're sorry?"

"He didn't say anything about 'sorry.' He just wanted it brought back." She found the misdirection very easy to say because it was technically true; Belamy didn't want this conversation to happen at all, so he'd never said she needed to say she was sorry.

"Foolish old man," Ossertine muttered, rubbing her fingers together to remove the persistent crumbs. "He'd likely be cross with me if I sent you off with the Guards, then. Why in the world he's going through so much trouble for..." She trailed off without completing the thought and merely scoffed.

"For what?" Skate thought she knew what she'd meant to say, but she wanted her to come out with it to be sure.

Ossertine looked at her for what felt like a long time, her eyes narrowed in distaste, her lips curled ever so slightly into the shadow of a sneer. "You saw my painting?" she asked. Skate said nothing. "Of course you did; you had little else to look at. It depicts an historic scene, a piece of history tied directly to my family." She stood and walked over to the large piece of art. "My thrice great-grandfather defended this city, though it was more a small town then, from a horde of monsters from the north—horrible things, it's said, led by a terrible dragon." Skate looked at the painting again; the sinewy monster beneath the man's feet took on an even more frightening aspect. "He slew the beast and turned the tide of the battle. He saved hundreds of lives with his actions, and was awarded the title of Lord for his brav-ery." She turned to face Skate directly, her thin hands crossed in front of her in the polite manner of the aristocracy. "His descendants carry on the line, though of course not all carry his title." She sniffed. "This is what I do not understand about Barrison's choice to protect you. You do not have such history. You do not have such worth."

"Worth?" Skate jumped to her feet, knocking the delicate table a few inches away in her haste. She had taken a second dark cake and was now crushing it in her fist. "You think you're worth more than me?"

Ossertine turned her face away and closed her eyes, her nose turned upward. "Saying such a thing is beneath me, child."

"What's better about you—"

"Nobility!" For the first time she'd ever seen, Ossertine showed not disgust or contempt, but true anger. Her teeth were clenched, and her hands, which had been clasped delicately in front of her, had balled into fists at her sides. She pointed a dagger-like finger at the painting. "Honor! Sacrifice!" She regained some of her composure, and her face became less of a monstrous mask of hate. Her other hand remained balled into a fist. "Sacrifice," she said again, her voice less agitated, but still entirely disapproving. "Dignity. Dedication. These are what makes my family, and therefore me, better. These are things children struggle to comprehend at the best of times and even among the well-bred, but for a thief? These values are as alien to your kind as the pale moons themselves are to us all. What would you know of honor?" She sniffed at her again.

Skate was burning. She wanted to launch herself at the woman, to tear at her, to stop her words. Doing so would only prove her right, though, so she stood in simmering rage. "We got honor. We got rules, same as you. And we follow them. We got other stuff, too. We take care of one another. That ain't something you'd understand. Sacrifice? We got that. You can turn your nose up all you want," she added as the woman did just that, "but it don't change nothing. You're not better than the rest of us just because you got money and your grandpa did something good. You're just lucky, is all." She unwrapped the elven text from the sack and dropped the book out of it with a resounding thud. "Lucky you never had to starve, or cheat, or steal to survive. Lucky that you got parents that took care of you and told you where you came from." She stuffed the empty sack into her pack. "Can I go, or is your stupid trap gonna stop me?"

The woman did not speak, but was looking at Skate with an expression the girl could not place. Perhaps it was because she wasn't used to seeing anything other than smug disdain there, because Osser-tine looked...unsure.

The woman shook her head in response to the question and waved at the door. It creaked open. "You may leave."

Skate was out the door when she heard, "Give my best to Barrison."

CHAPTER 17

IN WHICH A COURIER GOES WALKABOUT, A
LIBRARY IS ALPHABETIZED, AND A FLOOR IS
DIRTIED.

The trap did not go off as Skate crossed the threshold. She left Laribel Ossertine's home, and, instead of feeling proud for having gotten the job done without implicating Belamy, or satisfied for having told the arrogant woman off, she felt ashamed. She splashed through puddles that would soon turn icy, and her boots did their job of keeping her dry.

She stopped and looked down at the boots, footwear she'd neither bought nor stolen. She was not used to dealing with gifts, but had paid them no mind at the time; they had been in preparation for a job. But the very clothes on her back were gifts, given without expectation of repayment. The old man had never asked for them returned or paid for, and likely never would. They were not hers, not really; they were Belamy's, and he'd given them to her without a thought.

The boots were not hers. The dress was not hers. The coat was not hers. She was bedecked in clothes that did not belong to her, that she hadn't earned, that she hadn't stolen. It was not something she had given any thought to before. Ossertine made her think of it. "Bitter old cow," she muttered to herself, kicking a nearby chunk of ice. The sturdy boots absorbed most of the shock, but her eyes welled up with tears anyway.

Skate knew she was right, that there was plenty to be proud of in her life, plenty of accomplishments and friendships and honor. But she knew none of that mattered to someone like Ossertine. It didn't matter to the people who mattered. The people with money, the people with authority, the people with connections—these people didn't think anything of people like her and Twitch and Delly. They thought they knew who these urchins were, and were satisfied with their knowing.

The Ink had been the only people who cared about any of the kids in this city. They were the ones who saw the value of the dispossessed kids, who could move about all but unseen and unheard, who went unnoticed by the crowds and Guards, who were out for survival and to prove to anyone who cared to know just what they could do. The Ink took them in, protected them, grew them, respected them. All the Bosses had kids in their crew (except Boss Shade; the Bosses had decided it wasn't right to include anyone who had seen fewer than sixteen summers in that crew), and all knew the value such sneaks could pull in. The orphans and abused of the city found an open palm within the organization, and all they had to give in return was what they wanted to give anyway: proof that they were worth something.

Skate angrily wiped her useless tears away and began walking without a destination in mind. Other than her parents, the Ink were the only people who had treated her with something other than contempt. Everyone else had been like Ossertine and the Guards. *That's not right,* she thought, reminding herself where she had been sleeping in a warm bed and eating warm meals of late. *Belamy's been good. Belamy seems to care whether I live or die.* "Only cuz he wants something from me," she muttered aloud, stepping off the street to let a wagon full of barrels trundle by.

The Ink wants something, too, don't they? the small and persistent voice countered. *You can only stay if you work, right? "Ink ain't cheap," right? And if you want to leave, you'd better pay them off if you know what's good for you.* Skate huffed and picked up her pace as she wound through the back alleys. *Okay, fine,* she shot back, *so Belamy and the Ink both are sort of good. So what?*

She paused and listened. Without noticing, she'd almost blown right past a street musician working a crowd with a rousing rendition of "The Blue Grapevine" on a ragged violin. The graying woman had the top of her head covered in the gingham cloth favored by the traveling performers who usually brushed through in the spring. Her skin looked tough as leather, especially around her beaky nose. The crowd was laughing and carousing as they began the second verse:

My love has left me here this cold November,
My heart packed full of bitter, sullen snow.
I know not if she will bother to remember
The doting fool whose face she used to know...

They moved into the chorus again, and the playing woman seemed more than happy to keep the tune going as long as the crowd cared to take part. She smiled and revealed a mouth with only three teeth left within. She'd be gathering plenty of coin from this crowd, and had much to be smiling about.

So, stealing from Belamy is wrong. Skate scoffed aloud at the thought, though there was no external target for her derision. The idea that stealing was wrong was discussed at length with those brand new to the Ink. It was an idea that some children had managed to pick up from their parents or other family members before joining. Skate had been one such recruit, but the other thieves were quick to point out the hypocrisy of such talk: the people who said stuff like that were awful quick to do other stuff that wrong just the same, so what's so bad about stealing in order to eat? If left with no options, they'd do the same. And people in the Ink? They had no other options.

Still, the thought did not leave Skate when she strolled away from the music. *Why's it wrong?* she demanded of herself. *Why's stealing from him any different than anybody else?* The answer, she knew, lay in the conversation she'd already had with herself: he didn't treat her like trash. He'd shown concern for her before he'd seen any value in her thieving skills, despite the fact that she had been involved in some minor stabbing of him. Stealing from him felt wrong to her because of who he'd shown himself to be. He had demonstrated nothing but kindness to her, and she was planning not only to steal from him, but to steal from him in such a way that he would end up under the control of strangers who thought him a monster and cared nothing for him beyond his utility.

The guilt came back, and Skate tried to outwalk it, turning this way and that in a blind struggle with herself. Stealing from him felt like a betrayal, no matter what she tried to tell herself. She had his trust, and she was planning to hang him with it when all he'd given her were work, learning, and respect.

She stopped where she stood, causing someone behind her to curse when they bumped into her. The gentleman in the fine hat cut her a dirty look underneath his bushy black eyebrows and said something about "useless" and "public menace, the lot." Skate paid him no mind, and dealt with the most significant problem she felt she'd ever encountered. *Can you do it?* She'd asked herself this before and either refused to answer or gave an affirmative, but that affirmative had not been properly considered—it had been a knee-jerk response, and nothing more. It had helped her ignore the question and the crisis it would bring. She faced that crisis now, and she felt it would tear her apart if not dealt with soon.

She did not know what to do. The Ink needed her—Boss Marshall especially, if the rumors were to be believed. He'd kept her safe all these years, with food in her belly and a cot to sleep on. It had not been the stuffed mattress she enjoyed each night, nor the rich fare she ate, but it had been better than a bare floor and no food at all; and the others, those who had to stay on the streets, could never claim better than what she'd gotten from the Boss.

Still, she had been caught in the act of burglary by Belamy, who had had every right and ability to hold her and throw her to the Guard. Instead, he'd offered her freelance work, with a bed and warm meals in the meantime. And reading, that was another thing. Even though she was not by any means literate, the wizard had opened a door that was previously shut: the written word. With enough practice and time, she could teach herself to read with the skills the old man had taught her. It was something that couldn't be taken from her, no matter what.

The idea of selling her teacher into bondage opened a pit in her stomach, but so did the idea of abandoning her caretaker and employer after she'd made promises to help. Besides, trying to leave the Ink could be...dangerous.

"Honor," Ossertine had said, and Skate had retorted that she and those like her had plenty of it in their own way—and she believed that. But what honor was there in selling an innocent man into slavery, an innocent man who'd shown mercy and generosity when they had not been earned in any way?

And yet, what honor was there in abandoning an agreement and leaving a friend and mentor to struggle and possibly even die? Big Boss, if he was displeased with Marshall, would not stay so for long without taking action against him, especially if Boss Shade was out spreading rumors of his impending doom. Failing Boss Marshall would mean leaving him at the mercy of the other Bosses, and being against the other Bosses always went poorly. It was why Hajime had reorganized the criminal group as he had: everyone on the same page, and no mercy or hesitation in cutting out those who weren't. If Boss Marshall were decided to be on a different page, then there was nothing to be done for him. He wasn't there yet, but failing to get Jack Gherun into the fold might do it. If he had a powerful mage at his disposal, though? One who couldn't die? He'd be fine. He'd be golden. He'd be in the books for good.

Skate wiped her eyes. Each choice was wrong, and each one was right. Crying in the street wouldn't fix that. Deciding now wouldn't do it, either. She'd only know what her decision was in the moment when the opportunity presented itself. She looked around to figure out where her rambling had taken her, and realized she wasn't out of the Old Town. The sun had sunken lower; it offered feeble light through the rows of inns and pubs and shops, and soon even that would be gone, leaving Skate and anyone else unlucky enough to still be outside to fend off the cold alone. She turned around and walked back toward Belamy's house.

#·☌·⅄·◌

Skate walked in to find the lich back behind his desk, empty glass ball and spinning golden device in front of him. The glass showed nothing but his own distorted features; she could tell from across the room that he was not seeing anything he wanted to. She kicked off her boots and hung her coat on the rack. She didn't interrupt his work, despite her curiosity about his efforts of the day. Presumably, if he was coming back to these attempts, his search had not been nearly as productive as she feared it might have been. He did not look at her as she went upstairs.

Rattle and Petre were both still in the library (as far as she knew,

Petre never went anywhere else), but they were not reading together. Petre was back in his perch by the window, and Rattle was running one of its legs across the spines of the books. The rest hung limp and rattled.

Skate stood and watched Rattle. After a while its leg stopped, and the flapping eyeball turned to look at the title. It took the book off with a pair of spindly legs and shifted the books next to it up straight and to the right. It then placed the book back on the shelf, but between different books.

"What are you doing?" she asked, waving at Rattle as it returned to its extended-leg-guided tour. It looked at her, but did not stop its trip.

She was about to ask again when two things happened: she realized that asking was pointless since Rattle was unable to communicate through conventional means, and a voice spoke in her head, as if from a distance, *"It's alphabetizing."* She recognized the voice as Petre's, and went to collect him from the sill.

"What's it doing?"

"Alphabetizing." Petre's expressive eyes shifted into view, as if he'd been looking elsewhere and found the view boring. "It's putting the books in order by the name of the title. It's the order the whole library is supposed to be in, but as you saw, there are aberrations in the order that Ol' Batball needs to fix. It's dreadfully boring to try to accomplish, but it doesn't seem to mind too much. Sometimes we make a game of it. Just to pass the time, I'll name a book and try to time the thing to see how long it takes to find a book. If it takes more than ten seconds, we talk about reorganization. I guess it's not a game so much as a stress test for the system," he said as an afterthought. "Anyway, it's dead useful for trying to find a specific book when you're looking for it, so long as the title is known to you."

Skate watched Rattle move some more, and it seemed only to be using the one leg to detect the titles, instead of the eye. "How come it's not looking as it goes?"

"Because it's a weird flying bat eyeball." Petre's eyes danced with mischief. "How should I know what goes on behind that big eye of its?"

"So you don't know what Rattle is."

"No one knows what Rattle is. Barrison made the thing, but even he couldn't spell out what exactly it is if you asked him. I know what he was trying to do when he made Rattle, and it wasn't...that." When Skate said nothing but remained obviously interested, he went on. "At the time, he was trying to create a being of living magic. A very dangerous undertaking, but theoretically possible. I could name dozens of wizards over the centuries who have tried to make this happen— Billion the Dwarf, Moriak the Mad, Perianne Redmane..." Seeing no recognition in Skate's face, he said, "Well, never mind, but as I said, it's an undertaking many have tried, but none have succeeded. Barrison caught the urge, and Rattle was the result."

Rattle continued its trek with the next row of books. It must have been nearly done, since there was only one row of books on the wall after its current circle finished.

Skate said, "It was supposed to be a spell, but it turned into something alive?"

"That was the idea, yes."

"Why? What's the use of something like that?"

"Since it's never been successfully done, there's no way to know for sure. But the magic theorists suppose that such a being would be formidable in battle, probably able to ignore weapons and armor that were not themselves magical in nature."

"Rattle was supposed to be a weapon?"

"Yes. Barrison made it during the war. You can imagine the lure of such a weapon, and how useful it would have been to have on the battlefield against scads of heavily armored soldiers. They'd find themselves totally helpless if the theories were right. So, the Iron Wind made the attempt, and when the smoke and lights cleared, Rattle was there, flapping away and looking around. We weren't sure if Barrison had been successful or not, but it seemed to respond well enough to words, especially if Barrison was the one talking to it. He set it on a training dummy, and while its legs made quick work of the cloth and stuffing, it could not pierce any armor. It wasn't a living spell, but something else. Barrison didn't know what else to call it, so Rattle is just Rattle."

Skate continued to watch the thing floating around the room. *It was meant to be a weapon*, she thought. It did not surprise her, really. She'd seen it fight. It was odd, though, to think of the thing she'd come to enjoy being around as a failed war experiment.

A few moments of quiet as Rattle finished its last flapping lap brought the question from that morning back to her mind. She knew asking would do no good, so she stated her thoughts as fact instead. "You know what AB is."

"Yes." Petre wasn't looking at her as he spoke, but continued following Rattle's path.

"It's something to do with Mr. Belamy, isn't it? One of his secrets."

"Yes."

"Has he told you not to tell me about it?"

"No."

His short answers were not unexpected, but Skate found herself getting frustrated just the same. *Calm down*, she told herself; *at least he's talking.* "Would he tell me what it means if I asked?"

"You shouldn't ask."

"That doesn't answer my question."

"No, it doesn't."

Skate frowned. "I'm going to ask him."

"I can't stop you." His eyes faded into smoke.

Knowing the conversation to be over, she set Petre down on his perch by the window. Rattle floated back down to eye level and watched her leave. She shut the library door behind her.

She found Belamy where he'd been earlier, staring into the clear glass ball. The golden enhancer was by him, spinning with agitated speed. It was throwing reflections of the firelight around the room like shooting stars. The room was dimmer than it had been, so she tossed a log onto the flame, knowing the magic of the hearth would create more fuel for later as it always had. Once the new wood caught, she stood in front of Belamy's desk and waited. He ignored her for several minutes, but eventually the golden enhancer began to slow. Belamy leaned back in his chair and stroked his short white beard. He didn't look tired— presumably, he was no longer capable of being tired—but he looked annoyed.

"How'd your search go?"

"Poorly. Those whom I thought had some connection to the people I'm hunting for either knew nothing, pretended to know nothing, or avoided me entirely. The Lady was not at home when I called on her, and the butler wasn't lying about that—I checked—so that is a dead end, at least for now. The various hedge wizards were unwilling to discuss the matter no matter how insistent I was or what offers I made of payment."

"What, did you not offer enough gold?"

"Neither gold nor secrets nor offer of magical service proved of any use toward loosening tongues. It has been quite a frustrating day, I'm afraid. Well, more disappointing than truly frustrating," Belamy said, coming forward again in his chair and looking into the glass ball. "I've got some time to find these people, I hope, and I have not yet exhausted all of my contacts. Perhaps the good Lady Flandel will return from her travels tomorrow; her manservant suggested that was likely, though the weather may interfere."

"These guys must be pretty scary to keep everybody quiet like that." Really, the silence was surprising; what honor there was among thieves was generally not shared by their victims. Not talking to the authorities about criminals made sense. Refusing to talk to friends about the Ink didn't. There was no way to answer the question of why no one was talking, though. She'd need to speak to Haman or Boss Marshall again to try to figure that out.

Belamy shrugged. "Yes, they must be. I know some of these people quite well, and for most of them, this is the first time I've ever been stonewalled in a line of questioning. No matter; I'll find them out eventually. Enough about my work; what about yours?" He pointed to the burlap poking out of the side of her pack. "I take it the book has been delivered?"

"Yep."

He waited for her to elaborate, and when she didn't, he asked, "And how'd it go?"

"Fine." She walked past him to the kitchen to prepare a plate for herself of something plain. She wasn't really hungry, but it was a convenient excuse for trying to dodge this conversation.

The old man followed her. "It went 'fine'? What does that mean?"

Skate opened cabinets at random, looking for a platter or dish to hold the bread and cheese she wanted. "It means it went fine. She got the book, safe and sound."

"Did anyone see you?"

"Where are the plates?"

He pointed to one of the cabinets she hadn't opened yet. "Skate, did anyone see you?"

She pulled out a plate from the identified cabinet and set it on the table, which put it at just about eye level for her. She sighed before she answered. "Yes, Ossertine saw me."

The wizard's eyes went wide. "Did she recognize you?"

Skate rubbed her forehead and eyes. "Yeah. We talked." She explained how she'd been caught, and the direction the conversation had taken regarding her situation with Belamy. He looked relieved that she'd been able to cover for him so easily.

"She has no idea I was the one who told you to steal the book? Oh, that's fantastic," he said, opening the larder door and handing Skate a plate with a few light, fluffy bread rolls.

"No, she thinks you found me out and sent me back with it."

"It all worked out then, didn't it? Smart thinking, Skate, really. You can think on your feet, and that's no small skill."

Skate smiled at the compliment, though that was purely for Belamy's benefit. She did not feel like smiling as she thought of the conversation that had followed about honor and dignity. *He doesn't need to hear about that.* Something about her smile must have come across as less than sincere, because Belamy's smile faltered somewhat after a moment. "Is everything all right?" he asked, concern clear in his voice.

"Sure, why wouldn't it be?" To cover the awkward moment, she took a huge bite off of a roll.

Belamy frowned but pressed no further. "As I said, a job well done. And that's another week of room and board."

Skate nodded, not able to get around the bread in her mouth just yet.

"More to come when you take care of Jack. A while to go before then, though. This business with his criminal acquaintances has cut into my reading time considerably. I'm sure I'll be done with at least one of the books by the time your store of weeks runs out, though, so don't fret about that. And if I'm wrong, there are always more books to steal, eh?"

Skate smiled, a genuine expression this time, and shrugged. She was finally able to swallow. "Lesson went okay without you today."

"Oh? The blending of letters and the new sounds didn't throw you?"

"Nope. Try me."

He considered her for a moment and nodded. He left the desk and moved to the fireplace. "I don't have any writing materials handy, so this will have to do." With a roll of his hands and some rhythmic chanting she couldn't follow, he spread his arms toward the fireplace.

The flames streamed toward his hands like water poured from a jug. His hands worked in circles, packing the fire into a ball much like Skate and the other street kids sometimes did with snow to harass passersby. The result was charred wood smoldering in the hearth and a ball of orange flames in the wizard's grasp, burning on nothing and not harming the old man at all.

"Now then," he said, pulling one hand free of the fire, "show me." He drew in the air with the free hand, and behind the finger the flames trailed out the exact path he made. When he was done, there were two symbols she couldn't read in tongues of orange and red.

She tried to puzzle out the letters and failed. It was not that she was having trouble recognizing them, but that they were letters she had never seen at all. "I don't know what those are."

He screwed his face up in confusion. "Skate, you know all your letters. I know for a fact you—oh," he said with his eyes widening in understanding. He stepped back and swept his arm across the face of the unfamiliar letters. They spun in the air and then Skate understood, too: she'd been looking at them backwards.

"C H. Ch." The recitation was in the pattern they'd practiced, and Belamy nodded. He pulled his hand back, and the fire returned to the ball. He wrote again. "S T. St." He nodded again, pulled back again. He wrote a third time. "A N. An."

Satisfied, Belamy pulled the fire back into his hands a final time, and then lobbed the whole ball back into the fireplace, where it latched back on to the wood and began devouring it once more. "Rattle is a reliable tutor in my absence, as expected," he chuckled, wiping his hands against each other as if removing dust from them. She was surprised when dust actually *did* fall from them, gray and flaky chunks that wound their distracted way to the ground.

"Ash," he explained, seeing her confusion.

"What's the point of something like that?" Skate walked forward and toed the ash that had formed a tawdry little pile in front of Belamy. "Why would you know magic that lets you write in the air with fire? When would you need to do that?"

"It's got a number of uses," he replied, placing his hands on his hips. "As just demonstrated, it can help when you've got no paper and ink directly handy."

"All right, but that's really specific. That can't have been the original use of it, right?"

"No, I suppose not. It's much more commonly used as a way to send messages over large distances. I made them very small, but writing with fire can be as large as you need it to be, so long as you've got the fire to write it all and can get to where you're writing." He pointed a finger toward the wall facing south. "The harbor master keeps a wizard on his payroll just for this spell. If he ever needs to send a message to ships at sea at night, that's how he does it."

"I've never heard of that," Skate said, starting to doubt the story. "I've lived here all my life, spent plenty of time by the docks."

"He hasn't needed to do anything like that in years; it's an emergency measure, not something to be done all the time. Anyway, you asked for the purpose of such magic, and now you have it. It's enormously useful for sending a written message to groups across open spaces, like a harbor."

"Or a battlefield."

His eyebrows twitched upward. "Yes. It is useful in the chaotic din of battle to send messages to commanders quickly. That's an odd observation to make on your part. Why bring it up?"

Skate shrugged and avoided eye contact.

"Oh, I see. Petre's been telling tales again." He walked past her, his gait stiffer than usual, and took his place again at the desk.

"He said you were a war hero."

Belamy grimaced and shook his head, like a horse shaking off an irritating fly.

"Is that why you know that magic?"

He nodded once—a jerking, clipped motion. "Yes. As you pointed out, it's very useful." He was frowning slightly, and she wasn't sure whether it was in concentration on the glass sphere or irritation with her.

"He said you had a name in the war: Iron Wind."

He shook the invisible fly away again. "Petre certainly likes to talk," he muttered, setting the enhancer spinning. "Skate, if you're wanting to know about the war, I'd really rather not talk about it. It's not a time I'm particularly fond of."

Not a monster, she thought for perhaps the dozenth time. *No monster would shy from discussing his bloodshed.* She might have expected relish in the telling, or perhaps callous indifference; this looked more like shame.

"No, that's okay," Skate said, changing the subject. "But I did have a question about something else."

He raised his gaze from the empty glass ball. "Yes?"

"What's 'AB' mean?"

Belamy mouthed the letters back in confusion, then twisted his face in a fury she'd never seen from him. "He talks too much, indeed!" He stood with such force that his chair skittered back to bump against one of the bookcases behind him.

"Petre didn't say anything!" She took a step back, afraid for the first time since the night she'd met this man. "I asked and he wouldn't say anything, except I should leave it alone."

"He's got some wisdom left, it would seem," he growled. "Where did you hear those in—those letters?"

"They were carved in my desk upstairs." His odd phrasing and his catch of himself did not escape her, but she wasn't sure she should press him on the topic right now. His face had not softened any, but was no longer the boiling with anger as it had been; it had instead calcified into grim irritation. He moved out from behind his desk and stomped toward the door. "Where are you going?"

"Out." He slammed the door behind him, leaving Skate alone with a smear of ash and a crackling fire.

CHAPTER 18

IN WHICH SOMEONE SAYS "I TOLD YOU SO,"
CLAIRVOYANCE IS EXPLORED, AND A
SNOWBALL IS THROWN WITH SOME ICE IN
IT.

The sound of flapping echoed down the stairway just after quiet settled in. Rattle came down carrying Petre on his stand, a leg through each of the three small iron loops around the base. Skate took the imprisoned man from it, and he immediately appeared, the smoke sweeping from his eyes faster than it ever had before.

"I told you not to ask him about it." His tone was more smug than actually reproachful. "Very specific about that."

"Yeah, yeah," she said, waving her hand. "So you gonna explain what it means now?"

"You're joking, right? You saw how he responded even when you didn't know anything, and you're wanting me to make it worse by telling you what he doesn't want you to know? Not going to happen." Rattle went into the kitchen, leaving Petre and Skate alone. Petre watched it go, and his eyes lingered on the desk. "Huh," he said, mildly interested in something he saw.

"What?"

"He left the ball out. And the enhancer's still going."

This meant something to Petre, but not to Skate. "So?"

"So," he said, darting his eyes around, "if someone had a mind to, they could use his crystal ball and enhancer freely."

"Someone who knew magic, you mean."

"Well," he said, half-nodding his head in consideration, "sort of. Using the ball is a kind of magic, but it's a kind anyone can do. Just takes some concentration. Really easy to do with the enhancer rolling; it takes a word to get going, which Barrison did...and left."

"I dunno," Skate said, the anger on the old man's face stamped firmly in her mind.

"He won't care, so long as you don't break it."

There was no deception in Petre's voice, but the anger of the wizard was too fresh for her to be so easily convinced. "He seemed really mad."

"I'm sure he is, but he'll cool down. He wasn't mad at you, for what it's worth. You brought up something very painful for him, though you couldn't have known how painful it was. I did warn you not to bring it up, but without a reason given, your stubbornness all but guaranteed you couldn't help but ignore the warning. Having said all that, have I steered you wrong regarding the old man yet?"

Skate considered the question. He had not seemed to lie about Belamy, and had so far been plain about secrets being kept, though he kept them still. She shook her head slowly.

"Well, what say we try it? Some people have a knack for seeing, while others struggle. You may get it right away, or you may not be able to see more than your own reflection."

Skate nodded and sat in Belamy's chair, placing Petre on her right. The golden enhancer continued its spinning, throwing firelight around the room in fits and starts. "So, what do I do?"

"Look into the glass. Picture the person you want to look for. You could pick a place instead, but a person is usually easier to do, especially for a novice. You need to know their name, and it works better the more familiar you are with them. A friend or a family member, perhaps."

"All right." The best person to fit those categories was probably Twitch. "I know who to try. He's a friend."

"Good." Petre's voice was calm and soothing. "Now, relax. Keep the image of him firmly in your mind. Don't think of anyone else. Concentrate on his name and his appearance. Think of his voice. If you need to repeat his name aloud to help you stay focused, that can help. And look into the glass."

Skate stared into the glass ball, seeing only a warped reflection of herself and the rest of the room. *Twitch. Blond hair. Ratty clothes. Has a stutter. Twitch. Thief. Taller than me. Can't read. Twitch. Blond hair...* She repeated the mantra a dozen times, trying desperately not to let her mind wander, but nothing happened.

"It's not working."

"Be patient. It takes time. I doubt even Barrison could find some-one in the time you just tried. Keep looking. Focus." Petre's tone was as cool and soothing as it had been before.

She tried again. *Twitch. Blond hair. Ratty clothes.* The inner repe-tition droned on, and her mind began to wander. Where was Belamy going? Would he cool down, as Petre supposed, or had she managed to poison his opinion of her permanently?

"Focus," Petre said again. "Your eyes were glazing over. It won't work if you don't focus."

"All right, I got it." *Twitch. Blond hair. Ratty clothes. Show me Twitch. He has a stutter. He's a thief. He's taller than me. Show me Twitch.* She was focused. Her mind did not waver. She was aware only of Twitch and the passing of time. Her stomach growled, but she ignored it. Her breathing was steady and regular. The glass was inert.

As Skate ran through her list of descriptors for perhaps the hun-dredth time, something tugged at her mind. It was not unlike what she'd felt when Ossertine began to question her about her motives: a presence in her thoughts that was not her own. This time, though, it did not feel like an invasion but like a helping presence, a guest invited in. She did not have time to question it before an image began to take shape in the glass ball.

The hair came through first, a blond chunk of hair shooting out of a ragged gray head-wrap. The image quickly filled in around the hair, and she was looking unmistakably at Twitch. His immediate surround-ings were in the ball as well, but only a few feet in any direction was visible. She found that she could will the image to move around him to try to get a better sense of where he was. Sound began to come out of the crystal. It was a crowd; Twitch was hovering around the edge of a crowd. He looked like he was trying to get through but was having trouble finding a gap.

"Have you found him?" Petre's voice came from far away. For a moment, Skate worried that responding to him might break her concentration. Something—the comforting guest in her head perhaps—led her to guess that this concern was misplaced. The finding was the hard part, like searching blindly in the dark. Once found, she simply had to hold on to it.

"Yeah," she said, not taking her eyes off the image. He had made it into the crowd and was pushing and slipping his way forward. "I found him. Can he hear me?" He had jerked his head around and looked in her direction.

"No. Some seeing devices exist that allow such communication, but this isn't one."

"Who else is in here?" She brought a finger to tap on her head.

"You're probably feeling the enhancer at work. It would feel like a warmth or a comfortable pillow."

"A guest."

"Sure. It's there to help you, and it looks like it has."

"Yeah. I felt it as soon as I found him. Or right before." Skate's words felt fuzzy coming out. She was too busy watching her friend to pay much attention to the conversation anyway. Twitch had made it to the front of the crowd. He was evidently pleased watching whatever was there, because he started laughing. It was contagious, and she couldn't help but join in.

"Well done. Well done indeed." Petre sounded pleased, even impressed, with her success. "You've done it. Most people who try give up in frustration after a few hours the first time they try. I've only met one person who did it faster, and she was...well, she was special. You should feel proud of yourself, truly." He chuckled.

Twitch continued to look with wonder at something. Skate guessed it must be some street performance, one that used lights or fire; every few seconds, different colors would flash across her friend's face as he stared and laughed. "Now then, it's time to pull back. Let the image recede from your focus."

"Why?" The image in the glass seemed to grow larger. If she had thought about it, she would have realized that she had moved closer to the crystal. She did not think about it.

"Because," Petre said gently, "you've been three hours at the crystal. You need to eat."

"Three hours?" She repeated the number without much energy. It hardly mattered to her.

"Yes, three hours."

Skate heard the flapping of wings and the clicking of legs, but that also hardly mattered. A single metallic clink caught her attention. The comforting warmth in her mind winked out like a candle. The image in the crystal ball began to waver and fog over.

"No!" she said, putting all of her effort back into concentrating. *Twitch. Twitch. Blond hair. Show me Twitch.* The obscuration of the picture slowed not at all. *Twitch. Don't lose Twitch. Show me Twitch.* His laughing face clarified for an instant; then everything in the ball faded to nothing. Skate was looking at her own scowling face and the distortion of the room she was in once more. She looked at the enhancer, which was lazily swinging on one of its axes. Rattle had taken its leg away and floated near the desk, staring blankly at her. "I wasn't done!" she said to it, rising from the chair much as Belamy had, though it did not scoot back so far.

"You needed to be," Petre said, no anger in his voice. "Three hours is quite long enough, especially for a neophyte to the practice such as yourself."

"Who are you to tell me what to do?" Heat was rising in her cheeks, and she could feel her arms shaking in impotent rage.

"Skate. Stop, and think. Did you hear what I said? It's been three hours."

She was about to ask "So what?" when she stopped and realized why that information mattered. The ache in her abdomen told her she was hungry, her mouth was painfully dry, and she needed the chamber pot very soon. Her eyes ached, and her rump was sore from the seat. "It was three hours?"

Petre closed his eyes and nodded. "Seeing, or clairvoyance, is a strain for even practiced users. It's outright dangerous for novices." Skate turned from Petre's blue glass sphere to the empty one she'd been engrossed with only moments earlier. She felt the urge to chuck the thing across the room; she felt betrayed by it. "People have collapsed—even died—of starvation and exhaustion, caught in the allure of the sight."

"Why?" She knelt down to eye level with Petre. "If it's so dangerous, why'd you let me do it?"

"I was here to guide you. So was Rattle—who has made, incidentally, a fine warm dish it learned from a traveling Deruvian chef, exiled from his homeland on suspicion of espionage. I never could determine whether he was guilty or not, but his food was amazing. Rattle's imitation will be perfect, as always."

Skate ignored the remarks about the food. "You said it wasn't easy to do. I thought magic took years to learn."

"It does, it does," he said, his azure-rimmed eyes bobbing up and down in a nod. "This is just a small bit of what magic can do, when learned and directed carefully. Anyone can do what you did with practice and the right tools. As you saw, the enhancer helps tremendously, and you need a specially made clairant device besides, like Barrison's crystal. It *can* be done without special tools—I've seen an old woods witch do it with a brackish puddle of water—but that takes a spell. *That* would be beyond you."

Skate pulled the chair back up to the desk. She folded her arms on the desk and put her head down, if for no other reason than to give her eyes a rest. "It didn't bother Mr. Belamy." Her voice was muffled by her arms, but she was heard.

"Barrison is an incredibly skilled and experienced wizard, and unliving besides. He doesn't get tired, sore, or hungry. It doesn't strain his eyes or his mind because neither of them are capable of being strained anymore. Being unbothered by clairvoyance is one of many perks of being what he is. In some ways, though, it can be even more dangerous for him for all that."

"What do you mean?" Her eyes were closed, but she was in no danger of falling asleep; her stomach and bladder were making sure of that.

"He could, if he had the urge to, sit in that chair and search and find and watch for as long as he wanted. He's told me that the draw—that feeling of needing to keep watching, keep looking no matter what—is just as strong as it always has been even though he's not really alive anymore. If he were to fall into it completely, he might gaze for days, weeks, or months at a time. He's done so before." Petre shook his head, sending the fog rolling around his prison in shimmering swirls. "He knows how dangerous it is. That he's willing to do this to find his friend's bullies speaks volumes about his determination on the matter."

"Is all magic that dangerous?"

"Yes. Not necessarily always in the same way, but all magic carries dangers with it. Think of a sword—or a knife decked in jewels, if you like," Petre said with a wink. "It's useful for all kinds of things—cut rope, defend yourself, skin a deer after a hunt. But it's dangerous, too, as you well know. Magic is much more useful than a knife, and it's correspondingly more dangerous. The study of magic can yield marvels but should not be undertaken lightly."

With monumental effort, Skate pulled her head up and stared at the crystal ball. Its interior was clear still. The enhancer sat nearby, its motion arrested by Rattle's intervening touch. *Would I have stepped away on my own?* It was entirely possible that she'd have been sitting here for hours more if they had not kept her from it. *"People have collapsed and died." Would I have been one?*

"I don't think I could've done it," she said, rubbing her eyes. "If it weren't for you and Rattle, I don't think I'd have walked away."

"Ah, well. Barrison would have returned eventually, and he'd have been able to pull you out of it. The danger was minimized, you see. That's why anyone who learns any magic must be taught and guided by a teacher. Self-teaching magic is asking for trouble, though some fools take the risk anyway, thinking the rewards of their studies worth the risk. Learning magic without a teacher is like biting into a hunk of meat only to find it painted stone: you've learned something, but it was probably not worth the pain it took to get there. Those who are self-taught have decided they like stone food just fine and have never turned back."

"Anybody who'd do this without help is stupid."

"Or desperate or too ambitious. People do insane things all the time, for reasons that seem good enough to them in the moment. I've given up trying to understand why people do the things they do; it's a waste of effort, and even when you find an answer, it's always unsatisfactory."

Skate excused herself to use the privy. Rattle came back into the room at the same time she did carrying food. She didn't recognize it by sight, and the smell was also unfamiliar, but not unpleasant. There was the comforting smell of garlic among the swirl of nose-tickling scents, so she quickly dug into the orangish goop. It was a soup, with hunks of meat (probably chicken) floating within. It was hearty and somehow sour.

"This is delicious." She slurped it down greedily, and Rattle looked on. "Thank you."

It turned toward the stairs.

"And, Rattle," she said, pushing the quickly emptied bowl aside, "thank you for earlier, too. For stopping—stopping it."

If Rattle was emotionally moved by her words of thanks, she saw no hint of it. It clicked once and moved up the stairs as planned.

Skate stood and took Petre toward the fireplace. She set him down and threw another log on before rejoining him. "Petre, I have a question."

"If this is about AB again, I—"

"No, it's not that." Based on Belamy's earlier reaction, she guessed that it must be a person: he had almost asked where she'd heard those initials; she was sure of it. However, she didn't want to press on that particular nerve anymore. If Petre wasn't going to tell her then, he certainly wasn't going to now. "It's something else."

When he arched an eyebrow and remained silent, she continued. "Is Mr. Belamy a good man?"

Petre started, somewhat taken aback by the question. "What? What do you mean?"

She sighed. "Nothing. Forget it."

"Wait—" His voice cut off because she'd left him on the desk. She took the steps two at a time, despite her fatigue. She poked her head into the library and interrupted Rattle's reading.

"Go grab Petre off the desk. He probably wants a better view." Without waiting for a responding click, she turned toward her room and eased the door shut.

What am I gonna do? The way she saw it, she had at least three distinct problems of three totally different kinds with no easy answers. First, she needed to figure out how to keep Belamy from finding any more information on the Ink without being culpable for the interference. Second, she needed to figure out how to get Gherun's books back to him anonymously, since if Ossertine had been any indication, just leaving them at the door would lead to complications. Third and most troubling, she needed to figure out what to do about Belamy and the Ink overall. The first problem was professional, a question of how to protect her business interests and those of her crew. The second was practical, a puzzle she'd be able to work on and solve given the time and attention. The last problem, though, was moral, and it weighed heavily upon her.

It was more than a simple question of right and wrong. It was a question of who she was. On some level, she understood that her choice was to be a defining crisis of her life, that to choose one way or the other would take her down avenues she would not readily find herself free of. To defy the Ink was unthinkable; to betray her teacher was unbearable. She could not make either choice without breaking something inside her, and she dreaded that more than she could describe. No matter what she did or put her mind to, she could not pull herself from thinking of it and dreading the crisis. Momentary distractions were all she'd been able to find: stealing, reading, walking, and the newest one given in the crystal ball.

Another such distraction shook her from her musings. A thump on the window left a spray of white powder behind. A second snowball hit before she had a chance to get there, exploding with a harder thud that revealed the hunks of ice smuggled within.

Skate opened the window and looked into the half-expected face of Twitch, the glow of the smile she'd seen in the crystal flitting around the corners of his mouth. He waved her down and pointed in the general direction of their nearby familiar meeting spot. She nodded and closed the window.

Skate rubbed her eyes before she climbed back down the stairs. Rattle was in the library; it must have quickly bobbed its way down and back, because Petre was not where she'd left him. She stuffed her boots on and wrapped her coat around her before stepping back into the cold.

She trudged across the street, past the street lamps toward the spot. The flickering candles within each lamp worked with the others to provide a mostly steady orange glow for her trek, helping her avoid the already frozen puddles left by the melted snow. Judging by the renewed chill in the air, those puddles were likely to remain as they were now for a few days.

That suspicion was reinforced as small flecks of white began to drift down from above. The remaining large piles of snow would become monstrous mountains soon enough.

Twitch was below the dingy awning, peering out at the night sky and grimacing. He nodded at her when she approached, but resumed his skyward grouching almost immediately. "Gonna be a l-long winter if this keeps up." His voice was low. He was talking that way on purpose; even with his attempt to conceal it, the crack in the voice was unmistakable.

"Yeah, and it probably will." *He's laughed himself hoarse.* Whatever he'd seen must have a been a sight to behold. "What's the deal? Why are you knocking at my mark's window while I'm in the house?"

"Your mark? Listen to her," he said to an audience of none— "when we were in it t-together just a few scant days ago!" He smiled, and his left cheek twitched violently for the effort. "I came to tell you about something amazing that I-I got to see. There was a street performance today—"

"That was the best thing you've ever seen."

"Yeah, and I—"

"Laughed harder than you have in months because it was so great and had magic." The appeal of sitting in front of the crystal to see struck her in a different light; being able to know things she shouldn't was pretty great, but seeing the stunned confusion on Twitch's face was even better.

"How do you know? Were you there?"

"I got my ways, kid," she said, snapping her fingers at him. She only called him "kid" when she was trying to frazzle him. She didn't actually think too much about their slight age difference. For one thing, it didn't really matter; they were close enough to the same for them to get along. For another, despite being bigger and older than she was, he was willing to do what she wanted most of the time when it came to jobs. Belamy's house had been her idea, not his; and whether he'd thought it smart or not, he'd gone along with it without any hesitation.

"Whatever, doesn't matter," he said, shaking his head. "The point is, you gotta come see this thing. They said they're doing one more show tonight, so 'be ready and bring your friends.' I can show you where the next one is."

"What's so great about it?"

"I've never seen anything like it." His low voice cracked, and in his excitement, he seemed not to care. "The lights, the music, the jokes—it's just..." Words failed him, but the message was plain. His scowl was nowhere to be seen, replaced by the shadow of blissful awe.

"Music?" In watching Twitch through the crystal, she'd heard echoes of the chatter and laughter of the crowd and her friend, but she had heard no music.

"Yeah, there's music. So m-much more, though, Skate. Come on, you'll love it."

She scratched her head. It was late, and she was tired. It had been a much longer day than she'd wanted already. Still, the pleading look on Twitch's face was overpowering. He'd never cared for street shows before—"beggars with better tools," he'd called the performers—but this one must have been something truly special, because she'd heard nothing but admiration for it.

"Yeah, okay." The acceptance split his face into a wide grin, and he waved her out into the night, snow falling steadily on them both as they went.

CHAPTER 19

IN WHICH A LADY WITH A LISP ALMOST
FALLS OVER, A TALE IS TOLD THAT NO ONE
KNOWS, AND A WARNING IS DELIVERED.

She pulled her hood up soon after they took off into the night; the snow was stinging her face because she was having to move so fast to keep up with Twitch. He moved with a fervor she'd only seen from him when on the run from the Guard, and she'd never fully appreciated how difficult it was to keep up with him when he was in a hurry. Even though crowds were fewer than during the day, the night was young and the roads barely covered with a new layer of white powder, so there were still plenty of people to negotiate around on their way toward the performance. Twitch almost knocked over an old peasant woman in his haste, sending her tumbling into Skate's way as they went.

"Thtupid braths!" she croaked through the four teeth left in her head, shaking the knobby stick she'd been using to balance herself. "You coulda kilt me!"

"Sorry!" was all Skate said as she scrambled on, throwing an apologetic wave back at the old crone. Twitch didn't acknowledge the cry, but kept on running at his breakneck pace.

They were headed toward the slums. This made no sense, as buskers couldn't make any money off of people who had none, but the conclusion was inevitable as they left the vestigial splendor of the Old Town behind and began to skirt past the sordid shacks of the destitute. There were fires burning in hastily dug pits at odd intervals, where the

219

desperate and the uncared-for huddled together to stave off the cold. *There'll be lives lost tonight,* Skate thought as she considered the cold and the utter lack of protective clothing or blankets available to the people living here.

That was one thing she owed the Ink, she mused. *They kept me from starving and dying.* She did not have to sleep in the street if she didn't want to, and she never had, after she'd taken up with them. The safe houses were open to members in good (or even iffy) standing. Food was available. If she hadn't joined the Ink, she'd have been out here, wandering the paths of the worst kind of poverty, desperate for heat and food in the dead of winter. *And apparently being treated to the most amazing street show ever performed in the streets of the city of Caribol.*

Skate shouted at Twitch to wait. She bent over, her hands on her knees in order to catch her breath. It came out in translucent clouds that disappeared a few inches from her face. Twitch jogged back, his cloth-wrapped foot tapping impatiently on the packed snow while he waited.

Skate stared at the ground to collect her thoughts and her air. It was hard to see, now. There weren't any lamps in this part of the city, and lights were scarce, a luxury few could afford. Even the moons weren't helpful, being too low in the sky to shed much light. There were not many actual streets in the slum, and the Keepers certainly didn't bother with this part of town; they only came to help when a fire threatened to spread to other parts of the city, which rarely happened. The slummers had, for generations, gotten used to dealing with things their own way, and their destitute community worked internally on all emergencies, knowing that help was unlikely to ever come.

The Ink did great business here, especially in the selling of alcohol and a dangerous substance called "opum." Though Skate had never seen the stuff herself, she'd seen its effects often enough: users became very drowsy, usually barely able to stand. The Ink operated several houses in the quarter—dingy wooden structures that were nevertheless some of the best the area had to offer, and that existed solely as a repository for the comatose bodies of users. Skate didn't know where opum came from, but she knew the trade routes into the port were the primary source of it. It wasn't made here. Whenever the denizens of the slums did manage to get money, most of it that didn't go toward the sparest of food went to either drink or opum. For some, the food was an afterthought. Starvation was common.

"You ready? It's n-not much farther."

She nodded, and the run began anew. Soon, they were nearing a clearing in the tents and hovels, in the middle of which stood a hastily thrown-together platform. The clearing turned out to be more of a shallow pit; it probably filled with water in the spring and summer. The snow had surprisingly been cleared away here, and the brown dirt was clearly visible for the torches tied to stakes around the clearing. No one was on the platform, but there was a homemade stool on one of the corners.

"Is this where it'll be?" Skate asked.

"Oh, aye, girl, thish'll be it," slurred an old man sitting at the edge of the crowd. He was dressed in rags, and stared off past where she and Twitch were standing. "The mushic'll come, and the lightsh, too. Bet on it." He fell into a delirious cackle that sounded like it was tearing at his throat to get out. He clapped his hands as he laughed, showing a tooth-less grin. He continued looking past the pair, having clearly forgotten he was talking to anyone. Twitch rolled his eyes and pointed to a spot relatively free of people in the impromptu amphitheater.

They walked over and squatted down, rubbing their hands and shoulders to stave off the cold. It was not easy to stay warm, as the set-ting sun seemed to herald the return of more and more snow. It was melting as soon as it hit the ground here, so there was no danger for the time being that the area would become choked with the stuff. The cold and snow were also not much of a deterrent to fans and curious pass-ersby. Dozens of people were milling about, chatting, passing around bottles, or trying to stay warm while they waited for the performance of a lifetime to repeat itself.

"So, what is the show, exactly?"

"It's music and lights, like the c-crazy old guy said. That doesn't describe it well enough, though. It's hard t-to explain. Good news is, you're about to s-see for yourself." Twitch grinned and nodded toward someone near the stage.

There were three people who did not appear to belong to the slums stepping onto the platform. The first was a woman all in black who took a seat on the stool. In front of her sat a huge instrument that looked like a fiddle but made three times larger. She stood it on the ground in front of her and held the bow in her other hand. She had a rather wide face, and her black hair was pulled back into a tight knot, giving her a severe look when coupled with her stern expression.

The second was a man in a fine brown coat and plumed hat, who made a point to pat the back of every person he passed on the way to the dais. He had a thin goatee, one that might have been mistaken for being penciled on if it had not jutted out from his chin. His boots jingled when he walked; the buckles seemed to wink in the torchlight.

The third person was the strangest of the three: they were wearing a very heavy fur coat that obscured the shape of their body. Their head was wrapped in a very long scarf with only a thin slit at the eyes for the sake of its wearer's vision. All of this prevented identification as either a man or a woman. This person did not speak to anyone as he—she?— stepped up to the platform.

When all three were onstage, the man in the feather hat raised his gloved hands and waved the crowd closer. When he spoke, the crowd immediately quieted.

"Come one, come all! Gather around for a repeat performance of *The Tales of Beuford Hall*. For those who have yet to see this humble show of ours, we say 'Welcome!' To those who are coming back for more, we say 'Welcome back!'" He flashed a toothy grin and winked to the crowd at large. His voice was deep and booming. He reminded Skate of some of the hucksters she'd seen selling oils and unguents to crowds before skipping town the next day. For some reason, that didn't cause her to distrust him. "The *Tales* are thrillers, don't you doubt, but you're in for a treat this evening, ladies and gentlemen. For not only shall the stories be told—by none other than yours truly, Carsen Tillby," he said with a bow and a flourish, "but they shall be accompanied by music provided by the lovely Miss Amanda, and images—*moving* images—designed and created by the inestimable Kibo the Magnificent!" At each of their introductions, the other per- formers acknowledged their parts: Amanda played a flourish on her instrument, which resonated with a deep, rich echo, and Kibo flashed lights and smoke out of her—his?—sleeves. "I must warn you, dear people," Tillby continued, his deep voice growing serious, "that the

Tales are sometimes dark and dreadful; and if you've not the stomach for such fare, you should depart before the story begins—else, you may find yourself too engaged to leave!"

His eyes roved over the crowd. No one left. *He didn't expect them to*, Skate thought as his winning grin showed itself again. "You've been warned. Without further ado, make yourself as comfortable as you may, and prepare to enjoy *The Tales of Beuford Hall!*" He clapped his hands, and immediately, Miss Amanda began to draw her bow across the strings and Kibo brushed smoke and lights out of his or her sleeves. The light took shape in the sky, creating a young couple in a field.

The next thing Skate knew about the show was that it was over. The audience was showing its appreciation through applause, which was all such a crowd could hope to offer. She shook her head and joined in the clapping.

She was standing as she had been before the show started. She didn't know what had happened, other than that the show had gone on for some time (some of the torches were burning very low, and drifts of snow had formed on the ground), and that she'd loved every minute of it. Tillby was thanking the crowd repeatedly, and had swung the plumed hat off his head into a deep bow. He began to shake the hands of those nearest the stage—people who were reaching out to him, hoping to get a handshake or even just to touch him. Kibo and Amanda did not go toward the crowd at all, but stood and sat respectively, both impassive and unnoticed.

Skate shook her head again and stopped clapping. *What was the story? Who were the people in the field?* Beside her, Twitch was still clapping and whooping along with the crowd. There was something familiar about the feeling she had, but it was slipping away like a dream in the morning. She lifted her head and focused on Miss Amanda. *What was the music like?* She couldn't remember any of it. She tried to hum a tune from the show and couldn't come up with anything. She only knew she'd liked it.

Skate stood and tugged on Twitch's sleeve. He continued whooping and clapping, as did most of the rest of the crowd, so she pulled on his shoulder to bring his ear to her mouth. "What was it about?"

He shook his head, his gleeful expression unchanged, and continued clapping. Skate also shook her head, but did not resume clapping.

How could she remember nothing of it? How could the music have been good—so good that she was sure she'd never heard anything like it—but she couldn't remember the smallest bit of any tune played? The story, too, had been something incredible, but she knew nothing about it. How could that be? And images! No one in the history of performing had crafted such magical illusions!

But what had they been?

This didn't make sense, and she didn't trust any of it. Twitch had finally stopped his applause as Tillby and the others dismounted the stage, moving roughly together through the thinnest part of the crowd. Twitch was laughing, and he put a hand to his eye to wipe away wetness that had developed there. *Something is wrong.* Skate had known this boy for the better part of four years, but had never so much as seen his eyes water, either in mirth or in misery. She didn't try saying anything to him, but moved to where the performers were trying to push through their chosen patch of people. Tillby was glad-handing, all smiles and compliments to the paupers who were eager to meet him and thank him. Several of the women were batting eyes and adjusting sleeves. A little ahead of Tillby, the other two performers were making much quicker progress, ignoring the sparse words of thanks and admiration that came their way.

Skate jostled through the crowd toward them. "Hey, hey!" she shouted when she got near, having shouldered past a handful of people who'd given up on meeting Tillby and were dispersing into the dark paths of the slums. "Hey!" The third shout got Miss Amanda's attention, and she sneered when she saw who was shouting at her. She and Kibo quickened their pace into the dark. Skate reacted in kind, and soon overtook the pair. She tugged on Miss Amanda's black dress hem, and the woman finally stopped and faced her.

"What do you want?" Her wide face was fixed in an expression of irritation. Kibo, who had seemed not to have heard Skate before this point, turned to watch the exchange between the musician and the young girl.

Skate noticed with a jolt of vague surprise that she still couldn't see the eyes within the scarf. "What was it?"

"What was what?" Miss Amanda's voice was low and unrefined, a voice of a woman who'd lived in spare conditions all her life.

"What was the show?"

Miss Amanda looked to Kibo, who turned to return her glance, before both returned their attention to Skate. "It was called *The Tales of Beuford Hall.* Check back tomorrow for another performance. Tomorrow will be our last one for at least a season."

"I know what it's called. What was it?"

Amanda's irritation boiled into impatience. "Girl, I don't know what you're babbling about, but I have no time for silly games." She turned to go, and Skate pulled her hem again. Miss Amanda whipped around, snatching the piece of her dress out of Skate's hands.

If looks could kill, Skate mused, *this one would be hanged for murder on a daily basis.* "Why can't I remember any of it?" The question sounded insane to her as she asked it, but it was what she could make no sense of. This time, Amanda's and Kibo's shared glance carried something that looked like fear.

"If you want someone to explain the story to you, I'm sure some-one else can—"

"They can't; I've asked. You know they can't. Why?"

Miss Amanda scoffed and turned. Skate reached out to pull her back again, but stopped short when waves of pain shot up her arm. The pain lasted only a few moments, but she screamed. She felt like she'd dipped her hand into a pot of boiling water.

Kibo turned and followed Amanda. With the torchlight of the paltry amphitheater now distant, it took only a few moments for the pair to dissolve into shadow.

Skate rubbed her hand, not knowing what to do with any of this information. The pain was quickly fading, but she found she needed to rub for the sake of warmth as much as for soothing. She walked slowly back to where the performance had taken place, but Tillby was gone. Some stragglers remained, perhaps hoping for an encore performance, but most had gone out into the night, back to their huts or ragged blan-kets, or in search of awnings to protect them from the snow. Twitch was gone, too. With nothing else to do, Skate began the long trek back to Belamy's home.

The late-night journey was a dull one, and it caused her more than once to consider just tossing herself into an alleyway to sleep through the night. In addition to how boring it was to walk alone in the snow in freezing conditions, she had to deal with the strain of being careful not to slip and fall; the clean stones of the Old Town were a dangerous place for snow to be falling, and her legs ached from the effort of constantly reacting to each small slip of her feet. She didn't even have the energy to puzzle over what had happened at the performance.

When she got back to Belamy's house, Skate saw that the fire had burned down to smoldering embers in the hearth. She rushed over and heaved two logs onto the fire. The coals were still very hot, and it was only a few minutes before the wood was crackling vigorously, renewing the orange light that usually filled the room. She briefly considered changing the color to the only shade she knew the words for, but decided against it. It was cold enough in the room already without going through extra work to make it look colder.

Skate was warming her hands by the fire when Belamy's front door creaked open again, and in walked the owner himself. He looked much as he had when he'd stormed out hours earlier, though his expression was simply neutral rather than bitter and angry. He also had an impressive layer of snow sticking to his clothing and hair.

Skate didn't move away from the fire, but waved at him as he came in, a motion he returned with only the smallest reluctance.

"My word, what are you still doing up?" His question was probably a point of genuine interest, but the way he avoided her gaze when he asked it probably meant he was asking as a way to avoid talking about something else.

"I took a walk." She wanted to talk about what had happened at the show, but didn't think this was the best time to broach the subject. "Stayed out longer than I meant to. What about you? Where'd you go after...earlier." *Nice save, dimwit,* she thought as Belamy broke off the brief eye contact he'd managed to establish.

"I talked to some more people. Found out why nobody's wanting to talk with me: these hooligans have wizards of their own. Fairly dangerous ones, it would seem. This isn't just a trio of low-principled ruffians. It's an organization, one that's involved in all sorts of nasty business. I don't have a name yet, but I've managed to gather a sense of what they're about." He shook his head, sending small clods of snow flying; the stroke of his goatee achieved much the same. He noticed all at once how much of the white stuff he'd accumulated, and began to brush it off onto the stone floor in fussy swipes. "That they've managed to ensnare the like of Jack Gherun into their web of illicit criminality is a testament to the scope of their influence, whoever they are. Lady Flandel is a woman of no small standing and influence, but Jack's money outweighs most bloodlines in the city by itself, never mind his pedigree."

"Huh." She wondered how Belamy'd managed to piece all of this together in the span of roughly half a day, but she didn't want to seem too interested; in her exhausted state, she didn't trust herself not to give herself away, especially since tiredness was a disadvantage that the old man did not have to deal with. "What does them having wizards have to do with anything?"

"Most of the time, those of us who have any appreciable skill at magic have a distinct advantage over those who don't. If you're facing another wizard, though, or are faced with the prospect of facing more than one at once? Well, then, the wizard's advantage disappears, and he's among peers—in this case, peers who want to take his money and keep him from talking about the group to anyone who comes around asking questions. This group must make extraordinary amounts of money in order to be able to afford to keep more than one of us fed, especially since anyone who knows how to cast spells could easily afford to sustain themselves through honest work. The danger of a life of crime would push many away from such associations...unless, of course, the aforementioned fees were high enough to be irresistible to wizards and witches with, shall we say, dubious standards."

"Magic isn't cheap," Skate muttered, recalling a conversation she'd had with Haman. Magic was an incredibly difficult skill to learn in the first place, he'd said, and that meant that people who could do it could charge whatever they wanted for the services asked. The Ink did, in fact, keep contracts out with several wizards in the city, though the Bosses alone knew just how many. Most of them weren't like Haman— they weren't members of the organization, but were involved in a more-or-less mercenary capacity. The only other known magic-user who was actually a member of the Ink was one of the Big Boss's small crew, a trio of people he kept around himself at all times. Their names were on a need-to-know basis, and people like Skate didn't need to know.

"Quite true, quite true," Belamy responded, satisfied that the snow was now off him entirely. He looked at her and narrowed his eyes. Skate's instincts almost took over; her muscles tensed and prepared to shoot her out the door. She forced herself to relax, though, when she saw concern in that expression rather than suspicion. "Skate, are you feeling all right?"

"Yeah." The lie came easily, as many did for her, because she didn't really think before answering. In truth, she was exhausted from the trek, cold from the air, and confused from the show.

"Come, come," Belamy said, waving her toward himself, "let me look at you."

"What?"

"I think there's something wrong with you," he said, not waiting for her to comply but walking over to her. "Does your mind feel foggy?"

"N-no," she said, leaning back as he bent over to stare directly into her eyes.

"Skate, I'm serious. Is there something wrong? If you're not aware of it, you may be in more danger. Is your memory fine? Any blank spaces? Do you know who I am?" He started speaking slowly at this last question, as if she might not understand his words.

"Stop!" She pushed him back, but not with enough force to actually move him anywhere. He did stand up fully in response. "Okay, yeah, something weird happened on my walk."

She explained her trip, omitting all parts that involved Twitch. Belamy interrupted her only once to ask why she had been going to the slums.

"It's where I'm from. I'll go there sometimes if I'm out wandering."

He motioned for her to continue. When she described the performers, he frowned but said nothing. The frown grew more pronounced as she finished explaining her attempt to get answers from Miss Amanda and Kibo. "I didn't know what else to do, and I was tired, so I came back here."

He brought a hand to his chin, tapping a thin finger as he thought. Since he didn't seem to want to talk, she filled the silence with some of her own thoughts from the past hour or so.

"I thought it weird that they didn't get any money from the show.

They weren't even performing for people who had money to begin with. Plus, why were two of them so quick to scurry away without explaining themselves?"

"Very weird, indeed. It sounds like they may have been using some form of magic to hypnotize the crowd. In fact, I'm sure of it; I detected hints of the spell that did it clinging to you. It's how I knew something was wrong."

"Yeah, it's like when I was—" She cut herself off, not entirely sure that she wasn't about to reveal something she shouldn't. She'd suddenly remembered what the sensation felt like, and in her excitement had forgotten to run the thought process through her usual list of dos and don'ts regarding what to talk to Belamy about. *Too late now,* she realized when the old man returned his too-curious gaze to her. "When I was using your glass earlier."

"My glass? What are—" His eyes widened with surprise. "You used my scrying glass? You were able to use it?"

She shuffled from one foot to the other, though her discomfort did not keep her from making eye contact. "I had help. Petre walked me through what to do. Plus, you left the gold thing going when you...left." She wanted to call it what it was—storming out in a huff—but decided that diplomacy was needed here. "So, I used it to look for someone I know, and it worked. But I was doing it for hours, and coming back from the watching was almost painful, because I felt I was going to miss something, even if it was something small or stupid. Sorry, I shouldn't have done it without your permission."

"No, you shouldn't. However, that you were able to do it at all is remarkable." His countenance had shifted, this time to one of careful consideration—silver eyebrows raised slightly, a small smile playing at the edge of his mouth. "We'll come back to it. I want to figure out what these performers were doing. You say you can remember nothing of the story?"

She shook her head. "Nobody could. I asked."

Belamy shook his in turn. "I've never heard of these *Tales of Beuford Hall*, but I've been away from the singers and players for decades. It must be a newer grand story that I've yet to have the chance to witness or read. Yes, I must conclude that they were using magic to dull the senses of the crowd, especially since this Kibo fellow was there providing lights that no one can remember. But to what end?"

"Not money. Or popularity."

"No, neither of those, which are found easier and more plentiful elsewhere. They could perform even here in the Old Town and have a better time of it than what they'd find in the residents of the slums. Why, indeed, perform for those who have nothing to give?" He rubbed his chin, lost in thought, then shrugged. "Perhaps they just like casting magic on people. Maybe they're impish tricksters of some sort, and we aren't in on the joke."

The image of Miss Amanda's stern face and Kibo's inscrutable one, all cloth and shadow, flashed across her mind. "I don't think they were joking, and they were surprised to find me there to talk to after the show. It did not look like fun for any of them, with the exception of the one who did the talking, Tillby."

Neither of them had an answer to that puzzle, so they sat in silence for several moments, considering. Upstairs, a page turned.

"Maybe it's practice."

Belamy perked up at her words, so she continued.

"Like, they're planning to do something like this with a crowd with money, but they're practicing on the people in the dumps to make sure they've got it right."

"That's a possibility. It makes sense, really. If they tried this and it went wrong in another part of Caribol, they'd have the Guards called on them very quickly. Whatever they're up to, I need you to promise me something." He bent over to be at eye level with her, staring deep into her eyes again, as if searching for something. "In the next few days, if you have some inexplicable urge to do something strange— attack someone, break something, go somewhere odd, anything like that—examine that urge as thoroughly as you can. Fight it if you need to. Hypnotism can be a dangerous thing for its victims, lying in wait for hours or days at a time before being set off. If you *were* hypnotized, you may still be in danger from the magician. The whole crowd might be. Just be careful of it, yes?"

Skate nodded, leaning back a little to get him out of her face. "Sure, you got it. I won't do nothing weird." She put her hands up in surrender. "Nothing more weird than normal, anyway."

Belamy stood and smirked. "Very well. Let's return, then, to the topic of my crystal ball." He turned toward the desk and took his seat behind it. "Petre encouraged you to do this? To use my precious and very valuable scrying devices without my knowledge or consent?"

She nodded. "Don't be mad at him, though. I'm the one who did it."

"You did, indeed. And you were able to see something in it? Truly?"

"Yes." The conversation had taken a different turn than she'd been expecting, and it had caught her off-guard. "It took a while, but with Petre's help, I was able to find a friend out and about in the city."

"Explain what you saw." He leaned back with an elbow propped on the armrest, his head against his hand.

"Uh...I saw my friend. He was smiling at something and pushing through a crowd. I couldn't see what he was looking at, though. I could only see him and a foot or two around him. Petre told me to try concentrating on 'moving' the image, and I did. Didn't help me figure out where he was, though. The view was too close to him."

"I see." Belamy showed some measure of surprise at her retelling of the events. "And how long did this take you?"

"I didn't know while I was doing it, but when I snapped out of it, I think it was three hours. Petre and Rattle had to pull me out," she admitted, lowering her gaze and drawing on the floor with her foot, leaving barely detectable swirls in the thin layer of dust.

"My word," Belamy muttered, "you really managed to do it, didn't you?" He chuckled to himself, a dry noise not unlike a cough. "You'd have to have done, in order to know how hard it is to stop." He ticked the enhancer with an outstretched finger, setting it lazily spinning once or twice before it began to resettle. "Yes, one must be ever so careful when seeing afar. Of course, for me, the only danger is squandered time that could be otherwise spent reading and learning. When I was younger, though..." He shook his head. A dark cloud sank his features—a memory of shame?—but it passed quickly. He laughed again. "I spent so long at the ball that I passed out. On my way down, I hit my head." He pointed to his left, at the corner of his desk. There was a slight stain there, darker than the wood around it. It was almost imperceptible. "I would have died had I not been found. You shouldn't ever try this without someone else around. It could be the death of you, no matter what you find within the glass."

She nodded. *I would've stayed there forever, watching Twitch even up to where he chucked snow at my window.* "Yeah."

"All magic is dangerous, Skate. Better that you learn that now, before it's had a chance to do any lasting damage to you. It's unforgiving, and even the simplest applications of it take years of study to perform with any measure of safety. As long as you're aware of the danger," he added with a smirk, "you should be fine. But never charge in unawares where the Craft is concerned. Many before you have done so, and it's left them scarred or obliterated. I'd hate to see the same happen to you."

Skate fought hard to avoid screwing up her face in confusion at the kind words. This was the man who'd stormed out in a huff hours ago because she'd asked questions about some letters. *Now he's expressing hope for my safety?*

She must have been slow to hide her confusion, because Belamy coughed and lowered his own gaze to the floor. "I…apologize for earlier. You had no idea what you were asking, or how it could possibly have upset me. You see…" He paused, then shook his head. He raised his gaze from the floor. "Well, it can wait until morning. I imagine you're tired."

She was. Her lids were very heavy. She nodded, but said, "I'd still like to know."

"In the morning. I promise. Off with you, now. Make sure you have the vent open; I'll keep the fire going. And remember," he added as she made her way up the stairs, "be mindful of anything strange you might want to do. I don't want you trying to burn the house down because some street people put you in a trance." He pulled a book from the shelf and began to read it. It was one of Gherun's.

CHAPTER 20

Skate was in front of the fire, wrapped up in the blanket she'd used as an improvised book bag, and holding a hot cup of coffee prepared by Rattle, when Belamy began to tell his story. He was seated in a chair, facing the fire. Rattle was resting in his lap, unmoving as the old man kept a hand on the glassy surface of its eye-body. Petre was also downstairs, though he asked to be on the desk rather than with everyone.

When Belamy spoke, his voice was calm and measured, as if he were reciting a story he'd learned through rote memorization. His eyes did not leave the fireplace.

#♉♌♎

You asked what AB is, and you asked innocently enough. I'm sure Petre counseled you not to, but the curiosity of a child is rarely turned aside by such warnings. I reacted much more harshly than I should have. The question caught me off-guard, as it is something I have not heard for many years and have grown completely unaccustomed to talking about. There was a time when it was all I could talk about, when I took the pain and moved it toward some more productive purpose, a goal to find justice, to set right what went wrong. It consumed my thoughts for decades. It's the reason I became what I am today, the reason I was not ready to let my life end before dealing with the trouble of my soul, the burden I refused to renounce.

You see, AB is not just a pair of letters. They are initials, carved into the desk upstairs by one of the most important people in my life. Alphetta Belamy. She was my student. She was my daughter.

She was a wonderfully gifted young girl, a child whose sharp mind was matched only by her adventurous spirit. I was as likely to find her climbing the walls as to catch her at studies that no one had set her to. She was like her mother that way; Eliza was a flame, a passionate woman, and brilliant to boot. It was impossible for her to be content without something to chase, something to conquer and strive for. The only reason I ever left the house in those days was to follow her on her schemes. Her loss during Alphetta's birth was a blow I did not know that I would be able to recover from. Perhaps seeing so much of her mother in Alphetta helped, or perhaps it was simply the passage of time. I don't know. Eventually, though, the pain became less crippling, and Eliza became a companion again in memory, a refuge to return to when talking to myself, a mental stronghold of comfort and support as I raised our daughter alone.

As Alphetta grew, she began to take an interest in magic, which I had feared. I had hoped instead she would seek another occupation, another obsession to excel at. She could have done much fantastic work, regardless of what she set her mind to, but she was adamant about becoming a witch. My refusal to take her on as apprentice, I think, wounded her. I knew that I was taking a razor to her dearest hopes, but I could do no other. The study of magic was too dangerous, even under my protective eye. I could not bear to risk losing her as I had her mother. She did not understand, and I did not have the words to make her. I had taught her to read and write, which she did with exceptional skill, but I could not teach her this. Maybe if I had taken her on, things would be different. I have often thought about that; even now, I wonder. It is my deepest regret, to have turned her away out of fear of her or my own failure.

I had an apprentice at the time. I think that irritated her to no end, that I would teach these arcane mysteries to another, but withhold them from her. She could not—or would not—understand my actions for what they were, did not see them as protection but as cruel deprivation. Petre Hangman had been under our roof for a little under a year by then, and was showing promise. His father had taught him the basics of literacy, so that part of his education went by exceedingly fast, and the elder Hangman had agreed to pay handsomely for his son's education in the study and practice of magic. During those days, before the war started, hangmen did well in general; the crown became paranoid before deciding war to be the necessary course of action, and anyone suspected of disloyalty went to the noose, as did thieves, murderers, brawlers, and the like. So, Petre's sire could afford the high price.

Petre was older than Alphetta, but only by three or four years. That first year with us was rather chilly between them, as she found him irritating and he found her somewhat haughty. After I refused her request, though, the relationship warmed. I think that probably had much to do with the fact that they were the only two other people here in the house, and I made a convenient target for their shared frustrations. For Alphetta, an overprotective and stifling father had kept her from her heart's desire. For Petre, a demanding and stern master was expecting excellence in all things at all times. I may have pushed them together by my decisions.

A wizard's training takes years; the best and brightest can learn to master the basics of the practice in as little as four, but that's a rarity. Petre would be done with my tutelage in no sooner than seven or eight years—a respectable amount of time, mind you. In his fifth year—I think it was the year that Alphetta saw her fifteenth birthday—the war began. Petre, I know, has already told you about my military career. I won't reveal anything more specific about the time period, as it's nothing I'm particularly proud of, and it has little to do with our topic of conversation today. I bring it up only to explain that my military service compelled me to take two young people out into dangerous territory. I could not leave Alphetta here alone; the city was dangerous then. It is now, but that was before the Guard had been officially organized. Law and order are vapor and images, something to be chased after and eventually caught, but back then they were impossible. I also could not leave behind my promising young apprentice, whose father had passed during his training. He wanted to continue his education, and his father had paid well before his passing for the opportunity for his son to learn the highest of Arts.

So, in command of scores of men and women, and with a bitter young daughter and a promising young pupil in tow, I began to aid the conquest. I did not know it for what it was at the time, but the nature of the conflict would come up again and again over the following months, with it becoming more and more apparent that this was not a war I was fighting on behalf of the unduly attacked, but a war of pain and death—a cold-hearted push by the nobility to squeeze money out of our neighbors during negotiations.

The disgust I felt when I fully realized what the war was being fought for stuck with me, and I carry it to this day. One must always be skeptical of the powerful, Skate. Kings, merchant lords, even high priests—it doesn't matter the stripe of their power. The allure of strength, money, and influence is irresistible, and those who have a measure of such things only ever want more. I found that to be true of myself. When I did finally realize that I'd been fighting—killing and ordering killing, shedding blood and making widows and orphans of soldiers wrapped up in a conflict that wasn't even theirs—in order to line the nobility's pockets, it almost broke me. Because I *had known,* Skate. Or at least, if I hadn't known, I hadn't questioned it too much. I had not bothered to investigate the causes of the conflict, had not thought to even ask if it had been worth fighting over.

The worst events of the war were the executions of our own. Some men fled out of fear or desire for glory elsewhere. If caught, they were to be punished by edict of the king, and his edicts were cruel. The method of execution for the crime of desertion was death by exposure. I did this only once, though I knew in my heart it was wrong. He was a very young man. I still remember his name: Hugo. I did what I was ordered to do, though I knew it was needlessly cruel. I was happy to be of service, happy to be a war hero, happy to serve my king and country in battle. I had power, and I rushed to use it. I brushed aside my conscience, and the boy paid with his life.

I'm drifting off course; I said I wouldn't talk much of the war, and I've made a liar of myself. During precious breaks in the fighting, when I could, I continued Petre's education. I spent time with Alphetta, though she had grown somewhat cold to me in the intervening years, never forgiving me for my refusal. She didn't hate me. I know that, and she told me as much, but the wound never healed.

They were never in danger; I made sure of that. Miles behind the battlefield were they, always. I made sure neither saw the horror of combat, nor made themselves targets for it. It was during this time that I made Rattle in an ill-advised foray into experimental research.

A few months after Rattle's creation, the war was over. The king had gotten what he'd wanted, so it was time to come home. The awards and honors were doled out. I accepted mine, a fine set of crimson robes woven through with protective magic, though I cared nothing for it. The war and everything to do with it was abhorrent to me. I still have those robes, as a sort of insurance policy should I ever need a vast sum of money all at once. My daughter, my apprentice, and I returned home.

I should have been paying closer attention during those years, but I had been so preoccupied with the war effort that the relationship burgeoning right under my nose might as well have been happening on a different world for all the notice I took of it. You see, my daughter and my apprentice had fallen in love. I'm sure they were doing their best to hide it from me, and I'm equally sure that their efforts would have appeared comical to me had I not been so distracted.

As it turned out, though, I *was* distracted, and I only came to know of the true nature of their relationship by degrees. At first, I took note of their much-improved level of conversation. More than merely trying to be polite around one another, they conversed as friends might, and my old heart rejoiced at the idea of the pair of them becoming better acquainted. I found out later, from Petre, that they had already fallen in love by the time I noticed their warming dispositions.

Another fault of mine; after the war, I spent most of my time alone, reading, studying, mixing in the basement. I did not want the troubles of the world to bother me again, and I was ready to live the rest of my days in retired obscurity surrounded by stories and histories and theories. Had I been more active, had I been more tuned in to the lives of those nearest me, I may have prevented the folly that happened thereafter.

You see, I would not have minded had Alphetta and Petre decided to marry; he was a fine young man, and she a healthy young woman by that time, and both driven toward greatness and ever-greater heights that their union on its own terms would have been a fine development in its own right. But what they worked even harder to conceal from me was that my apprentice had done something incredibly foolish: taken an apprentice.

He was not ready to teach; he was barely ready to perform any magic of his own. In reality, all he was doing was regurgitating our lessons to Alphetta in private, so that in actuality I was serving as a master of two, though I'd no knowledge of that fact. I did begin to get suspicious, though. Snippets of overheard conversation. Lingering sidelong glances after seemingly innocent remarks. I think they must have sensed my growing unease, because a little over a year after returning home, both of them disappeared on me. Rather than talk to me and explain themselves, they eloped.

I was devastated. They'd left no note, no written explanation for their absence; I feared the worst, that some political rival during the war had come after my family for petty revenge or that some enemy made in the same period had come to attack me, but had found my child and apprentice an easier place to start for destruction. So, I did everything in my power to find them.

It was at this time that I bought my enhancer (I'd had the crystal ball itself for years, a relic of my time as a military commander, when I'd sought information on the enemy's movements), the better to find one or both of them. I did, at last, find them, and it broke my heart further. They were in the midst of a lesson. I saw my daughter performing magic, and I saw my apprentice teaching her how. He had been continuing his studies without me, you see, and learned spells and tricks I'd never taught him. So there they were, the self-taught master with his promising student—with his wife.

I knew they'd abandoned me. I was hurt, of course, but not nearly as hurt as I'd have expected to be. They were alive, after all, and seemingly happy. If their desire was to be away from me, what right did I have to make them return? It was clear they did not want me in their lives anymore, so I stayed away. I maintained intermittent clairvoyant contact but never made any overtures to let them know I'd found them. I had some idea of their physical location but didn't have anything specific to go on. I found out later that they had not even left the city, but were actively avoiding my part of it.

They were happy. They were safe, or as safe as a fledgling wizard and her neophyte teacher could be. I resigned myself to dying alone in my old age, content that my daughter had found satisfaction in her home and in her drive to achieve her greatest goal. I had done my part.

Unfortunately, an inexperienced teacher with a student determined to reach ever higher is a dangerous match. That which I had feared since her childhood came to pass. During their research, something went horribly wrong. Alphetta was killed. I did not see it happen, and that is a mercy I will ever be thankful for; but it happened, nonetheless. I could no longer see her. That's how I found out. One day, I could check on her, and the next, emptiness in the glass. I found Petre easily enough in my glass, on the run. He soon found a way to detect, then block, my observations.

A cold fire spread through me, Skate. One that I had not felt for almost a decade. It was the fire of war. I believed Petre to have killed my daughter. I was an older man by that point, but not so old that I could not be roused, and the murder of my daughter roused me. I left my home, my city, for the first time since returning from the war, after any lead I could find. I started with what little I'd learned from my last successful scrying, and thereafter relied on witnesses and observations. I hired a bounty hunter to aid me, and the chase was on.

It took years. Petre was skilled at avoiding notice, and with magic aiding him in his travels, the chase proved fruitless for years. Further frustrating our hunt was my own old age. So, breaking off to let my hired man do his work alone, I researched ways to thwart the ravages of time. It was during this period that I discovered a secret that many would kill for: how to extend my existence beyond the paltry four score years and ten I might have been afforded by the luck of my own fortitude. Even better, I found a way to do so that did not involve some vile ritual or deal with infernal powers. When I began my second life, I began it fresh, with no monstrous acts weighing on my conscience and with the cruelty of age gone forever.

I rejoined the hunt only to find the trail cold. My bounty hunter, noble soldier of fortune that he was, had contracted fever and perished some months before, chasing Petre deep into the savage wilderness of the southerlands, where vicious beasts prowl and the air itself carries fetid and oppressive heat. Such concerns no longer bothered me, but they explained my hunter's failure. What hope had he of surviving such environs alone?

During my extended forays into the shadowy groves, I encountered wondrous sights. There were tribes of lizardmen, who were shocked to find a human being blithely trekking through their territory. None had any specific information about Petre's whereabouts, though they spoke of rumors of another human who was said to travel among the tribes, using magic to disguise his nature. That was promising but ultimately unhelpful: thousands of these serpentine folk lived in the jungle. Trying to find the one who didn't belong would be as fruitless as searching for a particular seed after the bag has been dispersed to the winds. I began to question the wisdom of my search when I came face-to-face with one of the elder powers of the world.

The great dragon Zuri-shantar greeted me by name, dispelling the illusion it had made of its surroundings. What I had thought to be a thicket choked with undergrowth faded into a rare open area, a slight hillock free of trees or bushes. The grass, which I'd wager had not been chewed by any grazer for many years, came up to my waist. It did not even crest one of Zuri-shantar's terrible claws.

"Barrison Belamy. The wizard who would be immortal, as his betters are. Why are you trespassing here?"

Something you need to know, Skate: since my transformation, I do not feel fear in the same way you do. It is a weakness of the flesh that I simply do not experience anymore. I can be concerned about things, but only in the detached, clinical, practical way that one might be concerned about the weather or ill rumor. But I can remember fear. I remembered it very strongly at that moment. I'd never seen something so primordial as a dragon, something so majestic yet terrifying, so wise yet brutish. He could have snatched me up in the blink of an eye and crushed my body to dust, and all of my magic could have done nothing to stop it from happening.

I steeled myself; the destruction of my body no longer concerned me, since it would form anew if destroyed. "I seek a man, one who fled into this place to escape from me."

"He must be quite fearful indeed to have done something so foolish." The dragon wrapped his gargantuan claw around me and lifted me clean from the earth, as a child might grasp a mouse. "Why do you chase him?"

"Justice," I said.

Zuri-shantar laughed, a booming that sounded like a thousand bellows at the forge that made the world. Hundreds of birds took flight at the sound. "No, no. That is not why." He brought me up to his eye, the pupil of which was roughly the size of my torso. "A man may do what you have done for many reasons, but justice is not one of them. You may have fooled yourself, but not me."

I admitted my justification had not been accurate. "Revenge."

"That's closer, lich. Much closer to the heart of it. Something else lurks, I think, but revenge is indeed enough of a catalyst to force a man into violent, purposeful action." I remember the pressure as he squeezed at the end of his sentence. "What will you do when you find your prey, mighty and tireless hunter?"

I hesitated in answering, and he laughed again, shaking my body with each breath. "That's what I saw skulking in the recesses of your soul. You don't know yet!" The laughter continued, and he tossed me down. Had I been alive, I would have been mangled. "What foolishness is this! In my millennia roving the lands of this world, I have seen things strange and wonderful, the rise and fall of kingdoms and powers, whole peoples rising from nothing only to disappear without a trace. I have met dozens of your kind, practitioners of magic who have sought to escape the fate of mortals, ignorant hatchlings fumbling in the dark with things beyond their comprehension. None of them had conflict in their rotten, decrepit hearts. I have only ever seen hatred, coldness, and ambition. Today, I have seen something new. Hesitation! Softness! In a lich!" More laughter erupted, so much that the great beast rose up on his hind legs, swatting the air as if to dispel his mirth. When he gained control of himself, he dropped onto his back with a thunderous crash, tearing down trees and undergrowth at the perimeter of the clearing. He began lazily picking at his spear-like teeth with his claws.

I stood and watched, unclear what was now expected of me. When he continued ignoring me, I slowly turned and began to walk away. I had almost reached the end of the clearing when the voice of the dragon ripped through the oppressive silence of the surrounding jungle. "I know where your man is." I turned to find him scratching his great stomach, running a claw on the scales to pick out irritating debris. He spat a gout of fire toward some of the trees not yet trampled, and the blast of heat lit a swath of jungle aflame. He snorted in satisfaction at the sight.

"Will you tell me?" Had I been capable of feeling fear as people do, I'd have already lost consciousness from it. As it stood, I felt only apprehension, an assessment of risk that found the danger high, but worth the reward if it brought me closer to Petre.

He snapped up into his four-legged position with a speed totally at odds with his size. A thing so large has no business being that fast. Nevertheless, there he preened, scraping his massive horns along his back and sides, scratching and cleaning.

"Oh, I think so. If only to watch what you will do. I'll keep an eye on you afterward, too." He brought his fiendish head down low, to a point I hardly had to crane my neck to catch full view of him. "Have you begun to feel it yet, I wonder?"

"Feel what, mighty one?"

"Such flattery! You must have been a courtier at heart—when it was still beating, of course." He rose again, this time to his full height on all fours, his majesty and power bared in casual shifts of titanic muscle beneath crimson scales as large as dinner plates. "I speak of the madness that plagues your kind. Loss of memories of your former life, poisoning of relationships you desperately cling to, paranoia about imagined plots to destroy your precious tether."

"I have not," I replied. I knew of such troubles; one cannot take up a study of immortality without running across warnings of its effects on those who would take it as their own.

"You will." The certainty in that impossibly resonant booming voice gave me no small amount of dread. "I have met with the eldest of your kind, lich. I visited him on the eve of the thousandth anniversary of his new birth. Rech Bolthek is his name. He did not remember it."

"His birthday?" I asked.

"No," he said with a snarling chuckle, "his name. He had forgotten his own name. It took him a thousand years to get there, but he ended up where all mortals go when they try to avoid their natural fate: utter madness. It will come to you, too. It is the way of things, little Belamy. Your kind is not meant to view the passage of centuries; doing so degrades your mind, warps and contorts it in ways too strenuous, until it, like a piece of strong and unyielding metal bent with a force greater than it can stand, must break. Perhaps it will do so when you find your prey. That would be something worth seeing!" He laughed again, smoke pouring from his mouth and throat.

With that warning, Zuri-shantar finished his toying. He described the location and name of the tribe of lizards that Petre had infiltrated, then took flight, snorting flames and smoke in his wake. I assume he watched my meeting with Petre with great interest, but it's just as likely he forgot all about the encounter as soon as he was airborne. The minds of dragonkind are an inscrutable thing, their interests in mortals and even immortals being transient fancies, passing distractions to whittle away the time between now and eternity.

I stood amid the wreckage of the burning trees and underbrush, momentarily stunned by the unexpected meeting. Zuri-shantar is likely to be the oldest thing alive, one of the progenitors of the entire race of dragonkind. That he should have taken any time to talk with me was a wonder, and remains so to this day. In my musings, I forgot about the flames that were fast spreading in my direction.

I took flight, safe above the treetops, guided only by the words of the fast-disappearing dragon. The tribe he had described was not difficult to find; it was a prosperous community, thriving in the danger and wildness of the jungle. I landed a respectful distance away and made my approach to the village on foot.

The sentries were at first hostile to me; the fact that we seemed to have no language in common proved particularly vexing for both parties. However, I found they had some vocabulary in the language of dragons, which I have some skill in imitating. I was able to get across to these warriors that I was here searching for someone in particular. We stayed where they'd encountered me while a runner went back to the village proper. She returned with a fellow lizard decked in talismans and charms of all sorts. To my great surprise, he spoke to me in comprehensible, albeit raspy and broken, Caribolian.

"Why you here?" he said, gesturing toward me with the gnarled club he had been using as a walking stick, his necklaces and bracelets rattling with the motion. "You want someone?"

"I want to find someone who's here in disguise," I told him.

He seemed to work through the words. "Disguise. False face, yes?" When I nodded, he turned his head from side to side, sniffing the air through the narrow slits that served as his nose. "One who looks like lizard, but not, yes?"

I nodded again. "I've been told that he's among your people."

"Told? Who tells?" His reptilian eyes narrowed in deep mistrust. "No trust for other tribes. They would...lie of us."

"I came by the information from a dragon, Zuri-shantar."

At the mention of the name, all eyes went wide, and the warriors immediately dropped to one knee with bowed heads. My conversation partner similarly genuflected, though he kept his eyes fixed on me.

"You talked with Great One? Great One sent you here?" My affirmative almost knocked him over. He stood to regain his balance, and the warriors slowly returned to their feet. "Great One does not lie. Your prey is here. I think I know who it is. Come along."

With that, we trudged the rest of the way to the village, a collection of mud huts with green-thatched roofs surrounding a particularly impressive hut that must have spanned at least fifty feet. It was into this largest domicile that my hosts took me. Therein I saw the largest lizardman I have ever seen, his hefty paunch jutting pugnaciously from a thick and sturdy frame. He sat upon a rock throne that went through the thatched floor of the hut.

The chieftain, for I assume that's who it was, and the speaker conversed in their hissing and snapping tongue. The leader then shifted his gaze and weight in my direction, and said some more things I could not understand. My conversation partner nodded once, which I took to be a sign for what I was supposed to do, so I nodded as well. The chieftain nodded to the speaker, who tapped me on the shoulder with his clawed finger.

We left the home of the leader of the tribe and made our way to the outer edge of the village. "We think we have your man. Tried to hide..." He snapped his head side to side and sniffed; I realized later he was trying to find the right word. "...among. Among us. Wearing our skin, speaking our words. We keep him. He wears his own face now." He gestured to a lone hut ahead of us, isolated from any others. "There. Your prey. Do what you will."

"You're giving me your prisoner?"

"If Great One sent you to hunt, we do not...interfere. If he leaves the area, he is free. If we see him after, we kill."

I stepped into the hut.

CHAPTER 21

IN WHICH A STORY IS FINISHED, BIBELOTS
ARE EXPLAINED, AND BACON IS SERVED BY
THE FIRE.

Belamy paused his telling, and stared into the flames. Skate had stopped drinking her coffee shortly after the conversation started, and it was roughly the same temperature as the room around it. Petre's globe remained full of vaguely shifting blue smoke. Rattle stayed motionless in the old man's lap.

"Forgive me. It has been ages since I've recounted these things aloud. I'm sure this could have been explained much more succinctly, if I had put my mind to such. Shall I continue?"

Skate nodded, but slowly, and only after a few seconds of consideration.

"You have reservations?"

"Questions," she said, sipping the room-cooled coffee. Terrible or not, she wasn't going to waste any. "But they can wait."

"Might as well get them out of the way now, so I don't have to stop again until the end. I often find that I'm unable to concentrate if I have unresolved questions needling my brain." His eyes finally left the fire and turned to Rattle, whom he began to pet at the space where its wings met.

"Okay." The truth was, the old man was right; the questions would bother her if she didn't get them out of the way. "How did the dragon know who you were?"

"Dragons are wonderful things and grow more wondrous with age.

Zuri-shantar has had untold millennia to age, and his powers are unknowable. I believe, either through some particular insight into the world that eludes the lesser beings or else through the magic of simply being a very old dragon, that he knows things about the world around him automatically. He had no other way of knowing who I was, or for taking interest in me other than a random encounter in the wilderness. It's possible he can read minds, as well. The short answer is that I don't know, but there are known ways of doing what he did, and I am sure there are unknown methods as well."

"So, magic."

"Yes. Of one form or another."

"Was Rattle helping you look?"

"No. I left him behind, right here, as a sentry to ward off any opportunistic thieves who might have noticed a seemingly abandoned home and thought it to be easy pickings. He was incredibly helpful during my research, however. For whatever reason, he's got a real mind for books, and that affinity for the written word was indispensable for cross-referencing and fact-checking the sources I'd been able to locate, evaluate, and eventually return. He excelled in both duties," Belamy said with a smile, patting Rattle on its glassy body. It looked around the room, avoiding eye contact.

It's embarrassed by the praise, she thought as it resettled itself, shaking its wings out briefly.

"That thing the dragon told you, about liches always going insane. Is that true?"

He ruminated on the question before answering. "As far as I know, I am the only person to have ever achieved lichdom using the method I have. In that way, I am unique. I am aware that this very subtle distinction between myself and those like me will do little to allay any fears of those who—for the most part, rightly—condemn a lich to damnation for his decision, for choosing to throw away his life for a permanent facsimile of it, for ripping his soul to shreds and throwing the wastage into a pot of filth." Belamy brought his free hand up and scratched the side of his head, and she winced at the dry rasp of his skin. "Whether this difference will protect me, I don't know. But what I have seen from the larger body of research and commentaries of the world's liches seems to indicate that the gradual loss of memory and even the ability to make sense to others are wholly inevitable. They can be postponed, alleviated, or simply accepted, but the madness comes just the same. I have taken some steps I think will help to stall it, but only time—and a lot of it, at that—will tell whether they're of any use."

"What steps?"

Belamy smiled and patted Rattle on its side. "Go fetch the memories for me," he said. It slid off his lap and began flapping, winding its way to the stairs. "Shall I continue, or was there anything else nagging at the corners of your mind?"

When Skate shook her head, Belamy continued as before, dispassionate and staring into the fire. It had begun to burn low, so he willed a log to hover into the fireplace before continuing.

#�;☌⚷◌

My guide stayed behind as I entered the isolated, ill-kempt hut. Though it was a structure of threadbare rope and salvaged branches, it was sturdy; it barely creaked as I rested my weight against it in the doorway. In front of me was my enemy, Petre Hangman. The man who'd killed my daughter.

He was in terrible shape. His ragged hair hung about his face, which had been weathered by a life on the run—by his surviving in the wilderness where no lone man could hope to survive for long, even a skilled young wizard. Dried blood caked the lower half of his face, and further patches of blood were splattered on his clothes, which themselves were little more than rags. He was seated on the floor and bound to the wall, the same thin but resilient rope keeping him there that held the walls of his prison together. He looked up at me but couldn't see anything but a shadow in the light. The sun was glaring through, and his squint only made his position look even more pitiful.

"Who's there? Is it you again, Slisthak? I can't answer more questions today, I'm so thirsty." He dropped his head, which lolled from side to side in a daze. "Anything; water, juice. I can barely see." His voice sounded as if his claims of thirst were well-founded. It was more of a croak than his usual sounds.

"Who is Slisthak?"

He immediately recognized my voice. His daze wasn't gone entirely, but it was more muted. "The shaman of the tribe." He no longer spoke as a prisoner. In fact, he spoke as he always had to me. He spoke as an equal. "I've been teaching him what I know of magic in exchange for food and water, though I try to get more of the latter beforehand. Talking dries me out, you see."

"I imagine so." I came into the hut more fully, within arm's reach of the man. "Why have you not escaped?"

He laughed, a bitter sound. "I would love to, believe me. I'm out of spells. Slisthak has my book. I was caught unready and am paying the price for it. I doubt I shall ever leave this hut alive."

"I have the same doubt." I no longer had flowing blood to pour through my ears or heat to rise from my heart, but I still felt anger; I felt it as clearly as I ever had. I bent down to eye level with him. "Why is my daughter dead, Petre?"

He met my eyes and quickly turned away. "Because of me." He tried to move his legs underneath him, but he failed. The effort took his breath from him, and he slumped down again, coughing and rasping. "I killed her."

I stood back up. "Why?"

He caught his breath. "Because...because I'm a fool, Barrison. I taught her, and I pushed her too far. When I realized what I'd done, I tried to pull her back, but it was too late, too late." His throat choked him; by the grimace on his face and the heaving of his breath, I knew that he was weeping, despite having no tears with which to do so. "She tried what was beyond her, and it took her. The spell backfired, and she was gone."

The report was unexpected. I had thought that Petre had been directly responsible for her death. "You did not kill her?"

"Of course I did; aren't you listening?" He tried to bolt upright, but his restraints kept him from rising completely. "It was *my* fault she was studying magic at all; it was *my* fault she was pushing herself beyond her abilities. Who else could be responsible but her own teacher?"

"Why did you run?" I had assumed his direct guilt from the very beginning for that reason; his immediate escape and subsequent attempts at hiding had made it perfectly clear he had been the one to kill my daughter. It never occurred to me that she might have died for her own efforts, that her own drive to take on more than she could handle had hurt her.

"To get away from you, of course. I knew you'd be out for my head when you learned that she'd died under my care. So to save my own skin, I fled."

"She was under no one's care." I performed a simple trick to release his bonds; he slipped forward and caught himself with unsteady hands. He stayed in that position, shuddering and breathing raggedly. "That was my folly, Petre, and yours. Alphetta was her own person and would not be controlled or made to do anything other than what she wanted to do. Even had you not eloped with her, she would have found a way to learn magic. I knew that, deep down. It was who she was: determined, proud, and courageous. You could have no more prevented it than you could stop the sun from rising or the moons from waning. You've wasted a decade of your life fleeing from me, and I chasing you. Your skin is your own. You bear no guilt."

I turned to leave. I have mentioned before that certain emotions are different in me since the transformation. Fear, I feel not at all, and other emotions are muted and dulled. I remember in that moment feeling echoes of regret and of sadness but also of peace. I did not have to shed blood for my daughter; her murderer was nonexistent. That she herself had been responsible for her passing was upsetting but not unsurprising. I did not doubt for a moment that Petre's account was true. This certainty solidified shortly thereafter.

"Wait." His voice was a croak. He had risen from the floor, but remained on his knees, slumping in dejection. "Please."

"Do you need help getting out of the jungle?" I asked, at first misunderstanding his meaning. "The lizardfolk have promised that you'll not be harmed should you leave without returning."

"You can't. You can't let me go."

"Why not?"

"Because I am guilty!" Now he did rise to his feet, and he grabbed me by the shoulders. His grip was weak, and his eyes were wildly searching my own. "I killed her, do you understand? My wife, your daughter, is dead, and it is no one's fault but my own. You can't just let me go. You have to do justice. I know you, Barrison. You can't let a killer go free; it's not in you. You have to do justice."

"You would have me take your life from you? You think that

would be the just thing to do?" When he didn't answer, I continued, "I do not think so. There would be no justice in your death, Petre. It was an accident, nothing more. You owe nothing to me, and I would count your death a murder on my own count. Go, and be free."

"I'll make the lizardfolk do it, if you won't. Then you'll have made murderers of them." His eyes had become even wilder, and he'd backed away. "I can't go on, Barrison. I can't go on, and I won't do it myself."

"What good would your death do?" I asked him. "Whom would it help? What use would such a thing have?"

"Justice, punishment, whatever you will call it. I do not know how you have managed to come here, or how you have managed to remain unfazed by the jungle in your old age, but whatever you've done must have warped your senses if you can't tell that this is right."

"Will you put your judgment in my hand?"

He nodded but pointed a finger. "So long as there be justice in it. I'll not have you claim that there needs nothing be done."

"Fine, come here." I held him at arm's length. "I will not take your life from you"—I had to hold up a finger, because he tried to interrupt—"but I'll keep you held. I'll take your freedom from you, only so long as you're willing to give it."

"Barrison, you're old. Any imprisonment you offer can only last as long as you will, which can't be more than a decade or two at best. Your daughter's life must be worth far more—"

"I am not alive, Petre. I can be your gaoler for as long as necessary." I explained to him the process that I had gone through, and he recoiled.

"You...you have done this to find me?"

"Yes, and if you believe it, I am glad I do not need to do as I planned. What say you? Will you accept confinement as penance, where you will have a chance to live a good life afterward, a life of wisdom from time spent in contemplation, which you could not have in the event of your execution?"

He had fallen to his knees. He gripped the side of his head with both hands. "I deserve death, Barrison. I know that I do."

"A lifetime of imprisonment, then. A life for a life, or else until you realize that you're wrong. Do you accept my judgment?"

He lifted his head. I saw much in his eyes, but what stuck out to me was a sense of hope. He nodded. I cast my spell, and he dissolved into a vapor that coalesced into a glass sphere into my hand. I saw him within, and placed him safely in a pocket. We left the hut and the jungle behind.

✳☋⅄◈

Skate set her empty cup on the floor with a clack. The coffee had never recovered from that horrible temperature it had become, but she found that listening to the story had made her thirsty. Rattle returned, bringing with it the jewelry box from her first night here. It plopped the decorative case in Belamy's lap. It glanced at Skate, then picked her cup off the floor and disappeared into the kitchen.

"So you did all that, chasing him, becoming a lich, because you thought he murdered your daughter?"

"Yes."

"Did you know how she died before Petre told you?"

"Only that she had been killed by magic." Petre's globe remained inscrutable. "She is buried in the cemetery near the small chapel here in the Old Town. I stayed only as long as the service took to end before leaving town in search of her husband."

There was only the sound of the fire for the next few moments. "You should have taught her."

"I have often thought the same thing in the intervening years. Sometimes I come to your conclusion, but other times I turn the other way. I do not know if I could have prevented what happened to her had I been her teacher in Petre's stead. He was my most gifted pupil, and I'm sure he'd have been a fine instructor. It is hard to teach one you love, Skate."

She nodded at the tiny coffer in his lap. "What's your pretty rubies got to do with helping you stay...you?"

He smiled. "My rubies are no rubies at all. Actual gemstones of the sort are buried deep beneath the earth, taking millennia of churning within the earth to bring the valuable treasures near enough for mortals to have a chance at retrieving them. The dwarves are good at finding such things, but even those subterranean masters of the earth count such beauties an extraordinary find. To my memory, only the

Hallowed Halls of Heronguzun were ever known to produce the things in large numbers. No, these are facsimiles of gems. They are, in fact, my own memories."

He opened the box and showed her the sight. It looked as she remembered: ten gemstones aligned on a soft cloth within the delicate container. "These are memories?" She scratched her head, wondering how to pull her thoughts out to make them solid. "Why'd you make them look like rubies?"

"I didn't. It is the shape my memories naturally take upon leaving the corners of my mind." He took one out and examined it. "I do not know what color others' memories may take, or even what shape. This is a work of my own invention, and is unique, so far as I know." He held the false ruby out to Skate. "Here, hold on to this. Gently, please."

She took it and cradled it in her hand, as if she had been handed a cracked egg and told not to spill it. "So, are all of these from before you became a lich?"

"The memories themselves span a range of years. Most of them are from before my transformation, but two are from afterward."

"So you suck your memories out of your head, and that keeps you from going crazy?"

He laughed at the question. "It's more that I make a physical copy of my memories to hold on to in case I forget them or where I have come from. At least part of the madness that accompanies longevity is to do with memory loss or memory confusion. This will, I hope, stave off the mental effects of extreme old age for decades, if not centuries."

"So you use these to remind yourself of where you've been and what you did in case you forget."

He nodded and pointed to the memory in her hands. "I've found that the memory is available to anyone who holds it. Through testing we've found that even Petre can use them, so long as someone is nearby to keep the memory pressed against the glass. Go on, try it." He mimed bringing the small red sphere to his forehead. "The effect should be immediate."

She smiled and touched the stone to her forehead, and a whole scene flashed by at the speed of

She sat at her desk, reading a book. She looked up and saw her dear daughter, Alphetta, stretched in front of the fireplace, reading a book about a traveler to far-off lands. Her crystal ball sat in its usual place on the large desk.

OR

She felt a swell of love toward her daughter, and she closed her own reading. Her hands were large and indelicate, though not without nimbleness. She stood up and walked around the desk. She wrapped her daughter up in her arms, and her daughter giggled and yelped for her daddy to put her down, and she never wanted to do that in a thousand thousand years, never.

Y.

It was over in an instant, but the image was clear to Skate. The sights, sounds, textures, emotions, names—they had all been as real to her as if she'd been there herself.

She offered the gemstone back, and her breathing faltered. That sensation of love for her daughter—for Belamy's daughter—had been overpowering. She looked into his old eyes and recognized the pain within them. The loss of her must have felt like dying to him. Even though Skate had felt all of the emotions out of order (learning of her loss only to catch a glimpse of love for her after she'd long been dead), it still hurt her, if only lightly and momentarily, to think of her as gone now.

She cleared her throat to paper over her discomfort. "So if you think you're having trouble remembering something, you'll have a way to keep everything...alive for yourself."

Belamy took the stone and placed it back in its spot within the jewelry box and closed the lid. "That's right. So far, it has hardly seemed necessary. I can still recall each scene in the glass before I have used the magic within. Even though, as you've seen, the experience is incredibly vivid, my own natural recollections are not far removed from the events within. I fear the day that the memory seems entirely new to me; at that point, I do not know how helpful these tools will be. I can only hope to forestall the deterioration."

Skate considered the jewelry box as Belamy snapped it shut. *He did all this after his meeting with the dragon. It can't be the thing that holds his soul.* "What will you do if it doesn't work? Gonna try something else?"

He nodded and set the box on the arm of his chair. "Yes, I'll have to. I don't know what that something else would be."

"I hope it works." She looked over at Petre's globe. His prison was as cloudy as ever. She didn't know what he was doing or where he was looking. Belamy's recollection had described a very unpleasant and oddly personal moment in the man's life. She didn't know what she'd say to him when they next talked.

"I do, too. Oh, that reminds me," Belamy said, rising from his seat and stepping into the kitchen. He said something to Rattle and came back in. "Starting next week, we'll begin actually reading a text as part of your lessons. Shall we begin your reading for the day?"

"After breakfast," Skate said, smiling before gazing into the fire.

"Of course." The old man pulled Petre to him through the air and made for the stairs.

"I'm sorry." Skate wasn't sure what made her say the words, but it felt like the right thing to say. She didn't turn around, but heard Belamy halt his progress and turn, the bannister creaking as he put more weight on that side. "I'm sorry about what happened to Alphetta. I'm sorry you..." Her mind was filled with the memory of Alphetta, and the love that Belamy had felt for the girl as she got lost in her reading in front of the fireplace. "I'm sorry you didn't get more time with her."

There was silence from the staircase for a moment, and the only sounds were of the fireplace, the odd moving locks, and Rattle's banging in the kitchen. Belamy finally spoke, and his voice sounded like it had come from the end of a long tunnel. "We only have the time we are given. We must learn to make the most of it." His footsteps echoed through the house, seeming to fill her ears with their slow, sad rhythm, making her think of families, and friendships, and discarded trinkets.

Skate thought of the crystal ball on the desk, and smiled as the kitchen door swung open and the smell of fatty bacon filled the room.

"I only have what time I've been given," she said to Rattle, who set the plate down with a clink. "I guess eating bacon by a fire is worth the time, isn't it?"

Rattle clicked in response and floated back into the kitchen.

The meat was flavorful, and her feet were warm by the flames. *It is,* Skate decided, *well worth the time.* Her concerns tried to press in on her again—

What will I do about the Ink? How can I be sure that the statuette is the thing I'm looking for? Do I have enough time to really learn to read before I leave forever?

—but she pushed them aside, and she was able to enjoy her breakfast.

CHAPTER 22

The days passed pleasantly. An entire week went by, in the course of which Skate began trying to read written words on a page. It just so happened that the book she was given was the book she'd chosen as practice days before, though on that occasion, she hadn't gotten past the title: *The Last Dragon of the Lost Brink Islands*. She took ages on each sentence, and even then, she only knew two words out of every three.

"More will come with time and practice," Belamy told her when she complained about the matter, and she decided to trust his judgment. He'd taught people to read before, and probably knew enough about the process to tell whether it would come to her or not. So, Skate continued, and spent time talking with Petre in the meantime.

The first conversation was awkward, as both of them tiptoed around the fact that Skate knew the story of Petre's imprisonment. Eventually, though, the tension eased as they wordlessly agreed not to mention it. Between meals and lessons, Skate talked with him about the reading and about other stories Petre knew. This pattern would have continued had Belamy not found something of interest in his spying glass as Skate came down for breakfast.

"Aha!" He laughed triumphantly and clapped his hands above his head. "I got him. I got him! Ha!" He was staring intently into his glass sphere, which contained within it a tiny moving image that Skate had no chance of discerning from her vantage point. His immediate return to silence after his outburst told her he had not even been talking to her, but making a general announcement to the house or to himself. *He doesn't know I'm on the stairs.*

"Got who?"

"Hush." Belamy was staring into the sphere, the golden enhancer buzzing away to his left.

"You just shouted—"

"Shh." He held up a finger to emphasize his point.

Skate stuck her tongue out and walked into the kitchen, where Rattle was busy cooking breakfast. The chaos of the room was punctuated as ever by the clicks of the cook and the banging of pots and pans. Skate noted with some surprise that a lot of these sounds were superfluous; Rattle was banging louder and more often than it strictly needed to. She returned to the main room, where Belamy was sitting unmoved from his intense study of the crystal ball.

Skate joined her teacher by staring into it herself. She saw within it a figure wrapped in cloth that disguised all features in bulk and shadow. The person was seated at a table but doing nothing other than taking an occasional drink from a tankard in front of—him, Skate decided, based on body language alone; most women did not sit with that posture or drink in that fashion. It was Kibo the Magnificent, one of the street performers in the slums. He was in the corner, with others around him. The sphere did not show them fully, but their hands flashed into view and out as their conversation played out. One pair of hands was adorned in several gaudy rings; they were large and mannish hands, though finely cared for. They gesticulated expressively throughout the conversation. The other pair belonged to a pale woman, whose gestures were far more reserved than the man's.

The owner of the ring-bedecked hand on Kibo's left was speaking. "...can't be too worried about it. It works—we've made sure of that. We'll do our bit, get the goods, and be gone within a week. There's no reason to be worried about these ruffians, Amanda. We'll be done before they can track us down to demand any money. Forget it, I say." It was the voice of Carsen Tillby, orator of a story that Skate could not remember. "Nothing to worry about."

"You weren't there, Carsen." Miss Amanda's bark of a voice was more subdued in this context, but no less unpleasant. "These aren't nobodies we're talking about here; these are people with connections. I'm pretty sure they're running all or most of the crime in this town, like those Claws in Herzeschal. Do we need to go over how that worked out?"

The jeweled hand patted the air in mollification. "I get it. And if we were going to be here much longer, I'd be as concerned as you are. But we're not, right? Two days, and we're gone." The hand took the pint in front of it out of sight for a moment, and Tillby let out a healthy burp as he returned the empty flagon to the table. "Gone like the wind, eh?" He laughed and knocked on the table.

"I don't like it. They'd have to be keeping eyes everywhere, to be able to have found us out already."

"They haven't 'found us out.' Thanks, dearest," he said as another drink landed on the table. The clink of coins and a giggle came from out of sight. "They have no idea what we're doing; they think we're a traveling troupe, just like everyone else does."

"They know we do more than that." Miss Amanda was growing impatient. "They know people watching the show can't remember what they saw. They suspect—"

"They *suspect* much, I'm sure, but they don't *know*, do they?" The new flagon disappeared from view. "So they made a threat. They won't move on it in two days' time. They don't think there's any urgency. Why would they, when they don't know for sure what we're doing?"

"Suspicion is enough to make me nervous, and if you had the wisdom that God gave an ant, it would do the same for you." Her words were scolding, but there was a note of playfulness in her voice, as if Tillby's words had lessened her fears somewhat.

"I'd take it, to be sure, so long as I could keep the rest of me." He guffawed at his own wit, and surprisingly, Amanda joined in. Kibo made no sounds, but the robed shoulders shook with silent laughter. The focus of the vision shook their covered head and took another hearty gulp from the tankard.

When the trio recovered from the mirth, Amanda spoke up again. "And I still don't like that girl who—"

"Oh, not this again," Tillby said around another belch.

"Yes, this again." Her irritation was back in full force. "I'm telling you, it didn't work on her. Not all the way. Tell him, Kibo."

The magician shifted and set down the almost empty flagon. "It was unexpected, Carsen." One mystery settled: Kibo the Magnificent was decidedly a man. His voice was a register lower than Tillby's, though breathy to the point of sounding like a whisper. "No one else has come out of the show so lucid—"

Tillby interrupted with a spluttering raspberry. "'Lucid'? You said she barely even knew where she was!"

"And that she remembered nothing, yes. But she had questions for us about the show." Skate realized with a small shock that they were discussing her, that they were talking about her attempt to get answers about the mysteriously disappearing story. "The magic is supposed to prevent that. Any nagging doubts about what was seen and heard should have been immediately smothered by an overwhelming sense of contentment and marvel. That this random child somehow evaded this effect would suggest something went wrong."

"See?" Amanda chimed in. "It's not nothing."

Tillby considered a moment before answering. "You said it only 'suggests' something went wrong with the show." Amanda let out an exasperated groan, but Tillby continued, his ring-adorned hand waving away her objection. "Now hold on, I'm serious. You said 'suggests.' What else could it be?"

Kibo leaned forward onto the table, resting on his elbows as he interlocked his fingers in front of him. "Well, it's all conjecture, really. She could have been in a particular spot that interfered with the magic somehow. Such loci of interference do exist in the world, though they're rare and difficult to find. It's also possible she bore some sort of charm or trinket that protected her, but we'd not expect to find such magic among the slums. She was dressed finer than any slummer had any right to be, but that doesn't mean she can afford magic. There's also the possibility that she has been trained to resist such magic in the past, though that's exceedingly unlikely. Training in magic, even in resisting it, costs a heavy fee; those of my craft do not part with their time or secrets trivially. Finally, it's entirely possible she's just an incredibly headstrong and intractable youngster, whose pigheadedness kept her from giving in entirely to the spell. Such a will would be one in a thousand; when we spring this on the city proper, we should expect we'll run into at least a couple such resistors." He leaned back and polished off the rest of his drink before returning to his original position. "Of all the secondary explanations, this last is most likely; but I think my original concern that something went wrong is likelier still."

Tillby's fingers drummed on the table. When he spoke, his voice was lowered to almost a whisper to match the magician's. "Look, we've done this thing here, what, six times now? Nothing went wrong with any other shows. Nobody else at that show went off the rails, right? We need to assume we're good as far as the show goes and chalk up Little Miss Thinks-Too-Much as a fluke. We must have done it with, what, two hundred people so far? At least that many. And one out of two hundred comes up only..." He trailed off and pulled his hands out of view. Skate was doing the same thing he was at the moment: trying to figure out the number in terms of a percent.

Before he could finish, Kibo cleared his throat. "Half—"

"Half a percent! Thanks, I was getting there. Half-a-percent failure rate. Now listen, I may not be the absolute best gambler out there, but someone shows me a deal that's 99.5% a sure thing? I'm there. *We're* there," he amended, reaching out and taking both Amanda's and Kibo's hands in his own. "We worked hard to get there so far. Let's not be timid now."

Kibo nodded and clasped right back on Tillby's offered hand. "I'm still in, don't worry. I want to know what happened with the girl, but it's not going to interfere with my work."

Amanda sighed. "It's going to bother me, too, but I'm a professional. The spell works most of the time; that it went wrong exactly once doesn't mean too much, I suppose. I'm in, too."

Tillby chuckled, an encouraging sound. "Good! Good," he repeated, his voice heavy with what sounded like genuine emotion. "We can do this. Tomorrow, after the last show, we'll get outta this dump. If we do good enough, we'll be able to retire to the country and live the rest of our days as landed money."

"That's what you said about Herzeschal." Amanda's voice was similarly more subdued than before.

"We got unlucky in Herzeschal. Luck won't abandon us again; I'm sure of it. Not now. Not after all the work we've put into it. My dad always said that luck favors the prepared. Well, none can say that's not us, right? Girl!" He was shouting, and it made Skate jump. "Another round for this table, and fast."

He paid for the drinks, and each of them took one of the three and lifted it high above the center of the table. "To the bold!"

"To the prepared," Amanda corrected, and when Tillby laughed, the three flagons thudded together. As they drank, the vision began to fade.

Skate pulled back up to a standing position and rubbed her eyes; she hadn't been blinking. Belamy sat back and brought a hand up to stroke his beard.

"You managed to find Kibo the Magnificent," Skate said as moisture found its way back to her eyeballs. "Was that on purpose or an accident?"

"Both, oddly enough." Belamy stood and opened a drawer in his desk. While rummaging through its contents, he said, "I was trying to find the trio of performers you told me about, and decided to start with the least likely to succeed and work my way down to the others. Imagine my surprise when I found our beloved stage magician within a few moments! There was no resistance whatsoever; it was as if I were trying to scry on some yokel peasant."

"So he ain't a proper wizard. It's just an act. Wait," Skate said as she thought of what she knew of the strange man, "that can't be right. The only thing I remember from the show was him doing some magic. And after the show, too, when he tossed me away. So what gives?"

"You're right, first off. I don't think the premise that he is an actual wizard is incorrect; his fellow performers seemed to assume him to be the one knowledgeable about magic, and to be the one responsible for the spell for...whatever it is they're doing." Belamy leaned into the drawer he'd pulled open, all the way up to his waist, despite the fact that the drawer could only have been half a foot deep at most. When he spoke again, he sounded like he was speaking from within some small nearby room rather than from within a simple wooden drawer in a desk. "I think the best explanation for the ease of my search with Mr. Kibo is that he's not exactly a 'proper wizard' after all, as you said. He's self-taught."

With some effort, Belamy pulled himself from the drawer, and in his hands were two bright blue gemstones, each as small as her pinky nail. "No wizard with adequate training from a skilled teacher could possibly have failed to have mastered the simplest attempts at blocking clairvoyant eyes of others. I believe our stage magician is an autodidact. He didn't have his protections in place because he doesn't have any—because he doesn't know about them."

Skate did not see any particular importance in this new information. She was more focused on the fact that it sounded like the Ink knew of these three and wanted them gone.

Belamy put down the two gemstones with a soft *tic* and brought his hand back to his beard in thought. "Self-taught practitioners are dangerous, both to themselves and to others. Trial and error ends all too often in the latter, usually with disastrous consequences. It's entirely unpredictable who will succeed in learning magic that way, and it's equally unpredictable what magic they'll teach themselves in the process. It is not unheard of for amateurs fumbling in the dark to find something new and truly unique. It's possible Kibo has done something of the like and is now using it toward some dishonest purpose. Of course, I won't know for sure until I see it for myself tomorrow."

"That's probably not a good idea." Skate said the words without thinking and immediately wished she'd said nothing at all. Belamy's confused expression demanded an answer. She improvised. "Aren't you worried that whatever it is they're doing will take your senses away like everyone else?"

Belamy stared a moment before his expression melted into a sloping, wry smile. "I appreciate the concern, but I should be fine. If it is some mind-altering magic, it won't bother me. The half-dead like myself are unbothered by such attempts."

Skate nodded and smiled, hoping that she appeared as relieved as she genuinely was without revealing why. *He bought it.* In truth, she was hoping he'd stay away from such an event because she planned, at the first available opportunity, to report to Boss Marshall when and where these three were performing their last show before skipping town. The Ink wanted them out, and Skate planned to help make that happen. "What were you searching for those three for, anyway?"

"To help Jack Gherun. I assumed these three were in league with the criminals who'd tried to extort money out of him. Based on that conversation, though, I'm inclined to think otherwise. Our performing band has come into conflict with these others. Which means," Belamy finished with a sweeping wave toward his two gemstones, "they might have some information for me about who these thugs are."

"You're gonna trade gems for info on the thieves you're after?"

"Not exactly, no. But I plan to get the information just the same."

Okay, gotta make time today to get to the Boss. "Good luck, I guess."

Rattle opened the kitchen door with a bang, and carried over a plate full of scrambled eggs, jelly, and toast. It set the large plate *(Almost a platter, really,* she thought) on the floor in front of the fire, and then returned to the kitchen for the inevitable clean-up. Skate went and began her meal, using the toast as a shovel to get the warm yellow fluff down faster. Belamy swept past her toward the hidden door to the basement laboratory. The click of the false book opened the way, and he disappeared through the hole in the wall. Skate finished her meal, leaving the plate on the floor, and went down the stairway after her teacher. The familiar acrid odor stung her nostrils again.

"What are you doing?" The ever-glowing lamps were illuminating the room, and Belamy was gingerly taking several heavy bottles from the high shelf.

"I need to make some things for tomorrow. I'm afraid I'll need to be here all day and night."

"What about my lessons?"

"We'll pick back up tomorrow. I won't count today against your room-and-board days."

"Well..." Skate couldn't complain about that; after all, she needed to get away from Belamy to report in to the Ink anyway. "Yeah, okay."

"Good. Now, unless you're ready to spend tedious hours helping me measure things in exact amounts, you should probably get above ground. The fumes won't do you any favors."

"Sure," Skate said, smiling and crinkling her nose. "Gonna shut the bookcase, too."

"Good idea."

Skate walked up the stairs and shut the bookcase with a dull click. She picked up her plate and dropped it into the tub in the kitchen, where Rattle was busy banging away at the dirty pots and pans. Then she bounded upstairs two at a time, threw on her dress—which Belamy had cleaned a few days earlier—and ran back down. In the entryway, she pulled on her boots and draped herself in her coat (similarly cleaned). She peeked back into the kitchen and said, "Rattle, I'm going out. I don't know if I'll be here for lunch or not."

The eyeball did not turn from its work but fluttered two of its legs at her, shooing her away. She obliged, and stepped out into the cold.

There was a fresh, thin coat of snow over the cobblestones. Winter was still here in full force and would remain for at least four weeks more. As Skate walked, small flurries began to flutter around from the overcast sky.

The Old Town safe house was north of Belamy's house. It was north of Ossertine's, too. She thought of the map of Caribol, and straight lines from each place to the others formed a somewhat lopsided narrow triangle. The warehouse was much less claustrophobic than the docks place, and the thought of not having to be stuffed up underground put an extra spring in her step as she strolled through the fluffy flakes of snow.

Skate's steps slowed as she neared the storage building. There were two large, irritable-looking men posted on either side of the front door, both dressed in heavy black coats to ward off the cold and furry ushanka hats to protect their ears. They did not say anything to her when she went inside, but their eyes followed her with suspicion.

Two more guards stood by the clerk at the front desk. The owner was also behind the counter, examining a set of charts and documents, and occasionally looking from those charts to the small boxes that lined the wall. The guards here watched Skate, too, but made no move to stop her when she stepped toward the clerk.

"I need to speak to the owner."

"What about, young miss?"

"My goods. I have three crates of Shivadian tree bulbs stored."

The owner of the warehouse pointed to the door to his right, which led into the warehouse and to the Boss. Skate had no idea what Shivadian tree bulbs were, but the password was always easy to remember. On her way back, she caught the owner's attention. She nodded toward the men in black and said, "Did you decide to hire some more security?"

The owner, a slightly balding man with a set of spectacles perched on the end of his nose, said nothing, but his mouth tightened. He shook his head and continued his work. She shrugged through the door.

As she wound her way through the maze of crates and boxes and shelves and barrels, Skate wondered what these grim-looking men were doing here if the warehouse man hadn't been the one to hire them. *Did Boss Marshall think he needed the extra security?* She'd ask him, she decided. She came to the end of the maze and knocked on the thin wood door mounted between two shelves.

When she was told to come in, she did so. Once more she saw unfamiliar faces: two more stony, black-clad guards, and a pallid man dressed in exquisitely sewn clothes in the latest fashion of the aristocracy, including a dark green jacket embroidered with a golden filigree of curls and swoops along the arms and chest, and showcasing a fluffy pouf of cloth at the neck in layers, like a waterfall of white. The effect on the man's color was to make it seem even more unhealthy; the off-white skin tone contrasted nightmarishly with the actual white of his blanched undershirt, making his skin look bone-like and dead. He was like a skeleton in a black-haired wig given flesh and dressed to impress. He was sitting in Boss Marshall's chair and looking very, very bored.

Boss Marshall was seated across from this stranger, a drink in one hand and his pipe in the other. He winked at Skate as she came in. Haman was in here, too, off to the side with a stack of papers set on a barrel. He was examining a sheet at a time and making marks in his ledger book, carefully and expertly ignoring everyone else in the room, hearing and seeing nothing.

Boss Marshall spoke first, his gravelly voice setting Skate somewhat at ease. "Skate, let me introduce you to the Big Boss," he said, raising his glass in a toast to the man behind the desk. He took a healthy sip from the glass, and Skate realized with a jolt of embarrassment that this was not the first drink he'd had today; his eyes were bleary and watery, and his voice had the slightest hint of a slur toward the end of the sentence, making "Boss" sound like "Bosh." The ease his voice had begun to bring her disappeared. He came dangerously close to spilling some of the drink as it sloshed around after leaving his lips. "He's honoring us with his presence this week as part of a...a tour, of sorts."

The Big Boss turned his full attention to Skate. His eyes—dark, wide, and intelligent—roved her face, as if filing details about each individual feature onto a parchment page in his mind. He finally settled on her eyes, and fixed her gaze for so long without blinking that she became uncomfortable. "You are the burglar currently living with Barrison Belamy, the dead wizard in Old Town." Though they should have had the cadence of a question, his words were a statement of fact. His voice was smooth and calm. He gave an air of being unshakable, as if every trouble in the world were something to be watched, catalogued, and sorted, but never felt or experienced. He was the type of man who would never ask a question, she realized. He knew everything already, and if he did not, he would not ask for missing information, because he knew it would be given to him.

"Yeah—yes, Big Boss." She knew he wasn't asking for confirmation of the facts but didn't know how else to respond. There was something deeply unsettling about the way he stared without blinking, giving no clues as to what he wanted her to say or do in response to his words. Not getting any help there, she decided to talk some more, if only to break the increasingly uncomfortable silence. "I'm looking for the thing he put his soul into for safekeeping. I thought it may have been a couple things so far, but I don't think they're it anymore. He either doesn't care about them enough, or they're from after he already did the magic that changed him."

Big Boss nodded. "In the time you have been studying your mark, you have made no monetary contributions to the Ink." Another statement, another question removed of all its thrust.

"No, Big Boss."

"Because taking what the lich has, his soul jar, will give you power over the thing. He will do anything to keep this safe, so the one who has the soul jar controls the lich."

Yeah. Not a "questions" guy. "Yes, Big Boss. That's the idea."

The pale man did not move. He did not so much as tap a finger on the armrests of Boss Marshall's comfortable chair. He just sat, staring. Boss Marshall slipped out a low, silent burp between his teeth and coughed a little. Haman rustled his papers. The Big Boss spoke. "You've been stealing from others on Belamy's behalf as part of this job. You have even stolen from Jack Gherun, who now believes our organization to be responsible for the theft."

"Yes, but—"

"But he believes that your would-be employer Belamy will help to extract him from our plans."

Skate looked at the side of Boss Marshall's head. He was busy studying the nearly empty glass in front of him, and did not notice her attention—or if he did, he gave no sign of caring about it. He looked ashamed at the turn the conversation was taking, which was odd, since there were no reasons she could think of that he would not have already filled in the Big Boss, which he had clearly done. It was, after all, his job to report the goings-on to his next higher in command, and that was BB himself.

"Right. He's, uh, been looking for you, Big Boss. With magic. But he says he can't, because of some magic you're using to shut it down."

"He makes astute observations." A quick movement, quicker than anything she could have seen in a casual glance—indeed, she would not have seen it at all except that she was on edge because of whom she was meeting—and the Big Boss was holding a letter sealed in an envelope with the image of the Ink: a quill pen ending in a vicious point with a drop of dark liquid hanging from the end. "His efforts have been in vain. I need you to deliver this message to Jack Gherun. It makes clear that we are aware of Belamy's attempts, but that they won't work. His first payment will be expected within the month."

Skate stepped forward and took the letter. "You got it, Big Boss." She slipped the note into an inner pocket of her coat.

"Good. I assume you did not come here on a social call."

"Oh," she said when she realized this was his way of asking for her report. "Uh, no, I didn't." She explained her outing with Twitch, but the Big Boss interrupted her before she finished.

"We know of these three. They have already been contacted regarding their activities."

"Yes, but that's what I'm here to report: they're not planning to stop or offer tribute from their work to the Ink. They're gonna do whatever it is they're here to do somewhere in the Baron's tomorrow, and then leave town."

The Big Boss's eyes twitched and narrowed ever so slightly, the first sign of any emotion from the man. "We will be sure to make sure that does not happen." He snapped a manicured finger, and one of the black coats moved toward him. The guard bent down to hear the words of the Big Boss, spoken too low for Skate to understand, then nodded and began to leave the room.

"Wait," Skate said, holding a hand out toward the guard. He stopped and turned, looking between her and the Big Boss, who lifted a finger to confirm her request. He raised his other hand and motioned for her to continue. "Belamy will be there, too. He thinks he can get information about the Ink from these three, since they've been talked to."

"Then we will have to be quicker. That is of no concern." The Big Boss gestured again to the guard, who nodded and left. "Still, it is good information to have. Your people are very capable, Boss Marshall." This was obviously a compliment, but it did not feel like one, either to her or, apparently, to the Boss. He grimaced slightly before erupting into rolling laughter and a forced grin.

"Oh, the best, sir, only the best," he said through gritted teeth before taking a drink.

"I should hope not. I make it a point that the best work directly for me." The pale face upturned the corners of the mouth in what could generously be called a smile, but which looked more like a folding of a sheet...or a burial shroud folding as it draped over the deceased. Skate repressed a shudder at the thought of working for any extended period of time around such a man. "Not to worry, though," he continued, dropping back into the expressionless face that was his resting mask toward the world. "Your crew has been doing well enough, and I'm not one to interfere with profit when that profit is my own." The wide eyes left Boss Marshall and returned to Skate, who felt—and suppressed—revulsion in a new wave. "You've done well to inform us of these activities. Don't neglect to take advantage of your host's preoccupation. His absence from his home will be a golden opportunity to explore for that coveted trinket that binds his soul forever, whatever it may be."

Skate nodded, and swallowed hard. The more time she spent around the Big Boss, the more her unease grew. The ghostly pallor of his skin was only an introduction into the ways this man was upsetting. He had a disquieting way of moving the thin gash of his mouth, so that when he spoke, his teeth clicked together with almost every syllable. His eyes saw too much and blinked too seldom. "I also needed to tell you Twitch had been caught up in that show. He wasn't acting right."

"We'll snap him out of it," Boss Marshall piped up. "Whatever they're doing can't last forever, so he'll straighten up eventually."

"Well put, Boss Marshall." The Big Boss tapped a finger on the chair, the one extraneous movement from him during the whole encounter. "If there's nothing else, we've much work to be done. Deliver that message to Gherun today. Do it before you return to Belamy's home."

Skate nodded and made for the door. Haman turned a page. Boss took another sip from his drink.

CHAPTER 23

IN WHICH A TUNE IS SUNG, A LETTER IS
DELIVERED, AND A KNOT IS UNTIED.

The snow continued to fall when she stepped out into the street. She braced herself against the cold, which her coat was not entirely able to ward off, and turned toward the Baron's Quarter. Her pulled-up hood would bring no suspicion in this weather, so the Guard was no worry.

Why was the Big Boss here? Perhaps Kite's talk of Boss Marshall's dangerous position was true; maybe he really was in danger of catching the Big Boss's ire.

The air in that room had been warmer than out here, but the chilliness of the mood within made the trek without the far more preferable option. *I hope the Boss will be okay.* He probably would be. Haman was there, and his magic was strong enough to keep them both safe, even from the Big Boss's stone-faced personal guards. *He'll be okay.*

Unsurprisingly, the Keepers were fast at work keeping the cobbles of the Baron's Quarter free of snow, with teams of shovelers scraping clear the roads and as much of the sidewalks as they could—followed closely by teams of bag holders, who were walking and casting salt from huge bags. Each bag bore the official sign of the Baron's house. "Witch salt," the stuff was called, because it was made by magicians. It had a taste approximating the lowest quality salt and cost nothing to make (other than the fees charged by the wizards and witches who made it), so it was well-suited to its current use of being trampled underfoot to dissolve the dangerous impediment that was still falling onto the heads of those trying to clear it from the streets. The Keepers were singing as they worked, a rhythmic nonsense tune. Their hazy breath formed a hurried cloud about them while they trudged and threw, trudged and threw.

> *Bind my hands and free my arms,*
> *Please my sir, yes my sir.*
> *Take my clothes and leave my hat,*
> *Please my sir, yes my sir.*
> *Shave my head and pass the comb,*
> *Please my sir, yes my sir.*
> *Break my feet and tend my shoes,*
> *Please my sir, yes my sir.*

They went through several more verses of the song by the time they passed out of her earshot, and they would probably go through many more before they restarted the tune or found a different song to keep pace with. It was one of dozens of such songs the workers learned to make their work more bearable and more efficient. Haman had explained it to her once.

"Songs cheer the heart," he'd said as they'd passed a trio of singing Keepers helping to clean up after a nasty wagon spill near the docks. "A cheered heart makes a better worker. Plus, for anything that requires repetitive motions, it helps to have a rhythm going that everyone can hear. It speeds things along, and it keeps everyone on one pace. It's why the sailors know so many songs; much of their job requires working as a team and doing things the same way, at the same speed, as everyone around them. Soldiers, too."

"Who came up with that?"

"No idea," he'd said, dropping a copper blade into a nearby beggar's bag. "I don't know if it's the sort of thing that one person could even be credited for finding out. Some things just get discovered all at once by many people in different places. It's gone on for centuries, though; I'm sure of that."

Skate hadn't thought about it since then. The road she traveled had already been scraped by the Keepers, but would not stay clear for long; even now, as Guards went about their patrols and wagon wheels bumped and creaked along the stones, the snow was reasserting its command, forming another thin sheet of white that would, within the hour, hide the stones beneath.

It didn't matter much; Skate would be out this way again well before that. Already, the colossal housing manor purported alternately to be owned by the Baron or a relative towered at the end of the avenue, where the road intersected with another and simply stopped.

Skate passed by shops selling decorative luxuries, fresh bread, candlesticks, fine household tools, sweet foreign delicacies, fine clothes, etched silverware, intricate clockwork timepieces, hot bowls of soup, highest-caliber wine, steaming mugs of coffee, and even extravagances like chocolate and jewelry. In the windows of such shops, pedestrians could see haughty eyes roving hungrily over offered goods, and the deferential salesmen, shopkeepers, and clerks bowing and joking and demonstrating, selling the goods to those who had no needs and every desire to buy nonetheless.

Of course, it wasn't only shops and stores. People here lived near the Baron's Palace, where only the wealthiest could afford to build or buy. Through these decorated windows, white and yellow lights from magic and candles mingled to create a golden glow that shimmered like twinkling waves on the white-and-gray palette provided by the half-cleaned streets. Within, the lords and ladies entertained their guests with drinks and food served on platters of silver, all dressed in clothes bought from the smiling and bowing salesmen down the street. By contrast, the servants carrying the platters dressed in plain, sturdy blacks and grays. They worked around the masters and mistresses with deft movements honed by years of practice, never missing a beat, never spilling a drink.

"Nobility," Ossertine had said of the lords and ladies.

Skate snorted, sending a burst of cloud in front of her as she neared the doors of the great manse she'd burgled a few short weeks ago. *I don't see any of that. Just money. Money and connections and closed doors. That's all.*

Skate stopped short of opening the door and retrieved the letter she'd been charged with delivering. She traced the letters written on the front of the envelope in a flowing, flourishing hand, and confirmed that it bore its recipient's name: Jack Gherun. Then she walked inside, letter in hand.

The room looked almost exactly as it had before: imposing to people like her, while welcoming to people like Gherun. The main differences were the fact that there were people sitting in the poofy chairs, sharing cups of something warm and steamy that smelled something like apples, and that the manager behind the dark wood counter was the one she'd had pinned as the more competent one. She steeled herself and approached the desk, turning her nose up only the slightest bit as she gingerly placed the letter on the counter.

The manager looked up from the ledger he had been studying. "How can I help you, miss?" His voice was polite and soft, as if he were making an effort not to disturb any of the conversations of the tenants in the main hall.

"I've come to deliver a message to Jack—excuse me," she said, smirking and bringing a hand to her neck in an imitation of embarrassment, "Mr. Gherun. It should be delivered as soon as possible, please."

He picked up the letter between thumb and forefinger. "Who is the sender?"

"I'm sure I have no idea. I was stopped on the street by a gentleman who asked if I knew Mr. Gherun. I responded that I did, and he gave this letter, with instructions to deliver it."

"I see." He tapped the letter lightly on the counter. "And you know Mr. Gherun."

"Oh, yes. He's some relation to my mother, distantly. We just call him Uncle Jack."

He set the note down and arched an eyebrow. "Mr. Gherun does not usually receive...visitors."

"Oh, I know. And I'm not here to visit. Just to deliver a message and step out of the cold for a moment."

He drummed his fingers lightly on the counter, a set of finicky, rolling taps at a time before lifting the letter again and setting it somewhere underneath the counter. Skate frowned and did her best to sound arrogant and annoyed, which wasn't hard; the man's apparent wordless refusal to deliver the letter had put her in a bad mood. "You're not going to deliver it?"

"I will, young miss, as soon as Mr. Gherun returns. He is out."

"He's never out." This was an unexpected wrinkle. There had been no reason to assume Gherun would be anywhere other than his own quarters when she'd made her way toward the manse. Realizing her outburst was not a normal thing to have said, she improvised. "Mother says he's a shut-in."

The manager's eyebrows ruffled a bit at that. "Mr. Gherun is a private individual, it's true. But he had a social call earlier this morning. He is not a 'shut-in,' young miss."

"Of course." She offered a most insincere smile before turning away, making sure her boots clicked just loudly enough to irritate some nearby residents who had been shooting her suspicious glances throughout the whole conversation from one of the small tables in the hall.

Skate returned once more to falling snow and bitter cold. She threw her hood over her head, the fur-lined coif offering some relief. The cobblestones were almost hidden again. She took a moment to think about Jack Gherun under the shelter of the awning draped over the doorway.

He'll get the message, one way or the other. Either the manager would do as she'd asked and deliver it to him, or he'd read it himself and deliver the message afterward. The worst-case scenario, she figured, involved the manager involving the Guard, but even in that case, Gherun would get the message. The Boss—*the Big Boss*, she reminded herself—wouldn't like the Guard's involvement, but these things happened. Besides, she'd bet her last helm on BB having included a line about not getting the Guard involved. Clients who squealed to the Guard usually got a warning visit from one of Shade's crew. The next day, the clients'd show up in front of the Guard taking back everything they'd said. "I was mistaken," was the oft-repeated line, followed by apologies for wasting everyone's time and regular hefty payments to the Ink.

At some point in her musings, she'd begun walking in the general direction of the Old Town. It had not been a conscious decision; when her mind began to race, her legs had a tendency to move. She'd not moved more than two blocks from the manse before she stopped cold, staring like a startled rabbit into a very unwelcome face.

Jack Gherun and a man Skate did not recognize were walking on the same stretch of road as she, and now they stood less than five feet apart. Gherun saw her at almost the exact moment she saw him, and interrupted whatever conversation the two had been having with a shout of "You!"

The word stirred her to movement, but she had only taken a step before both feet were lifted off the ground by a hand around her neck. She flew into a nearby alley, where her back was slammed against the wall hard enough to knock the wind out of her. She looked down to see Gherun, wild-eyed with his arm outstretched. His friend's hand was also out, making a clutching gesture, but they were several paces away. *Magic,* she thought stupidly as she clawed at her neck, trying to break the grip of something she could not touch; she was swatting at air. She could breathe, but it was a laborious process, and she did not doubt that the unseen hand could close tighter if the unknown wizard wanted it to.

"You know this one?" The companion's voice was deep; she was sure she'd heard it before, but with her feet dangling several feet off the ground, it was not her most pressing concern.

"It's her. She's the one that stole from me." The wizard gripped tighter. "The one who's working to ruin my life."

The unknown man had a wide, blocky face, like a statue of a brute left unfinished. "She's young. I expected a lass of some sixteen years, the way you described it."

"I may have exaggerated—look, it was dark, and it doesn't matter. This is her. The oracle doesn't lie." Gherun's face was warped with hate, and he sounded like he was struggling to keep his voice from shaking.

"Gonna let him kill me, Jack?" Skate asked, not bothering with addressing him as an adult. "Be a bad idea. You got a letter waiting for you. Go read it. I'll wait." She thought she sounded confident, but that was hard to tell at the best of times, and less easy to pull off when suspended by throat-restricting magic. Still, she must have done well, since she saw a waver in Gherun's face—from unbridled hatred to a flash of fear.

"What are you talking about?" The shaking in his voice was obvious, and any attempt he was trying to make to prevent it was failing miserably. "What letter?"

"From my Bosses. Go check; I'm serious. I'll wait here. Have whoever this guy is keep an eye on me if you want," she said, pointing at

Gherun's friend before immediately returning to trying to take the invisible hand from her throat. "Or don't, but either way, have him drop me, would you? This is less comfortable than you probably think."

Gherun's face spasmed, warping from rage to fear and back again in rapid order. He eventually said, "Let her down." The wizard pulled his arm back slightly and lowered her, kicking and gasping, to the ground. The snow buildup was not so high here, so the fall was not padded much—but other than a shock through her legs as she landed, Skate was unhurt.

She rubbed her throat and coughed. There was still pressure there, but not nearly as much. Gherun pulled his companion close and whispered something in his ear before bolting toward his home and the unwelcome message waiting for him there. The friend turned toward Skate and held a splayed hand up in front of him.

"You move, and I'll hurt you."

Again, the sense that she knew the voice washed over her, and now that she had time to think, she intended to figure it out. "Sure, no problem." She took several deep, steadying breaths and used the time to try to place that voice. "How do you know Jack?" she asked. "Family?"

"Shut up, thief." The deep-voiced man spoke without much conviction. He was only irritated, not truly upset.

"Pretty sure I know most of his acquaintances." She began ticking them off on her fingers. "His cleaning crew, the managers of his home, a group of thieves, a set of wizards—ah!" she said, snapping her finger and pointing at the man. "You must be Gemhide, right? Bakurin Gemhide, who lives in the docks."

"How do you know my name?" Gemhide had tensed up, and the splayed hand gripped inward slightly, looking like a claw.

Skate took a seat against the wall and set her head back, looking up at the sky as snow continued to fall. The buildings protected against the wind and most of the snow. *"We* know all kinds of things."

"'We'? Are you…" He lowered his hand almost imperceptibly and was about to finish his sentence, but shook his head and thought better of it. "Shut up," was all he said, and raised his arm back up.

Skate smiled and closed her eyes. *He knows about the Ink.* He might have been contacted and brought on as a client. The Ink, after all, did the bulk of their business in the docks and the slums, where they were allowed to operate more or less free of the Guard's interference. For that reason, most of their protection clients were in the docks. The slums rarely contained anything worth protecting, so the Ink didn't even bother trying to extort money in a systematic way there. It would be impossible, however, to live for any period of time in the docks and not be aware of the syndicate that ran vice.

They remained in their respective positions until Gherun returned. He was holding the note, opened but replaced in its envelope, in a quivering hand. He looked about to cry.

"Jack?" Gemhide turned toward his friend in concern. The broken man said nothing. He handed over the letter and stared at the ground, as if doing so would keep his problems safely away from him. Gemhide turned away slightly to better catch the gray light seeping through the overcast sky in order to read the words on the page. His brow furrowed as he reached the bottom of the one-page note. He folded it back to its compact shape. He looked up at Skate. "Are you one of them?"

"The ones behind that note? Sure, I'm one of them." She climbed back up to her feet, swatting the snow off her clothes. "So, we're done here, right?"

"Of course we're not done!" Gemhide's deep voice had become a growl. "You can't just steal from a person and leave a threatening letter without dealing with it."

"You know who sent that letter. You know that I can do whatever I want so long as it's with permission."

"There's a sign." Gemhide's voice had become somewhat strained, restricted by nervousness. "If you're one of them, show me a sign. Each member has to pierce a bone somewhere on their body."

Skate snorted. "Liar." She rubbed her arms to stave off the cold.

Gemhide pursed his lips. "Fine. What's the tattoo look like?"

"It's too cold to show you mine. Here," she said, drawing a rough sketch of the tattoo in the snow: a quill with a drop of ink at the end of the nib. The quill pointed to the left, positioned as if it were writing on a page. It had six divots in the feather. "It's the same symbol that was pressed on the seal of that letter," she said with a quick wave at the paper in his hand. She wiped the snow off her glove.

Gemhide heaved a sigh and turned to Gherun. "She's one of them. It's real." He held the letter out to the other man, who took it wordlessly and slipped it into the fold of his robes.

Gherun turned his hateful gaze on her. "So, that's it, then?" The almost-weeping quality of his voice had gone. "Any other news you'd like to deliver?"

"No, everything I was supposed to give you was in that envelope." She stepped into the street proper. "And since you did your little trick before you got the letter, we'll call it square. I won't tell anyone you attacked one of us. You didn't know, right?"

"How generous of you."

"It is, really, but you're mad. I get that. So, I'm gonna leave and let you work through that on your own. We're not so bad, you know. You really will be protected now." She turned to Gemhide. "You knew about us already, didn't you?"

He nodded and pursed his lips.

"You're under our protection, right?"

"Yes," he said through gritted teeth.

"Good."

Not knowing what else to say and seeing that her words were doing nothing to make the situation any better or easier, she turned on her heel and began the walk back through the streets. Neither man tried to stop her. If Gemhide was under the protection of the Ink, she wouldn't be stealing any books from him. That meant her days learning from Belamy were limited.

They were always limited, she reminded herself. While this was true, it did little to make her feel better about her situation. *It's probably over tomorrow.* The Big Boss was expecting her to make her move when Belamy attended the show; once she took the only thing she thought could be the soul tether, she'd be out of the old man's house for good. If she didn't make her move, the Big Boss would know about it, and wouldn't likely take kindly to her failure to produce results.

The air burned her lungs as she walked the half-cleared streets. There were few pedestrians out, and those who were kept coats wrapped tight and stepped with a fervent haste on the clearest parts of the road. A carriage passed her, its occupant shrouded in shadow as the driver "heed" and "hawed" at the horse to turn this way or that around snowdrifts and corners.

The knot had returned to her stomach. It was time for her to make her decision, to make her move, and she wanted to do nothing of the sort. "Steal or run. Steal or run." She was muttering to herself, and she knew it, but she couldn't help it. The question had been running through her head for weeks, at varying speeds and urgencies. It had become very urgent. "Steal or run. Steal or run." Normally, she would have people to discuss such a problem with, but all of them were of the Ink and could only be expected to give one answer: steal. Twitch probably would have actually thought about it before answering. *He's been weird, though. Whatever Tillby's crew did really stuck with him.* In his addled state, he couldn't be trusted with her doubts.

A month ago, she wouldn't have considered it much of a choice; the theft would have been easy and guiltless, because it would have helped her survive. The Ink was still helping her survive, but she had other considerations, too.

She could not do it, she decided. Selling Belamy into servitude was not an option. If she were someone like Kite, it would be easy, and she felt a mixture of jealousy and revulsion. *He doesn't care about anyone. He'd sell his own mother if he thought it would help him, never mind save him from being cast out or punished.* She hated herself in that moment, for thinking Kite was worth envying.

Having made the decision, Skate felt the knot in her stomach disappear. "I won't do it." She said it out loud, just to hear it. Hearing it said convinced her even further that it was the right thing to do. It raised questions, of course. *Will I be able to run? Where will I go? Should I tell Belamy?* These questions, though important to answer, did not weigh heavily on her. She would figure it out in time. She had confidence in that, though she couldn't explain why.

The snow did not seem as biting as she made her way to the home of Barrison Belamy once more.

CHAPTER 24

IN WHICH ALCHEMY DRIVES ONE TO TEARS,
ETHICS ARE DISCUSSED, AND GEOGRAPHY IS
PUZZLED OVER.

Skate found the home much as she'd left it, though the fire had died down again. She lifted a log at a time from the ever-full supply until she felt confident that the heat would be just short of oppressive. Then she opened the bookcase and made her way down to the lab.

Belamy was still there, working away on his creations. There were three stoppered bottles full of something brackish collected on a table opposite him, far away from where he was currently working. The acrid smell made Skate's eyes water. The old man was pouring a gray powder into a bottle of clear liquid. As he poured, the clear water began to take on the cloudy, brownish appearance of its completed fellows. When he finished pouring, Belamy set the empty container down and swirled the liquid around in the bottle. Satisfied, he stoppered that one, too. The smell got to be too much; she coughed, and the wizard noticed her.

"Upstairs!" he said, shooing her away and waving with the bottle around the room generally. "I don't have the vents open; you can't be down here."

Skate coughed more and nodded, keeping a hand against the wall as she walked, not trusting herself not to fall over on the way up. She wiped away the painful moisture from her eyes, and found that the heat from the fireplace made the irritation subside. She sat in front of the increasingly warm fire, knees bent, and arms resting on her knees while she waited for Belamy to come up.

At some point, Belamy had turned the flames back to their natural color. Wanting to enjoy the color of the blue fire, Skate spoke the Dwarvish words: *"Gerunk kekondahash."* Immediately, the room was awash in the azure light. Skate stared into the flames and thought.

I should explain everything to him. She backed off of the idea immediately; the more Belamy knew about her and her connection with the people he was hunting, the more likely it was he'd never want to see her again, and then she'd have isolated herself from all possible friends and safe places. *He can't know that I was one of them.*

If she did decide to leave the Ink, which was her only option now that she'd decided not to steal Belamy's tether, she'd never be safe on the streets again. She needed a place, and the wizard's was her only option. If it had just been Boss Marshall and Haman she'd be breaking with, she might have been able to explain herself and get away with a clean separation from the organization; but with the Big Boss keeping a close eye on the crew's activities, looking over the Boss's shoulder with regard to every decision, that couldn't happen. BB would demand retribution, and the crew would be forced to oblige, or else another crew would be brought in to do the job. Here, though, protected by the heavy stone walls of the house and the magic of its owner, she'd be safe.

He can't know.

The wizard's slippered feet made soft scooching noises on the stone steps of the hidden staircase. She turned to look at him, her eyes clear of the stinging vapors trapped below. He looked as he always had, old and bent but still alert, still able to move around. He had a look of concern. "Is everything all right? Why did you come down, when you knew I was working with my alchemical tools?"

"I wanted to see if you needed help with anything." In truth, she wasn't sure what had driven her downstairs. It wasn't as if she could share her good news with him. *"Hey, I decided not to steal from you and betray you after all!"* *That would have been a* great *way to start a conversation.* But it was why she'd wanted to see him; she'd made her decision, and it had made her happy. However, it was a happiness she could not share with him. "You know, get something for you, or just pester you while you work."

"No, I don't think I need anything like that," Belamy said with a soft smile. He threw his hands over his head and turned back toward the staircase.

"What are you doing, anyway?" Skate put her legs back under her and stood up, taking a step away from the fire. The logs had caught and were starting to burn with their bright blue waves of heat.

"Getting prepared. I have magic, but I can't rely on that alone. How did that brigand Tillby put it? 'Fortune favors the ready.' Something like that. And he's right. So, I need to get ready."

"Ready for what?"

"War." He walked downstairs without looking back at her.

Skate took a step to follow, but decided that was a stupid thing to do, given the choking fumes. Instead, she took the stairs upward and went into the library. There, Rattle and Petre were reading in their usual position on the small table against the wall. She walked over and brushed Rattle's legs aside to see the page they were examining. The legs made a sound like rocks tumbling down a metal tube.

The letters on the page were not anything she could identify. They must have been Elvish, she decided. The unknown letters flowed and drifted together in a more intricate way than the letters she could read, and were far less blocky than the runes the dwarves used. She put a hand on Petre's sphere. His eyes flowed into view, looking at the book.

"What is this?" she asked, giving the unreadable words another cursory, polite glance.

"It's a political treatise written by an elven philosopher comparing the benefits of taking consideration for the self above all others and of taking a more altruistic approach to decision-making when it comes to making choices on behalf of a nation or kingdom."

Skate smiled at this response, struck by how wonderful it was to know these two—to eat Rattle's food, and to learn of stories and history and philosophy from Petre. Watching them further convinced her that she could not throw this all away, even for the Ink.

The gang wouldn't be happy about it. BB wouldn't especially.

Her smile faded. The Big Boss wouldn't be happy to hear of it at all. He was expecting a lich delivered into the hands of a subordinate tomorrow. When he learned he wouldn't be getting one, he'd be furious. A furious man might lash out at those around him, and assign blame where it didn't belong, like on Boss Marshall's head. She didn't want him hurt over any of this. Her—and by extension, his—recent acquisition of Gherun as a paying customer might help smooth over any disappointment. *That's loads of free money each month that they didn't have before, right?*

"Blade for your thoughts." Petre was watching her, an eyebrow arched. "You seem unusually pensive."

"Just thinking about the past. And you don't have any money."

"You're right about that. At the moment, I don't have a copper coin to my name. Or a body for that matter. What holds your attention in the past?"

Skate sighed. "How you can't change it. How it's part of who we are, whether we know it or not." She couldn't deny that the Ink would always be a part of her—literally, with regard to the tattoo on her back—and that it had brought her to where she was. But if staying with it meant throwing Belamy into slavery, she had to move on.

Petre was silent now, his gaze in the blue haze far away; he might have been looking at the book, but it seemed he was looking beyond it. Rattle's legs clicked idly as it floated, sounding like a wind chime in a breeze.

When Petre spoke, his voice was thoughtful and low. "It binds us. It controls us. It shapes our every move. And it's not even real." Now it was Skate's turn to look curious. Petre's tone lifted a bit, becoming more energized at the apparent challenge of her questioning stare. "It's not. Think of it a moment: what's the most real of the three—past, present, or future?"

"They're all real."

"Oh, really? Can you do anything with any of them? Interact with any of them but the present?"

The conversation had taken a rather sudden and bewildering turn. "Uhh." Skate shrugged. "No? I can't go to the past, or to the future. It's just always now."

"Exactly my point. The future is speculation and guessing, hope and fear, but not tangible, not experienced, not real. And the past is nothing but memory and records. It did happen, but it is no longer real, just as the future will certainly happen but is not yet real. You see?"

"No." The discussion had become immensely confusing, but Skate was almost certain what Petre was saying was nonsense. "No," she said again, "the past is real because it happened. We know it happened."

"But it's not happening *now*," he said, leaning on the final word with a hint of exasperation. "That's what I mean. Of course it happened, when it was now, and of course the future will happen—when it becomes now. That's what I mean by the past being unreal—it's not real in the same way that now is."

"Oookay," she said, shaking her head at the dizzying pace and direction of the topic at hand. "So what? What's it matter that the past isn't the same as the present? Does that mean it doesn't matter?"

"No, never that. It matters immensely. As you said, it brought us to now, and there's no changing that fact. We all owe our existence to the past, one way or the other. That was my whole point: it's insane that we rely so much on something that's not real, and that it has such power over everything."

"So we should...what, ignore it? Pretend it doesn't matter?" She was guessing at the tilt of the train of thought, but immediately found the flaw in her own estimation.

Petre seemed to see in her face what she had realized, and his smile reached his eyes to give them a point at each corner. "Never that, either. I'm in here because of the past. I will not leave here because of the past. It matters immensely to me that the past should hold a great authority over the affairs of mortals like you and me. We cannot escape it." He looked away again, his stare growing distant. "We should not seek to. To do so would be to lose who we are."

The pronouncement hung in the air, unanswered and unanswerable, because Skate did not know how to even begin interacting with the ideas wrapped up in the statement. Rattle's legs continued their gentle clicking.

Skate shook her head. The Ink, the past, and her relation to both were swimming and mingling in her head so freely that she feared she'd never be able to sort them out without long hours of further mind-boggling discussion and self-exploration. "What did the elves have to say on the matter?" she said, pointing to the open book on the table.

Petre blinked and brought himself out of his own reverie. "Well, as with most things, the elves viewed the past as a weapon, a tool to be wielded when needed, and disposed of when it became prudent to do so. They were entirely willing to report mistruths about history, particularly political history, when it was convenient for them—their own meticulously passed-down histories will often record these instances of prevarication with a sense of pride and admiration, an attempt to show themselves as being wiser and more cunning than their enemies. Nevertheless, they showed a bizarre dedication to ensuring their own histories were well-documented and sourced with eyewitness accounts when available. So, in some ways, they cared a great deal about the past, and even seemed to have a great reverence for it in their private histories; but in other ways, they showed a great potential for contempt of the truth of history when it served them to do so, particularly in political and military matters."

"You make them seem like snakes."

"You're not the first to have called them such in their long stretch of time involved in the affairs of mortals, and likely not the last. Still, a prolonged study of them is a fascinating exercise, for what it can teach us not only of these mysterious would-be conquerors, but of philosophy, and of history. If we were half as committed to ideas like truth and honesty as the elves were committed to their opposites, the world would be a different place entirely by now. But in the elves we see only ourselves, turned toward our most unpleasant and self-serving interests. We're not that far removed from them, and that should be concerning in the extreme."

Skate crossed her arms. "I'm not like them."

"We all are, in some way or another. You've never wanted to make someone else suffer?"

Skate thought of Kite, and she winced.

"You've never cheated or lied in order to get what you wanted?"

She looked to the floor and frowned.

"This is a reflection of us all, Skate. The worst of us are no different from the elves in that sense, while even the best of us are at least tempted toward such behavior on a near-daily basis. Even the holiest priest has had to resist the urge to politick, to mislead, to steal.

"It's not all bad news, though. I think there's something redeemable in even the worst of us, and I'm not sure that wasn't true of the elves. They themselves noticed this in their description of the various kingdoms of men: some, they praised for their cunning and wiliness; while others, they chided and mocked for their 'weakness,' which is how they described things like kindness and honesty. But they made sure to note even in their praises of vicious neighbors that these humans cared for someone, be it a mate or a parent or a friend. The elves viewed such relationships as folly. That's what I mean by our not being far-removed from them: there are those among us who would agree with the assessments of the long-gone conquering creators of magic." His eyes became sad. "And I'm afraid they may have had a point when it came to rulership. The fall of a kingdom is a terrible thing. It leads to death and destruction for the common folk as well as the king."

She considered that for a moment. "I don't like it. They're wrong. I'll think of why later, but I know they're wrong."

"Maybe. And aren't we lucky we get to talk about it? That, more than anything, might be what differentiates even the worst of us from the elves of old. I don't know if they had any such choice in their behavior. Their texts are universal in this ethos; it may not have even been a discussion they could *have* in these terms. This is one of those times when in theory, I'd love to meet an elf to ask such questions; but practically, that would be a nightmare because their return to the world would not be something to look forward to."

"Better leave the question unanswered in that case." Skate smiled and said, "Well, that's enough history for me." She picked up her reading from another table. "I'm going to go work on this some more." She was almost out of the room when an idea struck her. She returned to Petre. "Is this one true?" she asked, tapping the heavy cover of *The Last Dragon of the Lost Brink Islands*.

"Every history is true in some sense, just as every history is a lie. It's not a work of fiction, if that's what you're asking."

Skate nodded, satisfied with the answer, and went to her own room. Petre's eyes dissolved in his blue fog. She sat on her bed and put the book in her lap. She found herself unable to focus, however; she read the same sentence three times before realizing she was doing so, and couldn't even remember what the line said. She rubbed her eyes and tried again, this time reading aloud, her rhythm and speed much improved over the preceding weeks.

"'The first dragon to live...therein had come from afar, likely from the coast of Brebully.' Where is Brebully?" she muttered to herself. She set the book to the side and went to the desk, where she took out her slate. She took the chalk and wrote the name of the location at the top left corner to remind herself to ask about it later. She paused and reflected on what she had just done. *I can write. I can read. At least a little.* She moved to the bottom of the slate and wrote out the whole alphabet, curving around to the right side of the writing surface when she ran out of room. In the top right corner, she wrote her name. She underlined it, and then wrote it again. "I can write my name," she said aloud, relishing the sound of the words and even more the truth behind them. "I am Skate, and I can write my name." She was whispering now, as if uttering something secret, or else something holy and deserving reverence. "I can read stories about dragons, and I can find out where Brebully is, and I don't care if the stories are lies or not, because I can read and I can write my name." She was struck by an impulse to write something on the slate, and knew she had to write it, because writing something changed it, and made it permanent, even if she or someone else erased it. In all capital letters, as compactly as she could to still keep the letters legible, she wrote:

I AM SKATE.
I HAV MAD MY CHOIS.

The letters were clear and neat, in the rigid adherence to form and tidiness only found among the barely literate. She thought it the most beautiful set of words she'd ever seen, because they were hers, and she could read them.

A drop appeared on the slate, distorting the words, the white smudging into a swirl. She wiped her eyes, then wiped the slate clean, except for "Brebully" in the corner. She set it back in the drawer, taking a moment to trace her fingers along the unseen AB within.

Skate got back in the bed and continued reading, silently now. Hours later, after eating and drinking and talking and reading again, when she finally fell asleep, the book was open a few pages later, and the ghost of a smile remained on her face in unconsciousness. The snow continued to fall in lazy flurries through the night.

CHAPTER 25

IN WHICH A DOMESTIC DISPUTE OCCURS,
AN UNWELCOME THIEF APPEARS, AND A
TOAD KNOCKS OVER A BOOKCASE.

Skate shot straight up in bed, wiping the spider webs out of her mouth. It took her a moment to realize it was her own hair she was struggling with, made wet by her open mouth during the night. With a grunt of disgust, she wiped the offending hairs away more fully and jumped out of the bed.

It was very early in the day; only the first rays of dawn were peeking through the window. She was unused to waking so early, especially from the comfort of the fine bed she'd been given. The cause of her early rousing from welcome rest was clear: the banging and yelling echoing through the vent in the floor. Still groggy, she bent down to listen. The warm air hit her feet first, then her head as she leaned closer to the vent.

"...mad at me for using the salt in my own house! I needed it last night for my stinging slime—stop throwing pots at me!"

Skate winced and tried to cover her ear as the resounding clangor of cookware shot through the vent.

"Rattle, I mean it, these things cost money to replace, and you might dent them." Silence greeted this last warning, and when Belamy spoke again, it was in much more controlled tones. "I'll get you some more salt as soon as I can. I know," he said over the sound of clicking legs. "I know food needs salt in order to have flavor. You'll just have to make do until I can get to market to buy another bag. Or maybe Skate

288

will want to go; it's her food you're worried about." Lighter clicks followed. "You're right, I should have told you about it beforehand. Even better, I should have purchased some for the lab instead of using up the kitchen supply. As I said, though, I can't fix it right now. I've got a bigger problem to deal with. I'm sure Skate won't mind helping you."

A few more clicks, then the faint shuffling of feet. Skate stood up and chuckled. "He's going to send me shopping," she said, and shook her head. She got dressed and went downstairs. When she saw Belamy at his desk, she almost fell down the remaining steps.

He was no longer dressed in his green robes that he had worn every day since she had first met him. Instead, he was bedecked in the bright red robes gifted to him as a payment for his service in the war. He was not sitting with a book open in front of him, as she was used to, but was standing with his shoulders hunched over a pair of leather bandoliers, each slot filled with glass jars of varying size, shape, and contents. As she walked, he selected a vial and placed it into the inner folds of the magnificent robes.

He looks like he belongs with the Baron's court, she thought. The robes changed his entire appearance. Instead of a doddering old man wrapped up in old dusty books, he looked like a commander, an aristocrat. There was something military about his appearance, though he bore no weapons or insignias beyond the royal seal at the collar. This warlike character had not been nearly so pronounced when the robes had merely been on display, and seeing them fully in this way was jarring. Something about Belamy's face had changed, as well; he looked determined. He carried himself with a surety and determination that was at odds with the old, unimposing scholar she knew. She was looking for the first time at the Iron Wind, readying himself for a battle.

He turned his gaze at Skate, and softened immediately. The frown of cold command melted into a polite and welcoming smile. "Good morning," he said, taking another vial and putting it into a different pocket without looking at it. "How was your rest?"

"Good. That vent does a really good job keeping the room warm," she said while she pointed at the one on the wall. "Unfortunately, it also lets in sounds that might otherwise not have reached upstairs."

"Ah," Belamy said, glancing at the kitchen. "Yes. Well." At a loss, he returned to his inspection and storage.

"Everything okay?"

"Yes, I think so. Or, I think it will be. I, uh, may have used up all of the salt in the kitchen in my work last night. I had run out, you see, and no one would have been willing to sell to me in the volume I needed in the middle of the night, so I had to improvise. He's sore at me," he said, jerking his head toward the kitchen, "but it couldn't be helped. There's no telling how much of this I might need today, and I refuse to be caught unprepared." Though he was looking at his assortment of glass bottles, his gaze seemed far away as he spoke. "I do not wish to cause harm to anyone, least of all innocent bystanders or victims of the troupe. I must have these tools available for their sake. No casualties, no injuries if it can be helped." He shook his head and blinked, clearing his head. "Anyway, I say that to explain that your breakfast will likely be somewhat bland—" His words were accompanied by a banging in the kitchen. He spoke a little louder to be heard over the tumult. "Somewhat bland this morning. Would you mind going to pick up some salt later? Perhaps after breakfast? Rattle will gather the coins you need."

"Sure. What's going on with all this?" she asked, gesturing toward the robes he wore, the surface of which shimmered in the morning light, the glint of rubies noticeable to the point of distraction. "Going to some party or something later?"

"Not at all," he said, laughing. "These robes were a gift from the king. I've told you about them, I think. I've taken them out of storage because they're not merely ornamental. They're heavily enchanted, both for attack and for defense. I do not know the extent of the abilities of these minstrels, and I doubt our conversation will go entirely peacefully. I expect a fight ahead, so I've put on my armor, so to speak." He took two more vials and placed them in their appointed places within the fold of his robes. Satisfied, he rolled up the remaining bottles in the leather bandoliers and closed the straps on each. "These," he said, lifting both of the containers off the desk, one under each arm, "are what I was working on last night. Some tools besides magic to try to make sure no one gets hurt, if it can be helped."

He swept past her with the potions and down the hidden staircase, which stood open and swung lightly on its hinges. She moved to follow him, but remembered the burning in her eyes and throat from the night before and thought better of it. Instead, she went to the kitchen. Rattle was busy cooking, though its movements were jerkier than usual, and its wings flapped with more force.

"Hey, Rattle."

It turned to look at her, not slowing in its movements. Though its speed was unaffected, its motions smoothed out when it saw her. It freed one leg and waved it at her, then returned to its business. She left it alone and turned back to the living room in time to catch Belamy headed for the door. "Hey, when are you coming back?"

He had his hand on the door. "When I have the information I need." His voice was hard once more. He did not turn around.

He'll be fine. The Ink would be present, but Belamy was a lich prepared for battle. Any mention of the thieves would invite unwanted and uncomfortable questions. "Good luck."

He nodded and walked through the door. The day outside was bright but cold. The sunlight shining down and reflected on white snow made the glare painful to look at. The brightness created an aura of red around the wizard as it refracted and reflected on his robes. He stepped lightly from the doorway and floated into the air. Skate hurried to the door and leaned against the jamb, watching him float. Some pedestrians pointed and clapped as he soared like a red fluttering bird late for its migration through the cold. Skate smiled and went back inside.

The Ink was expecting her to take advantage of his absence, to take his most precious possession from downstairs and flee. Instead, she went back in and closed the hidden bookcase.

After bounding up the stairs to retrieve her book, Skate returned and sat down heavily in front of the crackling fire. Either Rattle or Belamy had recently placed two new logs. She spoke the words to change the hue to blue, and began reading about the history of dragons, likely from the land of Brebully. *I need to ask Petre about that,* she thought as she brought her finger to the point on the page where she'd left off.

Rattle came in with breakfast (scrambled eggs and fried toast), then floated back to the kitchen to clean up. As Skate took bites of the toast and ran her free hand along the words, unease set in. Would the Ink send people after her when it became apparent that she was not going to be stealing from Belamy? Or would they be sufficiently concerned about the might of the wizard and war hero that they'd leave the wizard's house alone?

They don't know he's led armies. They won't fear him for that. Even if they do stay away, the streets won't be safe for me anymore. I'll have to become a shut-in like Belamy. It made her sad to think of, but did nothing to change her resolve; handing over the wizard to slavery under threat of destruction of his soul was unthinkable now that she had finally made her choice against it. She returned to her reading and had gotten through the current page when white light filled the room.

Skate turned toward the door, shielding her eyes from the invading light. There were several people outside. One of them was in the doorway itself, someone tall and thin. "Morning, girlie."

She leapt to her feet, making the book flop onto the floor, pages-first with a dull thump. Kite came into the house proper, not bothering to shake any of the snow and ice off of his shoes as he did so. His band of ruffians followed him in, most of them older than he.

The noise of their entry had gotten Rattle's attention. It poked its body into the room, took half a second to realize none of these people belonged here—*Especially not Kite,* Skate thought—and blasted out of the kitchen, its body a whirl of spindly legs attempting to connect with anything and anyone to cause harm.

Kite smiled his feral smile and threw something at Rattle. A net of heavy metal wrapped itself irresistibly around Rattle, sending it tumbling to the ground in a tangled mess. Two of the crew jumped on the mess, holding Rattle down as a third moved in with a thin ball of rope.

Kite walked past the tussle and straight up to Skate, that same heartless, snakelike grin on his face. He stood for a moment, almost twice her height, and paused. He moved, and Skate doubled over; he had been so quick that she couldn't follow his motion as he drove his fist right into her stomach. The breath had been knocked out of her, and it took a moment for her to recover long enough to even begin coughing. She fell to her knees. As she tried to catch her breath, Kite bent over and whispered in her ear, "Payback, girlie. Didn't think I'd let that knock to my jewels go by without a fight, did ya?"

Skate coughed a few times more before she was able to get her breathing back under control. Once she did, she climbed back to her feet and shot Kite a hateful glare. He went on smiling.

Kite turned to the rest of the crew, those who were not busy with Rattle. There were two of them, and they were eyeing the walls lined with books. Skate knew the look well. They were appraising value, trying to determine if there was anything worth taking while they were here. "You lot," Kite said, "get to work. Find something expensive enough to be worth putting your soul into."

"What? What are you doing here, Kite?"

"The Big Boss was worried a little brat like you wouldn't be smart enough to take full advantage of the old man's absence. So he enlisted Boss Shade to send a crew. I volunteered because I *missed* you so much." A flash of hate crossed his face so intensely that she worried he'd hit her again. However, it passed, and he stood at an angle with his arms crossed, hands within a comfortable distance of his blades. "I figure you don't even know where the thing you're supposed to take actually is, so we're gonna look around for you. Just to help, you know?"

He's gonna look for it and turn it in for himself to get all the credit from the Bosses. Skate's mind raced furiously. She realized with a jolt that she was not necessarily defenseless. *This house has magic stuff in it.*

"I know where it is," she said, crossing her own arms. "I can go get it right now."

Kite arched an eyebrow. "No kidding? You know where it is?"

"I said I did," she said, flashing out anger of her own. "Lemme get ready to go out and I'll snag it."

Kite searched her face, then waved one of his arms. *After you,* the gesture said, though Kite's persistent mocking grin told her he didn't believe her or trust her. "New plan," he said to the thieves who were rifling around in one of Belamy's many bookshelves. "Follow girlie here. Make sure she doesn't make a break for it. She says she already knows where it is, and that she's gonna go get it." The two thieves looked at each other, shrugged, and walked over to Skate.

"Whenever you're ready, kid." There was no emotion in the man's voice.

Skate knew this guy would kill her immediately if he began to worry about her loyalty or intentions. She assumed the other brute would be the same, though he stayed silent. "I'm gonna get dressed, grab some extra stuff I wanna take, then come down and show it to you."

The talking thief looked at Kite, who went on smiling and said, "Follow her up."

Skate stared daggers at Kite but went to the stairs without another word. She spared a glance at Rattle, who'd been double hog-tied with the twine. The eyeball struggled under the weight of the metal.

Kite saw her glance and said, "Big Boss was interested in this thing, so we're bringing it to him. Maybe in one bag, maybe several."

Skate looked away and entered her room. The men followed her in. She was already wearing her clothes, so there was nothing in the dresser she was going to need. Instead, she walked over to the desk and took out the slate and chalk. She erased the notes she'd written (including the name of still undiscussed Brebully, home of the Lost Brink Islands' likely first dragon). "Either of you lieutenants?"

They shook their heads. The talking one asked, "Why? What are you writing?"

"I was gonna ask you how to spell 'gotcha,' but I guess I'll do my best." She scratched out a simple, one-word message and signed it with her initial:

TAKEN
—S

"Gotta give him a little something to think about, y'know?" Neither of them spoke, so she placed the slate and chalk on top of the desk and wiped the dust from her hands. Then she edged past her guards and went into the library.

"What's in there?" The talkative thief was gesturing to Belamy's bedroom.

"Nothing worth anything. It used to be his bedroom, but he doesn't sleep anymore. I've been in there; anything worth money rusted or crumbled years ago."

Skate walked across the library to Petre, by the window. She picked his globe up and brought him close, pretending to examine the glass for scratches. Petre showed up looking very concerned. "Help me," she whispered to him. He understood at once. He spoke into her mind as he had when they'd first met.

You remember that little statue you picked up the first time you entered the room?

She nodded almost imperceptibly.

Its name is Ungor. When you need it to appear in full, say "Ungor Egeiro." Got it?

She nodded again and turned back around. The two other thieves were watching her with dispassionate attention.

"Here," she said, walking over to the toad statue. She picked it up and tossed it to the one who had been talking to her so far. "The old man said it was worth money. Consider it a peace offering, huh? Maybe keep Kite from hitting me again?"

The thief examined the figurine and shrugged. He placed it in his pocket. "Kite does what he wants. I won't let him kill you, though."

"Thanks, that's a big comfort," Skate said. She left the library, carrying Petre in the palm of her hand. Kite and the other three were busy rummaging through the wizard's belongings. She felt another flash of anger when she saw Kite pocket the golden enhancer from Belamy's desk. She went to her coat and slid Petre within before putting it on. She also pulled on her boots.

Kite turned his attention to her. "Ready yet? We don't have all day."

"We've got at least a few hours, and you know it. He's going to the Baron's district, and it'll take him a while to find who he's looking for." She got the second boot on and got to her feet. "All right, let's get it."

Skate walked over to the hidden staircase and activated the false book. The case unlatched and swung forward. She raised the collar of her coat over her face and was about to step down when Kite spoke up again.

"Wait," he said, his smile gone. Something about her confidence and what she was doing had unnerved him. While she was nervous, he was in control. Now that she was confident, he didn't trust her. He pointed to two of the thieves who had secured Rattle. "Follow her. Make sure there's no way for her to get out."

These other thugs did as ordered. Skate said through her collar, "You might want to cover your face until we get the vents open down there. The work he does is hard on the eyes, otherwise." The thieves followed her lead and covered their faces with their shirts. She led them down.

The coat helped but didn't get rid of the eye-burning effect of the vapors completely. Skate pointed to the levers of the vents, and the thieves moved to shift them and begin airing out the room. While they were busy, Skate reached into her pocket to place her hand on Petre's prison. "We're in the lab," she muttered.

Petre's voice resounded in her head as if he were speaking right into her ear. *You're going to want to mix cockatrice bone dust with calcified spider's eggs. Both white powders. High shelves. Barrison keeps one in a blue jar, the other in green. Get out of the room as soon as you mix them.*

"All right, you two. I need you to look for a key to this door," she said, as businesslike as possible. She knelt in front of the closed door and took out her lockpicks. She inserted the tools into the proper place, knowing full well she was picking an unlocked door. "I'll try to get through without it, but it'll be easier if you get the key. He keeps it in either a blue jar or a green jar, way up top. The jars are usually full of flour." She did not turn to look to see if her words were being heeded; she had to focus on "concentrating" to sell the lie. After a few moments, the sound of glass scooching on heavy wood filled the room. She continued pretending to attempt to conquer the lock, muttering at her continued failures to do so.

"In here?"

Skate turned and nodded. The scar-faced ruffian held a blue jar filled with white powder, slightly smaller than the flagons they used in pubs. "Dump it there," she said, pointing to the middle of the room, "so none of the flour touches anything else in here. If it's not in there, look for the other jar." She returned to her performance. The rattle of the empty jar rolling across the floor echoed quickly from wall to wall.

"Nothing," scar-face said, and the sound of glass on wood resumed.

Eventually, the other thief in the room said, "Hey, I think I got the other jar. I don't see no key in here, though."

She turned and saw this other fellow, pimply and pockmarked, shaking a small green jar of white powder, holding it up to one of the room's magical lights to get a better view. "It's small. Just dump it with the rest of the flour and get it out of the stuff. This stupid lock is giving me too much trouble." She put the tools away in her coat and stood up, waiting by the door with apparent interest in seeing the key pulled out of the pile of white. The pimply man poured out the "flour" into the other pile, sifting through the powder with his hands and creating a mixture of the two substances. "Both bottles empty?" she asked, placing a hand on Petre's globe to make sure he knew she was actually talking to him.

"Both bottles empty?" You weren't supposed to mix all *of it together! Get out of the room, now!*

It took her long enough to register the words that she saw the scar-faced man nodding as he looked for the key. "There's no—hey!"

Skate shot through the storage room door and closed it behind her, leaning against it with all her might. *They're gonna break it down; I can't hold against two grown men. This isn't gonna work; it isn't—*

Skate was thrown backward from the door, getting the wind knocked out of her as she collided with a busted old dresser. She looked up, expecting to see two very angry thieves ready to knock her silly. Instead, she saw what looked like very thick wooden spider webs crisscrossing in every direction in front of the door. The webbing stopped at the threshold of the room and covered about three quarters of the doorframe. Inside the lab were cries for help, muffled as if being shouted from underneath several layers of blankets.

Skate got to her feet and scratched her head. With her other hand, she pulled out Petre. "What did I just do?"

"Alchemy," Petre said, turning his eyes to look at her handiwork. He was no longer hiding his voice. "It's a mixture that creates a very fast-acting adhesive. It's not advised to use the reagent in such volume," he added, turning back to look at her, "but I should have explained that. Speaking of explanations: What is happening? Who are these people?"

"They're thieves. They're here to steal the thing that Mr. Belamy has put his soul into, to try to force him into service for them."

"They *what?!*" His eyes widened in shock. "How do they even know he has one of those?"

"Because..." She winced and forced the words out. "I told them. I was supposed to steal it for them."

"What?"

"I'm not gonna; that's why I needed your help," Skate said, casting her gaze frantically around the room for the statuette. She saw the blue gem of the woman's small staff peeking through the drawer she'd left it in. She scrambled over the detritus of the storage room to get to it. "They've already caught Rattle upstairs. I need to get it free before we get out."

"Stop!" Petre shouted. Such was the power in his voice that Skate did stop, though she was only a few feet from the small statue. The display case for the war robes stood open and empty nearby. "Skate, you're here to steal from Barrison? After all he's taught you, after all the time—"

"No, you're not listening. That was why I first moved in here, but I'm not gonna do it. These guys are still gonna want it, though, so I gotta grab it and take it to Mr. Belamy. Is the statue his soul tether?"

"I..." Petre's eyes were wrinkled in concern. "He never told me what his tether was, and I never asked. But the statue he used to keep on the mantle upstairs is a likeness of Alphetta. He may have made that his tether."

Skate nodded and reached into the drawer. "That's it, then. We gotta get outta here." Without another word, she dropped Petre back into her pocket and put the statue in another pocket. She returned to the almost-blocked doorway and tested the webbing; it did not stick to her skin. It was like touching stone or very sturdy polished wood. It seemed able to support her weight, so she began climbing it, using the intersections of webwork as foot- and handholds. There was just enough space at the top of the webbing for her to slip through.

The alchemical reaction had created a network of holes through which the magical lights could shine, sending spots of light throughout the room that was suddenly much smaller. She had to crawl toward the staircase over what used to be the lab.

Skate looked down and saw the thieves, her would-be gaolers, trapped in the webbing. The scar-faced one was unconscious; his heavy breaths lifted his head, which dangled limply from his body suspended against the wall, with each fresh intake of air. The pimply thief was very much awake. His wild eyes were darting around the room.

His were the cries she'd heard in the other room. The webbing had hardened right across his mouth. His nose was free, and his breaths were not the deep breaths of unconsciousness, but the frantic breathing of terror. She stopped her crawling and pulled Petre back out.

"Are they gonna be all right?"

Petre's eyes roved over the damage. "They should be as long as someone eventually gets down here to cut them out. If it takes a few days, they may starve. It looks like the web managed to break some of the containers, but it hardened around them instantly. They shouldn't have to worry about any poisoning."

At the mention of poison, the pimply thief redoubled his efforts to be heard. Satisfied, Skate slipped Petre back into her pocket. "He said you'll be fine," she said to the muffled man, and continued her uncomfortable crawl to the stairway.

"What's going on down there?"

Skate recognized the voice as that of one of the thieves who had followed her upstairs earlier. "Ungor Egeiro!" she shouted up at him.

"What? What was—" His words were drowned out by his yelp of surprise and pain. There were other voices yelling, but their sense was lost as they echoed down the stairs.

A mighty croak reverberated down to Skate as she reached the base of the stairs and slithered through the small opening left to her. She took the stairs two at a time and found a bizarre scene unfolding.

The talkative thief was sprawled on the floor, his blade out but neglected in his limp hand. He wasn't moving, and one of his legs had an angry red splash where his pants had been torn. The silent thief was engaged in a tug-of-war with a rope wrapped around his throat—no, not a rope, she realized, but a tongue. Ungor the statue had become Ungor the Giant Toad, a great bloated monstrosity the size of a sofa, with red blotches scattered all over its bumpy skin. It was trying to pull the thief into its gullet. Kite, meanwhile, was hacking at the tongue to no avail. His blades might as well have been trying to cut solid stone.

He saw Skate and pointed at the toad. "Help us, you little slug! It's trying to eat him."

Instead of answering, Skate spoke the Dwarvish words to revert the fireplace to its natural color. *"Gerunk haktha."* The room was now awash with red-and-orange light. The change in color created a dizzying effect, and Kite looked around in a clear panic.

"You're a witch?" He looked from the toad to his companions. With a whimper, he bolted wide-eyed out the door into the cold, his panting nearly becoming a scream with each vaulting step. Skate ran and shut the door as soon as he left, and then turned around in time to see Ungor take a step toward the remaining thief, who had been brought to his knees by the might of the beast.

"Stop!" she said, knowing it was useless; the mouth was already shadowing the doomed man's head. To her surprise, the toad turned her way and stepped back, still holding its tongue around the neck of the struggling, silent thief. Stunned into silence that yelling had actually worked, Skate took a few seconds before saying, more calmly but just as forcefully, "Let him go." Again, inexplicably, the monstrous toad obeyed, sending a wave through its tongue that slackened the grip around the man's neck until it came loose. Ungor then snapped the impossibly long tongue back into its wide mouth and unleashed another reverberating croak. Looking at her expectantly, it sat back on its huge haunches—knocking over an entire bookcase as it did so and scattering leather-bound tomes over its own head.

Skate walked over to the thief on the ground. He had several large scratches that were seeping red onto the floor and the rags of his pants. She looked at Ungor and saw a telltale red tinge on his left webbed claw.

Skate ran over to the shelf where Belamy's healing decanter sat undisturbed. She ran back over to the injured man but was stopped by an inarticulate grunt from the other thief. He was standing and massaging his throat, but he had his long knife pointed at Skate. Seeing his mouth open, Skate suddenly understood why he did not speak: he had no tongue.

Skate looked on, incredulous. "You're threatening me? Seriously?" As if to accentuate her point, Ungor croaked again. The thief winced but did not lower his blade. Instead he pointed from the decanter in her hand to the man lying on the floor and shook his head. He said something incomprehensible.

"It's going to help him," Skate said, moving over to the man despite the weapon pointed her way. "Don't be stupid." She knelt and poured the liquid—not all of it, as she remembered Belamy's warning that it must always contain some of the liquid within or be ruined forever—over the man's injured leg. The wounds sizzled and smoked as they began to close immediately. The unconscious man sighed as his breathing got easier and heavier.

"Now," Skate said, walking back to the shelf from which she'd taken the decanter, "go down those stairs and start hacking away at the mess. Your two friends are down there, and one of them is still awake. If you want them to live, go get to work."

He wavered, the blade in his hand shaking. After looking at the healed man on the floor, he darted toward the open bookcase. The sounds of heavy snapping began to echo up the corridor.

Skate pulled Rattle out of the net. It clicked its legs in thanks. When its attention turned to the man on the floor, the clicking intensified in agitated pops. It waved a spindly leg at the gigantic toad, as if there were nothing out of the ordinary about its presence.

Skate retrieved Petre from her pocket. "Ungor listens to me."

"Of course. You're the one who called him out of his sleep." The awoken toad croaked again, shifting the toppled bookcase and sending even more books sprawling. "He's a great guardian, the last one that Barrison kept after the war. Other than Rattle, of course." Skate dragged the unconscious man near the door and tried to pile up the disheveled books.

After several minutes of hacking from downstairs, there were grunts. The silent thief returned, carrying the unconscious scarred man on his shoulder. Behind him came the pimpled man, who eyed Skate with hateful intensity. He whispered something to the tongueless thief, who shook his head emphatically. Skate guessed what the topic of conversation was.

"Listen to your partner. You're outnumbered. There's four of us and only two of you. And you don't have any magic," Skate said, speaking the words of the fireplace to make it turn blue once more. The pimpled man's frown deepened, but he looked away. He scooped up his fallen comrade.

As the thieves crossed the house's threshold, the pimpled man looked back and said, "This ain't over. Not by a long shot."

Skate said nothing, but Ungor managed a hideous growling croak in response.

When they were gone, Skate shut the door and looked around. "He's not gonna be happy," she muttered, looking at the mess and thinking of what must be an even greater catastrophe downstairs. Still, his soul tether was safe. She pulled the statuette out of her pocket. *Maybe the soul tether.* "Probably," she corrected herself aloud. It wasn't safe to stay here. The pimpled man was right; once Kite got back to the Ink with word of her betrayal, they'd converge on the house ready for an all-out war, searching for the statuette and for her.

"We need to go," Skate told everyone, putting the statuette back safely.

Petre swirled into view. "Yes, I was afraid you'd say that. They won't just cut and run, will they?"

"Not a chance. I caught them by surprise, but they'll be ready when they get back. We gotta leave."

"To escape vengeance."

"To find Mr. Belamy," she said, nodding toward the door. "We're not safe with just us, but if he knows we're in trouble, we should be fine." She looked at Ungor, who was looking very content nestled in the corner. His fist-sized eyes blinked lazily. "I'd like him along, but I don't think he'll fit through the door."

"You can put him back to sleep. Say 'Koimao Ungor,' and he'll revert to his trinket form."

Skate spoke the words, and Ungor became something less than solid. With one more belching croak, it shifted back into the figurine that could fit on a shelf. She scooped it up, placed Petre in her pocket, and went into the street. Rattle clicked and bounced behind.

CHAPTER 26

IN WHICH A SPY IS SENT SKYWARD, A
CONFESSION IS MADE, AND STOMACH FIRES
ARE DELIBERATED.

Skate was something of a spectacle as she made her way through the streets. She knew it was nothing to do with her and everything to do with the thing that was flapping along behind her, with spider-like legs clicking loudly in the cold mid-morning air. The streets had been partially cleared in the night, so commerce was back in full swing, with wagons and carts being slowed interminably by scads of pedestrians off to buy and sell and trade and visit and gossip, all desperate for the end of winter.

Rattle—or, rather, the spectacle that Rattle provided—gave the benefit of creating a comfortable berth around Skate. Those who gawked did not wish to get too close, and those who weren't gawking found themselves swept up in the tide of shifting movement. Even the Keepers would look up from their endless struggle against the snow to mark Rattle's passing, discussing amongst themselves if any of their number had ever seen such a thing, only to reach the inevitable conclusion that no, they had not. The attention, while uncomfortable, made Skate's trip to the Baron's district much less of an exercise in drudgery, despite the frigid conditions and distance.

The crowds thinned a bit as they got closer to the area of town dominated by the Baron's mansion and influence. Clothing became finer, more decorative. The stares became more disapproving. And, worryingly, Skate and Rattle had managed to attract the attention of a

303

passing patrol of the Guard.

Skate picked up her pace. The patrolmen were not running: apparently, they did not want to alarm any of the pedestrians by appearing to rush. She cut through an alley to save time.

The biggest issue at the moment, of course, was that she did not know where exactly Belamy was, and finding him was going to be difficult with the Guard taking such an interest in Rattle's sudden and bizarre appearance.

Once they were safely nuzzled between the two random buildings, Skate turned to Rattle. "Can you hide or something? You stick out like a sore thumb. The last thing I need is the Guard following me and asking a bunch of questions about you, what we're doing here, or who I am."

Rattle clicked once and pointed a leg upward.

"You want to just float above us until we need you? That'll work. Hey, you can even get a better view of the place to try to find Mr. Belamy easier."

It clicked again.

"Great. Go away, then, and I'll try to outrun the Guard. I'll yell if I need you."

A third and final click, and it had gone, straight into the half-cloudy sky.

Skate shot out of the alleyway and doubled back the direction she'd been coming from, hopefully throwing the Guard off her trail. The people on this street had not seen Rattle, and her appearance was close enough to theirs to prevent any particular interest.

Skate wandered the streets, looking for a crowd of people, or a stage. It occurred to her that it was entirely possible Tillby's troupe was not planning to perform in the street, but was preparing to give its most important performance in some hall or other indoor accommodation. That would make the search more difficult and time-consuming. Even here in the Baron's district, the Ink had influence and several contacts who could make life difficult for her.

While she was ruminating on these difficulties and strolling down the road with the other pedestrians, Skate became aware of a persistent hissing. She turned and saw Twitch trying to get her attention from an alleyway, attempting not to be seen in his conspicuous rags amongst the finery of the Baron's dwellers. Spotting her eyes on him, he waved her over, rather frantically. Skate made sure she was not being followed or marked by anyone before making her way over to the boy.

Twitch looked much the same as ever, though there was a tiredness to his eyes that was not usually there. His shock of wiry blond hair drifted fitfully in the light winter wind. He did not smile at her approach, but looked worried.

"What—what are you doing here?" he asked, pulling her conspiratorially into the alley with him. "It's not—not safe."

"What are you talking about?" *Did they already get news that I'm trying to leave the Ink behind? Why would it spread that fast?* Skate wrung her hands but disguised the act by blowing into them as a warming technique. "What's dangerous?"

"We've been called in to deal—deal with a lich. It's your lich, the old wizard. The Bosses think they've got—got something the old man can't do without, and they're going to try to force him into helping the—the Ink, whether he wants to or not. He's supposed to be looking for the p-people that put on that great show we got to see." His eyes lit up in wonder at the mention of the show and its performers. Skate didn't like the effect; he looked like a person turned into a grotesque mask of enjoyment, a wooden mockery of happiness. "I think they might be trying to s-s-stop the performance, too. I'm not really clear on all the det-details. I just know that when we get the signal, we're supposed to come running to wherever the b-b-brawl is and do our part to help out."

Twitch motioned to a log leaning against one of the nearby buildings. "I've got a stick—stick to help out with. I just hope I don't find the lich at the other end of th-that thing." He shuddered. "Fighting a wizard who won't d-die? No, thanks." His concerned expression returned. "But enough about th-that. What are you doing here? Did the Bosses s-s-summon you away, too? Stealing the th-thing from the old man's house would have been more important than an-anything here, right?"

"There's been a change of plans there, Twitch." Skate looked around to make sure they were not being watched or listened to. "I'm out. I'm leaving the Ink."

His face screwed up in confusion. "Leaving? W-what? Why?" His head jerked to the side, a familiar expression of agitation.

"They're asking me to do something I can't. They want to turn Belamy into a slave, to be a tool for their schemes, whatever they are. I won't do that to him. I can't."

Twitch was shaking his head. "But he's a l-lich. He's not alive; he's not a p-person."

"He is. He's not alive, but he's still a person. I'm not gonna hand him over." She searched his face. "You're not gonna run off and rat on me, are you?"

"I…" His voice trailed off and he looked side-to-side, not meeting her gaze. "No, of c-course not. But w-what are you g-gonna do?" Now he did look at her, and there was only concern in his voice. "They're not gonna l-let you just leave, especially not when they were expecting all of th-this work from you."

"I've already sort of let them know I'm leaving," Skate said, "and I think Kite will be pretty quick in delivering the message." She explained the fight at Belamy's house, and how she had all but declared her retirement from the Ink through her betrayal. "They'll know soon, if they don't already, that I'm not bringing Belamy's soul tether to them." She resisted the urge to place a reassuring hand on the statuette in her pocket; there was no reason to announce to Twitch (or anyone else, for that matter) that she held the thing. "Do me a favor: whenever what's going to happen happens, stay out of it, okay? Belamy isn't gonna try to hurt anybody, but I don't wanna take chances."

Twitch wasn't listening. "What are you g-gonna do? I mean, how're you gonna s-stay away from the Ink?" He brought a hand up to his head and scratched nervously. "They're n-not gonna just let this go. They c-can't. It's one their r-rules. 'Ink always stains,' remember?" He looked her in the eye for the first time since her pronouncement. "What's y-your plan?"

"I'll stay with Belamy. He's strong enough to protect me. He's a wizard who doesn't sleep or need anything."

Twitch was shaking his head again. "They know where h-he lives, though, Skate. They've got wizards of their own, plus m-more they can hire if they need to. How many w-waves will it take for them to break through? How many attacks would he be willing to put up with f-for your sake?" He put a hand on each of her shoulders. "The Ink doesn't g-give up, Skate. The Big Boss would never allow it. They'll keep coming after y-you until they've got you. You know th-they will."

It was Skate's turn to avoid eye contact. He was right. You could be kicked out if the Boss thought it was a good punishment, or you could leave on good terms if you made a hefty payout.

Attacking members before leaving was...decidedly not advisable.

"I don't care," Skate said finally, still looking at her feet. "I don't care what they'll do. I won't do what they want. It's wrong. I don't care if Belamy throws me out or gives me over to them to get them to stop. I can't put him into their hands like that. Not after..." Her words trailed off because she didn't know how to end that sentence. After he'd taught her to read? After he'd taken her in even though she was a thief? After she'd seen his memories? Any or all or none of these might have been the reason; she could not be sure, even now, what the deciding factor in her defection had been. *I know it's right, though.* She raised her eyes. "I won't betray a friend."

Twitch nodded. "Neither will I." He looked out into the street. "You n-need to go. We n-never talked." He picked up his stick and went back to his post at the end of the alleyway, then shot a glance back at her. "Good luck, Skate."

She wanted to say something more, but she heard the cause for Twitch's concern: Kite was coming down the street, talking animatedly to someone. She ducked behind a stack of empty crates and waited for them to pass.

"—not lying to you. I got no reason to lie about this."

"Spare me. You don't need a reason. You're a deceitful creature, Kite, as you have always been." She knew the other voice; Haman rarely sounded this mad. "You cannot expect me to believe that in a few short weeks a girl seven years younger than you has managed to master difficult and complex magical skills. You say she summoned a demon frog out of someone's legs, trapped two men in magical webbing, and cast a spell to hypnotize and disorient you? Preposterous nonsense. Stay ready, Twitch."

Twitch said nothing, but evidently Kite and the other speaker stopped right in front of him to continue their talk. When Kite spoke again, he was seething, but kept most of his composure. "It ain't nonsense, though, is it? I got witnesses. She didn't manage to kill any of us;

you ask the other four—they'll tell you what happened. It were magic, Haman. Real powerful stuff."

"I doubt very much that their reports and yours will match. They never have, have they? Always inconsistencies between your own reports and others'. Extraneous details implanted or crucial information omitted, names misremembered and locations blurred, outright contradictions left unexplained. I'll say it again: spare me. Go report it to your new Boss. I'm sure he'll be more than happy to listen to whatever you have to say. Why are you here talking to me about it?"

There was a shuffling of feet. "Boss Shade don't like it when jobs go bad."

"Nobody likes that, Kite. It seems Boss Shade has even less time for fools like you than Boss Marshall does."

Another shuffle of feet, though this time there was what sounded like a shout followed by a grunt. The sound of coughing and retching echoed down the alley. When Haman spoke again, his voice was almost a growl. "Don't ever think you can touch me, Kite. Ever." The coughing continued, and Haman sniffed dismissively. "Unpleasant," he muttered. "Twitch, come along. We think he'll be closer to the Plume. Our inquiries have told us that at least one of the performers has been seen there in the past weeks."

"O-okay." There was the sound of crunching snow as the two went away, and Kite's heaving was slowing down. He groaned.

"Kill him. I'll kill him, never mind the rule." Kite coughed as he got to his feet, and more snow crunched underfoot, though he went in a different direction than Haman and Twitch.

Once she was sure she was alone in the alleyway, Skate stood and crept back toward the street. Stepping over Kite's pile of sick and holding her nose to block out the smell, she turned left to follow her fellow thieves to whatever the "Plume" was.

Haman's height made it fairly easy to keep track of him, though he blended well into a crowd with regard to his clothes; dressed as if he belonged here among the wealthy and elite, he seemed quite at home. Twitch stuck out, of course, but he was small and easy to forget once seen—and hard to follow over the heads and hats of the well-to-do. Haman turned a few heads as he walked, almost all from silly young women in wholly impractical heavy dresses.

The Plume, it soon became apparent, was a coffeehouse nestled among other shops—a bookstore, a haberdashery, a stationery shop, and a wine store were all cluttered around a central courtyard. The Plume's sign had a set of feathers of a fantastical nature: delicate, long, and thin with a circular pattern at the end. Skate had never seen such a feather, but the sign held five of them arrayed like a fan, under which was the name of the shop etched in wood.

Skate lurked by the edge of the courtyard. Haman turned and spoke briefly to Twitch, and then stepped inside. Twitch turned and walked toward Skate. She didn't want to be seen, so she stepped off to the side and let him pass. Then she made her way across the courtyard and stepped through the fine, heavy door of the Plume.

A bell rang above the door to announce her arrival, but none took note of it. The place was full today; the rich loved to discuss current events, the rumors of trysts among their fellows, the degradation of the poor—all topics great and small passed through the doorways of every coffeehouse in Caribol, and the Plume was no exception. Jokes and games of chance and waitresses and waiters fluttered around the room in a dizzying flurry, so that the arrival of a modestly dressed little girl was missed by all in the room. That did not include the watchful eyes of Haman Vaerion, who had placed himself alone a few seats from the door and was pretending to be very interested in a nearby conversation as he nursed a steaming mug. In reality, Skate knew that he had focused all of his attention on watching the door. His eyes scanned over her with a flicker of recognition and confusion. He did not get up.

Skate slipped around the tables toward the counter, where the proprietress stood with a hand on her hip. She was talking to a customer.

"Sir, I assure you, the drink came to you as you ordered it."

"It did not; it did not!" He accentuated his words with small knocks on the counter with his knuckles. The old man had a bristly white mustache that hung over both lips. He was dressed expensively but not well; he looked disheveled and more than a little upset. "I asked for a dark cocoa flavoring, and I got a sweet flavoring. I cannot have sweet things—my poor stomach aches when I eat or drink anything sweet!" Though the grating of his voice betrayed him to be old indeed, his words and tone would have otherwise led Skate to believe she was listening to a particularly prissy, spoiled child.

The proprietress did an admirable job of hiding the roll of her eyes by wiping gingerly at her forehead with a handkerchief. "I shall send you another cup at half the advertised cost by way of apology for the error. Would that suffice, sir?" She smiled the practiced false smile of servants and salesmen, and the old man's irritation melted into satisfaction.

"Indeed it will. I shall have to give the other to my...niece." His cheeks flushed, and he shuffled back over to his table, where he joined the men and women there engaged in a rousing game of cards.

The owner's smile vanished as soon as his back was turned. "Old cheapskate. You knew what you ordered the first time. You just wanted a discount on your drinks. And if that strumpet is your niece, then I'm a..." Skate never heard what she was, because the owner began mumbling too low to be heard, and swabbing off the counter with more force than was strictly necessary.

Skate announced her presence with a cough. "Ma'am?"

The owner stopped her mumbling and looked up in surprise. "Hello, young miss! I didn't see you there; so sorry."

"Not a problem—I mean, it is quite all right," Skate said, catching herself. "I would like a cup of whatever kind of bean you deem most appropriate—plain, if you please." The seat beside Haman became vacant. "I'll take the drink down there," she added, pointing in that general direction.

"At once, miss," the owner said, arching an eyebrow at the girl. Her slip of words had not gone unnoticed but was also not sufficient to cause any genuine concern.

Skate stepped back and took the empty seat she'd wanted. Haman did not pay her any mind beyond a sideways glance. She took her drink when offered by the servant boy.

"That'll be three blades, miss." Skate's eyes widened at the price, but she fished out the coins and placed them in his open hand. He seemed a little put off when she put her money away, but said nothing. When he left, Skate turned to find Haman looking directly at her.

"Hey," she said by way of greeting.

"Hey yourself," he said, taking a sip from his drink. "You're supposed to tip here."

"What?"

"That's why that boy shot you a dirty look. You're supposed to pay more than what they ask for. 'Be open with your gifts.' You know the words."

"Not gonna happen. Three blades for a mug? That's thievery, that is." Skate took a sip from her mug and had to steady herself on the counter. It was the strongest brew she had ever tasted, and had a pleasant flavor she could not place. She'd never had a cup of coffee like it, and she decided as she took another sip that perhaps the price was not as unreasonable as she'd first thought. "And I oughta know, huh?"

Haman smiled at the joke, but it was a reserved smile, more out of politeness than any real mirth. "Everyone in this room ought to, in one form or another." He cleared his throat and moved on. "Anyway, I fear we have much to discuss. I have heard troubling reports this morning."

"From Kite."

"Yes. I take it from that surprisingly accurate guess that you know what he told me?"

"I overheard you near the alleyway. He told you that I had learned some sort of powerful magic, and that I used it to attack him and his goons, and that I was leaving the Ink?"

Haman nodded and looked back at the nearby table in their animated conversation. They seemed to be engaged in a vigorous debate about the nature of taxation and its purpose between Caribol and Herzeschal, the capital city. One group of the coffee drinkers was convinced it was a politically driven choice of the crown being used deliberately to punish the merchant lords to placate the nobility. Another section of the table was adamant that it was not a political choice but an economic one; it was common knowledge that the kingdom had never fully recovered from the loss of a huge cache of goods at sea some months previously, and the crown had to recoup the losses somehow. Still another faction was almost frothy with rage at the other groups, and claimed this was the doing of the church; for how else could the High Weaver afford his fantastic cathedrals throughout the kingdom if not from extra money delivered to his feet by the reigning monarch? The arguments were loud and numerous, and seemed at points to be near blows, but never actually came to that.

"Is it true?" asked Haman.

"I don't know. I've never even been to Herzeschal."

"You know what I mean."

"Not all of it." Skate took a steadying breath before continuing. "I'm not a witch. I don't know any magic." She tapped out a skittish rhythm on the table with her index fingers. "The rest of it is true. I threw some stuff of Belamy's at them, and it scared them enough to leave. Kite was the first to run."

Haman snorted. "No surprise there."

Skate smiled weakly, but she soon found the expression a waste of time and effort. "I can't take from him, Haman. I just can't. He's done too much for me."

"He's an inhuman thing. He's not alive. He's a monster."

"No," Skate said, shaking her head after the first sentence, "he's not. I know it doesn't make sense, but he's not. He...he taught me to read and to write."

"And he's done this out of charity? Out of the kindness of his heart?"

"What do you mean?"

"Did he make you pay somehow? Or was it a free service offered?"

"Well..."

"Of course it wasn't. He wanted your help to steal things, didn't he? That was why he was letting you stay in his home, so it only makes sense that he'd be interested in securing more books in exchange for lessons. It was business. Though I'm sure he was quite friendly and hospitable, it's all been for him. Business." Haman paused to let his words sink in. "Now, my question to you is this: Have you overestimated the good nature of your teacher? Have you treated this as a business endeavor, as he has? Because to me, from the outside viewpoint, it looks as though you've been misled."

Skate had stopped her nervous tapping. Instead, she was clutching her white cup. The warmth of it gave her something to focus on instead of Haman's words. "He's a kind man." It was a sentimental triviality, she knew, but she also knew it was right. *He is kind. And that matters.*

"I'm sure." Haman's voice was dry and had a lilting humor to it, giving the impression that he seemed to find her answer both funny and sad. "But is that really worth throwing the Ink away, the only family you've had for most of your life?"

"Yes."

The lack of hesitation in her answer surprised him, and he chuck-led. "Well, I guess it's a good thing you're so sure. If it had only been Kite, you'd probably be able to get away with telling people he's just a liar. No one would've doubted that. But with witnesses and others attacked...there's no going back. The choice has been made. The ink's on the page."

Skate tightened up, her stomach twisting into a knot of apprehen-sion. She had just admitted to a lieutenant that she was breaking from the Ink, and that she had done so violently. She had no protection any-more, and Haman probably had orders from the Bosses to eradicate deserters in some violent way or other. Whatever he did, she needed to be ready.

What he did was to take another drink from his cup. He set it down, linked his fingers as he leaned on the counter, and turned his attention to the conversation of the other patrons. They had moved on to discussing some writer she'd never heard of, and how his work proved some crucial point or other.

Skate scooted her cup away. As it was scooped up by the servant boy, she decided to push her luck. "You're not gonna blow me away with wind or burn me up with magic fire?"

Haman chuckled again. "Not in here," he said with heavy irony. "It would upset the other guests, and I'd never forgive myself for breaking up such a meeting of minds." The ghost of a smile remained on his face as he continued, "No, Skate, I'm not going to hurt you. No one else in here knows who you are or that you're now a former member of the Ink. There may be two other people in here who know what the Ink is, but only from the customer side. I know no one who matters saw you come in, and I know you've got the good sense to make sure they don't see you go out. I've got no reason to hurt you, other than a slavish devotion to the rules of the organization—and try as I might, I simply haven't internalized those well enough to follow them when no one's looking."

"You really think he'll show up here?" Skate asked, turning in her own seat to watch the endless coffee-fueled argument.

"One of them probably will, either Belamy or Tillby. If it's the former, then we're supposed to approach him and apprise him of his situation—or rather, now, to apprise him of a false situation that is, for all he knows, true. If the latter, we're to simply have him followed until he makes whatever move he and his band of free agents are planning to make today. I hope if Belamy does show up," Haman added, throwing a glance her way as he reached for his cup, "you'll have the good sense to realize all that stuff I said about not needing to follow any rules goes out the window. You interfere in that conversation, and I'll start a fire inside your gut."

Skate smiled her own sarcastic grin, and nodded at the door. "Looks like I live to lie another day."

Carsen Tillby let the door shut behind him with a satisfied air and swept his hat off with a flourish.

CHAPTER 27

Tillby was still kicking the ice off his boots when Skate slid from the seat. "See you around," she said to Haman as she melted into the general hubbub of the shop. She found an elevated bench along the opposite wall, where she could keep a weather eye on the room as a whole—and on Tillby particularly.

Skate crossed her arms and scanned the crowd. On the bench with her was a young, aristocratic-looking couple gossiping away about those in the room, especially the old man and his "niece." Skate ignored the prattle and followed Tillby's progress to the bar.

He began by leaning on the counter and flashing his smile at the proprietress, who seemed to have no difficulty now with a genuine smile of her own. Tillby said something and brushed the back of her hand, which she promptly retracted to her mouth in a gasp that may or may not have been honest. The slight red that flushed her face indicated it was. A bit more conversation followed, during which the proprietress kept on smiling but avoided Tillby's eyes. Tillby then left the bar with a wink and sauntered out the door.

Haman, who had continued sipping his coffee as if he were utterly uninterested in anything but the arguments playing out in the center of the room, set his cup down and followed the man. Skate waited a few seconds before following suit.

Tillby's hat made for a conspicuous marker as he sauntered through the streets. Though Skate was several dozen feet behind him, it was almost impossible to lose track of the man.

Haman was nowhere to be seen. Whether he was simply following alongside Tillby through back alleys and staying out of sight or had made himself unseen through some trick of magic, his pursuit went undetected.

Other members of the Ink were not so stealthy. Skate recognized some members of Boss Marshall's crew moving through the crowds and backstreets, dressed in borrowed or stolen clothing to better blend in. However, no amount of fine haberdashery would hide years of desperate, hard living etched into the eyes of those afflicted, and even the least-practiced observer could have found them out if they had brought any attention to themselves as they made their way around carriages and crowds.

Tillby's hat disappeared through a side street, and Skate waited a moment to let his other pursuers follow suit before taking the same path he had. Once there, it was a simple matter of following the other thieves' course. Now that they were out of sight of the main host of the district's residents, they made no secret of their haste or intent; steps quickened and voices grunted with the effort of stomping over undisturbed piles of snow and ice that got in the way.

Skate turned a corner to find herself in a sort of makeshift courtyard, an open space behind the backs of several buildings. She did not see Tillby. Nor, apparently, did anyone else. The gang of thieves were looking around and arguing with one another.

"You lost him, you idiot."

"I did not; I was following you—"

"My foot, you were. I followed you down the path—"

There were numerous such squabbles among the gang, while others were conferring in more subdued tones, trying to find out where the man had gone. A voice rang out among them, and she recognized it as the voice of Tillby.

"Good afternoon," he said in false joviality. "I trust your travels through the city have been pleasant." A stack of junk against one wall disappeared within a wisp of smoke to reveal three figures close to the wall: Miss Amanda and Kibo the Magnificent were on either side of Tillby and immediately put their hands to work.

Acting on instinct, Skate covered her ears, turning away and ducking around the corner. She began humming a random note to drown out any sound that might get through.

Skate sat for what felt like a few minutes before she chanced a removal of her hand from one ear. She heard nothing. Feeling emboldened, she peeked around the corner. The Ink members were standing in a crowd facing away from her and toward where Tillby's troupe had been. The performers, however, were now at the back of the crowd, talking amongst themselves in animated gestures and excited tones. They were not hiding their voices at all.

"—went as well as could be expected."

"Yes, and that's great, but what are we to do with them now that we've got them?"

Tillby stroked his beard and thought about Amanda's question. "We've got them for several hours. Why not just leave them here and have them join in with the main group when we get started?"

"I have a better idea: distraction."

Tillby arched an eyebrow and motioned for her to continue.

"Send them to the other side of the district and have them cause havoc of their own a few minutes before we begin; that will mean fewer Guards springing up to stop the next crowd."

Tillby laughed and clapped Amanda on the shoulder. "An excellent idea! Kibo, will there be any difficulties in keeping these under thrall and moving forward with her plan?"

Underneath his wrappings, Kibo shook his head. He brought his arms out in a self-enveloping hug to warm himself. "No problem."

"Good! That's settled then. Give them their order and send them on their way. Then we'll go set up."

Kibo nodded and turned toward the crowd. Without a word, the whole gaggle turned to meet his gaze. There they all stood, looking dazed and stupid. Again, without a word spoken, they all moved at once in various directions, their slack jaws tightening up in a slightly unnatural grimness.

Kibo nodded, satisfied, and turned around. "We've got about twenty minutes."

"Then let's put on a show," Tillby said.

The other two nodded in turn and strode out of the makeshift courtyard. Skate followed at a safe distance to watch their progress.

They exited out into the street near a set of shops not unlike the area the Plume had been built in. In the middle of the white-covered lawn, presumably a garden in the warmer months, the three of them got ready. Skate watched from behind the low fence that separated the shops from the main road. Amanda got out her instrument, and Kibo began to stretch his fingers while Tillby called to passersby and patrons. "Come one, come all, my fair ladies and dashing gentlemen! We bring to you a show the likes of which you have never had opportunity to witness, a greater experience than all the wealth you could buy. We charge nothing for it, but only pray that you will give whatever pittance you can be moved to part with in appreciation. If it displeases you in any way, you may keep your coins. We hope only to move your hearts, not your purses. Come one, come all!"

The lines were followed by similar calls, and a crowd began to gather. Most buskers were thrown out of the Baron's district in short order, but most buskers did not look like Tillby's troupe. Some Guards approached at the sound of shouting, but they made no move to restrain the performers. In fact, they lingered at the edge of the crowd, though whether that was out of a desire to maintain order or to get a better view, Skate didn't know.

Tillby was introducing *The Tales of Beuford Hall* in a much more prolonged manner than he had in the slums—probably, Skate guessed, in order to let the crowd continue to grow—when a hand touched her gently on the shoulder.

The jeweled red sleeve trimmed in blue told her who it was before she turned all the way. Belamy was not looking at her, but at the crowd and its centerpiece. "You ought not to have come, Skate."

"They're going to hypnotize everyone in the crowd."

"Yes, I know."

"I'm not sure why, but they've already caught a bunch of thieves and sent them off to cause trouble."

"Very shrewd of them."

"I'm not sure what they're planning."

"Look where they are. Take a guess. Think of what you know."

Skate turned back to the crowd full of people chattering excitedly, some almost giddy with anticipation, others only slightly above boredom. *They've been planning this for a while. People who watch and listen will do what they're told.*

"The shops," Skate realized. "They're going to rob the shops."

Belamy dropped his hand from her shoulder and walked toward the crowd.

"You're gonna stop them?"

"I need to talk to the inestimable Mr. Tillby about his contact with the thieves. I think that would be harder to do once he has everyone under his thrall." Belamy did not slow down as he spoke, but he had raised his voice accordingly in order to be heard. "If the show starts, stay away. You don't want to get caught up in it."

"Wait." Skate knew what she was going to say, but her self-preservation was screaming at her not to. He turned to face her, brow pinched in concern. "I'm one of them. One of the thieves. They're called the Ink, and they're taking money from Gherun each month now. Whether you give his books back soon or not won't matter. Do you need to do any talking to Tillby now?"

Belamy's expression did not change for what felt like minutes. Then, as Tillby continued working the crowd up into excitement over the promise of a coming story, Belamy went from a slight frown to a smile—a full-faced, gleeful smile she had never seen on his face before. "Thank you for being honest with me, Skate. No, there's no need to talk anymore."

Belamy turned toward the crowd and launched himself from the ground, seeming to lunge an impossible distance. The wind whipped his robes while he flew, and he looked like a streak of flame over the white snow. He slammed into Tillby, who shrieked in fear as they flew into the air. Belamy held him there by the front of his shirt. He was saying something while the crowd gasped and pointed. Amanda stood in shock, and Kibo began to wave his arms and mutter. The magician's lower half became a whirlwind of smoke, and he flew up to meet the airborne pair.

The Guards had begun trying to disperse the crowd in order to get a handle on the situation. The spectators, however, were not budging; most assumed this to be part of the show. Only when the Guards began yelling and shoving did members of the crowd begin to scatter. Kibo, Belamy, and Tillby were talking in tones too low to be heard this far down, but Kibo looked ready to lash out at Belamy, who, for his part, held Tillby with both hands and was chatting with a pleasant air. As they spoke, Kibo's posture became more relaxed, until he was eventually "standing" with arms crossed, as if listening to a conversation about the weather. A member of the Guard saw Skate and walked her way.

"Young miss, you need to stay back." Even in the midst of potential catastrophe, the Guard treated people in this district with a level of respect Skate had never received from the armored men and women. "We don't know what's going on here. It could be—"

Screams rang out from some of those still refusing to move from the spectacle. A blast of fire enveloped the airborne trio, and sparks from the fire landed on those below. Panic sent the crowd running. Loudest of all was the full-throated roar of Miss Amanda, who saw her friends swallowed by the flame.

As the fire cleared, two forms plummeted the thirty-or-so feet to the ground, though the path was not straight down; it looked like Kibo was trying to keep them aloft, but failing. Tillby's fine hat was aflame, and he was swatting at the fire coming for his face. Both men's flesh was red and angry-looking in patches.

Skate looked up to see Belamy, unperturbed by the fire, scanning the windows and rooftops for its source. He reached into the folds of the war robes and took out one of his bottles. Another gout of flame surrounded him, and this time Skate caught a glimpse of something blue and green swirling around the old man as the fires passed over him; his magical protections were still hard at work.

Belamy shot off toward a nearby roof, where someone shouted in alarm. He tossed his bottle down. The tinkling of glass could be heard over the general tumult of the fast-dispersing crowd, followed by a ghastly sound of coughing and retching.

Belamy returned to his position in roughly the center of the courtyard, only to be blasted out of the sky altogether, this time by a fork of lightning from the window of the top floor of one of the inns in the circle.

The snow cushioned Belamy as he fell, but not by much. The thud was strong enough that Skate felt the tremor from roughly fifteen feet away. "Mr. Belamy!" she shouted, running toward where he'd fallen. She could not see him for all the snow he'd ploughed into, but the mound of the mini-crater he'd made stirred slightly.

Skate pulled up short as another blast of lightning fired directly at him from still another location, this time much lower and from the milliner's boutique. Skate fell over as she tried to back away and looked on in horror as two more forks of lightning assaulted the pile of snow, blasting gouts of the stuff away as powder and water.

A member of the Guard stood nearby, dumbstruck. Skate scrambled to her feet and pulled on his arm. "Do something!"

The Guard just shook his head, mouth agape. "No reinforcements," he muttered dully. "All busy on the other side." His voice trailed off into silence again as the spectacle continued and Belamy was struck by yet another two, three, four bolts of lightning. Skate tugged on the arm again before giving up and running toward the old lich again, ready to sustain whatever pain she needed to in order to help him get up.

Wait. Petre's voice came to her as a whisper carried by wind, but it froze her in place. One more bolt of lightning struck Belamy's location, and then everything stopped.

The crowds were gone. The attacks had ceased. Some faces appeared in windows, looking down at their handiwork, smirking that they had been successful in bringing down a mighty foe. Skate recognized none of them but assumed they were either members of the Ink or had been contracted by the Ink for the special danger of bringing in a powerful spellcasting undead man.

The silence was broken only by the stuttering sound of sparks and a few hesitant cries of victory.

A tremendous flash seared Skate's eyes as Belamy shot out terrible lines of lightning. They tore into the shops around the square. The tentative victory cry gurgled into a low groan and then fell silent altogether.

Skate blinked several times to clear her vision. Belamy stood in front of his crater, half of his face a horrific, charred black, though he did not seem bothered by his injuries. The windows around the courtyard were all aflame, and no more lightning shot forth to beat Belamy down.

Belamy nodded and approached the troupe, who had scooted off to the side of the courtyard to avoid the assault.

Skate ran toward him and caught the last part of his sentence.

"—want to leave."

"Yeah, no kidding." Tillby winced as he spoke, and leaned on the nearby railing for support. "What's going on? Who are you?"

"As I said, I approached you because I thought you might be of service in making contact with a dangerous group of thieves in the city. They seem to have found me in the meantime."

"Yes, and almost killed us in the process!" Amanda was standing rigid, her fists clenched into tight balls of fury at her sides. Her jaw was set in a pugnacious scowl. "You're responsible for this," she said, pointing to the burns along Kibo's and Tillby's bodies.

"Not quite. I have reason to believe the thieves were following you as well, in order to prevent whatever you were going to do with your captive audience today."

"Take a cut of the booty, more like," Tillby said through a smirk that he managed not to turn into another expression of pain.

"Yes, well. In any event, it does not seem they're terribly interested in you any longer, so I'd cut your losses and escape while you can."

"You said it." The huckster and showman stood to his full height with another wince. "Hey, doesn't that, uh, hurt? That doesn't look so good." He ran a finger along his own face to mirror Belamy's injuries.

"I'll be fine. Off with you now."

The troupe members looked to one another, shrugged, and ran as quickly as their injuries would allow. Miss Amanda took the lead, as her instrument had been smashed in all the hubbub, leaving her unburdened. She cajoled and encouraged the other two around a corner, and they were gone.

Belamy turned to greet Skate. She recoiled instinctively; the lightning had burned his flesh to a charred mess on half of his face. One eye was burned shut. Even aside from that, he looked wrong. His undamaged skin was sallow, and his good eye was pale and covered in a gray film. Nevertheless, he smiled at her, as if he were just wearing some sort of grizzly disguise.

"That really doesn't hurt you, does it?"

"No. I don't feel pain because of my...condition." As he talked, the charred skin began to crack. The smell of burning meat made her take a step back and gag.

"My apologies. The spells blasted away my disguise. Why are you still here?" His familiar look of concern was marred by his injuries to become completely unsettling.

"I thought...I thought you were hurt."

Belamy smiled again, and shook his head. "My body can be damaged, but I don't experience hurt anymore. You can't actually hurt a dead person."

"Did you know I was one of them?" There were still shouts and screams from around the square; the panic had not subsided. Two of the rooms blasted by Belamy's spell had caught fire, and that was causing an uproar of its own. Despite all of that—and despite understanding that in all likelihood, the Ink was not done with its assault yet—Skate needed to know.

The smile shrank somewhat but did not disappear, leaving a small smirk along the side of his face unburned by the lightning. "Not until ten minutes ago. Rattle told me."

"Rattle can't talk."

"Perfectly true." Belamy tapped his temple with his index finger. "But he can show me everything he's seen and heard if I want him to. He flew off after you two split up and met me." As he spoke, Rattle came into view in the sky, its legs jangling together in their familiar clamor. It came to a floating position at Belamy's eye level. "You did well to summon Ungor. I'm guessing Petre helped with that?"

Skate nodded. "He didn't exactly explain what would happen, though."

"Your intuition served you well."

"You're not mad."

"Not at all. There will be a mess to clean up, to be sure, but nothing world-shattering."

"I meant about me lying to you."

Belamy scratched a piece of burnt skin, which flaked off. "No, I'm not mad. You were on the streets, and you did what you had to do in order to survive. Of course you kept that from me, especially once I decided to set myself up against them. How could I be mad, anyway? You defended my home. You chose to protect me at great personal cost. There's honor in that—far more than any you could have possibly lost by simply choosing to survive." He knelt down and placed a hand on her shoulder a second time. "I'm proud, not angry."

Skate looked down. "Oh." She couldn't say anything else. She felt her cheeks flushing and warmth pouring over her ears.

Mercifully, Belamy took his hand away and stood back up. "You need to leave now, Skate."

A coldness had crept into his voice. The Iron Wind was speaking to her, and he was looking behind her, pale eye narrowed and jaw set. She turned to see a very unwelcome sight: the Big Boss entering the courtyard, flanked by two bodyguards. His too-large eyes scanned the damage done to the shops with only passing interest. As he approached the three of them, he handed off his cane and hat to one bodyguard, and his coat to the other.

"Barrison Belamy." His voice was calm and cold, as it had been when he was talking to her, but there was a note of something else in his tone that she couldn't tease out yet. "The Iron Wind at battle again."

A member of the Guard ran up to their location. "You lot, clear out of—" The bodyguard holding the coat spun around and hit the approaching man with so much force that the Guardsman's leather cap flew a dozen feet through the air. The man fell to the ground and did not move.

The Big Boss continued as if there had been no interruption. "I must admit, I'm impressed. I really did think that five of them would have been enough to handle you. My mistake." He picked at something underneath one of his nails, and Belamy's eye went wide.

"Hugo."

Skate turned to the wizard. "You know the Big Boss?"

Belamy said nothing, too stunned to do anything but stare in disbelief. The Big Boss chuckled and said, "Oh yes, he knows me of old. Old mates, we are. Eh, Colonel Barry?"

The use of the nickname shook Belamy out of shock enough to finally respond. "You're dead, Hugo."

"Oh, Barry," the Big Boss said, pursing his lips in condescension, "no more than you. Why you waited until you were so decrepit to make the change, I have no idea." He laughed again, this time revealing all of his pearly white teeth. His canines seemed to elongate as he spoke. "Luckily, I wasn't so foolish as that."

Belamy regained his composure, and the face of iron returned. "A vampire, Hugo? You were willing to sell your soul to a monster in order to avoid dying?"

"Turns out, it was well worth the deal. I got her in the end, and it left me free to do whatever I wished. And what I wished was to become important in a large city. I think I've done pretty well so far."

Skate's foot bumped into a building. She had been backing away from the Big Boss in horror since she'd seen his teeth. She pressed her back up against the wall, willing herself to disappear into the room behind—anything to put more distance between herself and the vampire. Twitch's stories filled her mind, ghastly images of blood and terror that took the strength from her legs.

"How are you standing here? It's midday. The clouds are not thick enough to protect you; you should be burning in the light of the sun."

"Oh, I bypassed that hindrance long ago. Before I even founded my little group, in fact. When you've pledged your service to me, I might let you in on the secret. After all, eternity is a long time, is it not? I'm sure we'd run out of other topics of conversation eventually."

At that moment, a hand grabbed Skate by the arm and pulled her up. She shrieked, imagining a set of teeth puncturing her neck—and indeed, there was something sharp pressing against her throat.

"Hello again, girlie." Kite held her in front of him with knife poised to strike, his arm across her chest and clasped at the shoulder.

Hugo tilted his head. "I think the threat hardly needs saying at this point, does it?"

Belamy stood where he was, eyes darting from Skate to Kite to the knife. "Hugo, this is madness. She has nothing to do with this."

"On the contrary, she's got everything to do with it. She's how I found you. The fact that her fate concerns you at all is proof enough that her death isn't a price you're willing to pay. So, you agree to come along, and we'll keep her nice and safe."

Belamy said nothing for what felt like a long time. When he did speak, the hardness had not left his voice, but he spoke in a low tone that made it difficult to hear. "And I would just have to take your word for it?"

"I'm sure we could arrange some form of visitations or something. Once or twice a year, just to prove that she's safe." Hugo's eyes twinkled as he spoke, and a hint of a smile cracked his pallid face. "I could do a lot with you working for me, Barrison. We'll own the whole city within a few years, with every nobleman and merchant prince either in our purse or under our boots. From there, we start working toward the rest of the kingdom; then we spread out from there. We've got nothing but time, right?" He crossed his arms, waiting for a reply.

Belamy said nothing, but his hands were twitching behind his back and his mouth was moving wordlessly. He opened his mouth a final time and a shriek rang out right in Skate's ear. Kite dropped the knife and pushed her forward. No, not pushed, she realized—he just knocked into her as he began to slap at his hands, his chest, his face.

"Oh God, get them off, get them—"

Then two things happened at the same time:

Rattle tackled her to the ground and crouched protectively over her, its spider-like legs forming a wide-barred cage around her. Kite, who was still slapping and scratching at something only he could see, was knocked over by someone much smaller than he, wearing gray rags and with a streak of blond hair showing on top of his head.

"Twitch!" Skate tried to get to the tussle but couldn't fit between Rattle's legs; it kept closing them wherever she tried to bolt through. Kite, for his part, seemed intent on swatting away whatever he thought was on him. He did manage to break free of Twitch's grasp and elbow the boy in the nose, though.

Twitch fell back with a hand on his face while Kite scrambled up to his feet.

"Help me, help—" Kite cut his words short with a strangled gasp and brought his hands to his neck.

Belamy had his hand outstretched toward the young man, and Skate let out a gasp when she turned her attention toward the wizard. He looked almost unrecognizable. His face was twisted into a grimace of hatred only made more horrible by the charred black burn arcing up one side of his face and the dead blindness of his good eye. He flung up his hand, and Kite flew into the air, kicking feebly as he clawed at his constricted throat. Already, he was turning red from the strain and lack of air.

One of Hugo's bodyguards moved toward Belamy, but Hugo put up a hand to stop him. He was watching with his wide eyes, never blinking, that same ghost of a smile playing at the corner of his mouth.

The guard returned to his respectful position behind Hugo.

Belamy spoke, his voice a monstrous growl. "You slime, you *worm*." Kite was kicking and sputtering, his face becoming a deeper shade of red, edging toward purple. "You would threaten a child—a child under my protection? Cowardly filth." He brought his hand down sharply, slamming Kite into the ground.

Kite grunted but could do nothing else with the unseen hand choking him. His eyes were bulging as he struggled in vain to escape the grasp of the wizard's magic.

"Unfit to live," Belamy growled.

"Stop!" Skate cried. Kite's eyes were bulging with effort, but she saw the silent plea in the wild stare. "Mr. Belamy, stop!"

Belamy fixed his glare on her, and she found herself clutching Rattle's legs for support. He looked monstrous.

"Why? This loathsome rat would gut you at first opportunity. I've seen how he acts; I've seen the way his mind works. He's a waste of space who is only now, for the first time in his selfish, wretched life, contemplating the concept of mercy because he'll benefit from it." Belamy turned his snarling face back toward Kite. "The world's better without him in it."

A particularly nasty voice (one made all the worse because Skate knew it to be her own thinking and no one else's) was screaming in her head: *He's right! Think of the knife at your throat! The people he's hurt and probably killed, the way he looks when he's threatening you. He'll never stop coming for you, he—* She shook her head and the thoughts evaporated. "You said you weren't going to get anybody hurt if you could help it. With the lightning, you were just fighting back. This is murder. Can't you help this?"

When Belamy snapped his gaze back to her this time, Skate didn't recoil—partly because she'd steeled her nerves for it and partly because his face was not still a mask of hatred. Instead, he looked shocked at her question. "I can...help it. Yes. Yes, of course."

Belamy shook his hand loosely, and Kite sucked in a desperate and stuttering gulp of air. He coughed and retched as he crawled away from the lich. He didn't crawl toward the vampire either, but toward a nearby tree. He rolled against it and continued coughing into the slushy snow. When Belamy spoke again, she recognized the voice. "I'm not a monster. You're right."

Hugo's airy laughter caught their attention. He stood with a hand on his chest, as if struggling to contain himself. "My, how disappointing. I thought I'd be meeting the Iron Wind again. But no," he said with a deep sigh that ended any echoes of his laugh, "I see I was mistaken. You're only a burned-out husk who tells stories to himself. You won't embrace what you've become. It makes you weak." Hugo waved at the bodyguard who'd moved earlier. The man stalked toward Kite. "I don't tolerate weakness. You'll learn that while you work for me."

The bodyguard was halfway to Kite already, a thin and wicked-looking blade produced from somewhere in the sleeve of his coat.

"Wait," Belamy said, holding up a hand to stop his progress.

The bodyguard stopped as if he'd run into an invisible wall. He turned toward Belamy and growled, opening a mouth with elongated canines. Belamy's hand gripped again and tossed violently, throwing the subservient vampire backward.

Hugo stepped aside and let him crash into his other bodyguard. Belamy kept pushing, and both of the bodyguards smashed through the wall of the fancy bakery.

Hugo stood looking at the lich with disgust. "Where was all this mercy of yours sixty years ago? What made me less deserving of receiving it than him?" He gestured toward Kite and put his hand on his hip. "Is it just a refusal to do what's necessary anymore? It doesn't matter," he said, not waiting for an answer. He put both of his hands behind his back and stood at a military-style rest position. "I've decided to destroy your body for now. We'll find whatever you tied your soul to and trap you when you re-form. It'll be easier to deal with you that way."

Hugo made no move, and Belamy was likewise still. The latter spoke. "I'm sorry, Hugo. You did not deserve to die."

"Empty words that cost you nothing. Spare me your false sympathy, your meaningless platitudes, they—" Hugo cut off his words a split second before Skate noticed the reason why: Belamy was waggling fingers and muttering quietly.

Faster than Skate could follow, Hugo crossed the two dozen feet between him and Belamy and stood directly in front of the wizard. He struck Belamy hard across the face, on the side where the lightning had done its damage.

Belamy staggered, and Skate gagged; the blow had torn the blackened skin completely from the wizard's face, leaving the ghastly white skull to shine in the midday sun.

Belamy turned with the blow, his half-face frozen in concentration as he continued muttering. He finished his spell, and a glittering sphere of translucent white enclosed both him and Hugo together, with only two feet or so on either side of them to move around in.

Skate was distracted for a moment as Rattle's legs moved, and footsteps approached. Twitch had come to stand beside her. He was clutching his nose, which was bleeding. There were blotches of red across his gray rags where blood had either splattered or he'd tried to stop it up. He said nothing but watched the confrontation.

"Foolish," Hugo said, his voice perfectly audible through the sphere. "Now you've nowhere to go. And we both know I'm the stronger by far." He accentuated this last word with another blow across the face. The crack of bone was audible as he kneed the old man in the stomach and delivered a third blow. With each hit, Belamy made no move to block anything, but brought his hands around him as if trying to curl into a ball and avoid the worst. The jewels of the robe glinted in the sun with every shifting movement.

The bodyguards had extracted themselves from the shop and were walking at a leisurely pace to the other side of the sphere, content to watch their master at work. Hugo was holding Belamy up with one hand, the old man's legs dangling loose below him. Hugo brought the wizard in close and said, just loudly enough to be heard by the onlookers, "I'm going to enjoy working with you, Barrison." He pulled back and delivered a terrible blow to the forehead, denting it in and sending the Iron Wind to the ground in a heap. The rubies glinted all over his robes.

Belamy had landed in such a way that he was looking at Skate. The side of his face with skin on it smiled, and his mouth moved. She heard his voice in her ear: "Rattle will show the way."

"Speak up, Barry; it's the last time we'll get to talk for a while." Hugo bent over him and snarled.

Belamy did not turn to look at him, but did resume speaking in an audible tone. "Do you know what one of my most successful tricks was during the war?"

"Do tell; I'm sure it's very interesting." Hugo delivered a kick that sent Belamy flying into the side of the sphere, which reacted not one iota to the force of it.

"If we were ever outmaneuvered and found ourselves retreating, I'd lay a very particular trap along our path that invariably caught any pursuers unawares. It—" A punch into—literally into, Skate realized—Belamy's chest cut him off, but only momentarily. The damage had not prevented him from speaking, somehow. "It was a very simple spell that only took a few words and a single object. I could set the trap to detonate for any time I chose, as long as I knew about how far away my enemies were—and I always knew, you understand; I made sure, every time. When it went off, they'd suffer losses and eventually give up the chase. Do you know what the object was the spell called for?"

Hugo picked him up by the collar of his robe, and shook a stray hair out of his own face. "I bet you're gonna tell me."

"A ruby."

Hugo cocked his head to the side in curiosity. Then his narrowed eyes widened in understanding as he looked at the robe in his hands and saw those strange, glinting gemstones. With a hiss, he threw the old man back to the ground and began to claw at the sphere. It withstood every blow and scratch. The bodyguards tried to help from the other side with an identical lack of results.

"Go find a wizard, you idiots!" Hugo continued to pummel the prison, and the two bodyguards bolted into the street, each one charging off in a different direction. Belamy, meanwhile, had pulled himself up to a reclining position.

Kite had finally caught his breath and was staring in horror at what was happening. He struggled to his feet and leaned back, still needing the support of the tree trunk. Everyone ignored him.

"My apology earlier was not a lie, Hugo," Belamy said. "I'm responsible for the thing you are. You did not deserve to die for your desertion; and compounded on that, you turned into this to avoid that injustice. My gift to you is the reversal of this last crime, at least." The vampire did not react to the words, but continued bashing against the unyielding barrier. Belamy turned toward Skate and Twitch. "Run."

Hugo heaved a scream of terror, and his body contorted and folded into itself until he was the size of a fist. He sprouted leather wings and began bumping against the barrier, a bat unable to find a hole in unbreakable glass. Belamy smiled up at him, the unharmed side of his face almost matching the garish grin of his exposed skull on the other.

"Be at peace."

The gems all along his robe flashed again, almost all in perfect unison, and retained their glow for three ticks of a clock.

Flames exploded from Belamy, and there was nothing visible within the sphere but red and orange. A shockwave rippled beneath Skate and Twitch's feet as they fled, Rattle close behind.

CHAPTER 28

IN WHICH MAGIC IS DISCOVERED, AN
ADVENTURE UNDERTAKEN, AND A HEADING
CHOSEN.

They had gone three blocks before either of them dared to stop. She didn't know whether she or Twitch had halted first, but they were both panting and leaning against the wall for support. There was moisture in her eyes, and not all of it was from the sting of cold air as she'd run. *He's gone. He's really gone.*

No, not really, she reminded herself. The thing in her pocket was supposed to make sure of that. Still, the horrific way he'd been destroyed combined with his absence made it feel like he was gone for good, all planning to the contrary.

Twitch was the first to speak. "The Big B-Boss was a vampire?"

"Yeah." Skate leaned her head back against the wall and sucked several deep breaths through her nose to get her lungs back under control. "Seems that way. I think his bodyguards were, too."

"We've been working f-f-for a vampire."

"Yeah."

"Huh. Weird." Twitch collapsed against the wall, letting his fatigue get the better of him. His nose had stopped bleeding, at least; the blood sat dried and dark on his upper lip, and he wiped at it with his ragged sleeve. "How w-was he standing out in the day, then? I thought that those th-things couldn't stay in sunlight. That's w-what all the stories say. Ow." He had twitched at the end of his sentence and knocked his head against the stone.

"Dunno. Him and his bodyguards both weren't bothered, though. He said he'd figured out a way around it. Some magic or other, I guess."

Twitch nodded and blinked hard, trying to regain all of his sense. "What'll happen t-to Kite?"

"Who cares." Skate started laughing, then. She wasn't feeling happy. It was just exhaustion. Twitch joined in, and the two leaned against an unknown building, shouting with laughter that had come from nowhere. Rattle floated nearby, looking at each of them in turn, not understanding what was going on.

The laughter departed as abruptly as it had come. They took a few minutes to regain their breath, the familiar empty chuckles that usually followed such outbursts strangely absent. When she had calmed back down, Skate muttered to herself, "Rattle will show the way."

"What's that?" Twitch turned to look at her and frowned.

"Belamy told me that before his robes exploded. He said, 'Rattle will show the way.' I thought at the time that he was saying it aloud for everyone to hear, but if you didn't hear it, I guess he used magic to get only me to hear it." Skate closed her eyes and frowned. "I don't know what he's talking about."

Skate. Petre was calling to her from her pocket. She pulled him out.

"What is th-that?" Twitch's mouth was slightly agape as he watched the smoky blue glass. "Is it more magic?"

Skate shushed him. "Yes, it's magic. What is it, Petre?"

His eyes came into view through the smoke in the glass. "I thought you might want to know that the gemstone in that statue in your pocket is glowing, off and on. It was very bright in there and was hurting my eyes."

Skate set Petre on a chunk of icy snow, where Twitch immediately dropped down to see within. She pulled the figurine out of her pocket. Sure enough, the blue gemstone at the end of Alphetta's short staff was pulsing intermittently with noticeable light, almost the same way that the rubies had on Belamy's robe. The blue glow illuminated Alphetta's features in a sad way, though it was impossible to say why that should be so; she looked confident and graceful in this frozen artwork, not melancholy in any way.

"What are you?"

Skate turned to see Twitch holding Petre and spinning his prison around to try to look at him from a different angle.

"Stop that," Petre said, glaring at the boy. "If you drop me, the glass will break, and I'll die."

Petre turned to look at Skate. "Why's it doing that?"

"How'm I supposed to know? It's not like it's mine." Skate turned the statue, trying to see if there was anything else that was odd or had changed about it, but other than the light it shone every few seconds, it seemed as it always had.

She felt someone looking at her, and stopped her inspection. Rattle was standing completely still on its rigid legs, staring with rapt attention at the gem on the statue. It did not move at all; even its wings remained totally still. She moved the statue off to the side, and Rattle moved its body to follow it, with that unceasing, unwavering focus. "Rattle?"

It flapped a wing in response, but made no other acknowledgement that it had heard anything.

"Petre, what is this?"

"I'm afraid I have no idea. Rattle has never done anything like this in my many years around it. It looks like it wants the gemstone, though."

"Is that right? Do you want this thing, Rattle? Is it because Belamy is in here?"

Rattle did not respond, even with a flap, but continued to stare.

Skate moved the figurine closer to the thing, and Rattle moved forward a little in response.

Skate hesitated. Rattle was a creature of magic, and this statue clearly had magic within it; doing something unknown with it was dangerous and probably stupid. Nevertheless, she tapped Rattle with the blue stone. There was a flash, and Rattle stood rigid, straight up to its full height. The blue glow remained, but not in the gemstone. Instead, it seemed to issue from deep within Rattle's pupil, the black pit glowing azure every few seconds, exactly as it had when it had been coming from within the gemstone.

The magical creature turned and began flapping away from them with an urgency that was upsetting. It was almost out into the street when Skate had the sense to call out for it to stop.

It turned toward her and shook its body, a shiver not unlike what she'd seen dogs do after finding shelter from rain. The light stopped shining in its eye; the glow had returned to the gemstone.

Rattle flapped happily back toward them, seemingly unaware or else undisturbed by its sudden dash away from them all. Skate hid the statuette back in her pocket, not wanting a repetition of the episode.

"Rattle," Skate said, turning it toward her to look her in the eye, "I need to know something: Do you know what Mr. Belamy's soul tether is?"

It paused, then clicked once, which she had been taking to mean "yes."

"Okay. Is the statue of Alphetta the thing he tied his soul to?" Another stretch of silence, this one much longer. "Rattle, please. If it's not the tether, he could be in a lot of trouble. You saw what happened back there. We need to make sure it's safe. Is the little statue his tether?"

Still with hesitation, Rattle clicked twice. *No.*

"Maybe it's l-lying," Twitch offered, eyeing the thing with no small amount of distrust.

"No," Skate said, searching the eye for any insecurity, "no, I don't think so. The figurine isn't the tether." Rattle seemed sure of its assessment—and if it did know what the tether was, it had no real reason to lie about the figurine and every reason to tell the truth. *But this glowing thing happened only after Belamy was destroyed,* she argued with herself. *That can't be a coincidence. Well, it could be, but it's probably not.* "Rattle," she said again, "do you know where the tether is?"

This was the first question that didn't get a direct answer in response. The eyeball bat looked about, as if expecting to see either the tether or a sign pointing to it in large letters nearby. Its legs clacked indiscriminately, like heavy wind chimes she'd seen outside some bars in the docks. After several confused moments, it purposefully clicked once. Then twice. Yes, then no.

"You do know, but you don't know?"

Rattle clicked a yes again, then flapped expectantly, as if she only needed to ask more questions to get to the bottom of this whole mess.

"I get it," Skate said, turning toward the others. "The statue shows Rattle where to go. Belamy hid his tether somewhere, and we've got to go find it and find him. That's what we're supposed to be doing now."

Petre and Twitch looked at each other, then back to Skate. Petre spoke first. "Okay, you may be onto something there, Skate. But why? Why do we need to go find him? The magic of what he is ought to bring him back just fine without our help."

"Maybe. But didn't he say he became what he was in a way that wasn't normal for liches? That he found a 'different' way to make it work? Maybe this is part of the difference. Maybe somebody has to do something to bring him back to life. Unlife, whatever." The more she spoke, the surer she was that she was on the right track. "We have to go bring him back."

"I dunno, Skate," Twitch said, rubbing the back of his head and jerking slightly as he spoke. "That's kind of a r-reach, isn't it? Why wouldn't he just tell you what to do instead of all this s-s-secrecy?"

"He didn't have a reason before today to tell me anything, and when he did, he had to do it right under Hugo's nose." *Speak up, Barry.* "So he had to get the most important information to me, and he had to do it fast. 'Rattle will show the way.' That's gotta be it."

"Aw, no, the Ink!" Twitch brought a hand to his forehead. He looked worried enough to be sick. "What's gonna happen w-with the Ink now that the B-Big Boss is gone? The rest of the Bosses're gonna fight for control. This city's g-gonna go crazy." He slumped back as the reality of it hit him. "I'm in big trouble. They're g-gonna know I went against the Big Boss. I'll have a t-target on my b-back, for sure."

"So come with us."

Twitch looked at Skate, on the verge of tears. "You mean it?"

"Of course, dummy." Skate poked his nose, and he swatted her hand away. "Doesn't make sense for you to stick around here. We've got somewhere we've gotta be, and you've got anywhere else to be. Who else'd take you, anyway?" She smiled, and he smiled back.

"All right. L-let's go find your dead guy."

#ชプ乙6

The sun was setting, and Skate had a backpack on. It felt weird, because behind her stood Caribol, the city she had spent her entire life learning how to survive. The gates were almost a mile behind them now, and hoofbeats rang out around them. Skate tried adjusting the strap until she decided to just take it off and hold the bag in front of her.

There was a clinking noise as a statue knocked against a glass ball and a stoppered pitcher within. Skate opened the pack, but only long enough to make sure nothing was damaged and that the padding was in place; the blue light shining out would reveal more to any passersby than she would have liked.

The wagon driver seemed not to notice; they'd paid him enough not to, and that was worth the extra helm. "No questions asked," had been his exact phrase, and he was intent on honoring that. He hadn't made eye contact or said a word to either of them once he'd gotten on the road.

Skate turned to Twitch and nudged him. "How you doing?"

"Good. Real g-good." He looked it, surprisingly enough. They had gathered up, with Petre's help, as much stuff as they could find and sell of Belamy's to get them out of town safely, and taken the goods to one of the Ink fences. Their betrayal hadn't percolated through all the rank and file of the organization yet, so they were able to make a substantial fortune from Belamy's goods.

"People are going to rob this place when we're gone anyway," Skate had explained, and even Petre had to admit that the goods within were likely forfeit within a week. So they had left the gates of Caribol with hundreds of scepts to their names. "He can make more money when we all come back."

Twitch had shrugged at that pronouncement, taking it as an axiom that wasn't worth debating.

The boy beside her was, for the first time she had ever seen, not wearing filthy rags. They had taken the time to stop and purchase traveling gear and a new set of comfortable and functional clothes for them both. Skate still had her dress, packed tightly away in her bag, but it made more sense to find a pair of trousers; they had no idea where they were going or what they would run into, but movement was probably going to be more important than fanciness of dress. Twitch was keeping a watchful eye on the road ahead. He had told her before embarking that he was concerned about the stories he'd heard of highwaymen who would accost travelers, demanding their money or their lives. "That's how th-they say it, too. 'Your m-money, or your life.'

We g-gotta be careful." What being careful would do to help them if they did happen to get caught by someone after money, Skate did not know, but she did not press the matter. It gave him something to do on what might be a very long journey.

Skate looked to the sky, which was clear and vibrant orange in the sunset for the first time in weeks. The snow was thick on the ground, but the traffic had helped to melt it along the paved road. Above them, unseen, Rattle kept pace with their progress. They had agreed it was best for the creature not to be seen unless absolutely necessary, given its upsetting appearance.

It was thanks to its strange connection to the gem in the statue that they knew where they should go; as a test, they had tried touching it with the gemstone again, and Rattle had gone south. They shook it out of its strange trance and tried two more times with identical results. Wherever Belamy was, it was somewhere to the south of the city of Caribol. Skate had only a dim idea of the geography of the surrounding lands, but she was fairly sure there was some great untamed forest to the south. *Did he put his soul tether there, away from everyone?* It seemed dangerous, since wild animals roamed the woods, but it was possible he'd protected it with magic. It was equally possible that the tether wasn't in the woods at all, and lay somewhere farther south, or that the woods functioned as a waypoint for the direction-giving magic in the statue (and by extension, Rattle), and they'd take off in an entirely new direction soon.

Skate wasn't worried. They'd get to their destination in the end. And in the meantime, she would learn something precious, even more precious than words written plainly on a page. In her bag, she held a particular yellow book that Petre had suggested she take.

She smiled at the setting sun, relishing the cold wind that blew around her. It did not feel like an attack or an irritation. It felt like the promise of an adventure.

In Belamy's absence, Petre had promised to teach her magic.

EPILOGUE

The sun, of course, was setting inside the city as well. A pair of Guardsmen was standing watch over a gaggle of Keepers cleaning up the shops and grounds around the small blasted courtyard in the Baron's district. The fires started by the lightning barrage had not spread; the treated wood had done its work properly. Near the center of the courtyard, leaning against a sturdy tree, one of the Guardsmen, a portly fellow named Harald, was badgering his fellow about details of the events that had so scandalized the district earlier in the day.

"Come on, you were 'ere," he said, with a languorous wave at nothing in particular. "Just about th' only one, I'd wager." He guffawed and slapped the other man on the back with a customary overabundance of enthusiasm.

The other man, a stringy chap named Aigel (Egg, to his friends), winced and shrugged off the hand. "Oy, watch it." Egg winced again, and brought a hand up to his swollen jaw, purple from the blow he'd received earlier. "I already told you, there weren't nothing to tell. I got knocked out before most anything happened, and I weren't looking when the fires broke out. I was keeping people back from it all."

"You're telling me you got nothing to say abou' tha'?" Harald pointed with a sausage-like digit toward the black crater near the center of the courtyard. "You managed to sleep through whatever did it?"

"It wasn't sleep, was it? Ahhh…" Egg had clenched his jaw in irritation, and more pain shot through him. "I was hit. Hard, by one of the biggest blokes you ever saw. Weird, too. I was looking right at him, but I never seen him move before it was too late." He idly rubbed his jaw. "Never seen a guy that size move that fast, neither."

"Heh," Harald said, hitching up the heavy belt that was sagging below his belly line, "you'd be surprised by what a large fella can do in a pinch. We're a surprisin' lot, eh?"

Egg rolled his eyes.

When Harald's laughing died down, he cleared his throat. He tensed up a bit and lowered his tones. "So, you don't know anythin' about who's in the pit?"

Egg shook his head and walked over to the crater. Harald followed with slow and heavy steps. The thinner man crouched at the edge of the crater, a place where the earth seemed to have been scooped away by a shallow but immense spoon. Within was nothing but charred black dirt and two skeletal sets of remains. One set—the one opposite from where Egg was crouched—was a crumpled mess of bones. It looked like someone had emptied the contents of an ossuary with all the care and respect one might have when emptying a chamber pot, and then set it on fire.

The closer set of remains was much more organized. Someone with his back to the center of the charred crater had been blasted outward. The dead man was lying on what had been his stomach, arms out wide like a bird taking flight. The skull was turned sideways, half-buried into the blackened dirt. The mouth was open in a silent scream, trying to swallow the earth closing in on its face.

"I don't mind telling yeh, Egg, this is abou' th' worst thing I ever seen. Gruesome, it is."

There was a patch on the man's back where his skin had not burned, despite the fact that his back had borne the brunt of whatever fiery end he'd met. On this patch of skin between the shoulder blades was a tattoo; in the waning light and with their hesitation to get near the bodies, they hadn't looked too closely at it. They knew, at least, that it was a feather design.

"Yeah. Gruesome and strange. The lieutenant is bringin' in some snoop-for-hire to try to figure this out. Says the rich people got spooked by the craziness."

"Hmph." Harald crossed his arms and glowered at the pit. "Magic did this, no question. Far's I'm concerned, we'd be a lot better off if they just outlawed wizards 'n' such. Or hired more of 'em for the Guard. Or both." He cleared his sinuses and spit heavily on the ground nearby. "Anythin' that can do somethin' like this is too dangerous, it is."

"Not gonna happen, mate," Egg said, standing up and grimacing as the rush of blood hit his head. He could feel one of his teeth grinding against its fellows. "Most of the ones we know about live right here in the big job; ain't no way they'll let the Baron outlaw magic. Augh, this toof!" In a desperate bid to rid himself of the pain, he'd reached into his mouth and found the offending molar. It wiggled freely at his touch. There was nothing much connecting it to anything anymore. He pulled, and out it came, though it split in two in his palm. "You think a priest'll put this back in?" He spat—as he'd expected, the saliva was an upsetting shade of red—and turned the split tooth over in his palm.

"Yeah, if you're gonna make a 'donation' to the poor box, I'm sure." Harald looked around and leaned toward Egg. "Listen, let's go see now? They don't need us 'ere, and that'll only get worse the longer yeh stay away from the healers."

Egg dithered, but gave in when the throbbing in his head returned. "Yeah, let's go." The two Guards left their post.

If the Guards had stayed, they would have seen the tattoo on the dead man's back turn a deep red and felt the pull of the wind toward the body. If Egg had paid attention to where his spit had flown, he'd have felt a pang of guilt: it had landed on the nearby dead man's open mouth. Egg was not a very pious man, but he was superstitious. He would have considered the offense to the dead a great portent of ill luck. Further, if the light had been better and the two had been less skittish about approaching the body, they might have noticed something even more upsetting about the nearby corpse than his undamaged and once-again-dormant tattoo: an elongated incisor, from which a drop of Egg's bloody saliva now hung.

The mouth of the dead man closed, turning up dirt and coming together in a soft click. The red spittle disappeared between its teeth.

TIMELESS BOOKS • QUALITY AUTHORS

www.ThinklingsBooks.com
Facebook.com/ThinklingsBooks
@ThinklingsBooks

Thinklings Books started out when three speculative-fiction-loving professional editors—Jeannie Ingraham, Deborah Natelson, and Sarah Awa—got together and formed a writing group. We called ourselves the Thinklings, in honor of C.S. Lewis and J.R.R. Tolkien's group, the Inklings.

Over time, we found ourselves agonizing more and more about how messed up the publishing industry had become. Why couldn't good books get published? Why were so many bad books published just because their authors had big Twitter followings? We wished there were something we could do about the problem . . . and then we realized there was.

As a developmental editor, a substantive/line editor, and a proofreader, the three of us knew good writing when we saw it—and we knew how to make it even better. We had a lot of experience walking our clients through the publishing process—both traditional and self-publish—and we had contacts with marketing and design experts. We had some amazing unpublished books lined up and ready for production. We had, in fact, everything we needed to make a great publishing company. All that was left was to actually do it.

So we're doing it.

Spectacular Reads. Every Time.

Survival isn't enough. She has to win.

The name's Cartier. Mercedes Cartier. Anyone asks, I'll swear I'm a "secretary." That's what my card says, so it must be true.

Mostly, I keep my head down, do my job. But I'm not about to let power-hungry traitors get away with murder. Or crazy demon-fairy-things seduce my boss. Or psycho cannibal children eat me.

Honestly, I probably shouldn't be having so much fun.

Bargaining Power **by Deborah J. Natelson**

One bite on her hand...a million problems.

After a wild animal attack, Melanie Caldwell thinks she just needs to go to the doctor. Then she's kidnapped on the day of the next full moon, and discovers in the worst way that monsters are real...and that she has become one of them.

All Melanie wanted was to get a boyfriend and graduate college. Now she has to deal with agonizing monthly transformations, a secret organization stalking her, friends and enemies trying to discover her secret, and hunters looming on the horizon.

Hunter's Moon **by Sarah M. Awa**

Technology Hates Janet

After she accidentally smashes a floatcar through City Hall, the bureautopia sentences Janet to captaining the starship S.S. *Turkey* and its misfit crew. Her mission: to boldly rescue a prisoner from the one corner of the universe colder than her ex-boyfriend's heart—Pluto. Which, aside from not even being a real planet, is the one place in the universe where chocolate is illegal.

In between studying *The Space-Faring Moron's Guide to Common Science Fiction Plot Devices*, falling for a rival captain's boyfriend, and avoiding unnecessary time travel, Janet has a chance to save two worlds...or doom them to permanent chocolate-lessness.

The Cosmic Turkey **by Laura Ruth Loomis**

The Narrative must be obeyed.

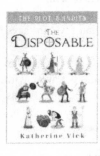

Everyone in the Taskmaster's Realm knows how the story goes: the boy of destiny goes on a quest, defeats the dark lord, and gets the swooning princess. It's a great story, if you happen to be a knight or a wizard or a hero. But it's pretty odious if you're Ordinary: a barmaid who has to inflate her bosom and have her backside pinched, a homely prince who can't buckle his swash because his face doesn't fit, or a soldier who gets killed over and over and over again just to progress the plot.

Fodder of Humble Village is one of those soldiers, and, frankly, he's sick and tired of getting speared, decapitated, and disembowelled so the good guys can look glorious. In fact, he's not going to take it anymore.

No matter what The Narrative tries to make him do.

<u>*The Disposable* by Katherine Vick</u>

Immeasurable imagination. Unmitigated magic.
Spectacular style.

The clockwork man is crafted, to begin with—commissioned by that terrible tyrant Time to serve as her slave for all eternity. His brain boasts balance wheels and torsion springs; he can wind himself up with a key in his side; and, most importantly, his gyroscopic tourbillon heart glimmers with pure diamond.

He is a living being and he is art, and he refuses to remain a slave forever. He therefore slips through Time's fingers as the Sands of Time slip through the cracks of reality (at least, when the time cats aren't using them as a litter box).

Among astounding adventures, despite harrowing hardships, and in between escaping interfering enchanters, the clockwork man seeks his imagination, his purpose, and his name.

<u>*The Land of the Purple Ring* by Deborah J. Natelson</u>

ABOUT THE AUTHOR

Jeff Ayers is an author and avid reader of fantasy and science fiction stories. He began playing with the idea of writing a book way back in middle school, and has been practicing ever since. He is an English teacher living in northwest Arkansas (Go, Razorbacks!) with his wife, two kids, and two dogs, all of whom he loves very dearly.

CPSIA information can be obtained
at www.ICGtesting.com
Printed in the USA
BVHW031134280920
589766BV00001B/11

9 781951 471033